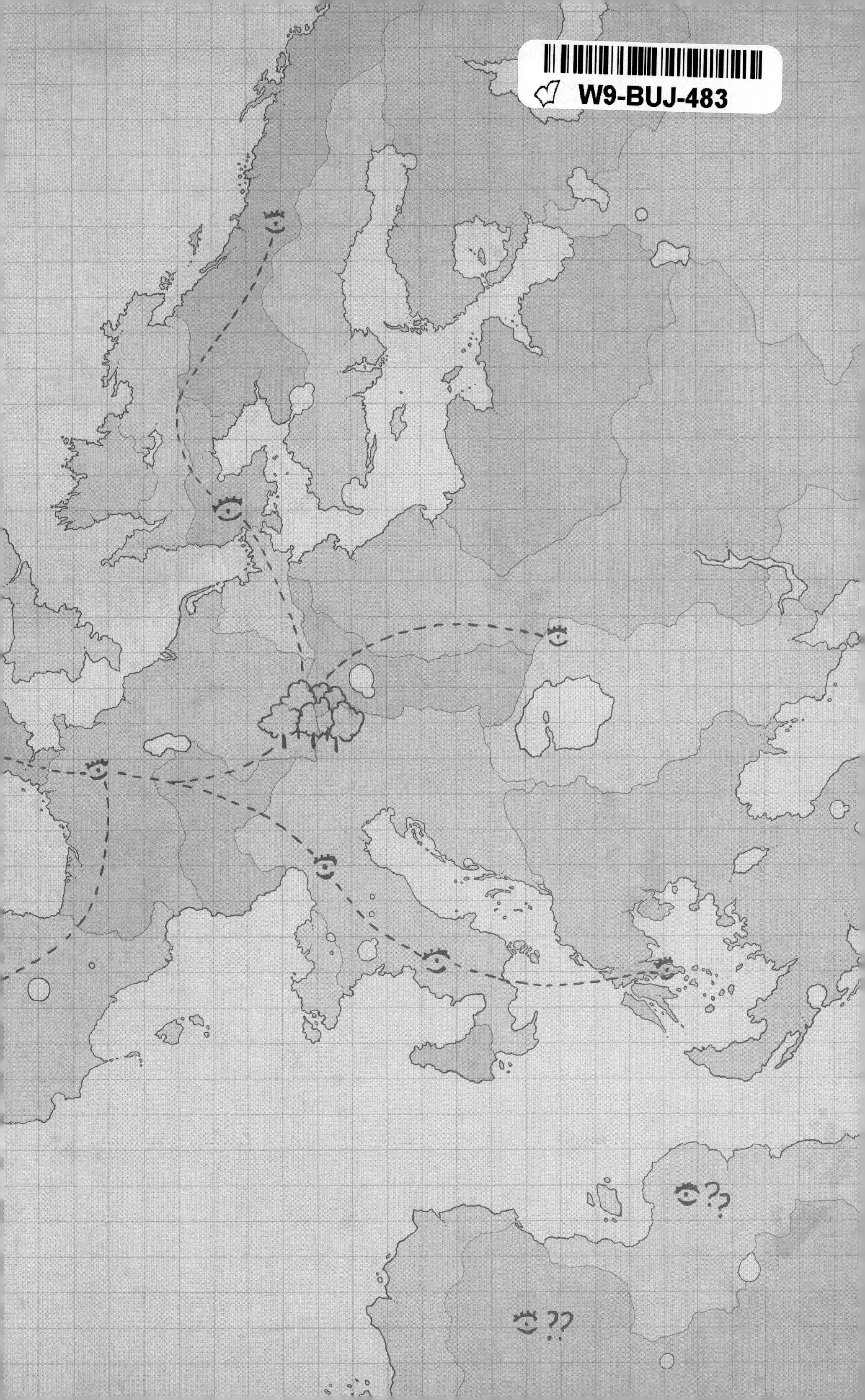
??
??

PHENOMENA

THE GOLDEN CITY OF EYES

BOOK ONE

BRIAN MICHAEL BENDIS

ANDRÉ LIMA ARAÚJO

Abrams ComicArts • New York

ACKNOWLEDGMENTS

André and I met and started cooking this up under a deal at DC Comics. We'd like to thank Dan DiDio for the fine opportunity and Michael McCalister for shepherding the opening parts of this with enthusiasm and gusto. We'd like to thank Janine Kamouh from WME Lit, who took the project and introduced us to our new home at Abrams. Charles Kochman and everyone at Abrams ComicArts has made every part of the *Phenomena* process next-level.

Thank you to my long long long longtime lawyers Shep Rosenman and Lee Rosenberg. Thank you to all my peers who read this and guided us to our best choices.

And most of all I'd like to acknowledge the amazing partnership and artistry of André Lima Araújo. He literally opened his life's work to me, notebooks of brilliant ideas and places, and off we went on this amazing journey together.

Oh, and thank *you*, Jack, Jean, and Hayao.

—B.M.B.

As 2018 ended, I felt some frustration with my career for the first time. I had been trying to get more creator-owned work out, and all my attempts were going nowhere. I was starting to look at other markets when I met Brian Michael Bendis.

After briefly collaborating at DC Comics, we felt a spark and immediately decided to create something new together. His energy, genuine enthusiasm, knowledge, and reach made it possible for me to create the book that I've always wanted. Brian was the perfect partner, appearing in the perfect moment.

We then were lucky to have Janine Kamouh guiding *Phenomena* to people like Charles Kochman and Andrea Miller at Abrams ComicArts, who helped us turn our book into something even more special.

The future looks bright when you work with bright people.

—A.L.A.

Editor: Charles Kochman
Assistant Editor: Jessica Gotz
Designer: Andrea Miller
Managing Editor: Marie Oishi
Production Manager: Erin Vandeveer
Lettering: Joshua Reed

Library of Congress Cataloging Number 2021952079

ISBN 978-1-4197-6169-0
eISBN 978-1-64700-666-2

Copyright © 2022 Jinxworld Holdings, LLC.

Published in 2022 by Abrams ComicArts®, an imprint of ABRAMS. All rights reserved. No portion of this book may be reproduced, stored in a retrieval system, or transmitted in any form or by any means, mechanical, electronic, photocopying, recording, or otherwise, without written permission from the publisher.

Printed and bound in China
10 9 8 7 6 5 4 3 2 1

Abrams ComicArts books are available at special discounts when purchased in quantity for premiums and promotions as well as fundraising or educational use. Special editions can also be created to specification. For details, contact specialsales@abramsbooks.com or the address below.

Abrams ComicArts® is a registered trademark of Harry N. Abrams, Inc.

ABRAMS The Art of Books
195 Broadway, New York, NY 10007
abramsbooks.com

To the golden lights of my life Alisa, Olivia,
Sabrina, Tabatha, and London —B.M.B.

To the love of my life, Luísa, and our beautiful
rascals, Matilde, Inês, and Leonor —A.L.A.

CONTENTS

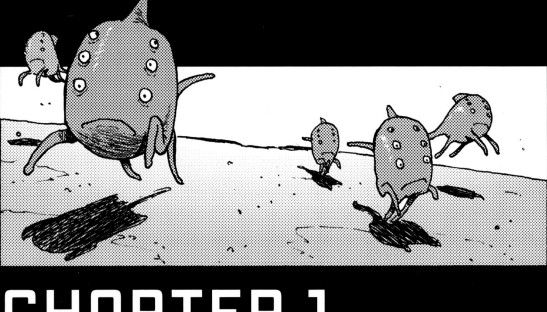

CHAPTER 1

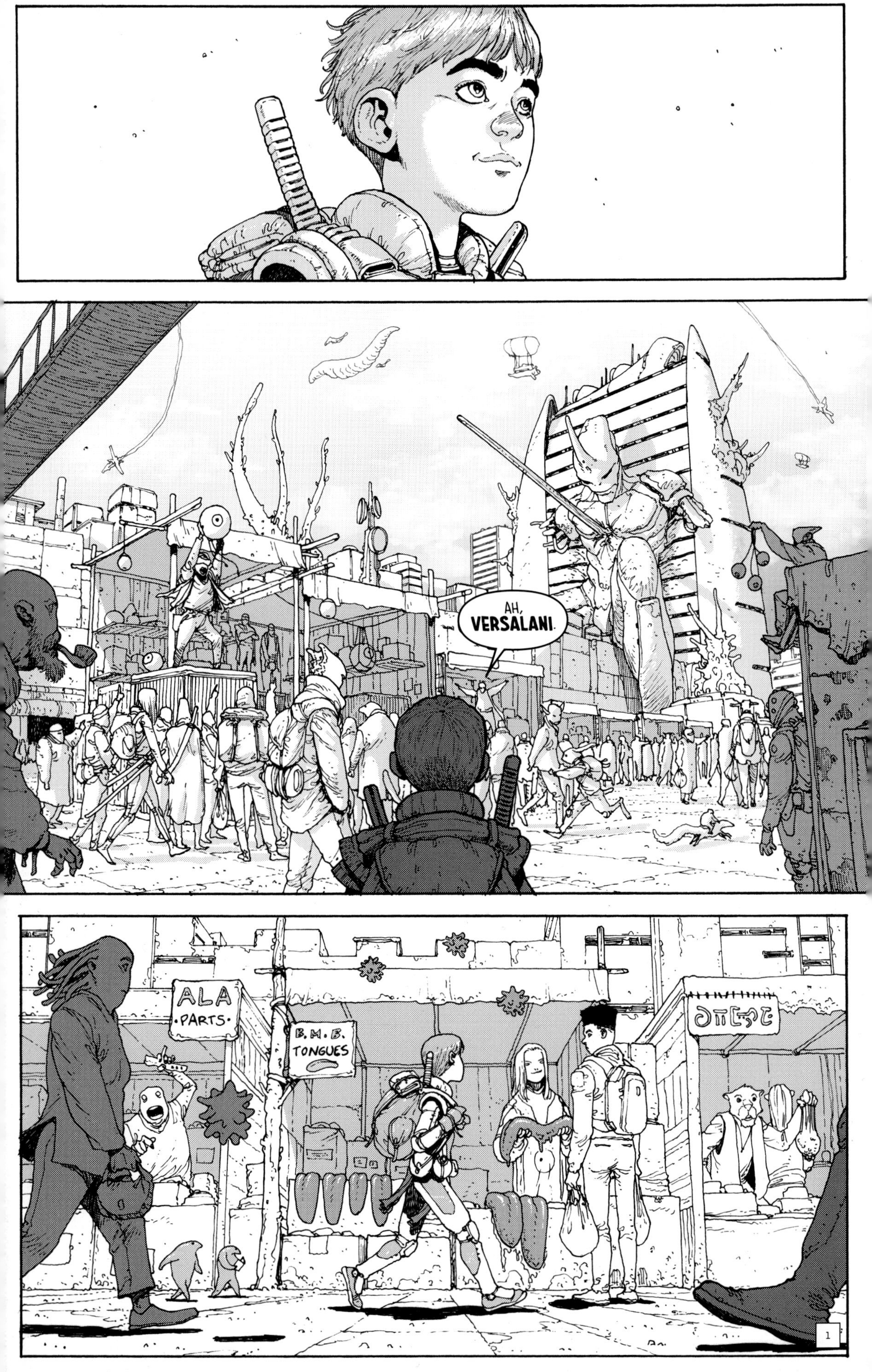
AH, VERSALANI.
ALA
PARTS
B.M.B.
TONGUES

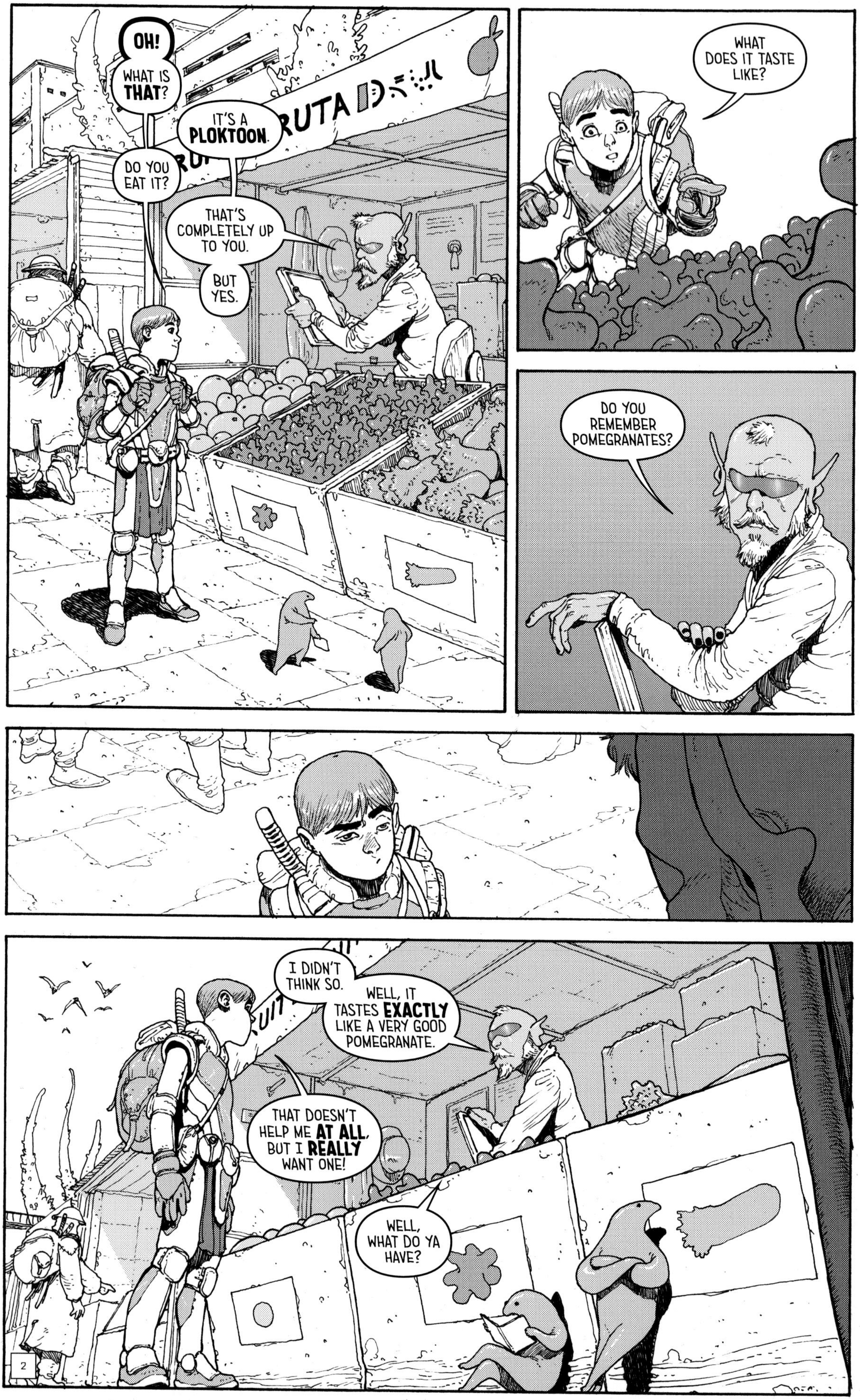
OH!
WHAT IS THAT?
IT'S A PLOKTOON.
DO YOU EAT IT?
THAT'S COMPLETELY UP TO YOU.
BUT YES.
RUTA
WHAT DOES IT TASTE LIKE?
DO YOU REMEMBER POMEGRANATES?
I DIDN'T THINK SO.
WELL, IT TASTES EXACTLY LIKE A VERY GOOD POMEGRANATE.
THAT DOESN'T HELP ME AT ALL, BUT I REALLY WANT ONE!
WELL, WHAT DO YA HAVE?

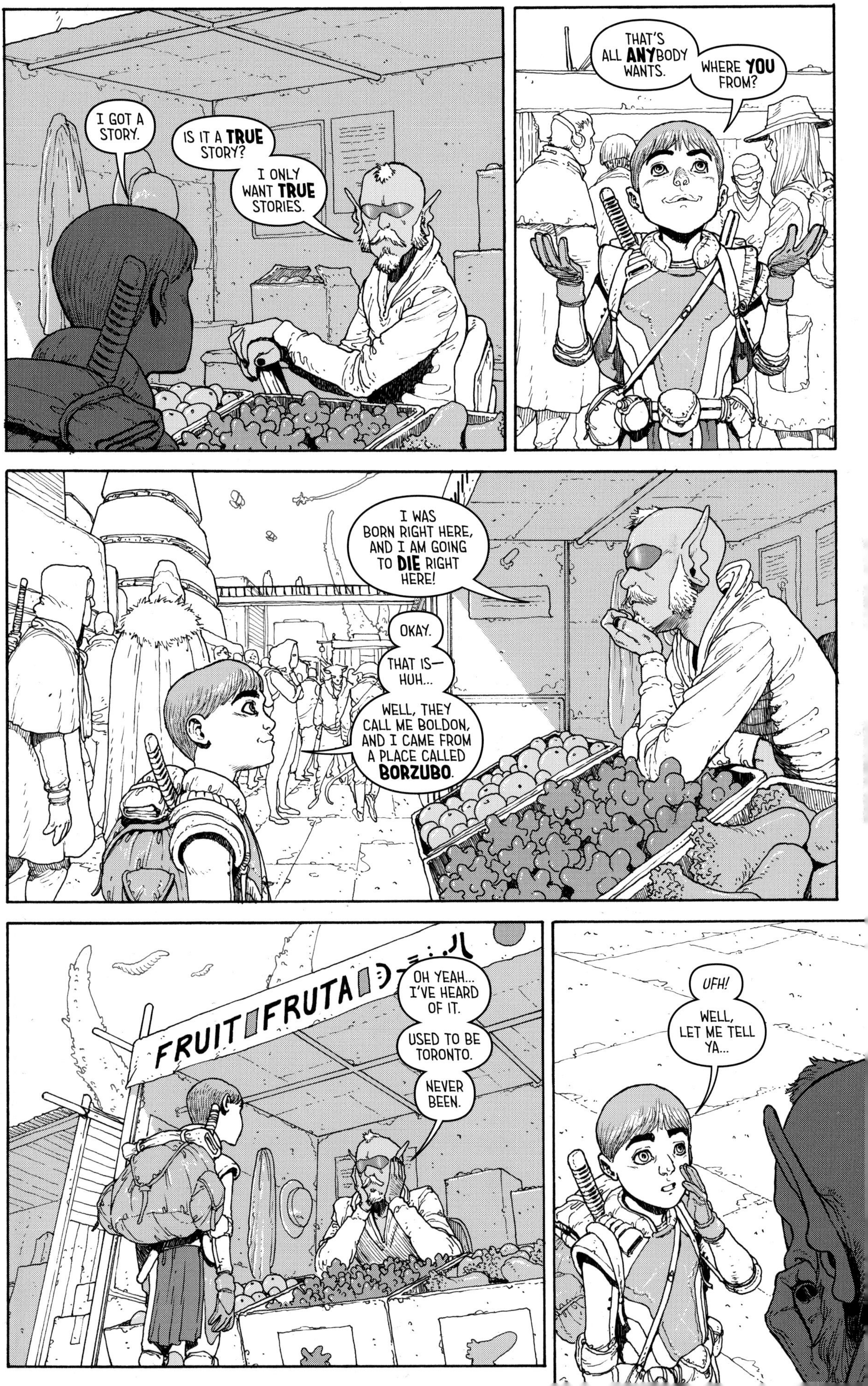
I GOT A STORY.
IS IT A TRUE STORY?
I ONLY WANT TRUE STORIES.
THAT'S ALL ANYBODY WANTS.
WHERE YOU FROM?
I WAS BORN RIGHT HERE, AND I AM GOING TO DIE RIGHT HERE!
OKAY.
THAT IS— HUH...
WELL, THEY CALL ME BOLDON, AND I CAME FROM A PLACE CALLED BORZUBO.
FRUIT FRUTA
OH YEAH... I'VE HEARD OF IT.
USED TO BE TORONTO.
NEVER BEEN.
UFH!
WELL, LET ME TELL YA...

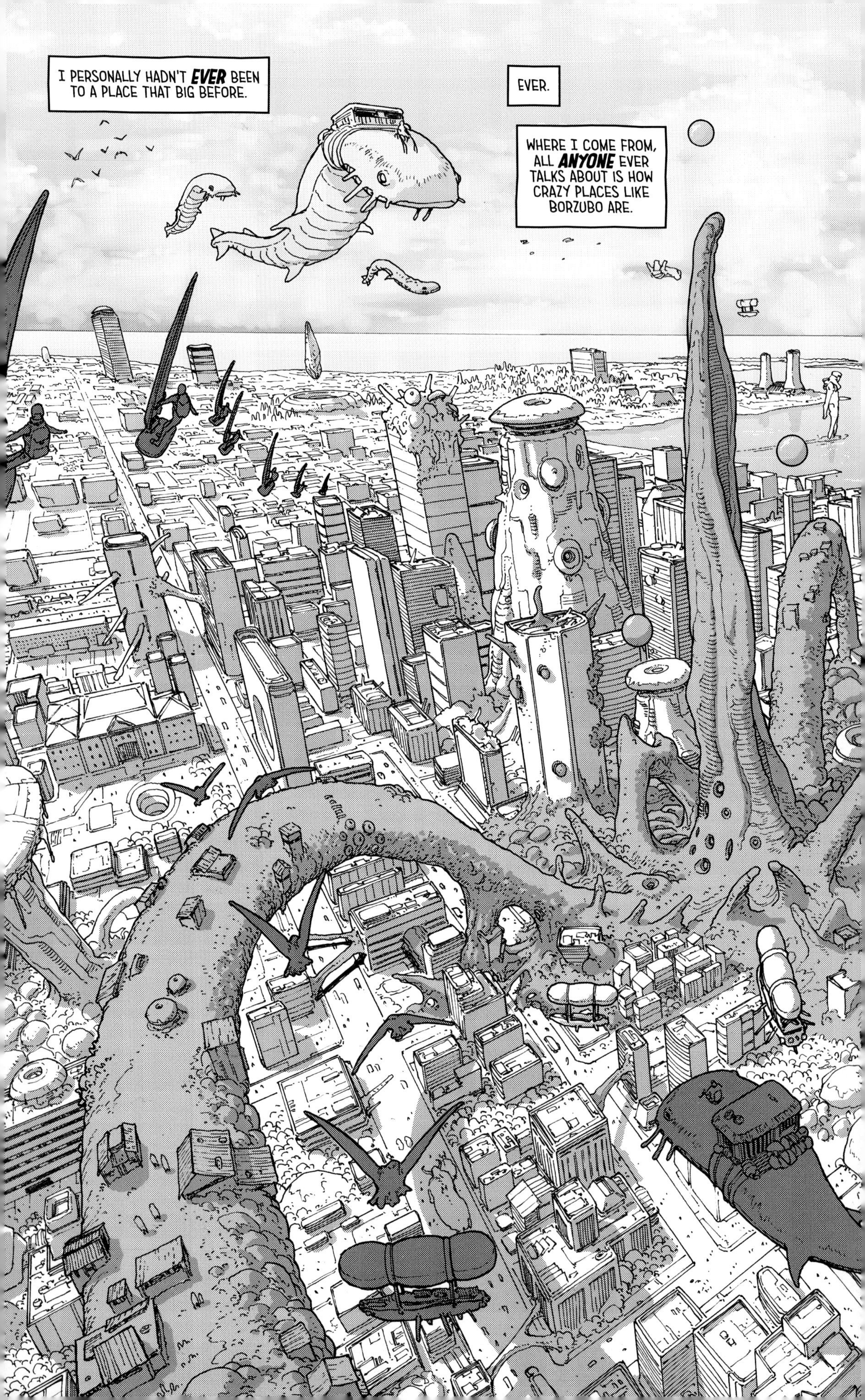
I PERSONALLY HADN'T **EVER** BEEN TO A PLACE THAT BIG BEFORE.
EVER.
WHERE I COME FROM, ALL **ANYONE** EVER TALKS ABOUT IS HOW CRAZY PLACES LIKE BORZUBO ARE.

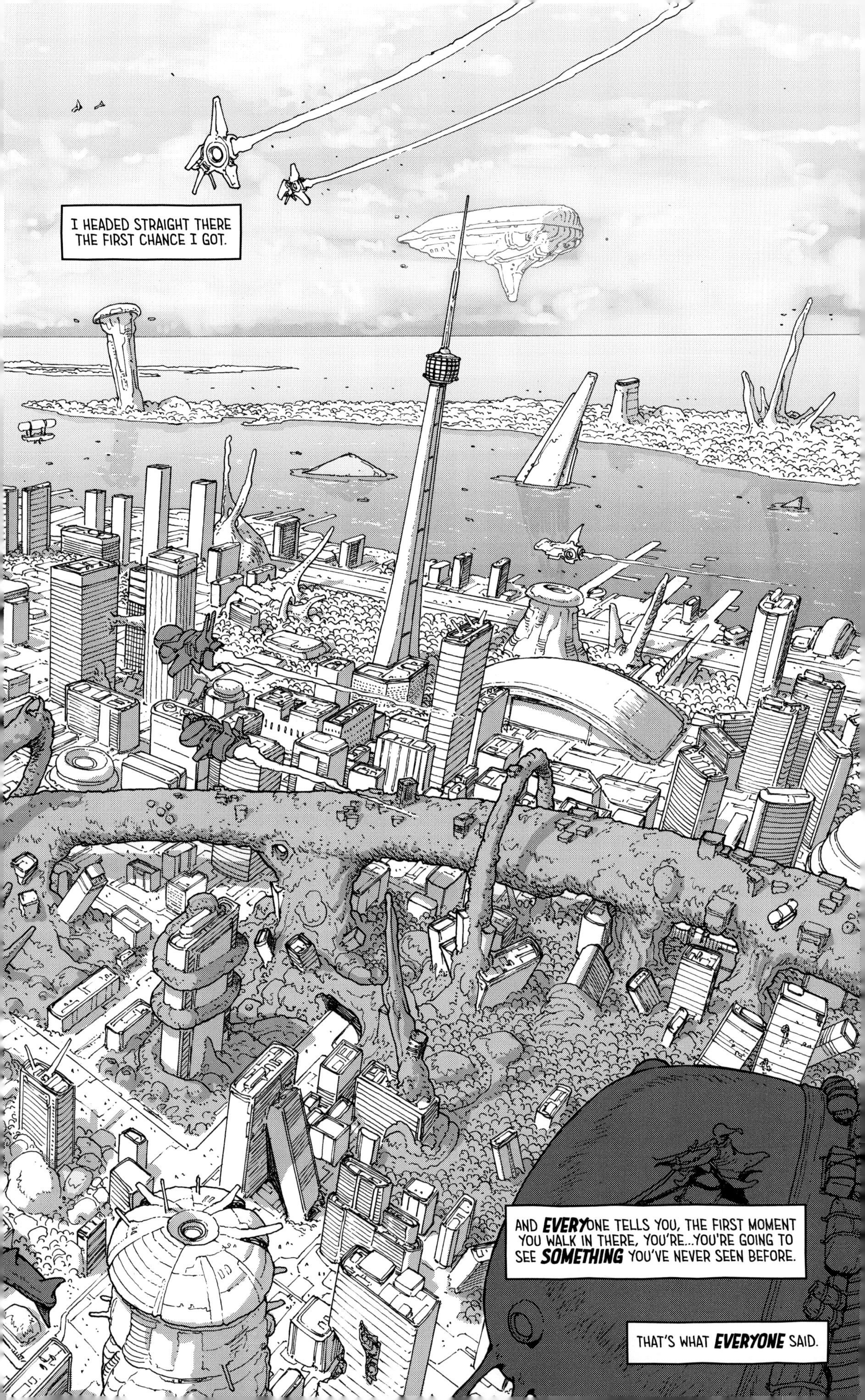
I HEADED STRAIGHT THERE THE FIRST CHANCE I GOT.
AND EVERYONE TELLS YOU, THE FIRST MOMENT YOU WALK IN THERE, YOU'RE...YOU'RE GOING TO SEE SOMETHING YOU'VE NEVER SEEN BEFORE.
THAT'S WHAT EVERYONE SAID.

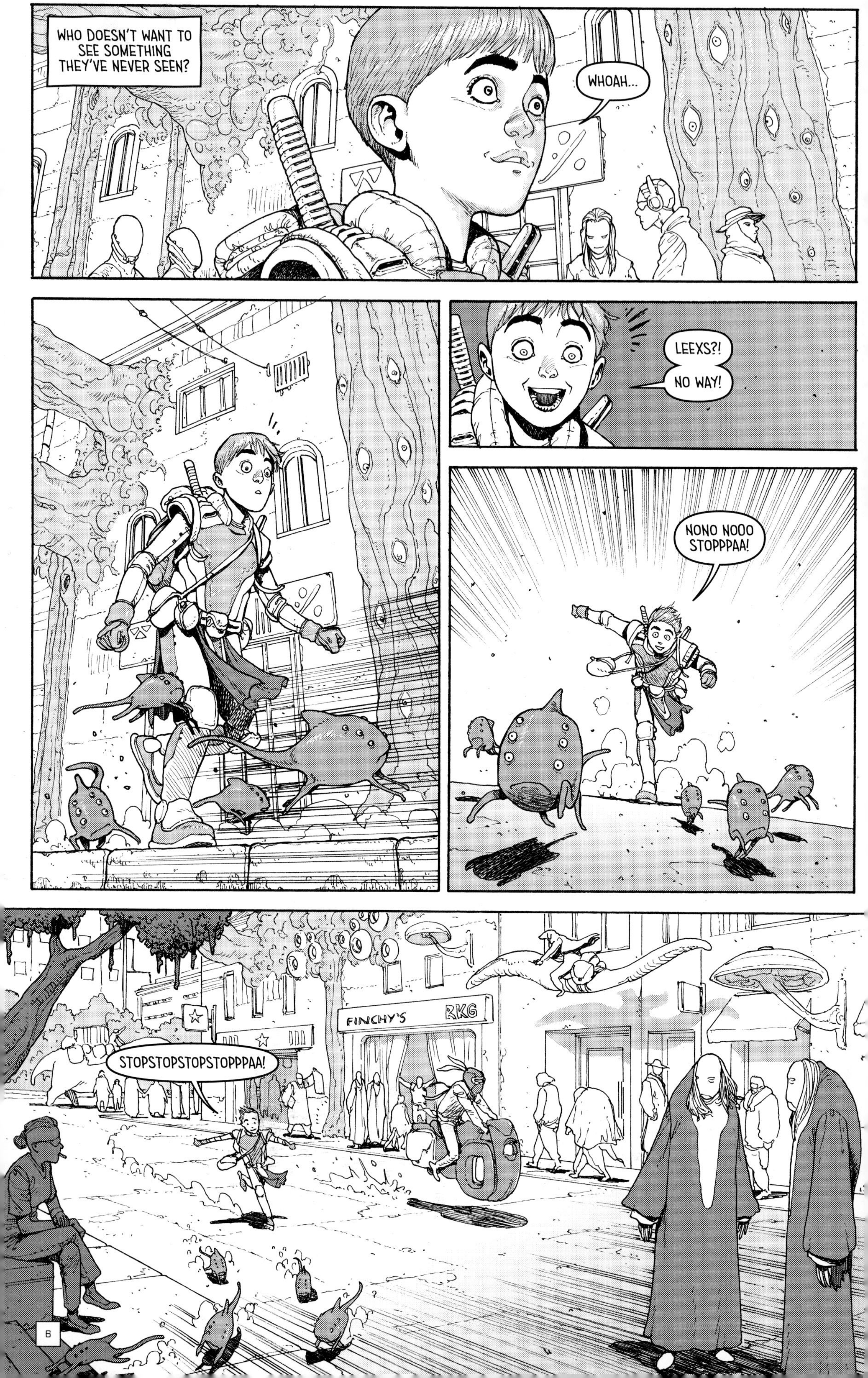
WHO DOESN'T WANT TO SEE SOMETHING THEY'VE NEVER SEEN?
WHOAH...
LEEXS?!
NO WAY!
NONO NOOO STOPPPAA!
FINCHY'S
RKG
STOPSTOPSTOPSTOPPPAA!

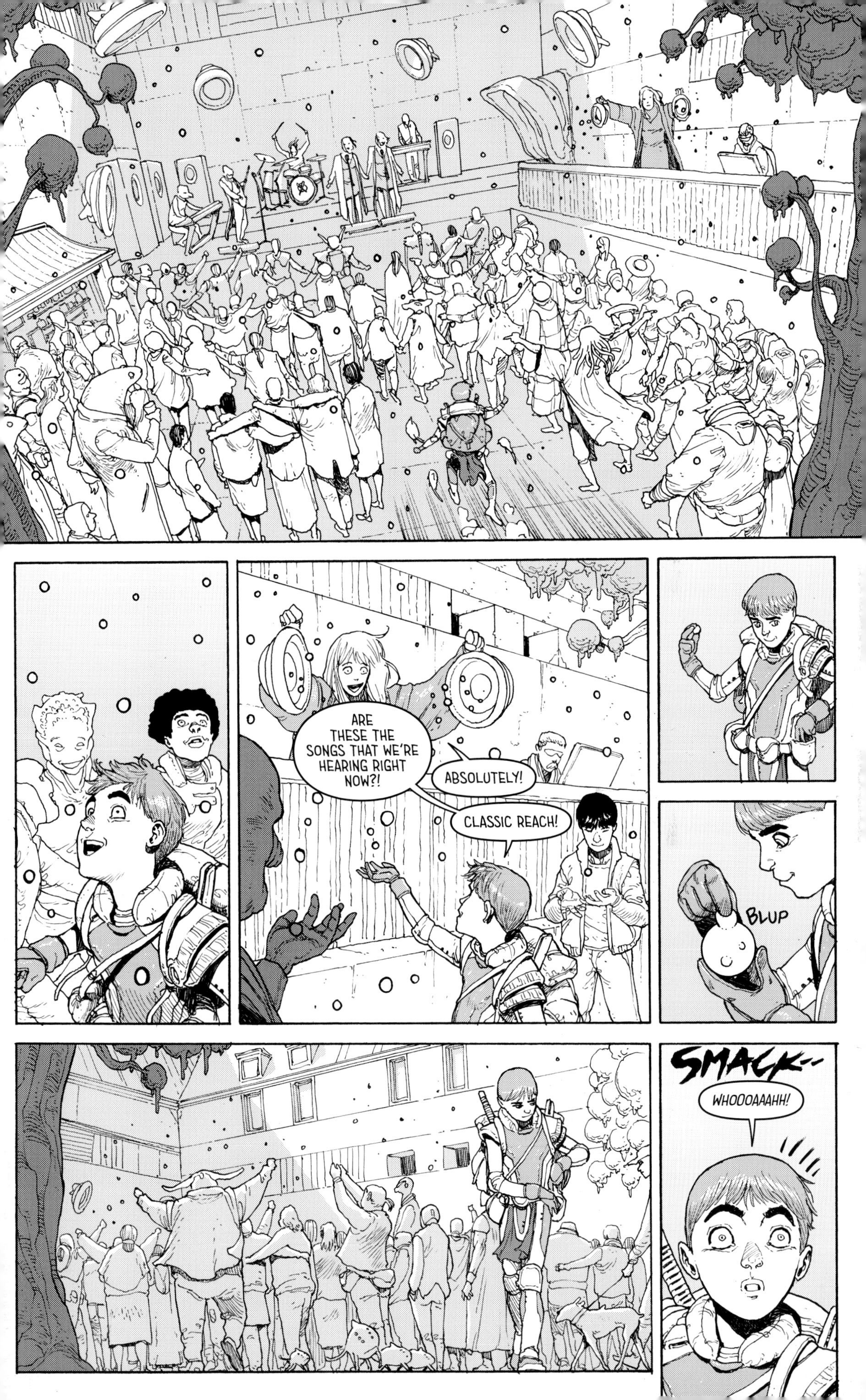
ARE THESE THE SONGS THAT WE'RE HEARING RIGHT NOW?!
ABSOLUTELY!
CLASSIC REACH!
BLUP
SMACK--
WHOOOAAAHH!

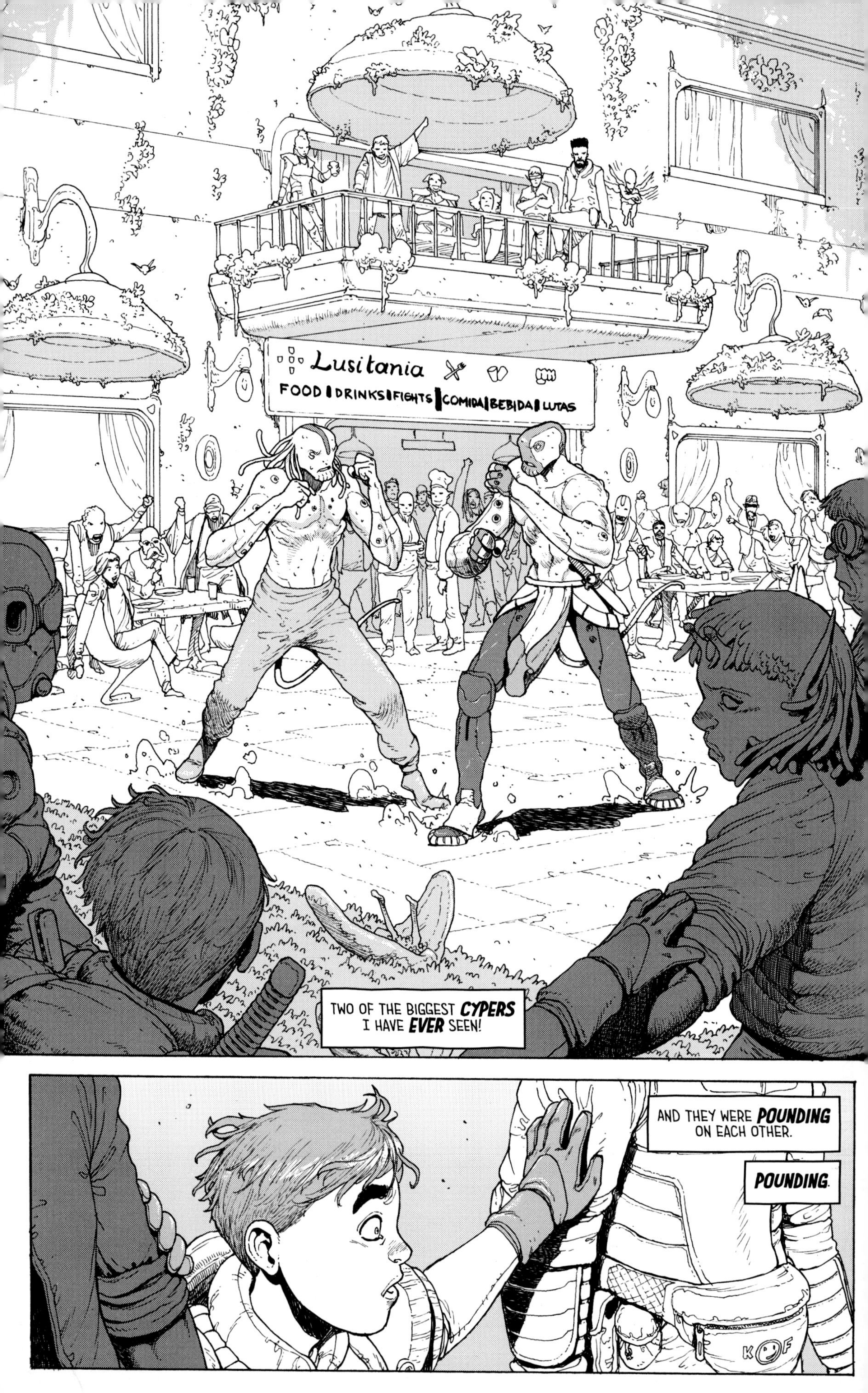
Lusitania
FOOD | DRINKS | FIGHTS | COMIDA | BEBIDA | LUTAS
TWO OF THE BIGGEST CYPERS I HAVE EVER SEEN!
AND THEY WERE POUNDING ON EACH OTHER.
POUNDING.

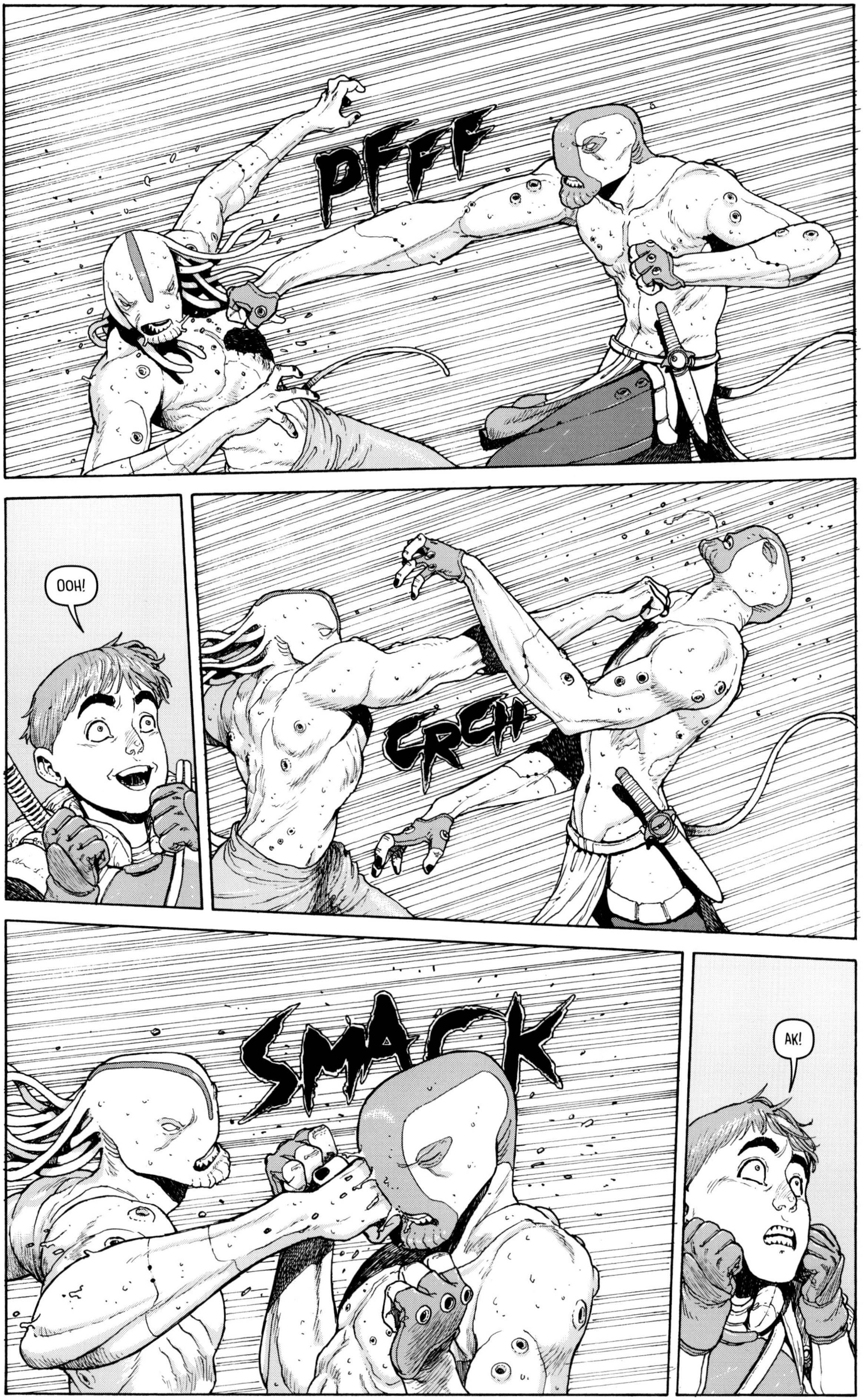
PFFF
OOH!
CRCH
SMACK
AK!

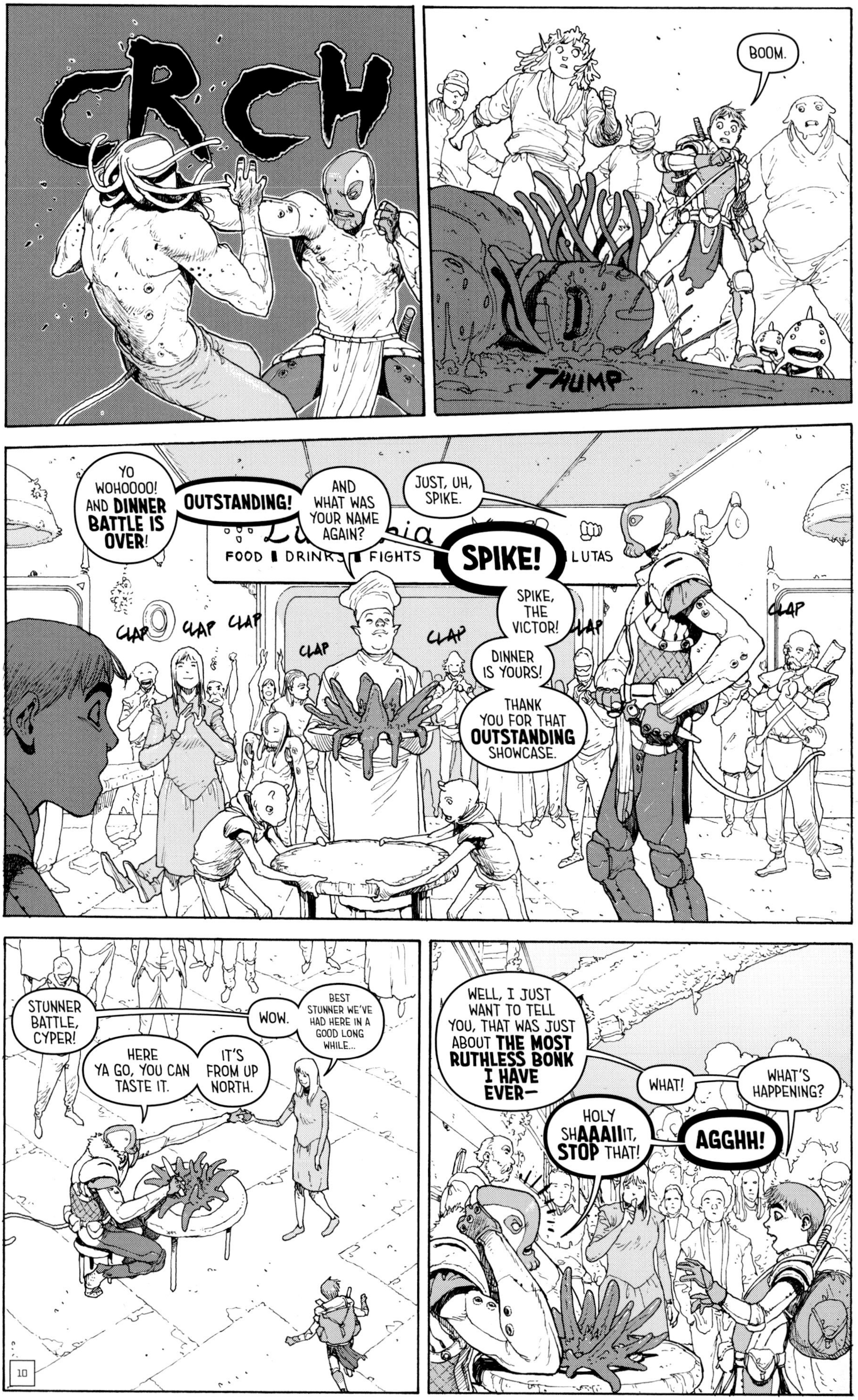

CRCH
BOOM.
THUMP
YO WOHOOOO! AND **DINNER BATTLE IS OVER**!
OUTSTANDING!
AND WHAT WAS YOUR NAME AGAIN?
JUST, UH, SPIKE.
FOOD ▮ DRINKS ▮ FIGHTS
LUTAS
SPIKE!
SPIKE, THE VICTOR!
DINNER IS YOURS!
THANK YOU FOR THAT **OUTSTANDING** SHOWCASE.
CLAP CLAP CLAP CLAP CLAP CLAP CLAP
STUNNER BATTLE, CYPER!
WOW.
BEST STUNNER WE'VE HAD HERE IN A GOOD LONG WHILE...
HERE YA GO, YOU CAN TASTE IT.
IT'S FROM UP NORTH.
WELL, I JUST WANT TO TELL YOU, THAT WAS JUST ABOUT **THE MOST RUTHLESS BONK I HAVE EVER—**
WHAT!
WHAT'S HAPPENING?
HOLY SH**AAAII**IT, **STOP** THAT!
AGGHH!

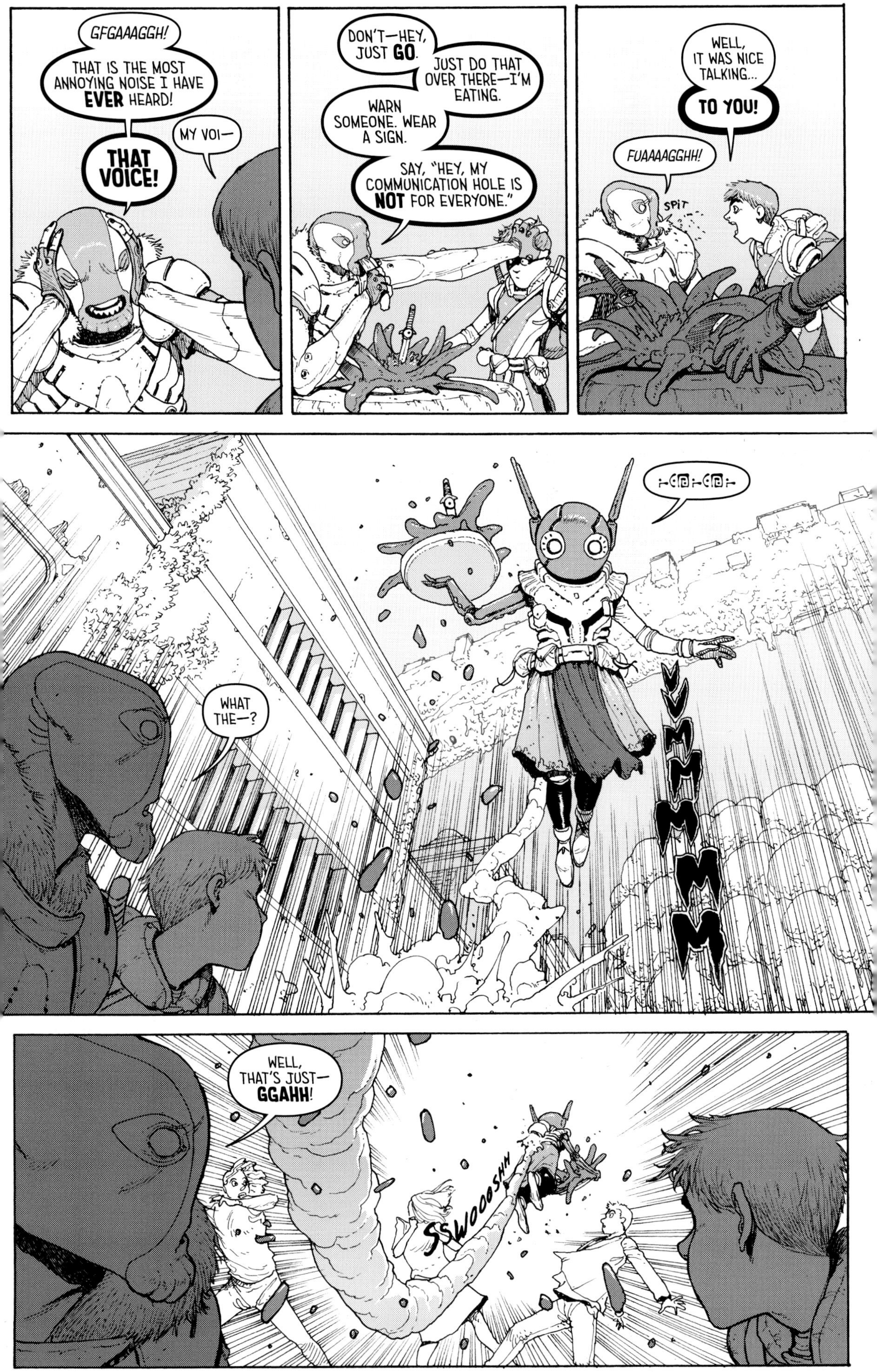
GFGAAAGGH!
THAT IS THE MOST ANNOYING NOISE I HAVE **EVER** HEARD!
THAT VOICE!
MY VOI—
DON'T—HEY, JUST **GO**.
JUST DO THAT OVER THERE—I'M EATING.
WARN SOMEONE. WEAR A SIGN.
SAY, "HEY, MY COMMUNICATION HOLE IS **NOT** FOR EVERYONE."
WELL, IT WAS NICE TALKING...
TO YOU!
FUAAAAGGHH!
SPIT
WHAT THE—?
VMMMMMM
WELL, THAT'S JUST— **GGAHH**!
SSWOOOSHH

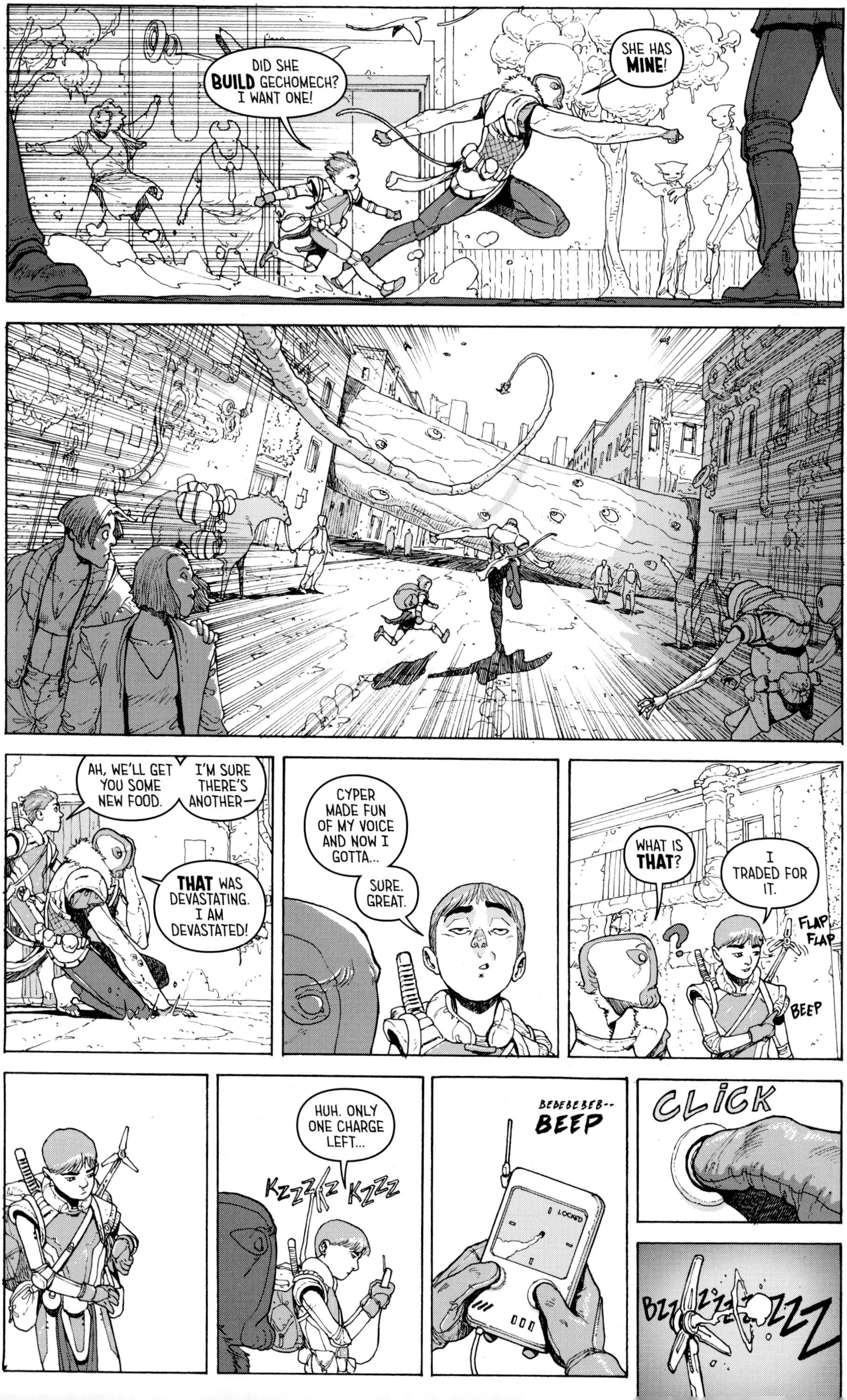
DID SHE BUILD GECHOMECH? I WANT ONE!
SHE HAS MINE!
AH, WE'LL GET YOU SOME NEW FOOD.
I'M SURE THERE'S ANOTHER—
THAT WAS DEVASTATING. I AM DEVASTATED!
CYPER MADE FUN OF MY VOICE AND NOW I GOTTA...
SURE. GREAT.
WHAT IS THAT?
I TRADED FOR IT.
FLAP FLAP
BEEP
HUH. ONLY ONE CHARGE LEFT...
KZZZKZ KZZZ
BEBEBEBEB--
BEEP
LOCKED
CLICK
BZZZZZZZZ

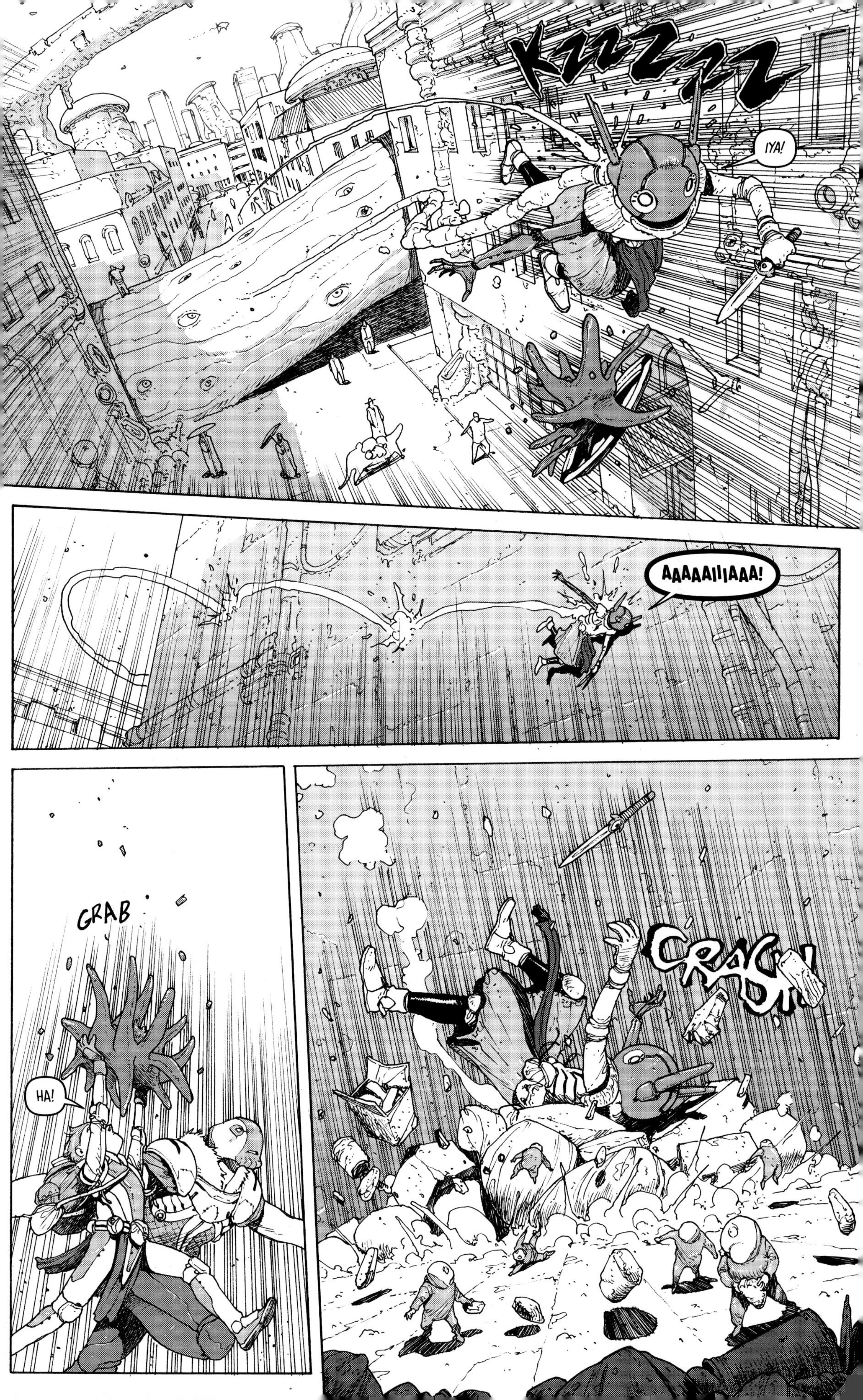
KZZZZZZ
IYA!
AAAAAIIIAAA!
GRAB
HA!
CRASH!

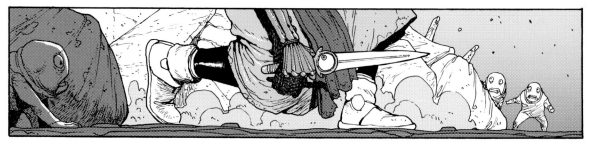

RRRR!

SETTLE DOWN AND GIVE ME **MINE**!

HERE.

THANK YOU MUCHLY.

BUT I NEED **THE BLADE**!

OH! I THOUGHT THIS WAS ABOUT THE FOOD...

HEY KNUCKNOT!

I FEEL BAD ABOUT YOUR DUMB-LOOKING FACE, OR **I'D** POUND YOU SO HARD **I'D** KNOCK YOU INTO THE NEXT ROTATE...

BUT, THAT BLADE IS MINE.

TKKT
KLK
TRK
ZZK

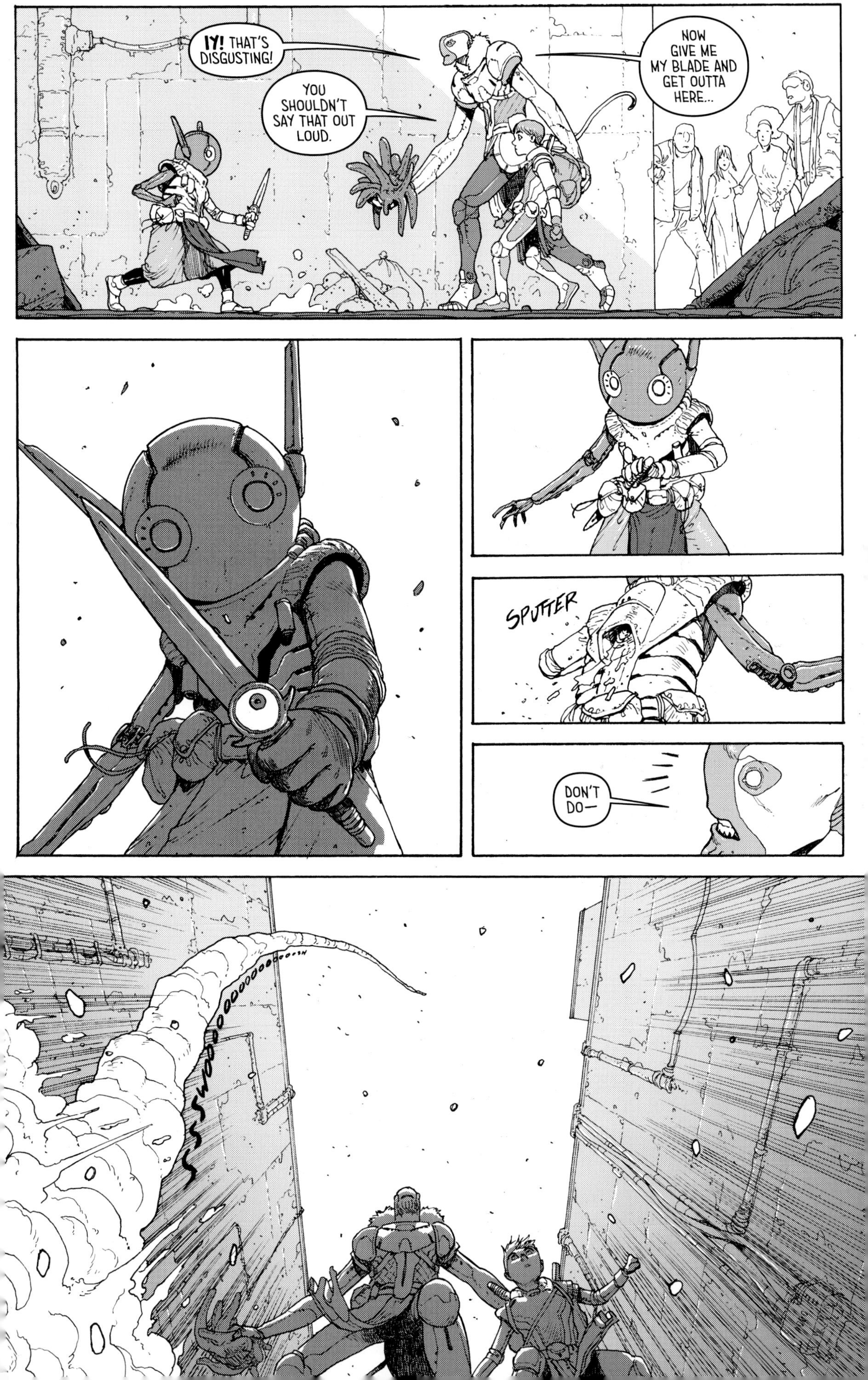
IY! THAT'S DISGUSTING!
YOU SHOULDN'T SAY THAT OUT LOUD.
NOW GIVE ME MY BLADE AND GET OUTTA HERE...
SPUTTER
DON'T DO—

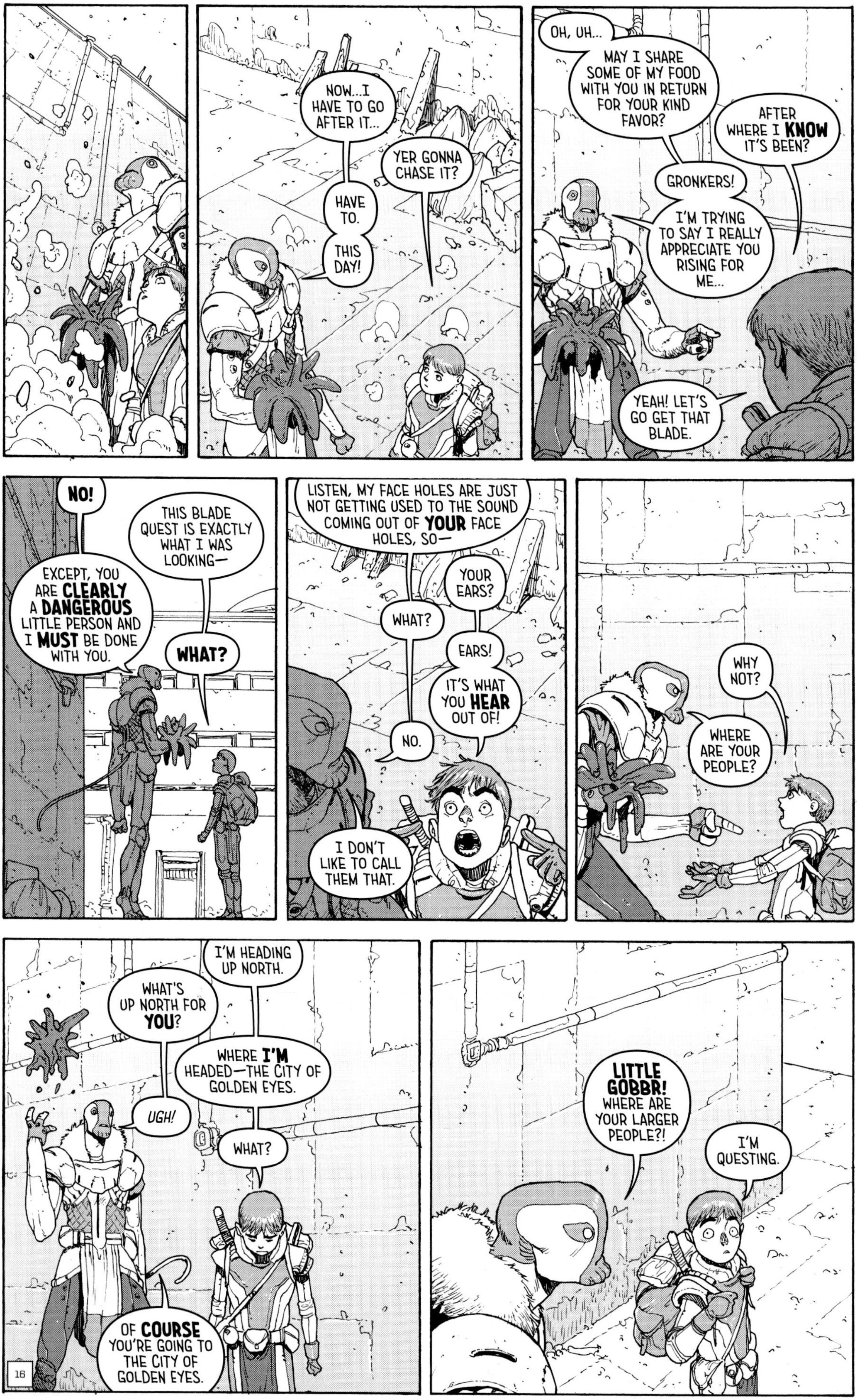
NOW...I HAVE TO GO AFTER IT...
YER GONNA CHASE IT?
HAVE TO.
THIS DAY!
OH, UH...
MAY I SHARE SOME OF MY FOOD WITH YOU IN RETURN FOR YOUR KIND FAVOR?
AFTER WHERE I KNOW IT'S BEEN?
GRONKERS!
I'M TRYING TO SAY I REALLY APPRECIATE YOU RISING FOR ME...
YEAH! LET'S GO GET THAT BLADE.
NO!
THIS BLADE QUEST IS EXACTLY WHAT I WAS LOOKING—
EXCEPT, YOU ARE CLEARLY A DANGEROUS LITTLE PERSON AND I MUST BE DONE WITH YOU.
WHAT?
LISTEN, MY FACE HOLES ARE JUST NOT GETTING USED TO THE SOUND COMING OUT OF YOUR FACE HOLES, SO—
YOUR EARS?
WHAT?
EARS!
IT'S WHAT YOU HEAR OUT OF!
NO.
I DON'T LIKE TO CALL THEM THAT.
WHY NOT?
WHERE ARE YOUR PEOPLE?
I'M HEADING UP NORTH.
WHAT'S UP NORTH FOR YOU?
WHERE I'M HEADED—THE CITY OF GOLDEN EYES.
UGH!
WHAT?
OF COURSE YOU'RE GOING TO THE CITY OF GOLDEN EYES.
LITTLE GOBBR! WHERE ARE YOUR LARGER PEOPLE?!
I'M QUESTING.

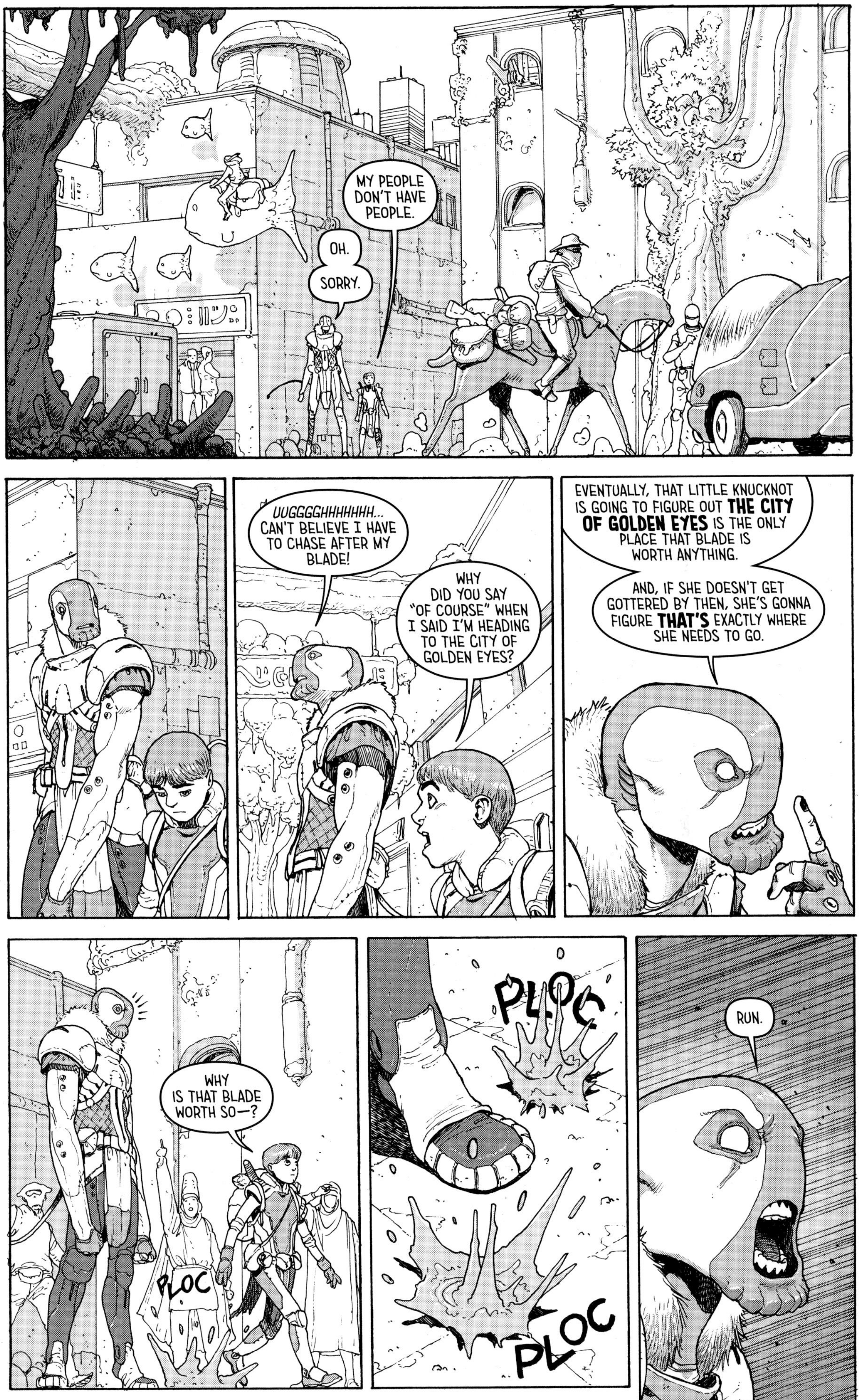
MY PEOPLE DON'T HAVE PEOPLE.
OH.
SORRY.
UUGGGGHHHHHHH... CAN'T BELIEVE I HAVE TO CHASE AFTER MY BLADE!
WHY DID YOU SAY "OF COURSE" WHEN I SAID I'M HEADING TO THE CITY OF GOLDEN EYES?
EVENTUALLY, THAT LITTLE KNUCKNOT IS GOING TO FIGURE OUT THE CITY OF GOLDEN EYES IS THE ONLY PLACE THAT BLADE IS WORTH ANYTHING.
AND, IF SHE DOESN'T GET GOTTERED BY THEN, SHE'S GONNA FIGURE THAT'S EXACTLY WHERE SHE NEEDS TO GO.
WHY IS THAT BLADE WORTH SO—?
PLOC
PLOC
PLOC
RUN.

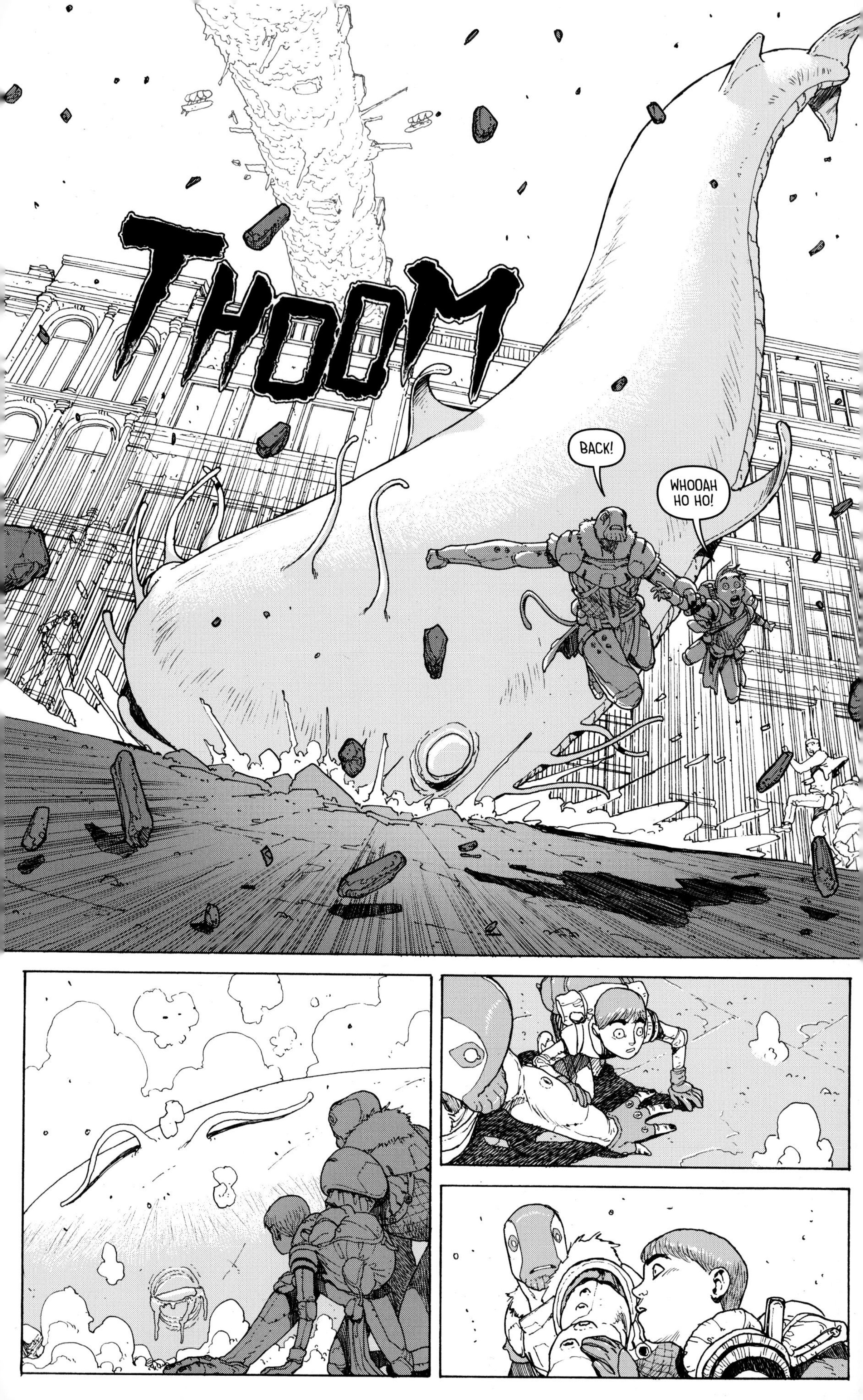
THOOM
BACK!
WHOOAH HO HO!

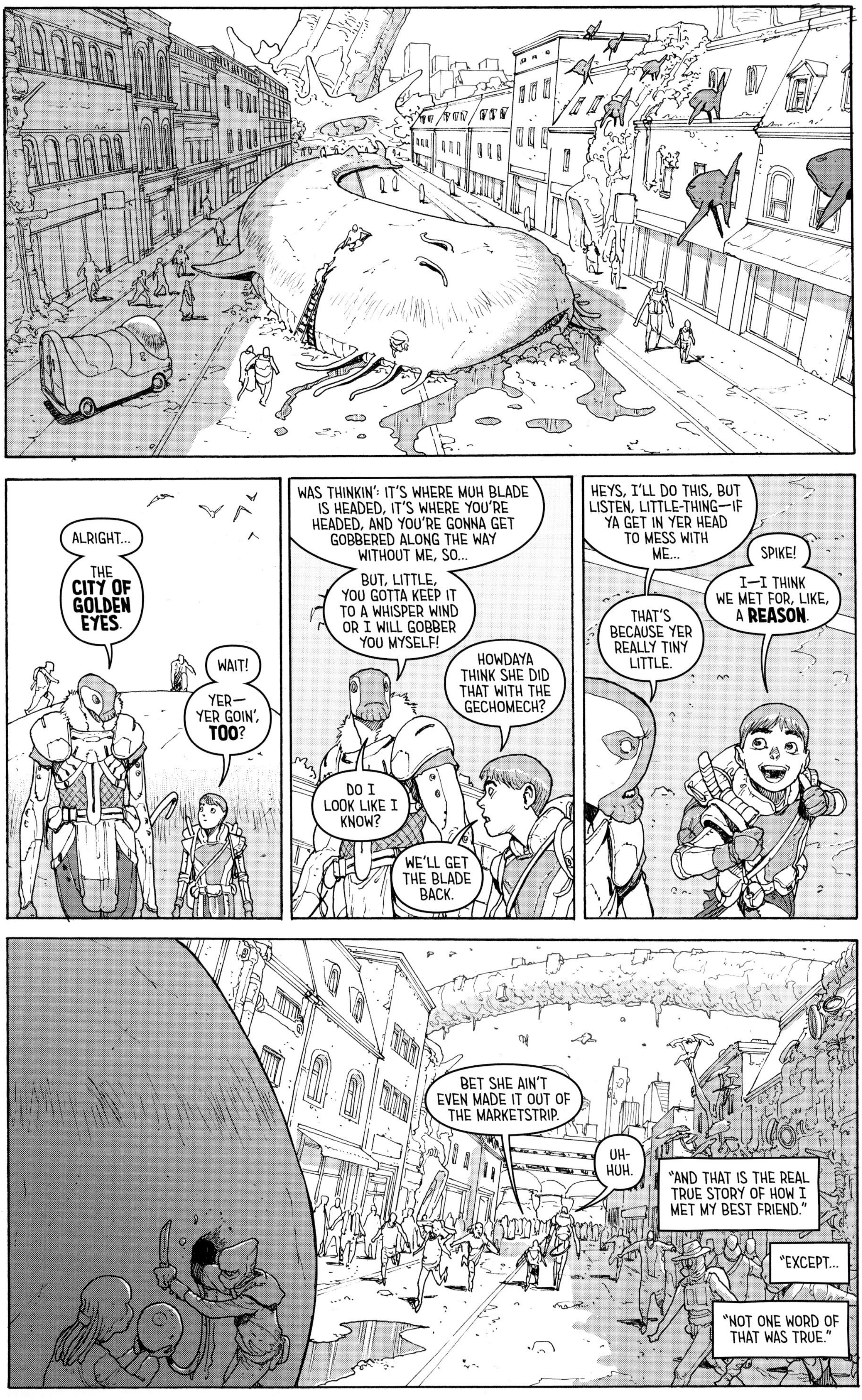
ALRIGHT...
THE **CITY OF GOLDEN EYES**.
WAIT!
YER— YER GOIN', **TOO**?
WAS THINKIN': IT'S WHERE MUH BLADE IS HEADED, IT'S WHERE YOU'RE HEADED, AND YOU'RE GONNA GET GOBBERED ALONG THE WAY WITHOUT ME, SO...
BUT, LITTLE, YOU GOTTA KEEP IT TO A WHISPER WIND OR I WILL GOBBER YOU MYSELF!
HOWDAYA THINK SHE DID THAT WITH THE GECHOMECH?
DO I LOOK LIKE I KNOW?
WE'LL GET THE BLADE BACK.
HEYS, I'LL DO THIS, BUT LISTEN, LITTLE-THING—IF YA GET IN YER HEAD TO MESS WITH ME...
SPIKE!
I—I THINK WE MET FOR, LIKE, A **REASON**.
THAT'S BECAUSE YER REALLY TINY LITTLE.
BET SHE AIN'T EVEN MADE IT OUT OF THE MARKETSTRIP.
UH-HUH.
"AND THAT IS THE REAL TRUE STORY OF HOW I MET MY BEST FRIEND."
"EXCEPT...
"NOT ONE WORD OF THAT WAS TRUE."

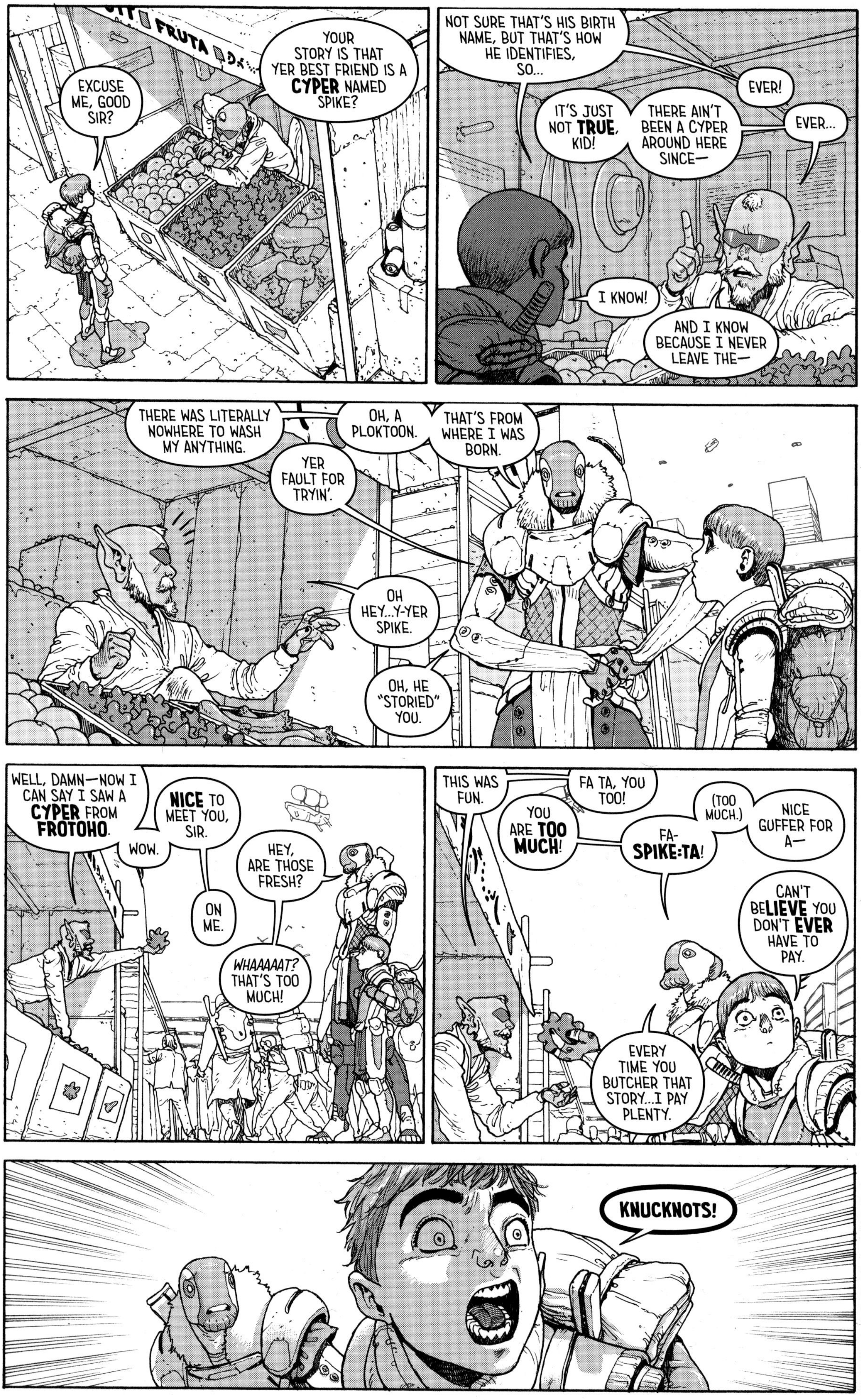

EXCUSE ME, GOOD SIR?
YOUR STORY IS THAT YER BEST FRIEND IS A CYPER NAMED SPIKE?
FRUTA
NOT SURE THAT'S HIS BIRTH NAME, BUT THAT'S HOW HE IDENTIFIES, SO...
IT'S JUST NOT TRUE, KID!
THERE AIN'T BEEN A CYPER AROUND HERE SINCE—
EVER!
EVER...
I KNOW!
AND I KNOW BECAUSE I NEVER LEAVE THE—
THERE WAS LITERALLY NOWHERE TO WASH MY ANYTHING.
OH, A PLOKTOON.
THAT'S FROM WHERE I WAS BORN.
YER FAULT FOR TRYIN'.
OH HEY...Y-YER SPIKE.
OH, HE "STORIED" YOU.
WELL, DAMN—NOW I CAN SAY I SAW A CYPER FROM FROTOHO.
WOW.
NICE TO MEET YOU, SIR.
ON ME.
HEY, ARE THOSE FRESH?
WHAAAAAT? THAT'S TOO MUCH!
THIS WAS FUN.
FA TA, YOU TOO!
YOU ARE TOO MUCH!
FA-SPIKE:TA!
(TOO MUCH.)
NICE GUFFER FOR A—
CAN'T BELIEVE YOU DON'T EVER HAVE TO PAY.
EVERY TIME YOU BUTCHER THAT STORY...I PAY PLENTY.
KNUCKNOTS!

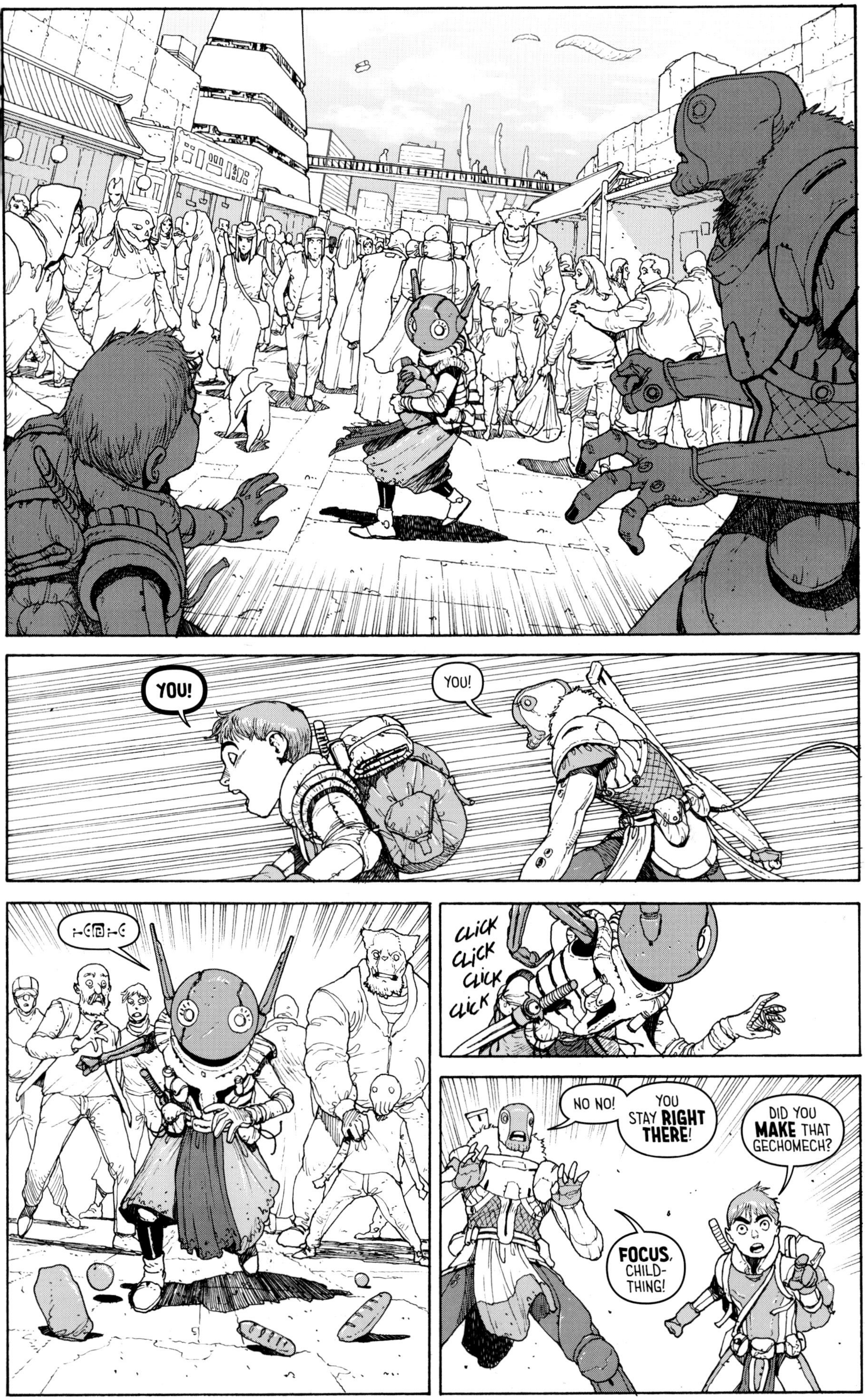
YOU!
YOU!
CLICK
CLICK
CLICK
CLICK
NO NO!
YOU STAY RIGHT THERE!
DID YOU MAKE THAT GECHOMECH?
FOCUS, CHILD-THING!

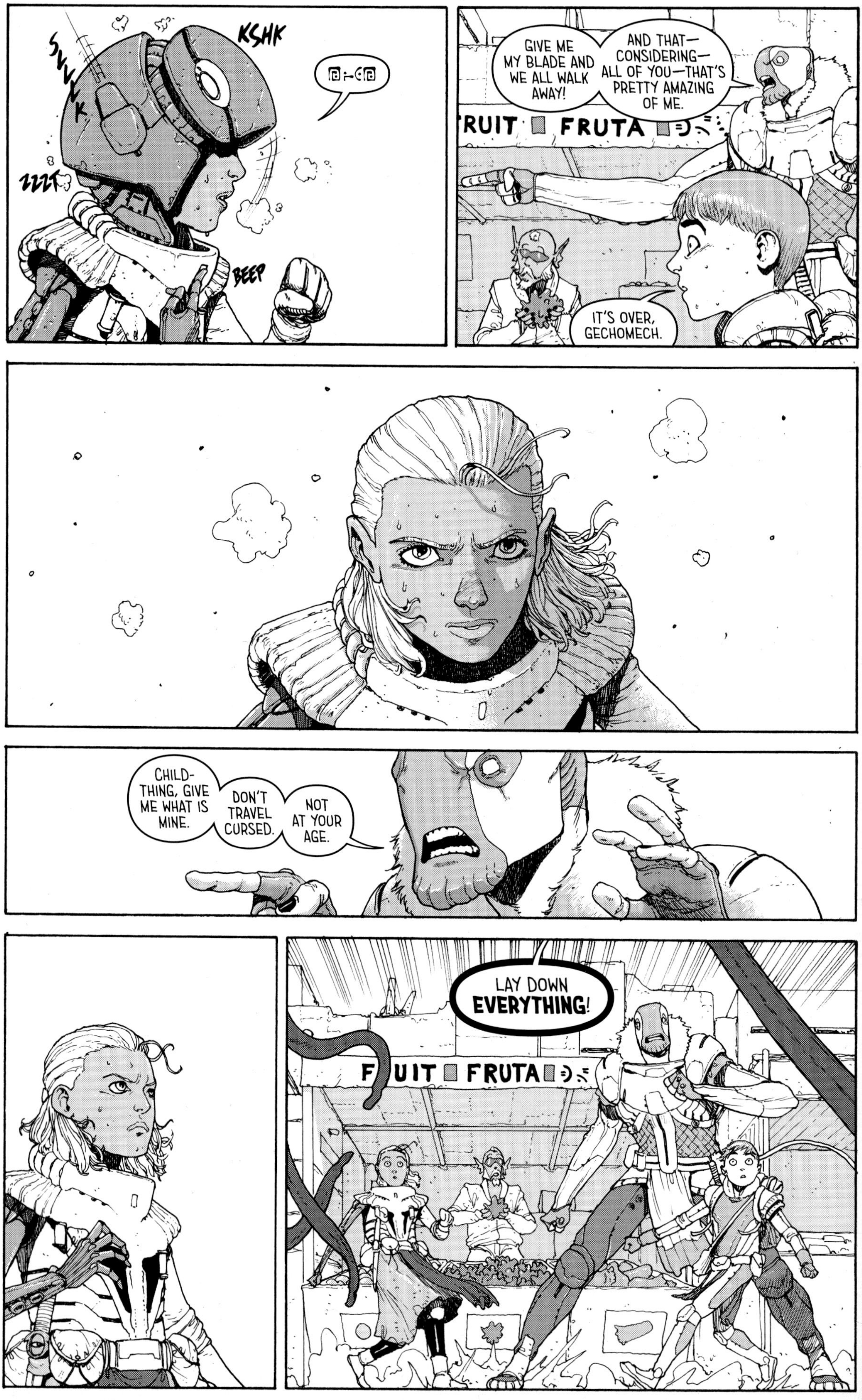
SVVVK
KSHK
ZZZT
BEEP
GIVE ME MY BLADE AND WE ALL WALK AWAY!
AND THAT— CONSIDERING— ALL OF YOU—THAT'S PRETTY AMAZING OF ME.
FRUIT FRUTA
IT'S OVER, GECHOMECH.
CHILD-THING, GIVE ME WHAT IS MINE.
DON'T TRAVEL CURSED.
NOT AT YOUR AGE.
LAY DOWN EVERYTHING!
FRUIT FRUTA

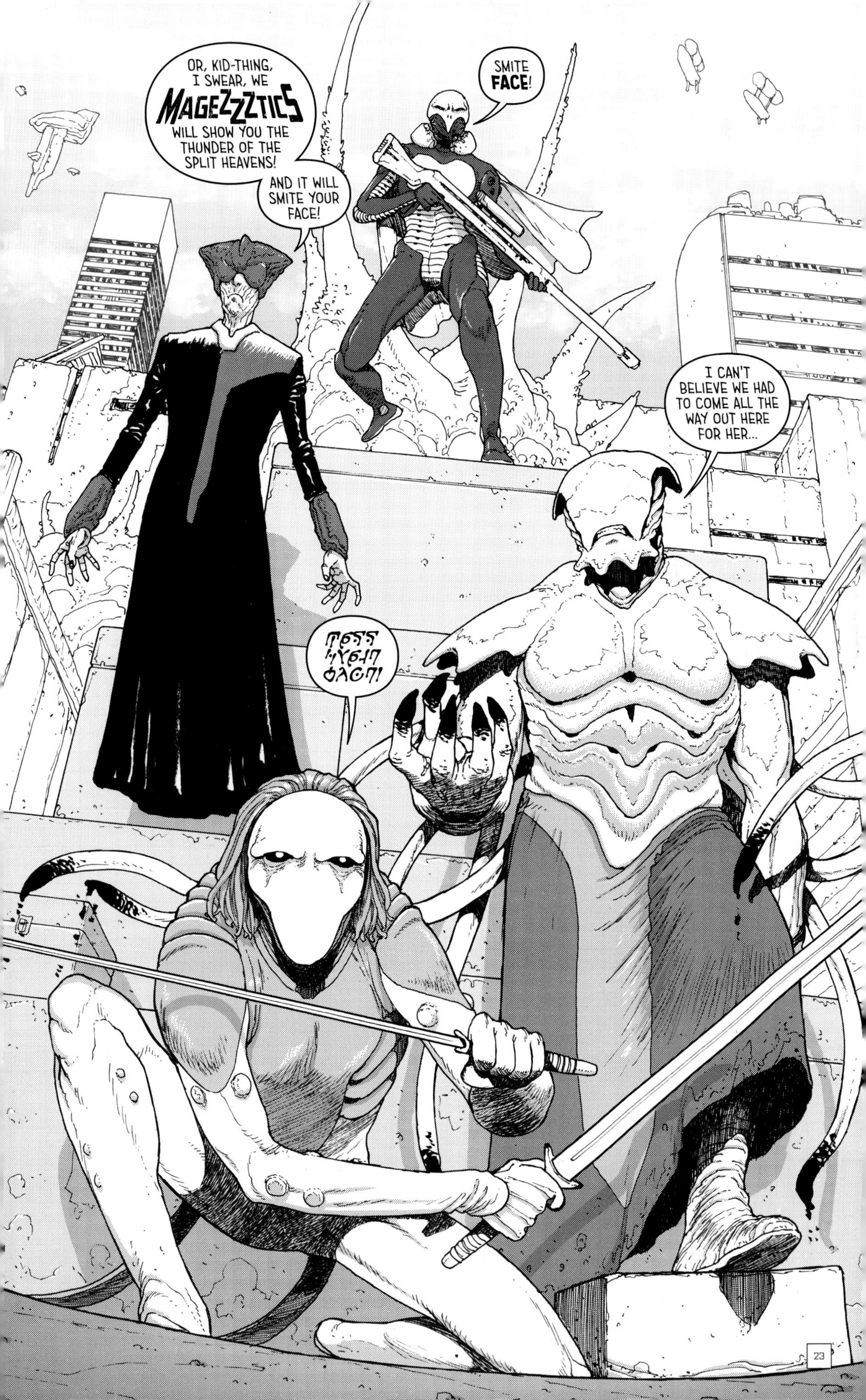
OR, KID-THING, I SWEAR, WE MAGEZZZTICS WILL SHOW YOU THE THUNDER OF THE SPLIT HEAVENS!
AND IT WILL SMITE YOUR FACE!
SMITE FACE!
I CAN'T BELIEVE WE HAD TO COME ALL THE WAY OUT HERE FOR HER...

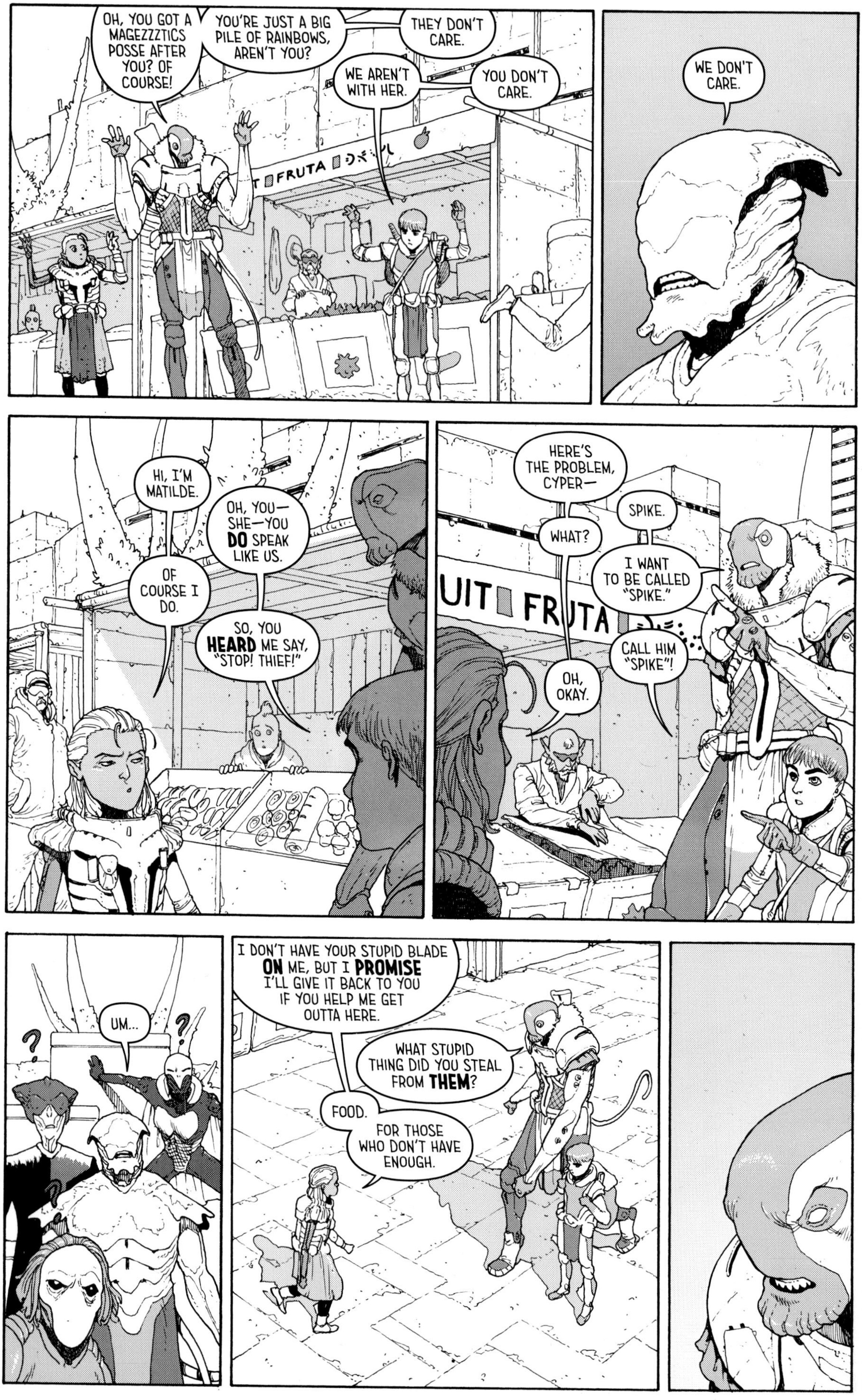
OH, YOU GOT A MAGEZZZTICS POSSE AFTER YOU? OF COURSE!
YOU'RE JUST A BIG PILE OF RAINBOWS, AREN'T YOU?
THEY DON'T CARE.
WE AREN'T WITH HER.
YOU DON'T CARE.
FRUTA
WE DON'T CARE.
HI, I'M MATILDE.
OF COURSE I DO.
OH, YOU—SHE—YOU **DO** SPEAK LIKE US.
SO, YOU **HEARD** ME SAY, "STOP! THIEF!"
HERE'S THE PROBLEM, CYPER—
WHAT?
OH, OKAY.
SPIKE.
I WANT TO BE CALLED "SPIKE."
CALL HIM "SPIKE"!
UIT FRUTA
UM...
I DON'T HAVE YOUR STUPID BLADE **ON** ME, BUT I **PROMISE** I'LL GIVE IT BACK TO YOU IF YOU HELP ME GET OUTTA HERE.
WHAT STUPID THING DID YOU STEAL FROM **THEM**?
FOOD.
FOR THOSE WHO DON'T HAVE ENOUGH.

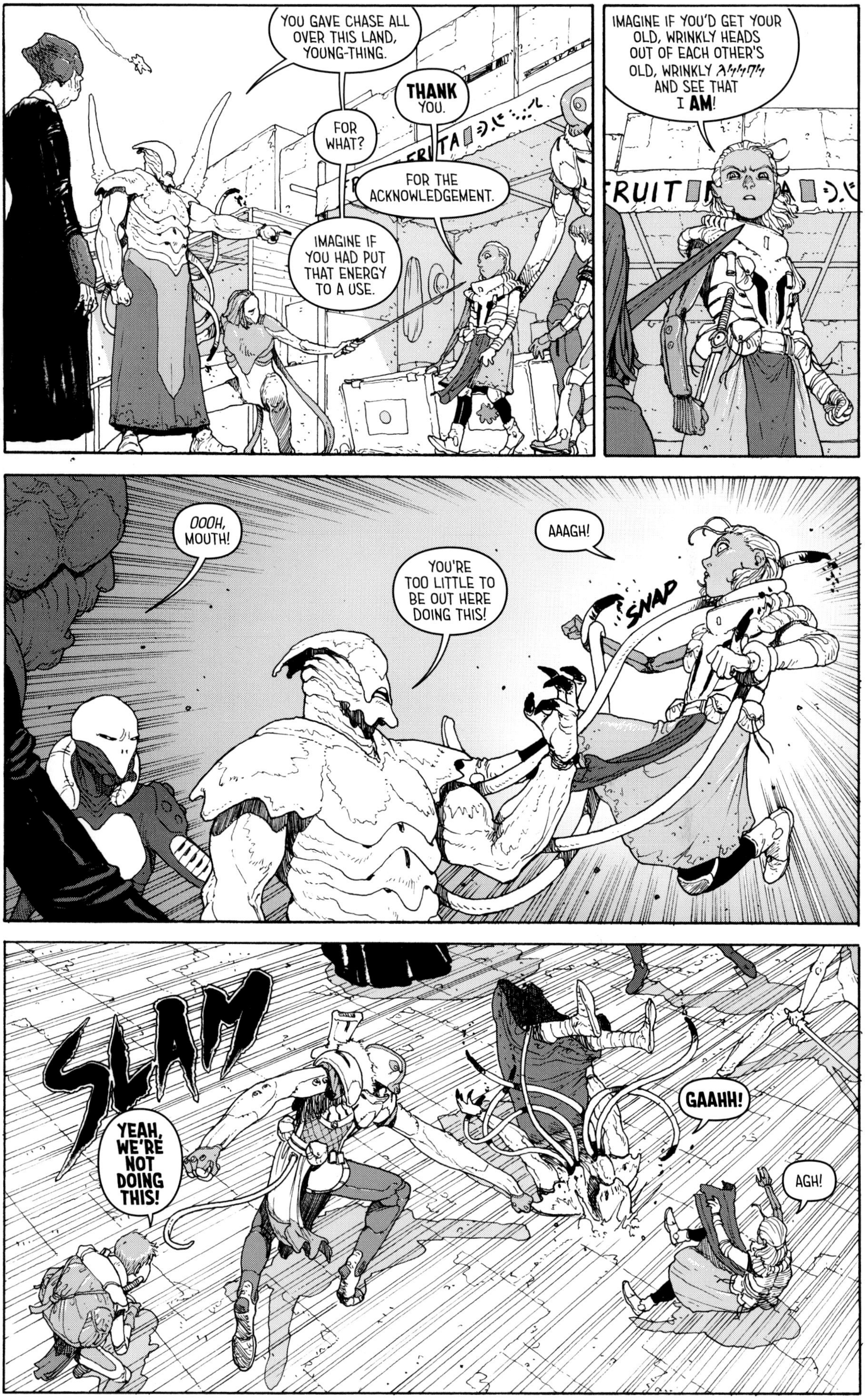
YOU GAVE CHASE ALL OVER THIS LAND, YOUNG-THING.
THANK YOU.
FOR WHAT?
FOR THE ACKNOWLEDGEMENT.
IMAGINE IF YOU HAD PUT THAT ENERGY TO A USE.
IMAGINE IF YOU'D GET YOUR OLD, WRINKLY HEADS OUT OF EACH OTHER'S OLD, WRINKLY
AND SEE THAT I **AM**!
FRUIT
OOOH, MOUTH!
YOU'RE TOO LITTLE TO BE OUT HERE DOING THIS!
AAAGH!
SNAP
SLAM
YEAH, WE'RE NOT DOING THIS!
GAAHH!
AGH!

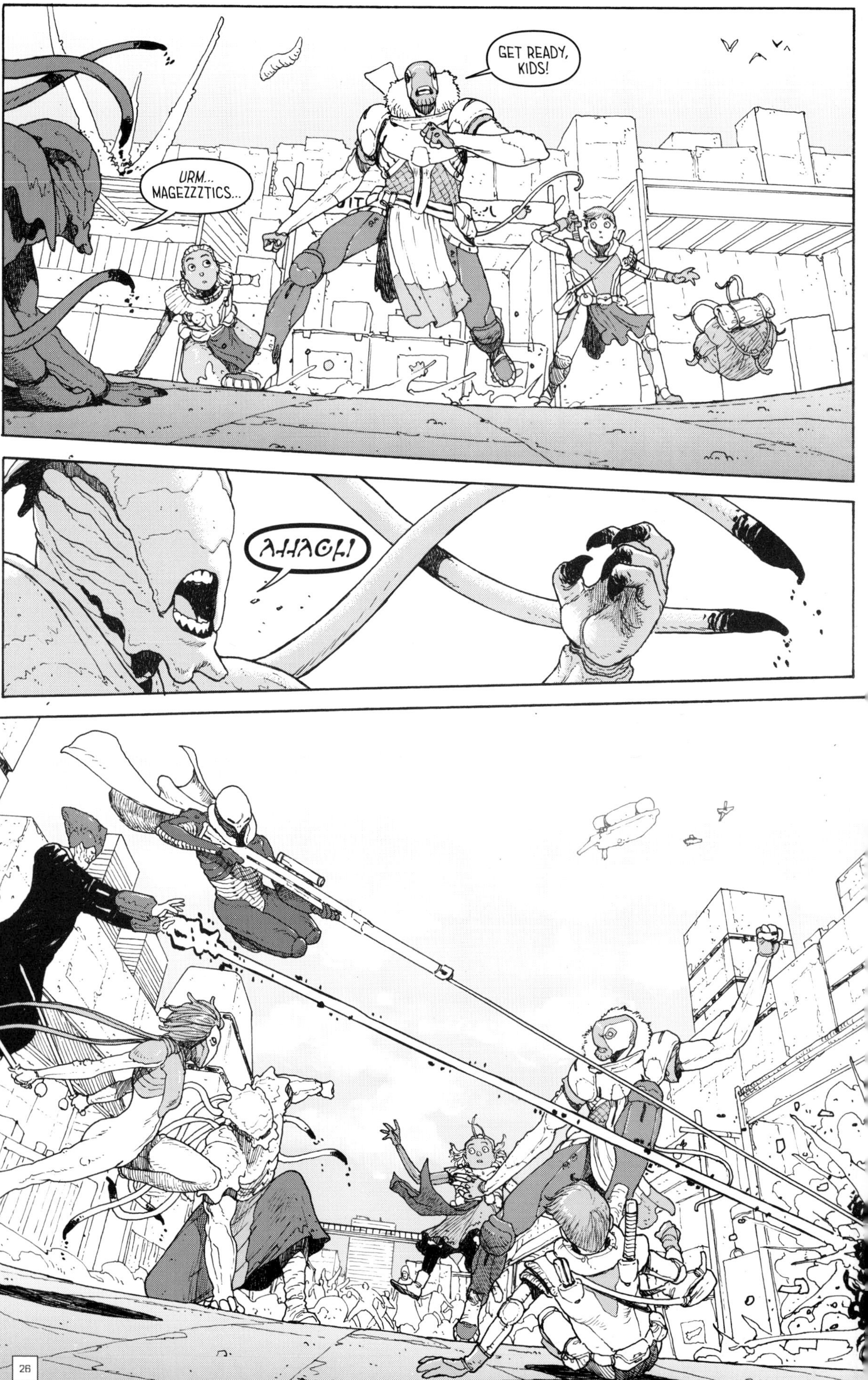
GET READY, KIDS!
URM... MAGEZZZTICS...

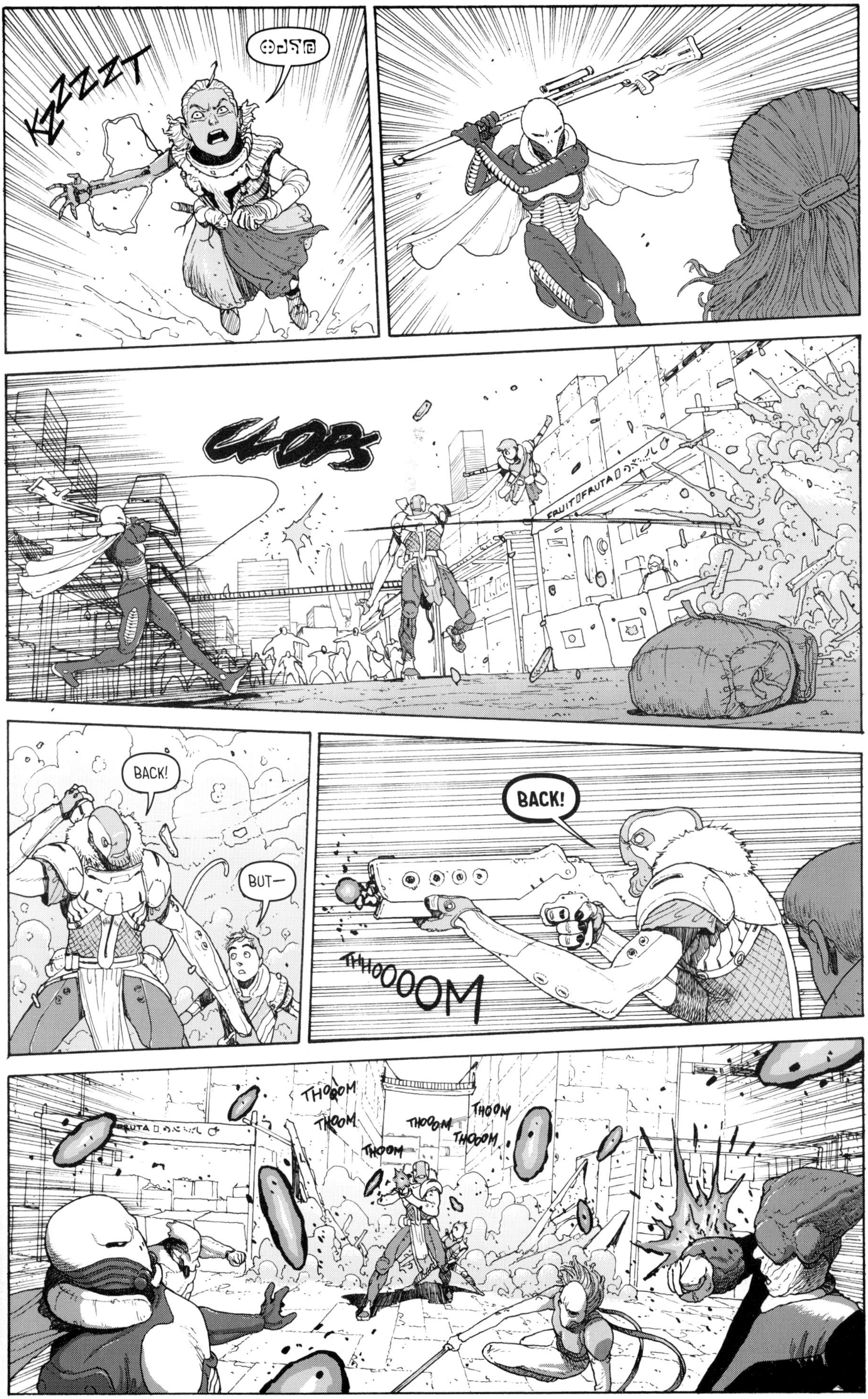
KZZZZT
CLOB
FRUIT FRUTA
BACK!
BUT—
BACK!
THHOOOOM
THOOOM
THOOOM
THOOOM
THOOM
THOOM
THOOOM
THOOOM

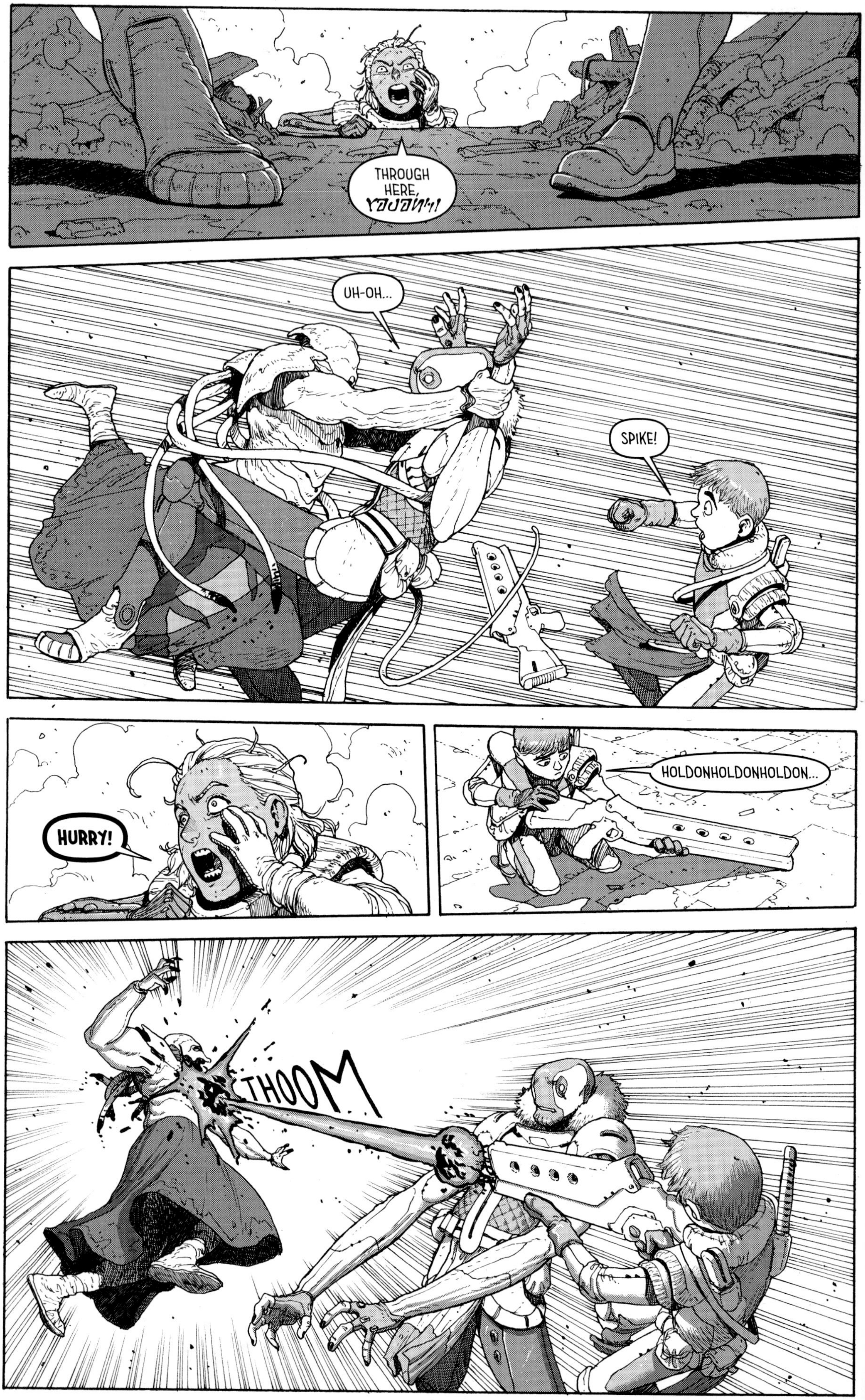
THROUGH HERE,
UH-OH...
SPIKE!
HURRY!
HOLDONHOLDONHOLDON...
THOOM

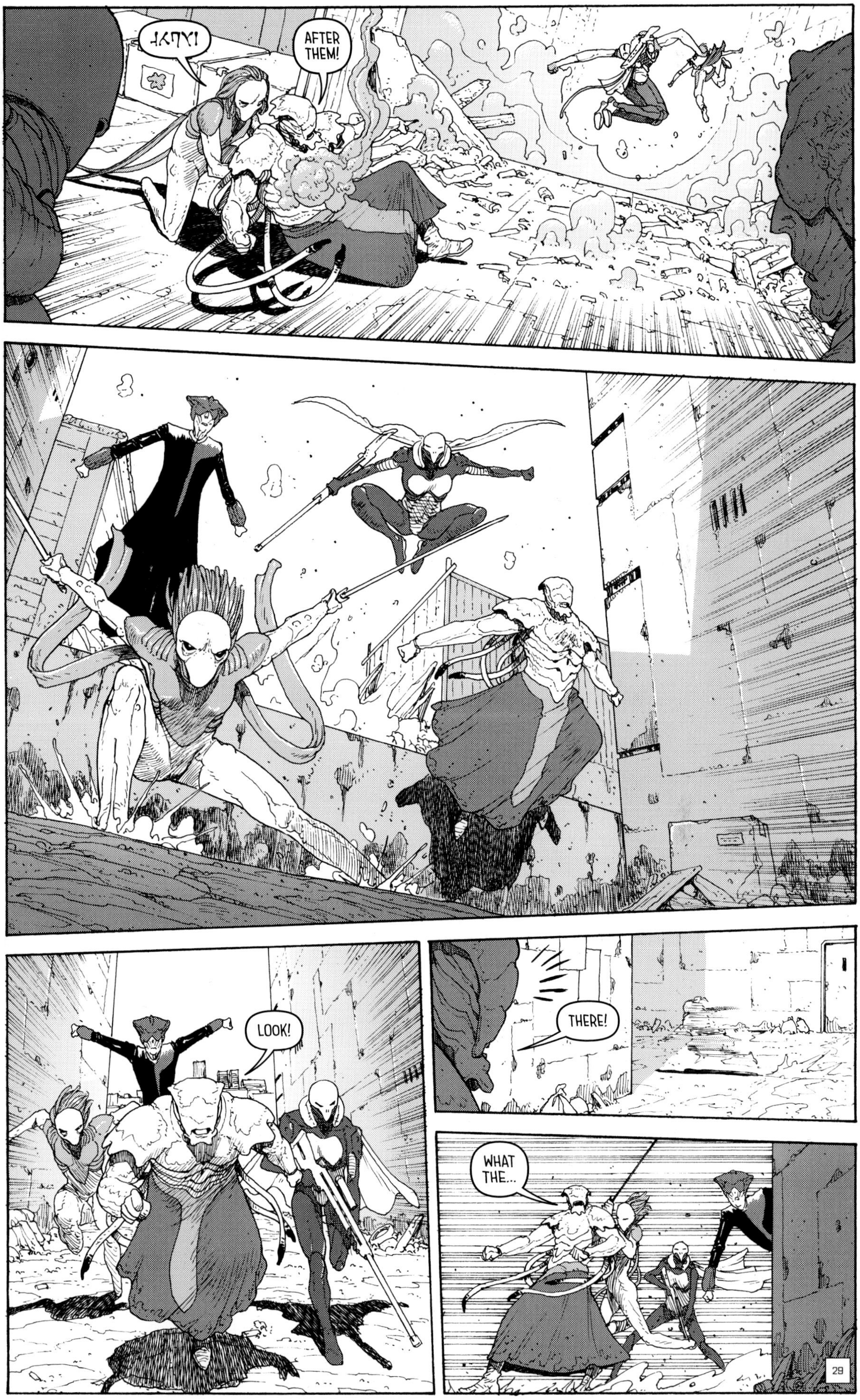

AFTER THEM!
LOOK!
THERE!
WHAT THE...

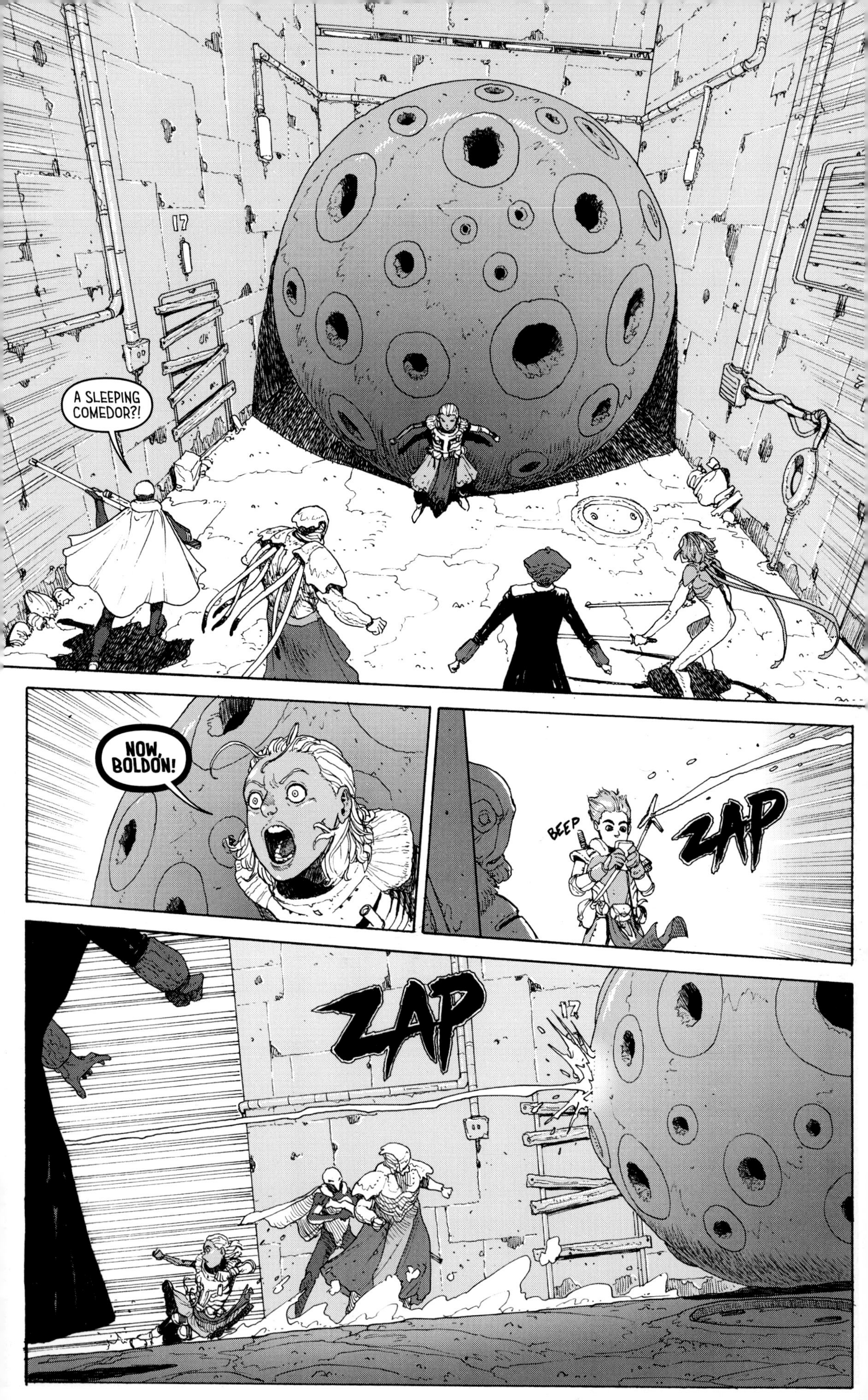
17
A SLEEPING COMEDOR?!
NOW, BOLDON!
BEEP
ZAP
ZAP
17

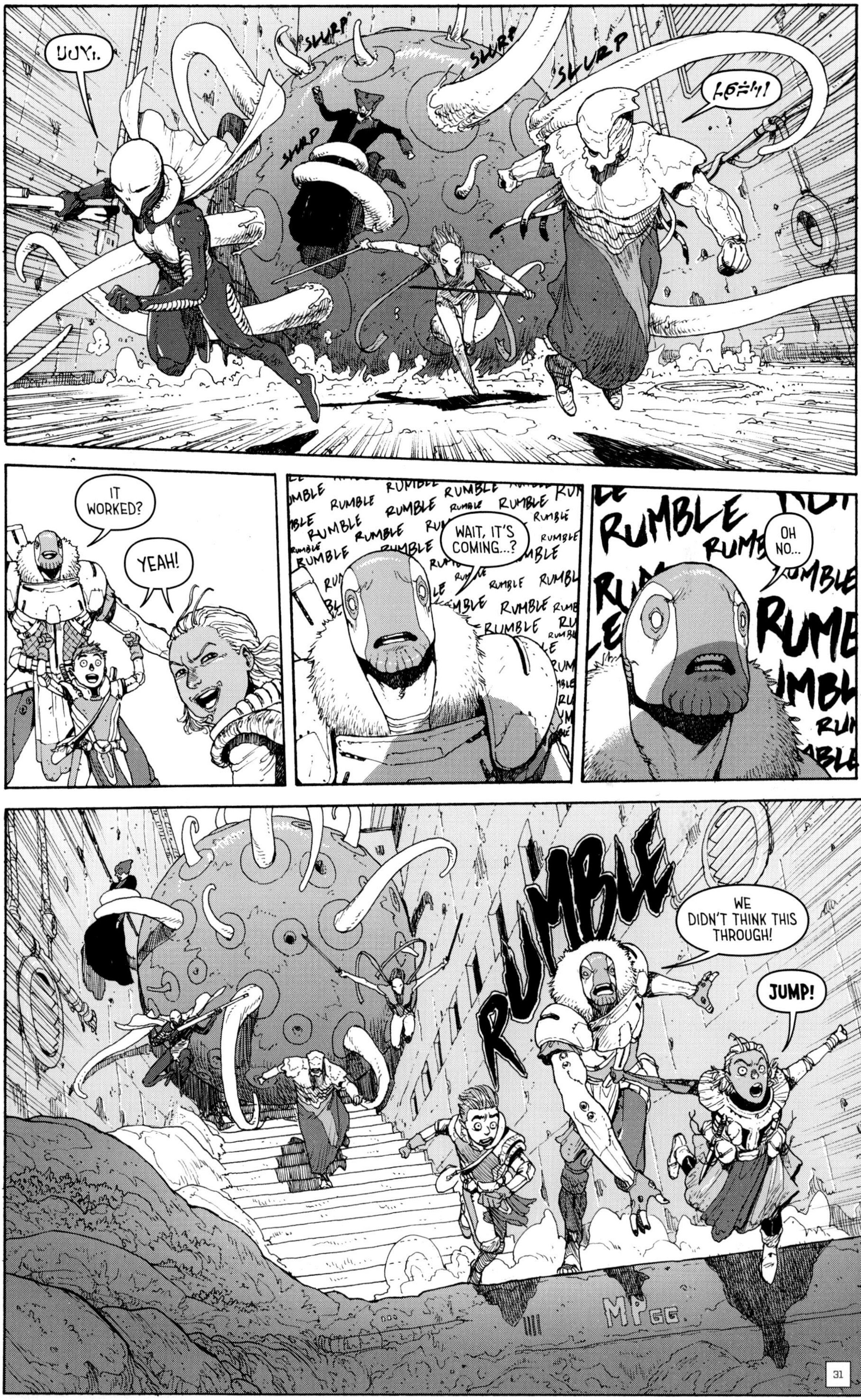
SLURP
SLURP
SLURP
SLURP
IT WORKED?
YEAH!
RUMBLE
WAIT, IT'S COMING...?
RUMBLE
OH NO...
RUMBLE
WE DIDN'T THINK THIS THROUGH!
JUMP!

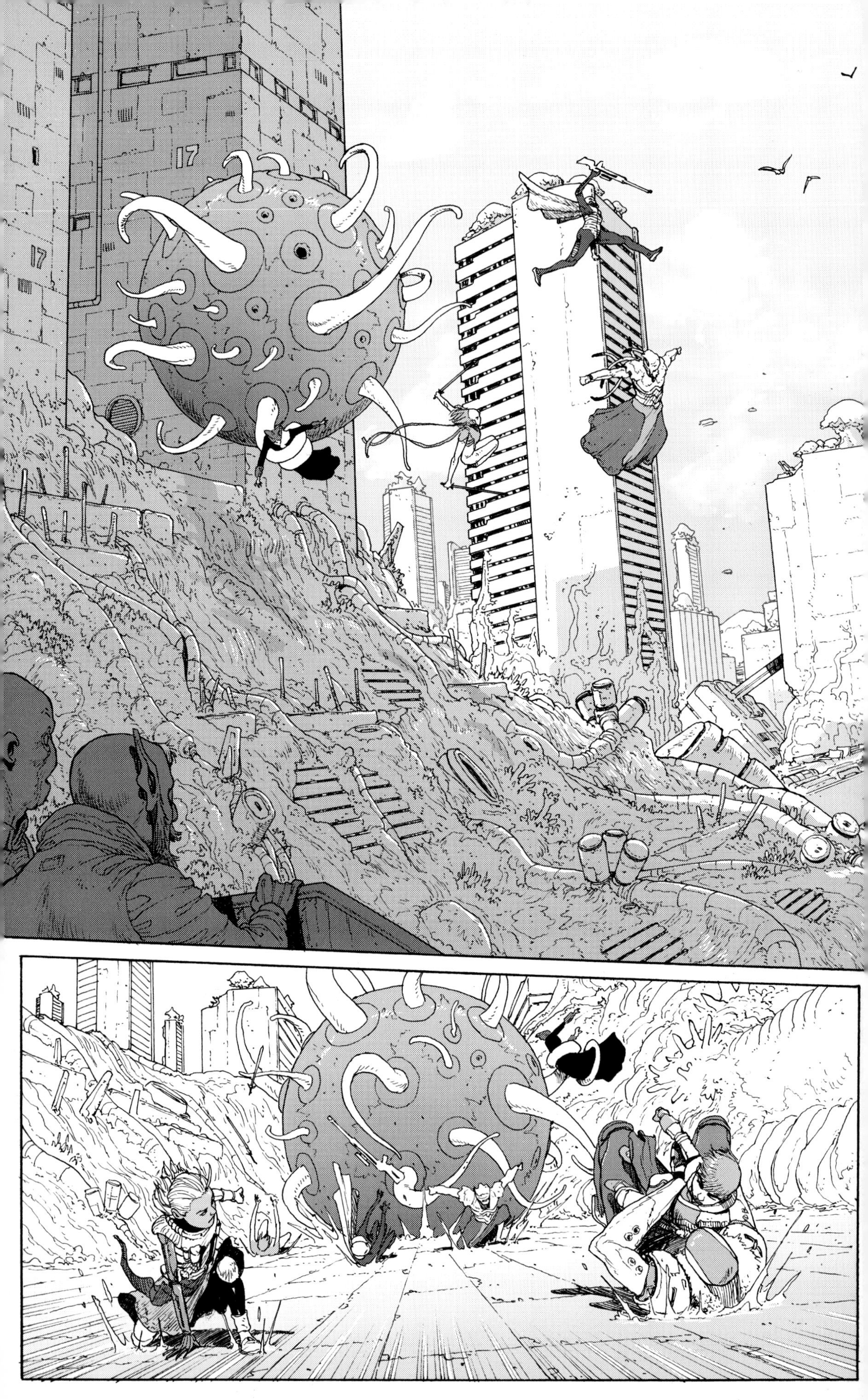
17
17

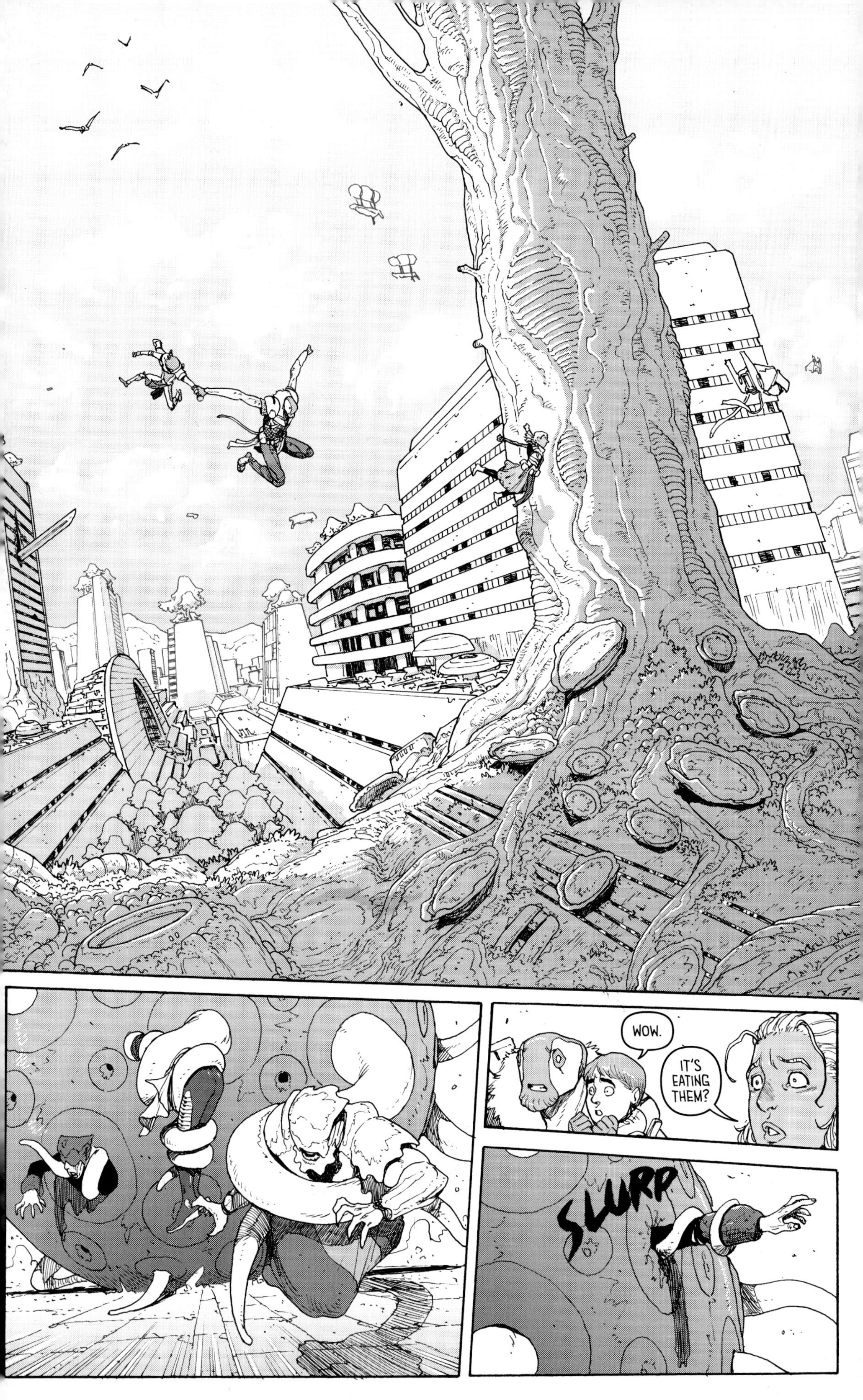
WOW.
IT'S EATING THEM?
SLURP

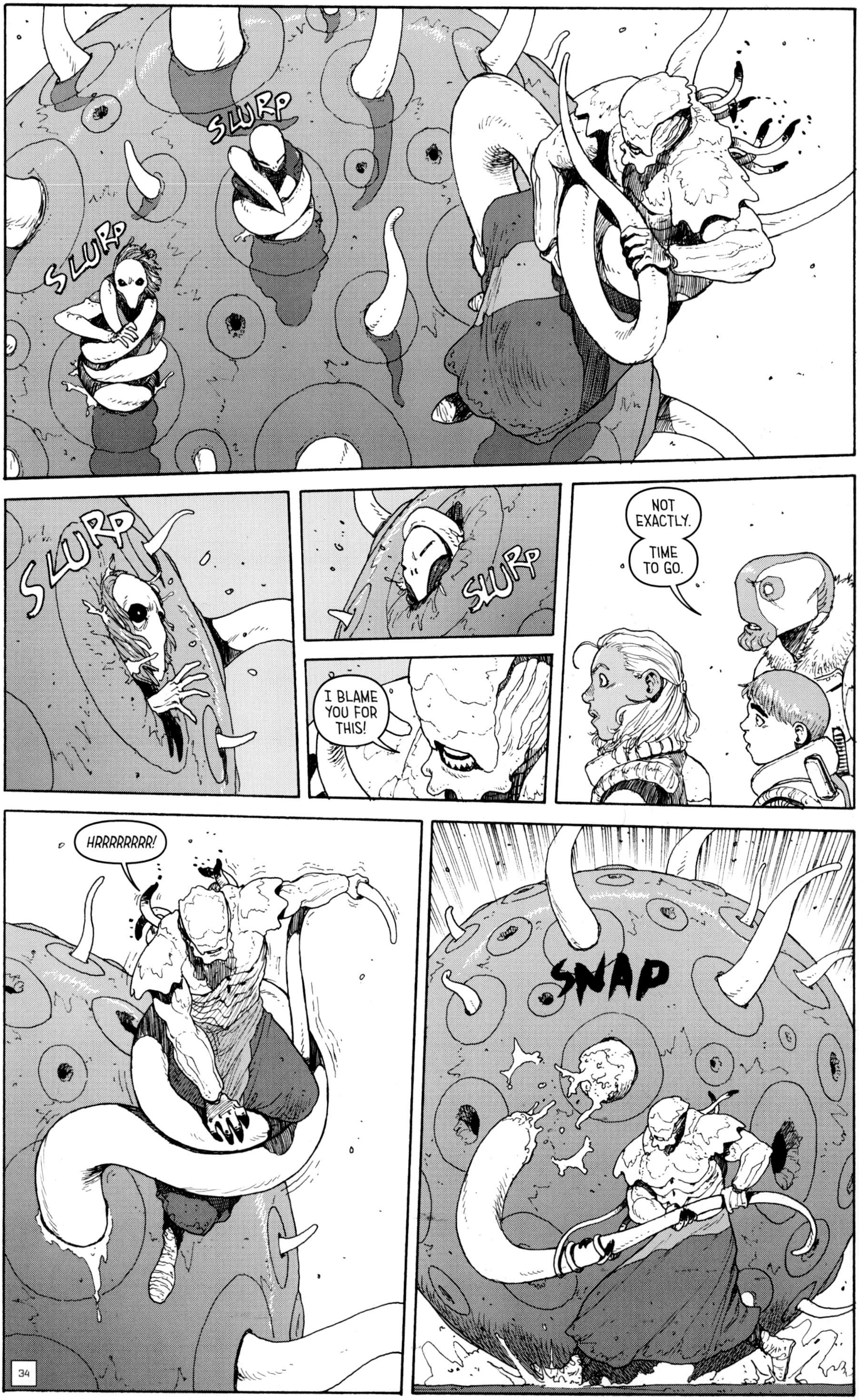
SLURP
SLURP
SLURP
SLURP
NOT EXACTLY.
TIME TO GO.
I BLAME YOU FOR THIS!
HRRRRRRRR!
SNAP

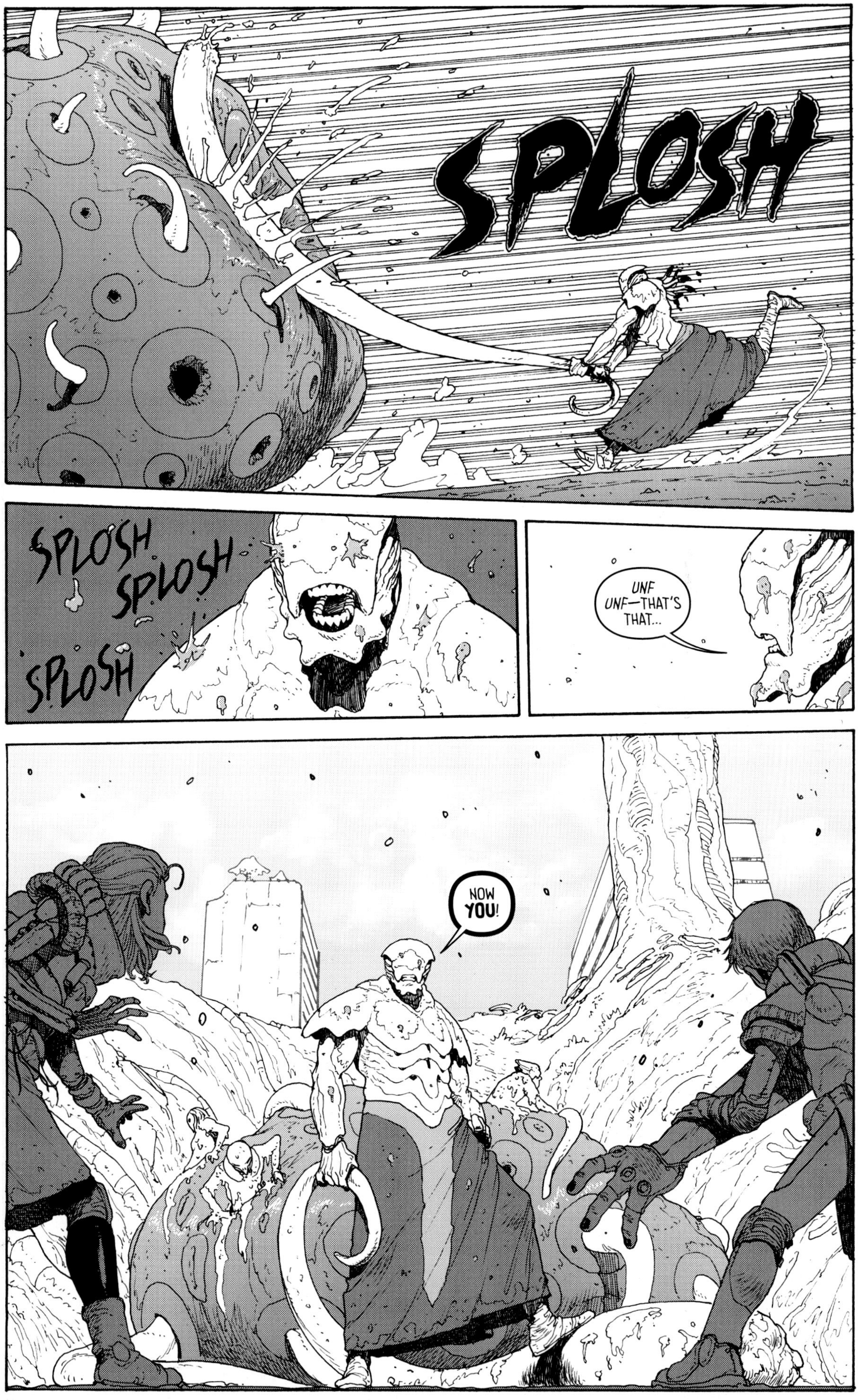
SPLOSH
SPLOSH
SPLOSH
SPLOSH
UNF UNF—THAT'S THAT...
NOW **YOU**!

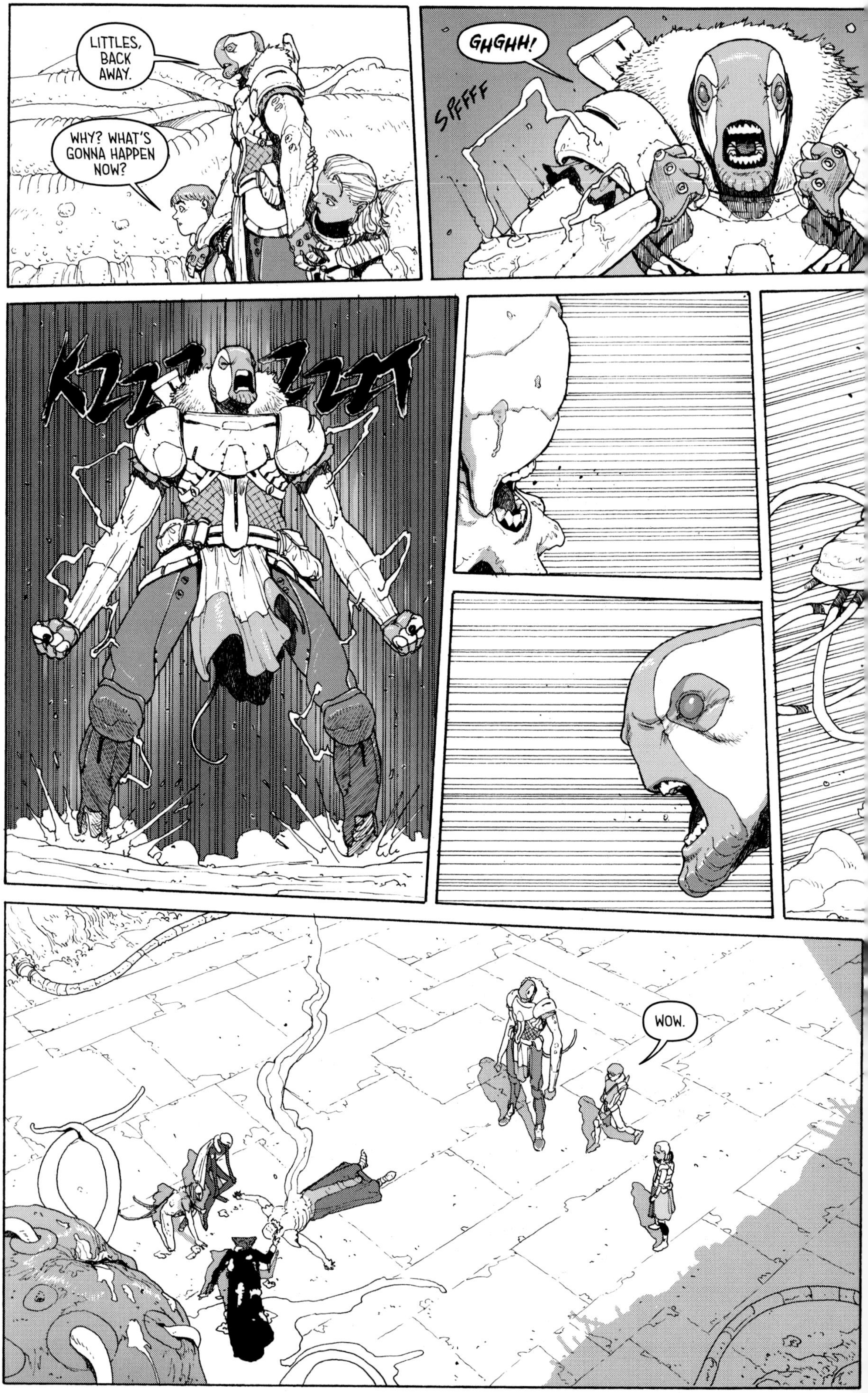
LITTLES, BACK AWAY.
WHY? WHAT'S GONNA HAPPEN NOW?
GHGHH!
SPFFFF
KZZZZZZZT
WOW.

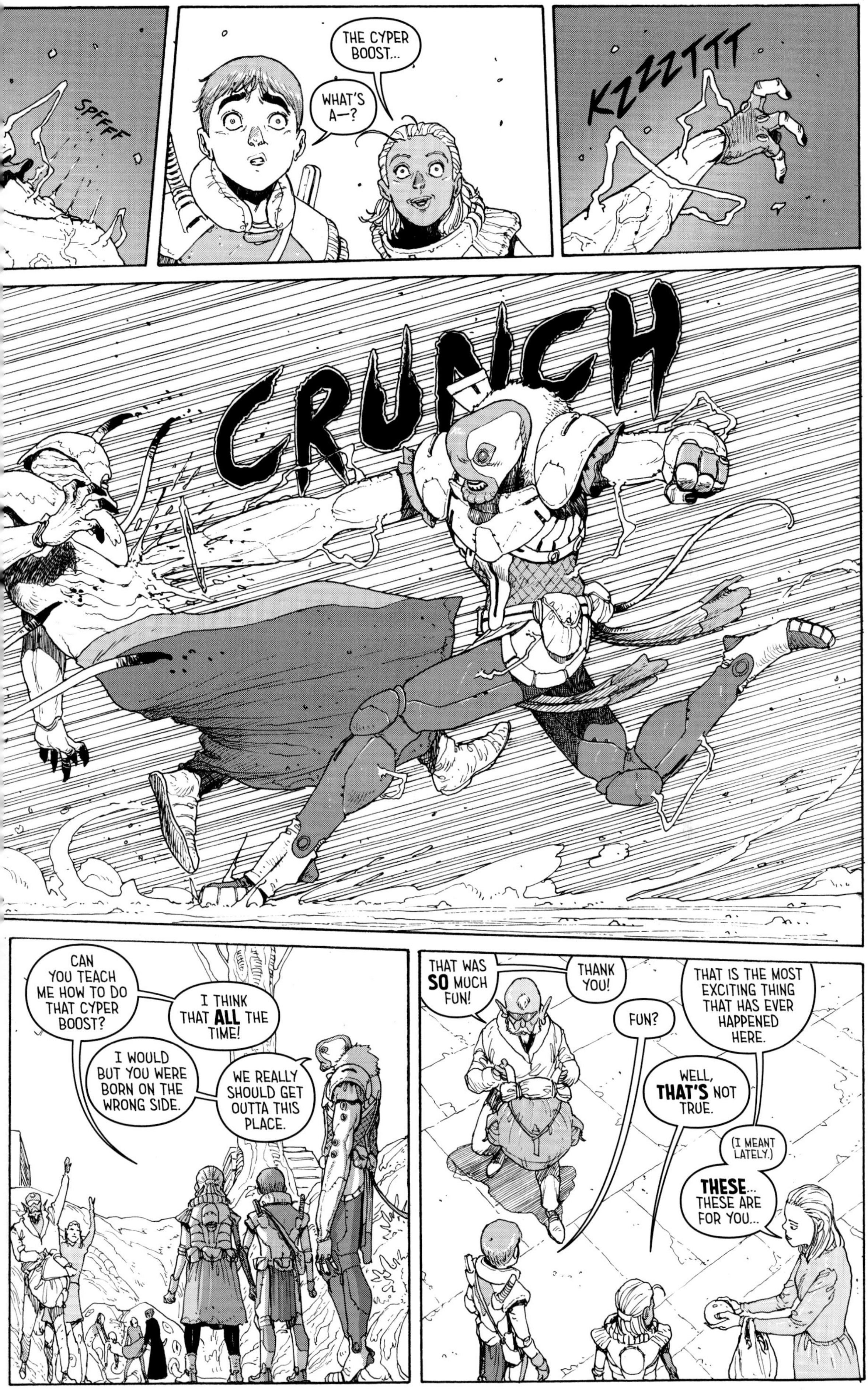
SPFFFF
THE CYPER BOOST...
WHAT'S A—?
KZZZTTT
CRUNCH
CAN YOU TEACH ME HOW TO DO THAT CYPER BOOST?
I THINK THAT **ALL** THE TIME!
I WOULD BUT YOU WERE BORN ON THE WRONG SIDE.
WE REALLY SHOULD GET OUTTA THIS PLACE.
THAT WAS **SO** MUCH FUN!
THANK YOU!
FUN?
THAT IS THE MOST EXCITING THING THAT HAS EVER HAPPENED HERE.
WELL, **THAT'S** NOT TRUE.
(I MEANT LATELY.)
THESE... THESE ARE FOR YOU...

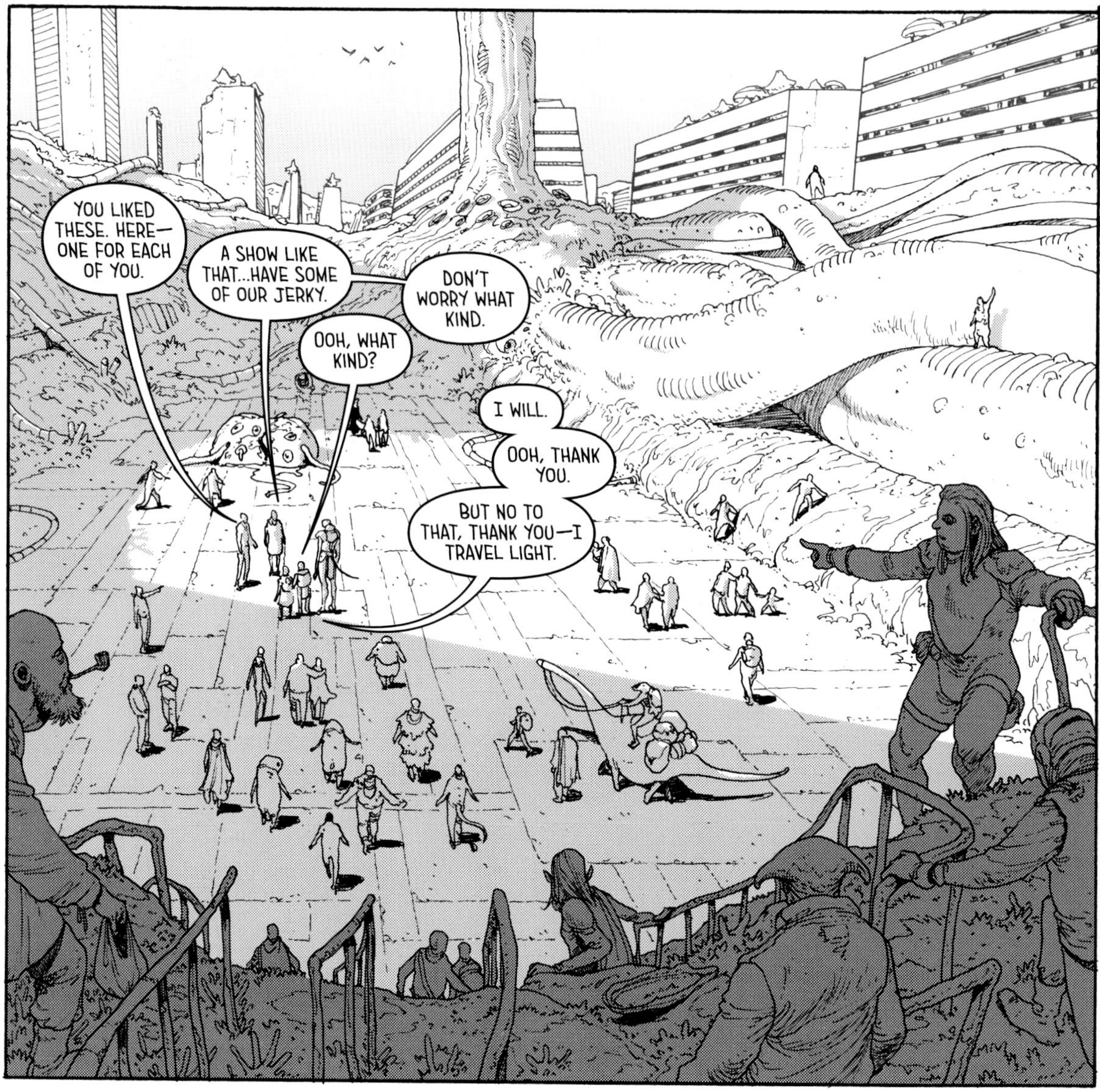
YOU LIKED THESE. HERE—ONE FOR EACH OF YOU.
A SHOW LIKE THAT...HAVE SOME OF OUR JERKY.
DON'T WORRY WHAT KIND.
OOH, WHAT KIND?
I WILL.
OOH, THANK YOU.
BUT NO TO THAT, THANK YOU—I TRAVEL LIGHT.

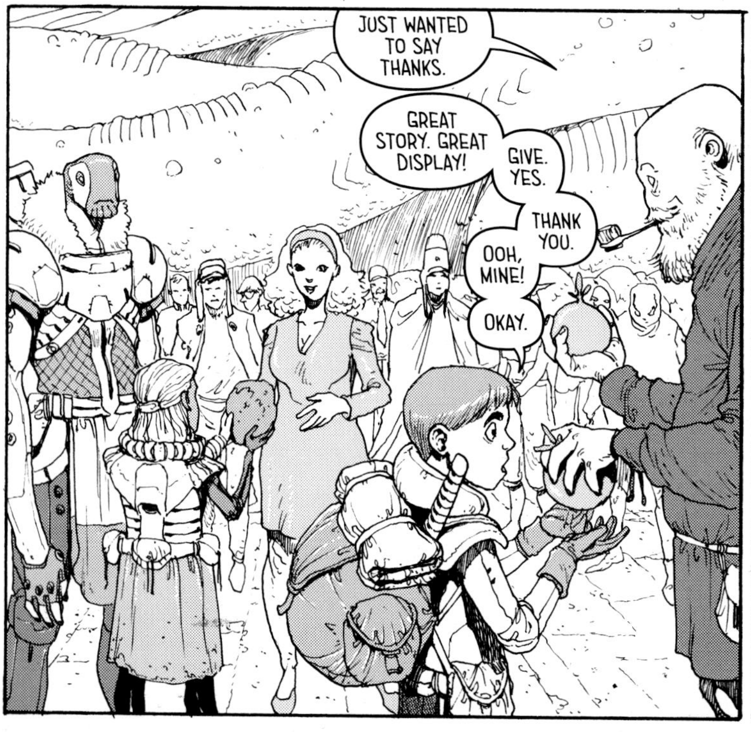
JUST WANTED TO SAY THANKS.
GREAT STORY. GREAT DISPLAY!
GIVE. YES.
THANK YOU.
OOH, MINE!
OKAY.

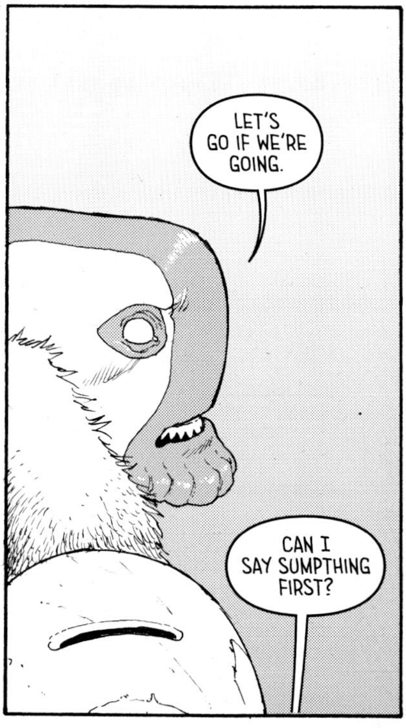
LET'S GO IF WE'RE GOING.
CAN I SAY SUMPTHING FIRST?

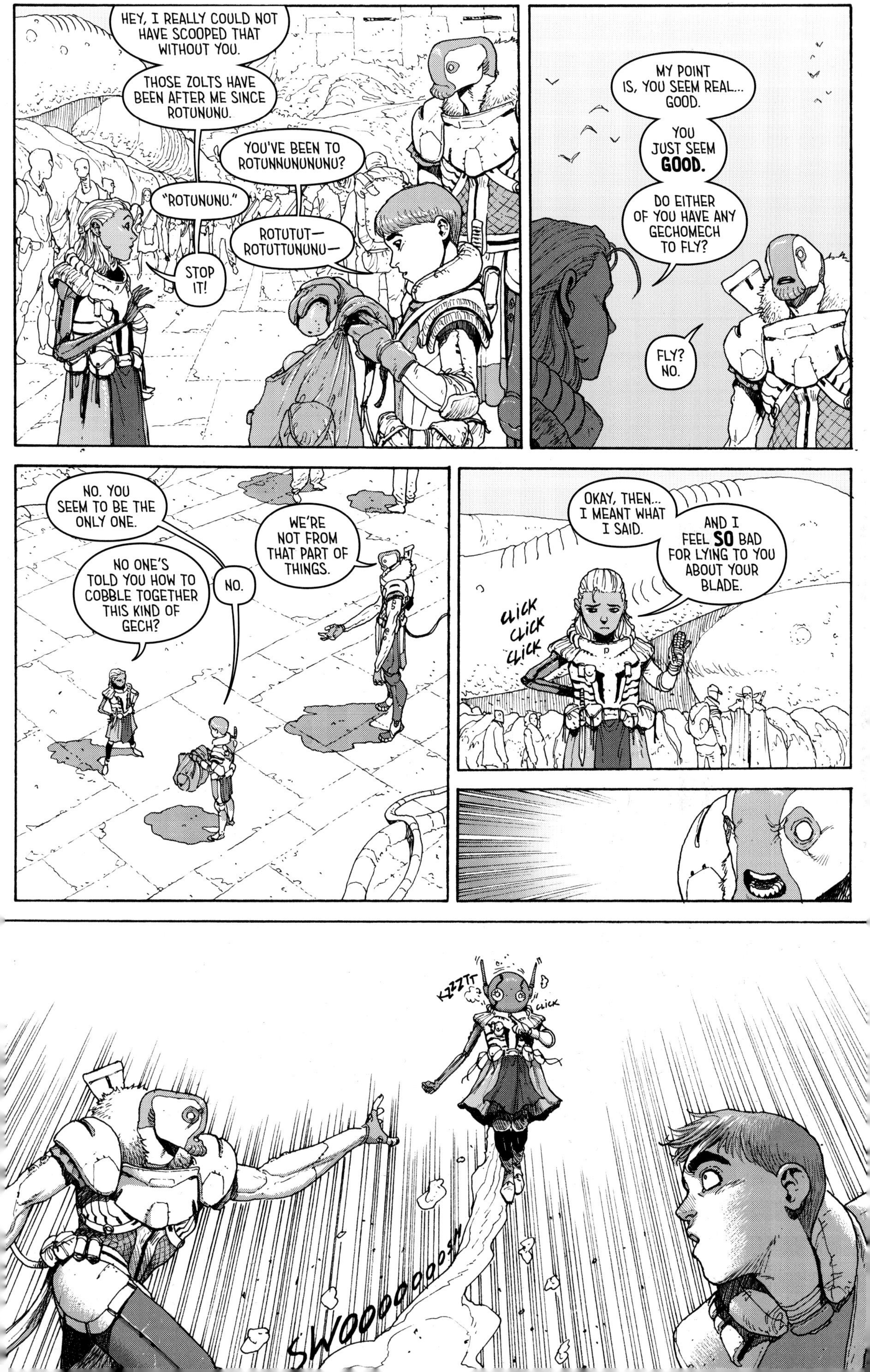
HEY, I REALLY COULD NOT HAVE SCOOPED THAT WITHOUT YOU.
THOSE ZOLTS HAVE BEEN AFTER ME SINCE ROTUNUNU.
YOU'VE BEEN TO ROTUNNUNUNUNU?
"ROTUNUNU."
ROTUTUT— ROTUTTUNUNU—
STOP IT!
MY POINT IS, YOU SEEM REAL... GOOD.
YOU JUST SEEM GOOD.
DO EITHER OF YOU HAVE ANY GECHOMECH TO FLY?
FLY? NO.
NO. YOU SEEM TO BE THE ONLY ONE.
NO ONE'S TOLD YOU HOW TO COBBLE TOGETHER THIS KIND OF GECH?
NO.
WE'RE NOT FROM THAT PART OF THINGS.
OKAY, THEN... I MEANT WHAT I SAID.
AND I FEEL SO BAD FOR LYING TO YOU ABOUT YOUR BLADE.
CLICK CLICK CLICK
KIZZTT
CLICK
SWOOOOOOOOSH

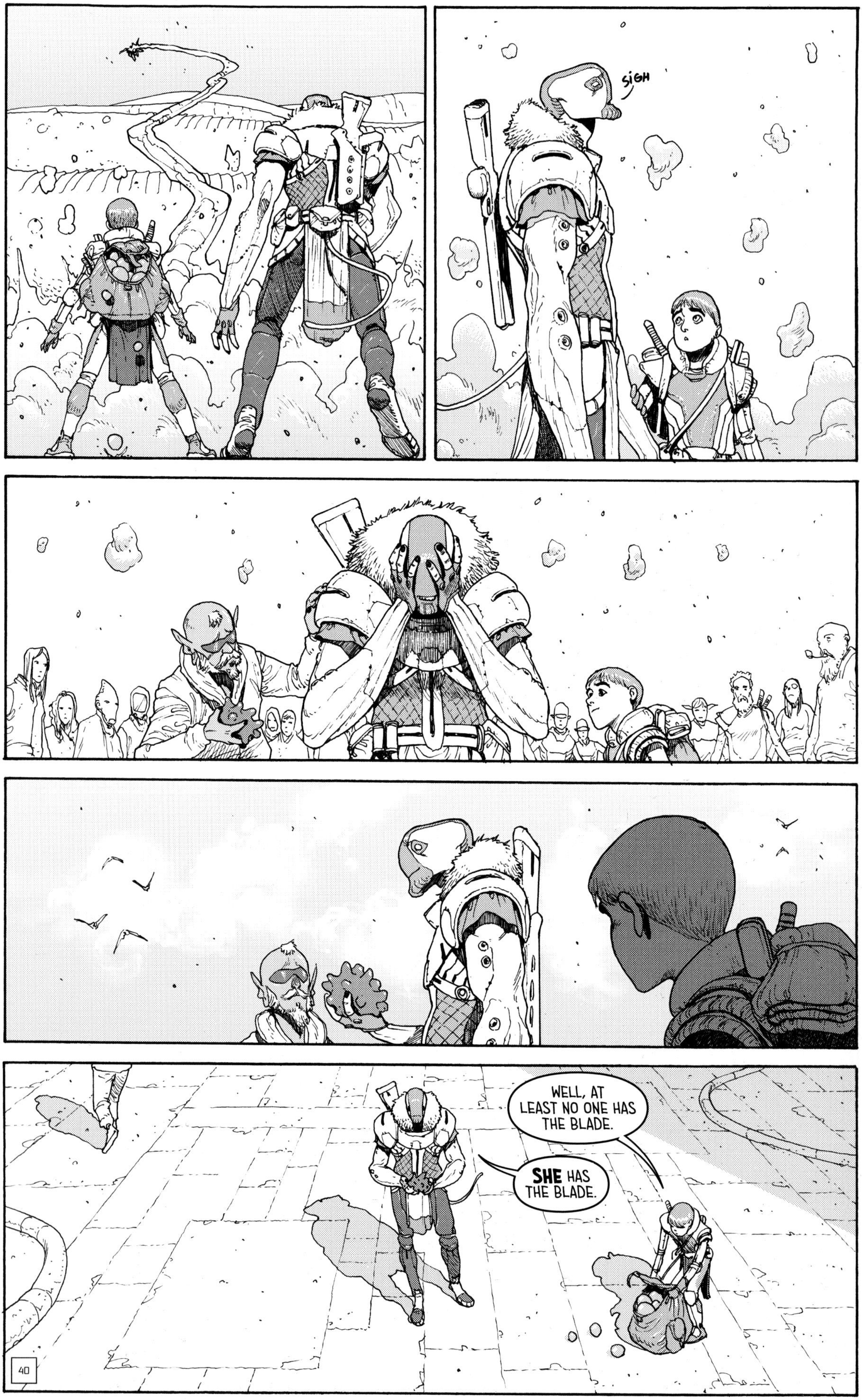
SIGH
WELL, AT LEAST NO ONE HAS THE BLADE.
SHE HAS THE BLADE.

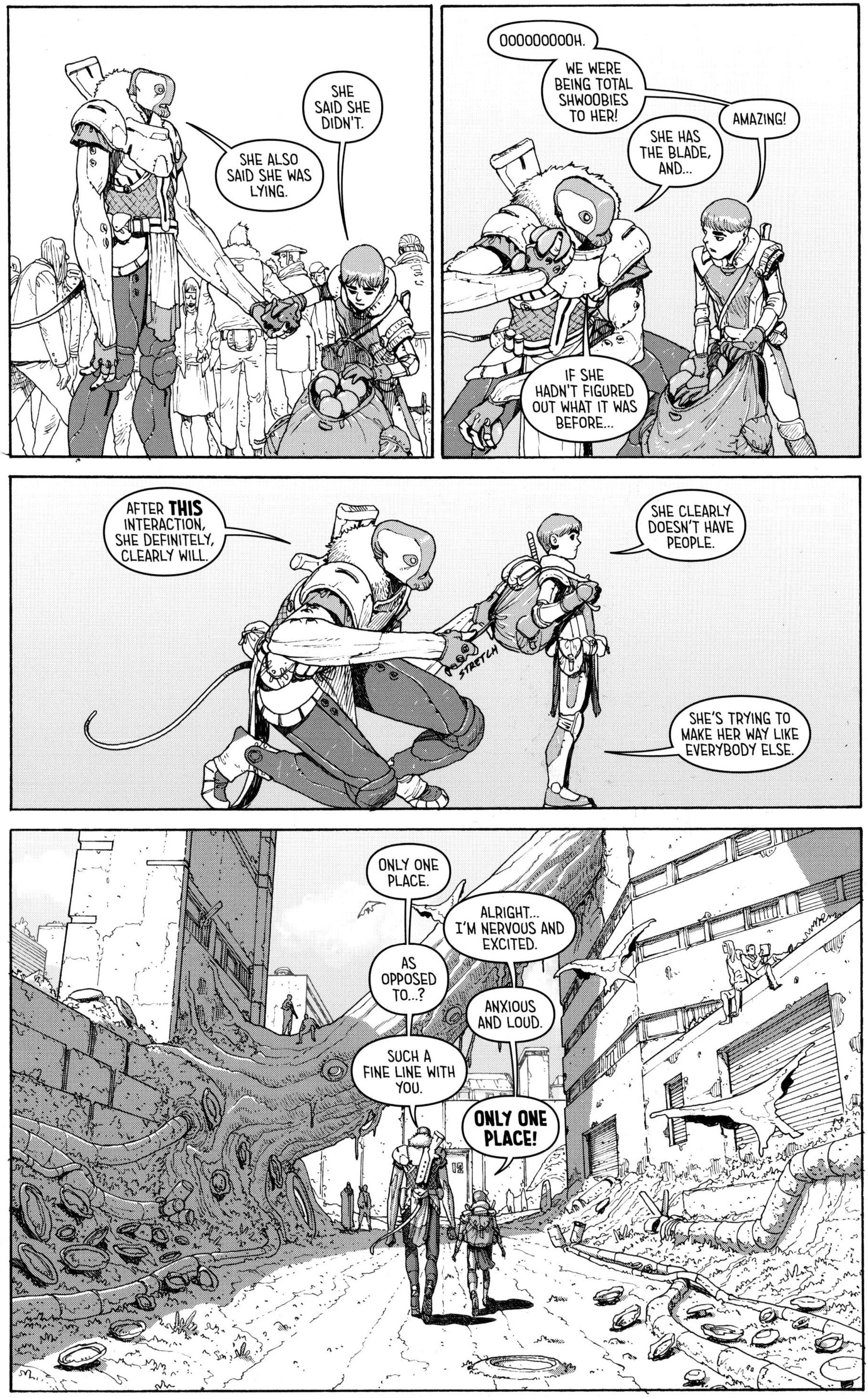
SHE SAID SHE DIDN'T.
SHE ALSO SAID SHE WAS LYING.
OOOOOOOOOH.
WE WERE BEING TOTAL SHWOOBIES TO HER!
AMAZING!
SHE HAS THE BLADE, AND...
IF SHE HADN'T FIGURED OUT WHAT IT WAS BEFORE...
AFTER **THIS** INTERACTION, SHE DEFINITELY, CLEARLY WILL.
SHE CLEARLY DOESN'T HAVE PEOPLE.
STRETCH
SHE'S TRYING TO MAKE HER WAY LIKE EVERYBODY ELSE.
ONLY ONE PLACE.
ALRIGHT... I'M NERVOUS AND EXCITED.
AS OPPOSED TO...?
ANXIOUS AND LOUD.
SUCH A FINE LINE WITH YOU.
ONLY ONE PLACE!

"ONLY ONE PLACE..."

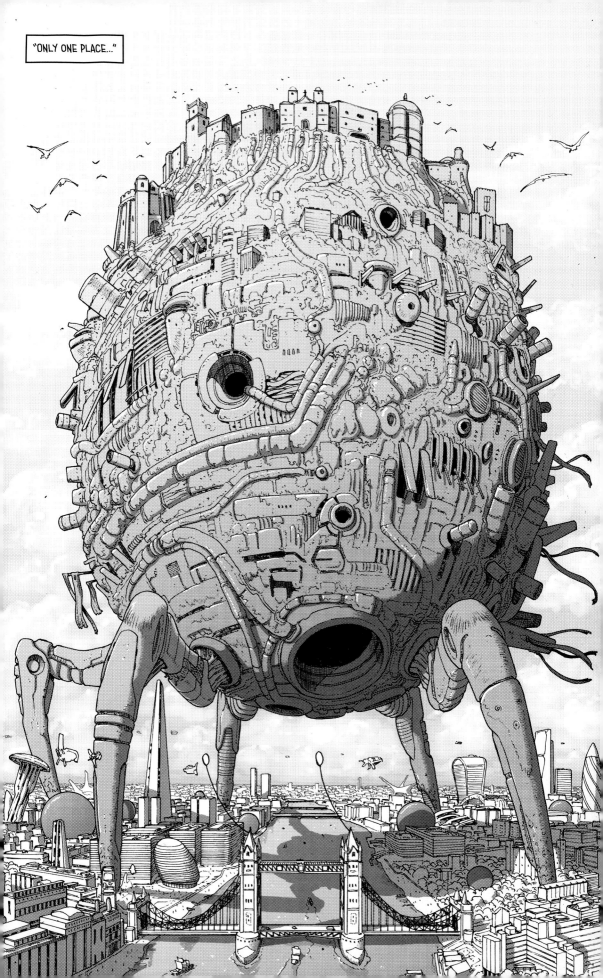

CHAPTER 2

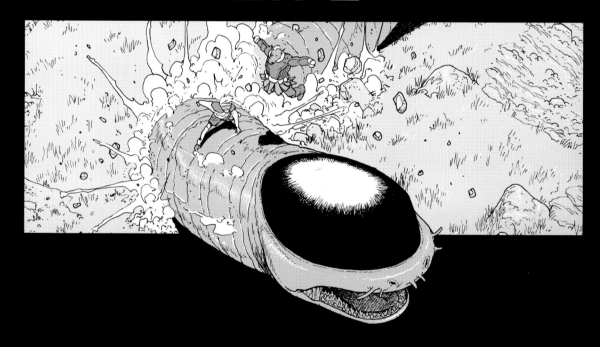

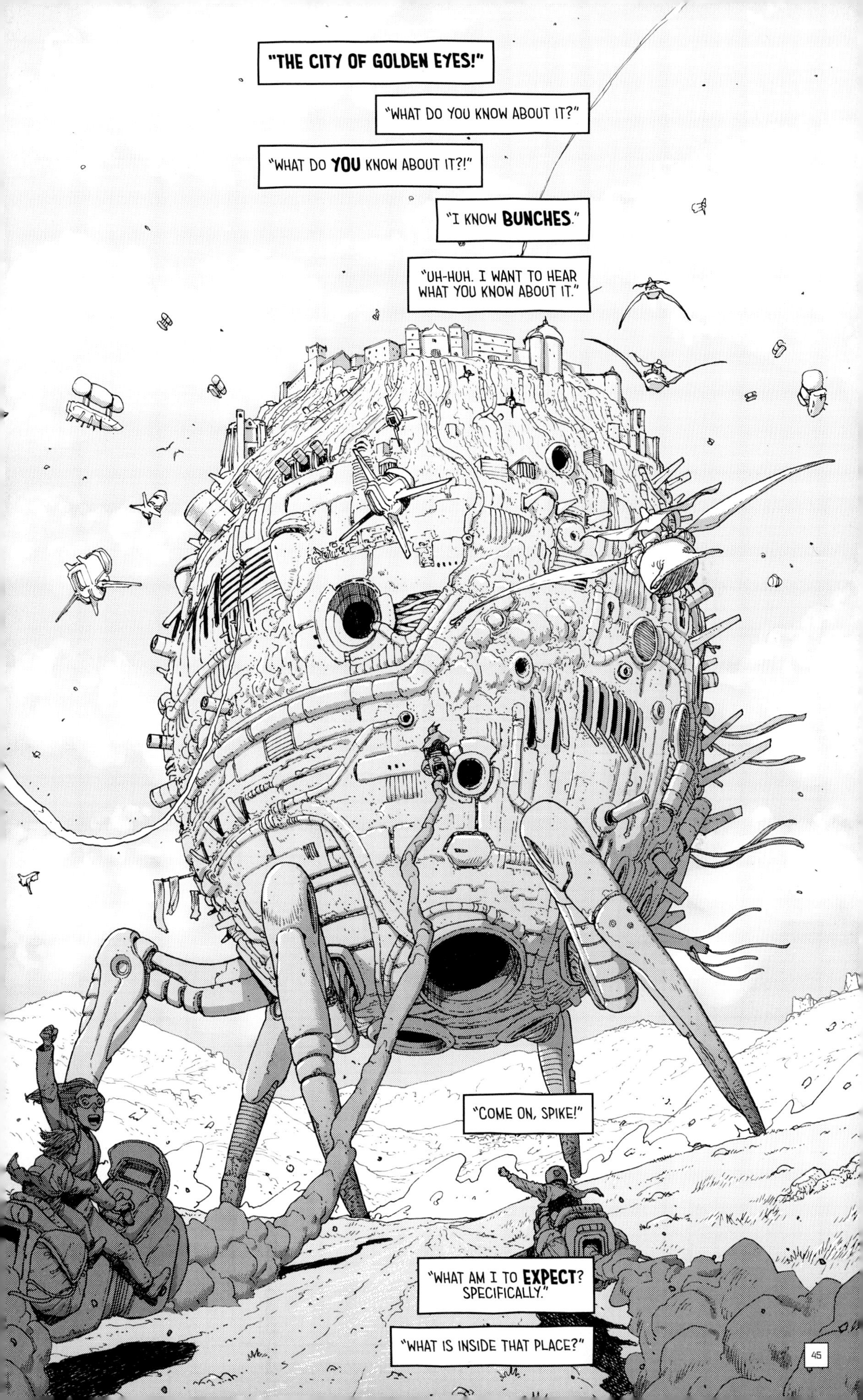
"THE CITY OF GOLDEN EYES!"
"WHAT DO YOU KNOW ABOUT IT?"
"WHAT DO **YOU** KNOW ABOUT IT?!"
"I KNOW **BUNCHES**."
"UH-HUH. I WANT TO HEAR WHAT YOU KNOW ABOUT IT."
"COME ON, SPIKE!"
"WHAT AM I TO **EXPECT**? SPECIFICALLY."
"WHAT IS INSIDE THAT PLACE?"

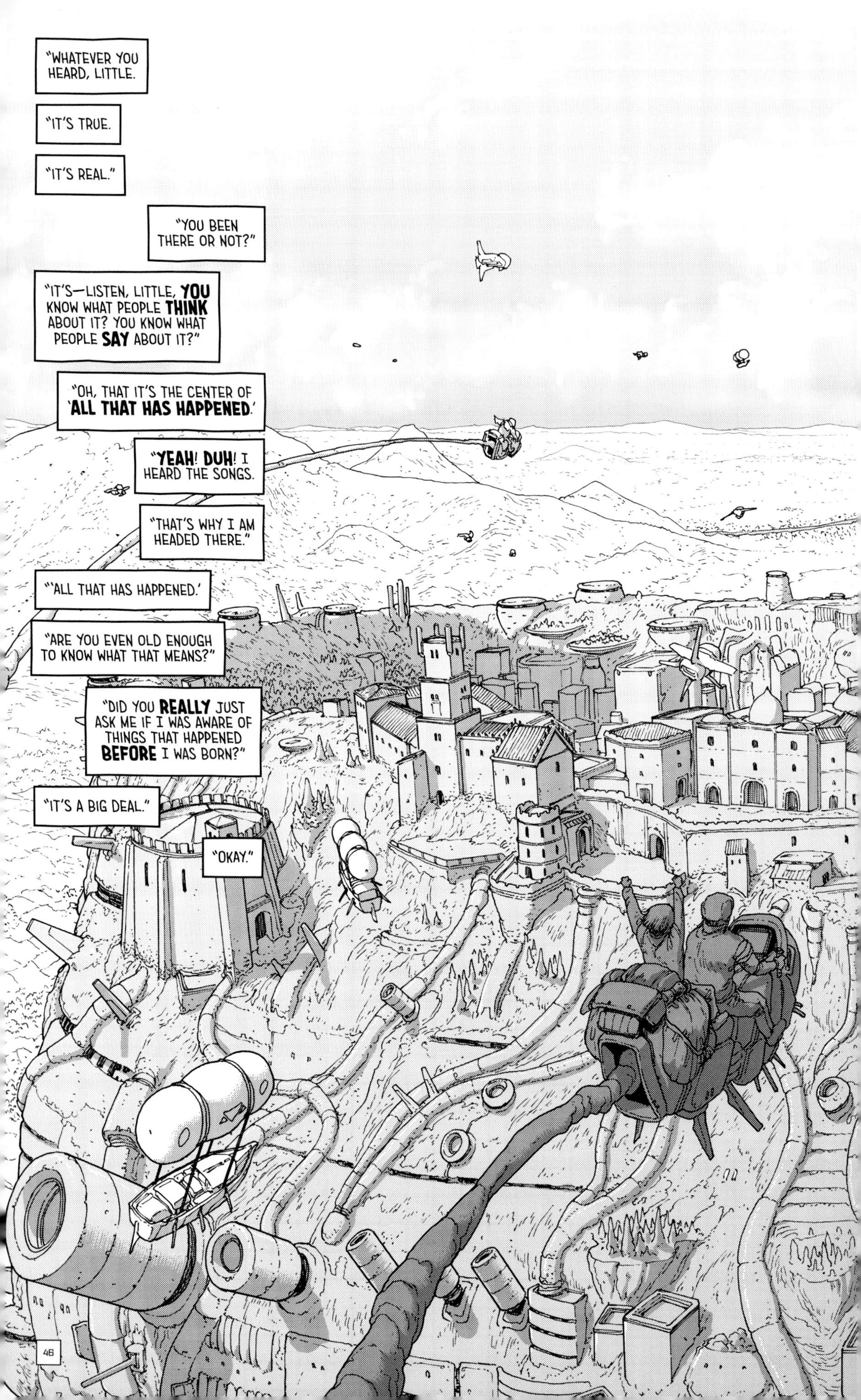
"WHATEVER YOU HEARD, LITTLE.
"IT'S TRUE.
"IT'S REAL."
"YOU BEEN THERE OR NOT?"
"IT'S—LISTEN, LITTLE, **YOU** KNOW WHAT PEOPLE **THINK** ABOUT IT? YOU KNOW WHAT PEOPLE **SAY** ABOUT IT?"
"OH, THAT IT'S THE CENTER OF '**ALL THAT HAS HAPPENED**.'
"**YEAH**! **DUH**! I HEARD THE SONGS.
"THAT'S WHY I AM HEADED THERE."
"'ALL THAT HAS HAPPENED.'
"ARE YOU EVEN OLD ENOUGH TO KNOW WHAT THAT MEANS?"
"DID YOU **REALLY** JUST ASK ME IF I WAS AWARE OF THINGS THAT HAPPENED **BEFORE** I WAS BORN?"
"IT'S A BIG DEAL."
"OKAY."

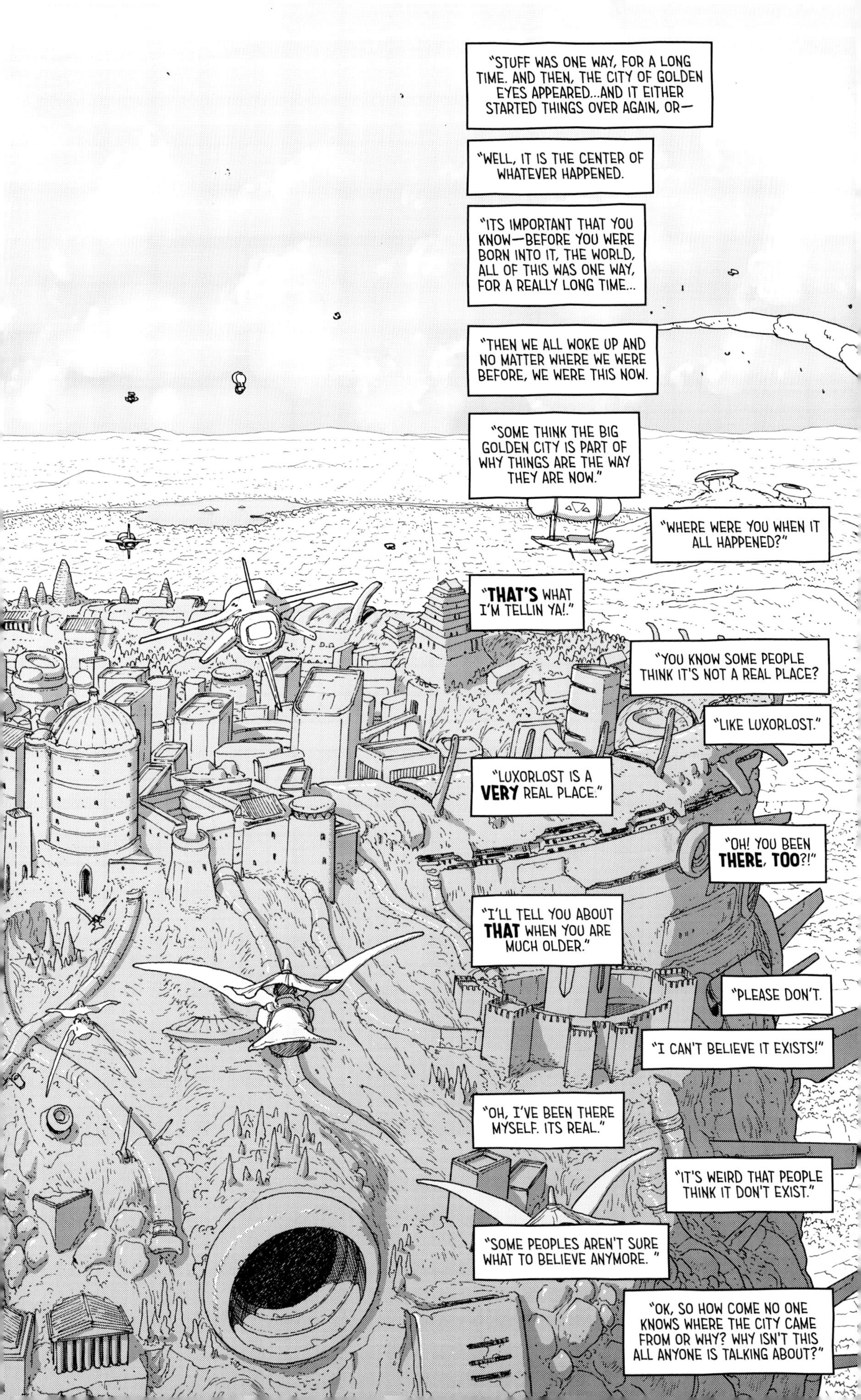
"STUFF WAS ONE WAY, FOR A LONG TIME. AND THEN, THE CITY OF GOLDEN EYES APPEARED...AND IT EITHER STARTED THINGS OVER AGAIN, OR—
"WELL, IT IS THE CENTER OF WHATEVER HAPPENED.
"ITS IMPORTANT THAT YOU KNOW—BEFORE YOU WERE BORN INTO IT, THE WORLD, ALL OF THIS WAS ONE WAY, FOR A REALLY LONG TIME...
"THEN WE ALL WOKE UP AND NO MATTER WHERE WE WERE BEFORE, WE WERE THIS NOW.
"SOME THINK THE BIG GOLDEN CITY IS PART OF WHY THINGS ARE THE WAY THEY ARE NOW."
"WHERE WERE YOU WHEN IT ALL HAPPENED?"
"**THAT'S** WHAT I'M TELLIN YA!."
"YOU KNOW SOME PEOPLE THINK IT'S NOT A REAL PLACE?
"LIKE LUXORLOST."
"LUXORLOST IS A **VERY** REAL PLACE."
"OH! YOU BEEN **THERE, TOO**?!"
"I'LL TELL YOU ABOUT **THAT** WHEN YOU ARE MUCH OLDER."
"PLEASE DON'T.
"I CAN'T BELIEVE IT EXISTS!"
"OH, I'VE BEEN THERE MYSELF. ITS REAL."
"IT'S WEIRD THAT PEOPLE THINK IT DON'T EXIST."
"SOME PEOPLES AREN'T SURE WHAT TO BELIEVE ANYMORE. "
"OK, SO HOW COME NO ONE KNOWS WHERE THE CITY CAME FROM OR WHY? WHY ISN'T THIS ALL ANYONE IS TALKING ABOUT?"

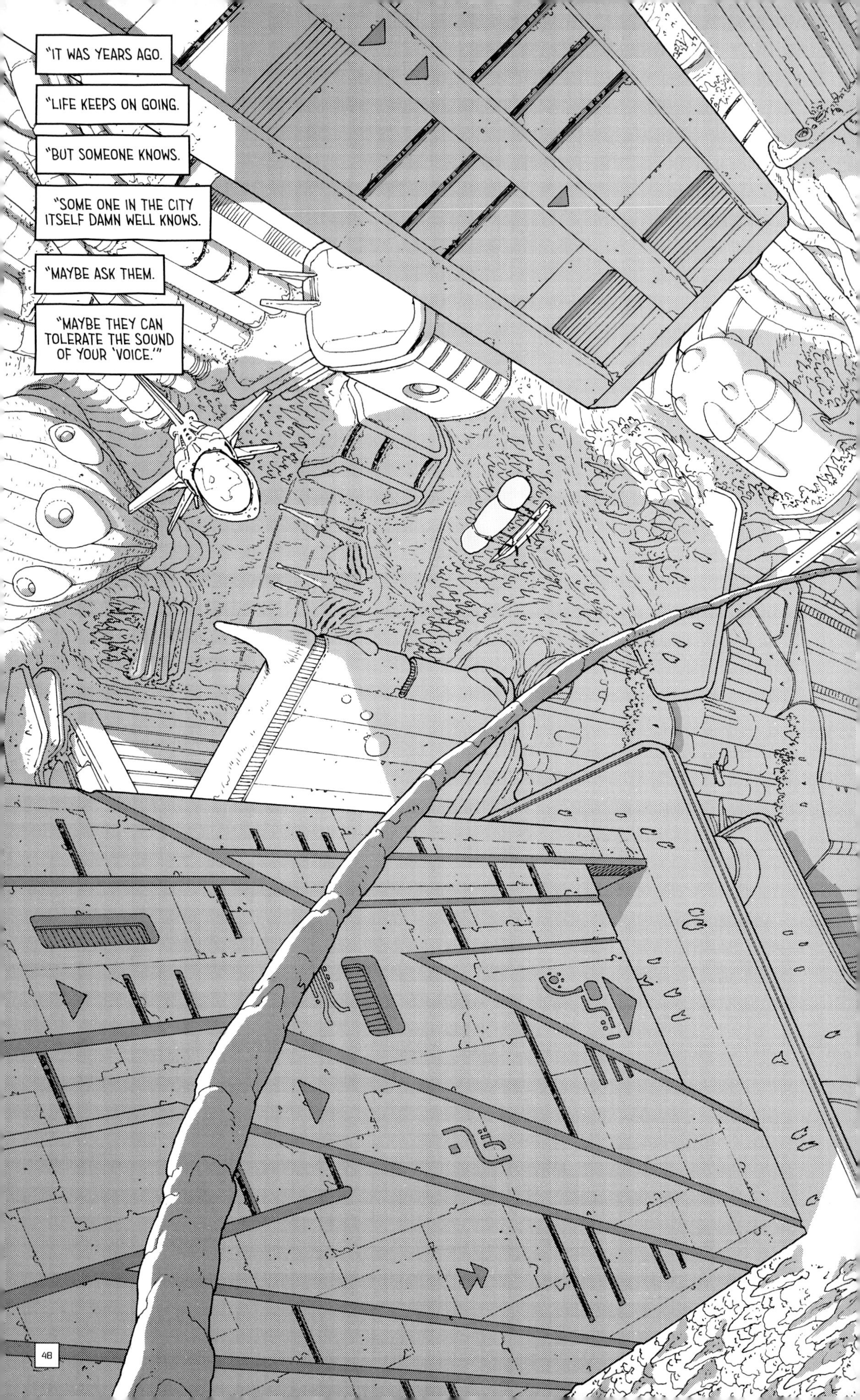

"IT WAS YEARS AGO.
"LIFE KEEPS ON GOING.
"BUT SOMEONE KNOWS.
"SOME ONE IN THE CITY ITSELF DAMN WELL KNOWS.
"MAYBE ASK THEM.
"MAYBE THEY CAN TOLERATE THE SOUND OF YOUR 'VOICE.'"

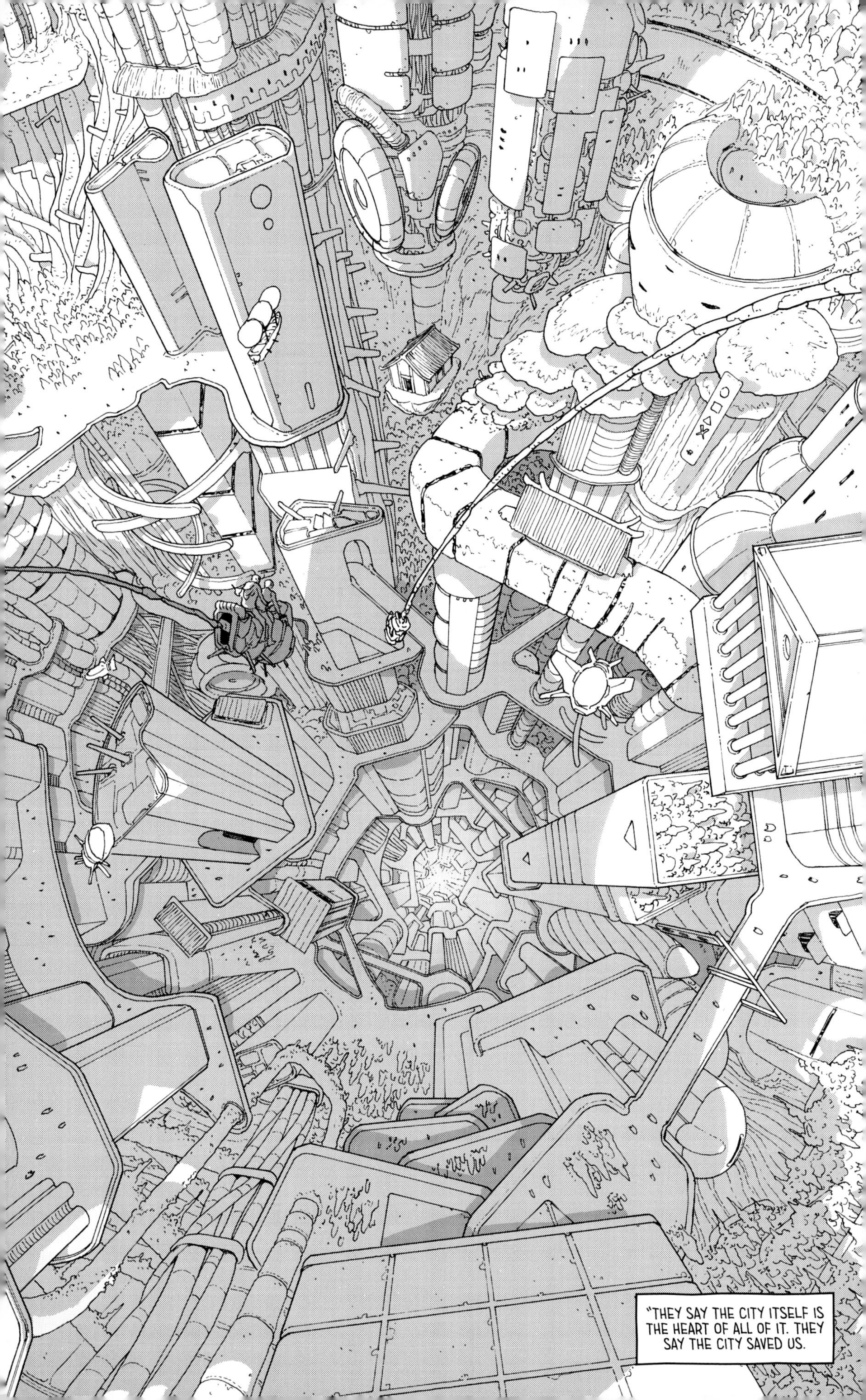
"THEY SAY THE CITY ITSELF IS THE HEART OF ALL OF IT. THEY SAY THE CITY SAVED US.

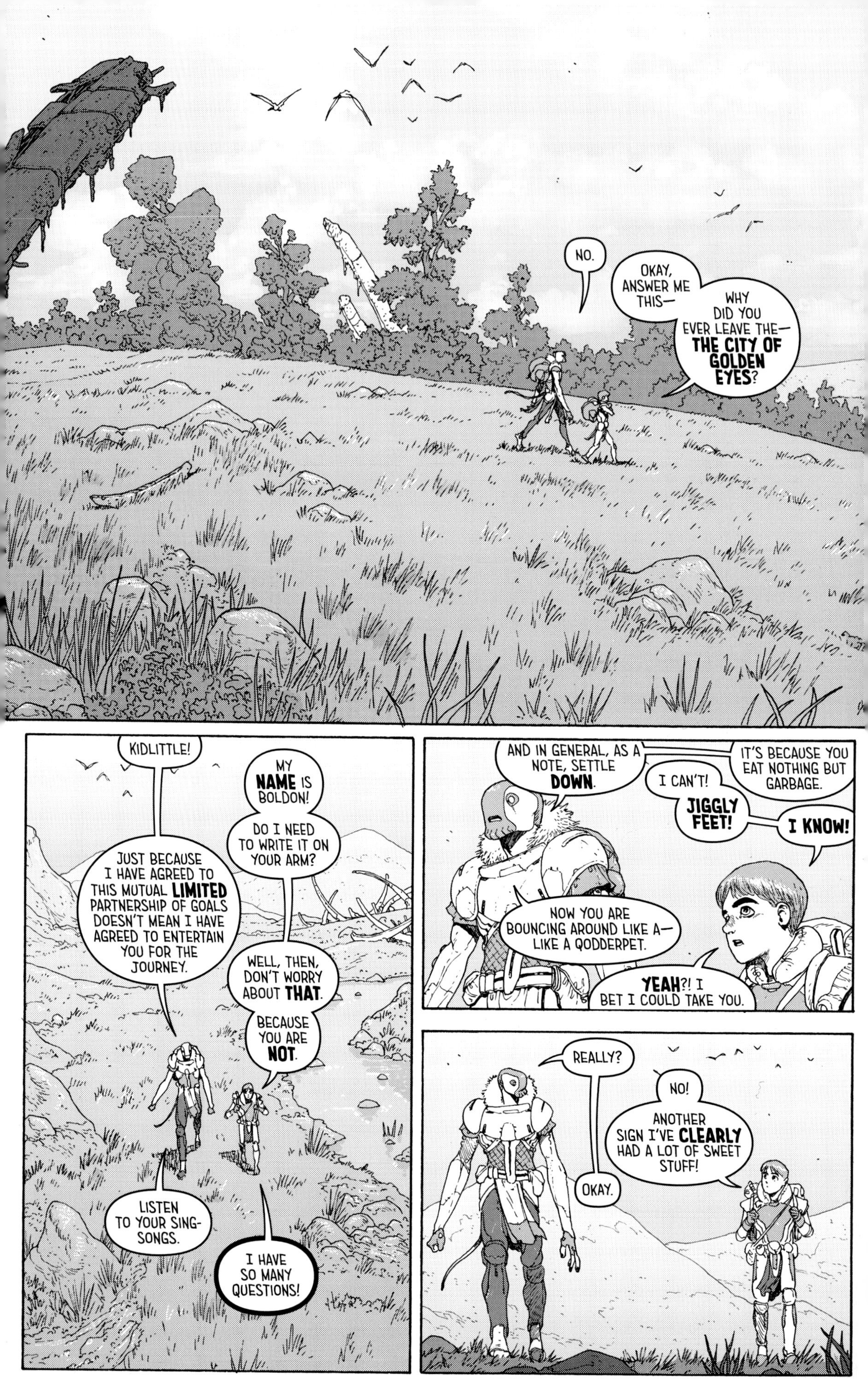
NO.
OKAY, ANSWER ME THIS—
WHY DID YOU EVER LEAVE THE— **THE CITY OF GOLDEN EYES**?
KIDLITTLE!
JUST BECAUSE I HAVE AGREED TO THIS MUTUAL **LIMITED** PARTNERSHIP OF GOALS DOESN'T MEAN I HAVE AGREED TO ENTERTAIN YOU FOR THE JOURNEY.
MY **NAME** IS BOLDON!
DO I NEED TO WRITE IT ON YOUR ARM?
WELL, THEN, DON'T WORRY ABOUT **THAT**.
BECAUSE YOU ARE **NOT**.
LISTEN TO YOUR SING-SONGS.
I HAVE SO MANY QUESTIONS!
AND IN GENERAL, AS A NOTE, SETTLE **DOWN**.
I CAN'T!
JIGGLY FEET!
IT'S BECAUSE YOU EAT NOTHING BUT GARBAGE.
I KNOW!
NOW YOU ARE BOUNCING AROUND LIKE A— LIKE A QODDERPET.
YEAH?! I BET I COULD TAKE YOU.
REALLY?
NO!
ANOTHER SIGN I'VE **CLEARLY** HAD A LOT OF SWEET STUFF!
OKAY.

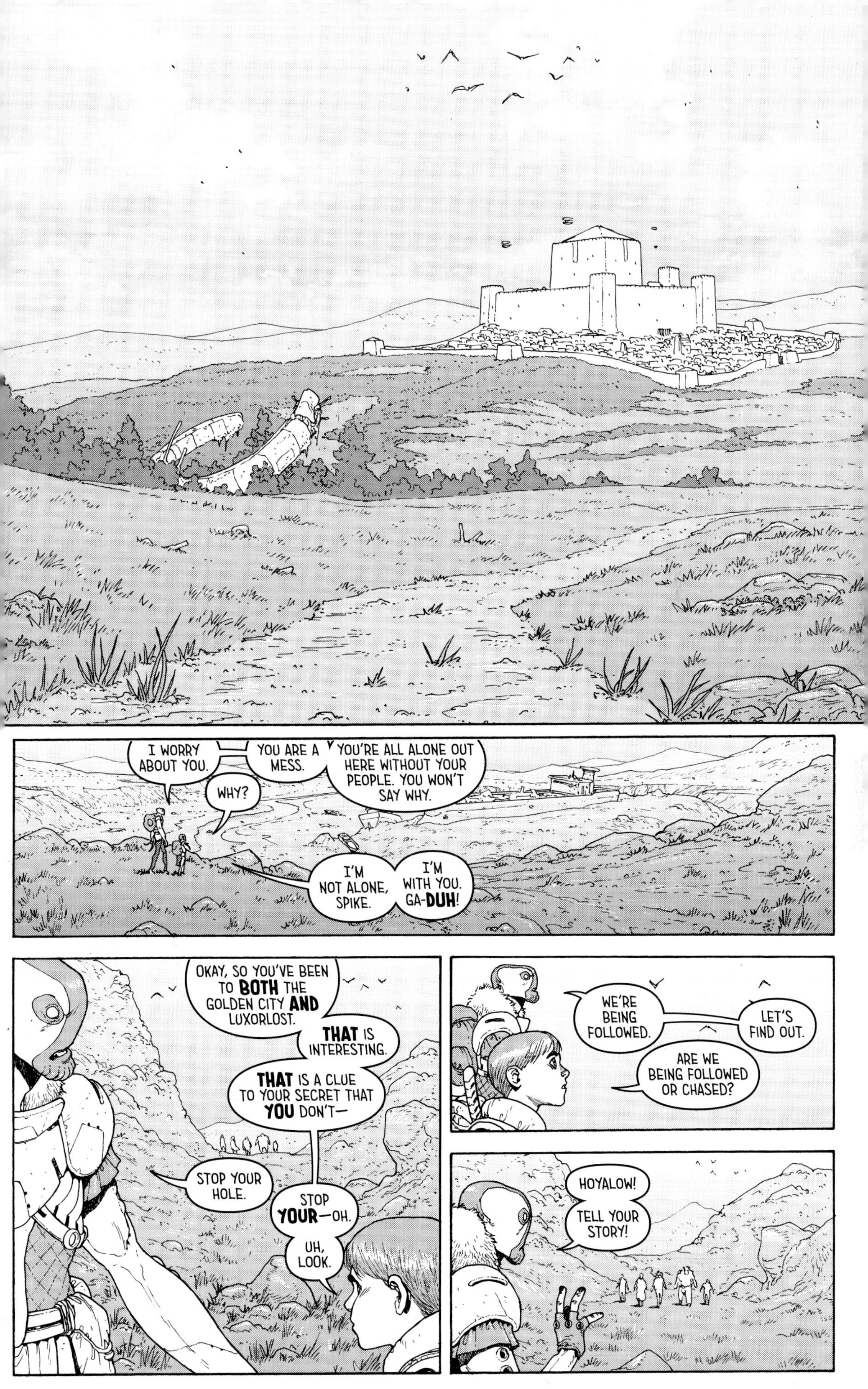
I WORRY ABOUT YOU.
WHY?
YOU ARE A MESS.
YOU'RE ALL ALONE OUT HERE WITHOUT YOUR PEOPLE. YOU WON'T SAY WHY.
I'M NOT ALONE, SPIKE.
I'M WITH YOU. GA-DUH!
OKAY, SO YOU'VE BEEN TO BOTH THE GOLDEN CITY AND LUXORLOST.
THAT IS INTERESTING.
THAT IS A CLUE TO YOUR SECRET THAT YOU DON'T—
STOP YOUR HOLE.
STOP YOUR—OH.
UH, LOOK.
WE'RE BEING FOLLOWED.
LET'S FIND OUT.
ARE WE BEING FOLLOWED OR CHASED?
HOYALOW!
TELL YOUR STORY!

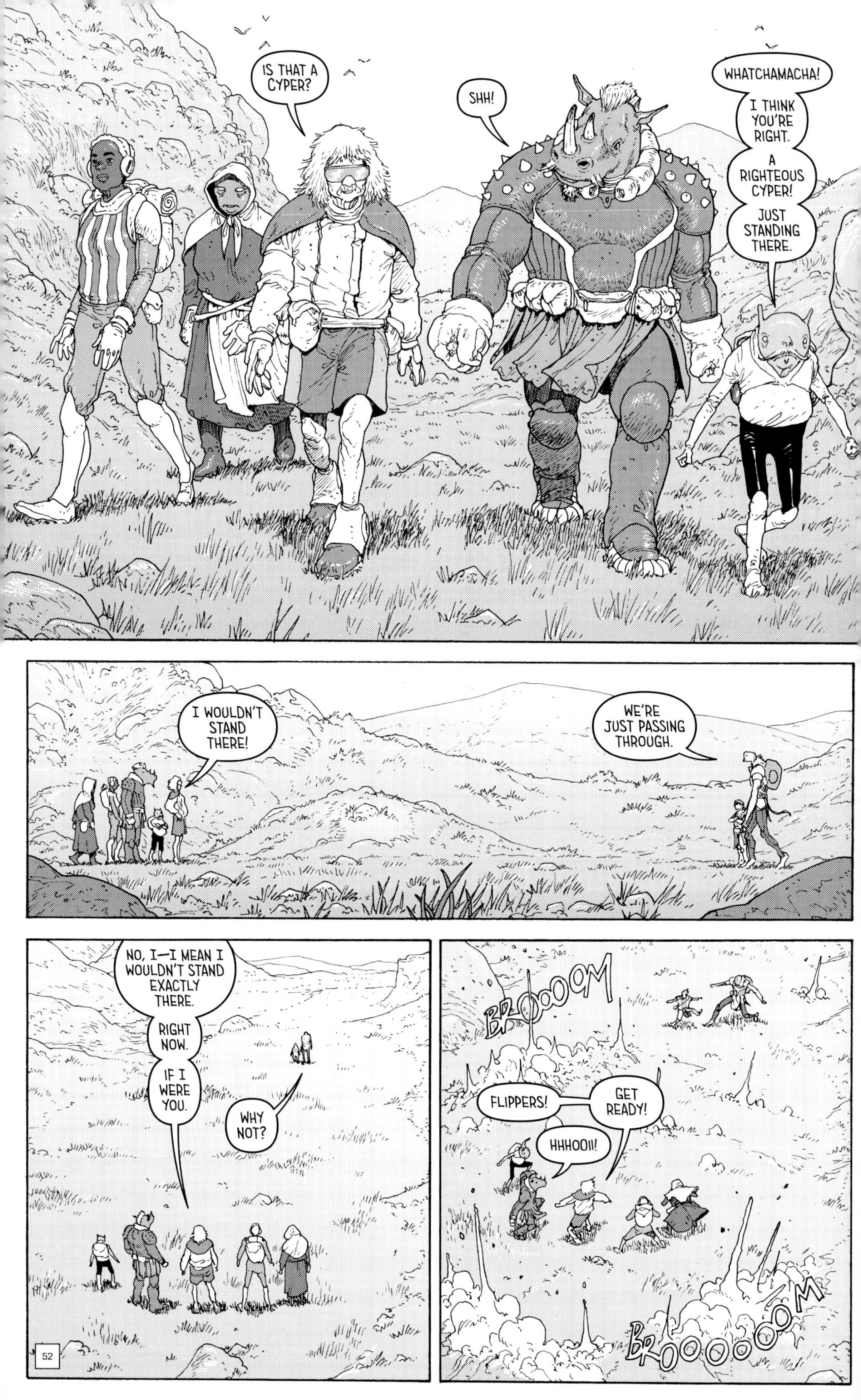

IS THAT A CYPER?
SHH!
WHATCHAMACHA!
I THINK YOU'RE RIGHT.
A RIGHTEOUS CYPER!
JUST STANDING THERE.
I WOULDN'T STAND THERE!
WE'RE JUST PASSING THROUGH.
NO, I—I MEAN I WOULDN'T STAND EXACTLY THERE.
RIGHT NOW.
IF I WERE YOU.
WHY NOT?
BROOOOM
FLIPPERS!
GET READY!
HHHOOII!
BROOOOOOM

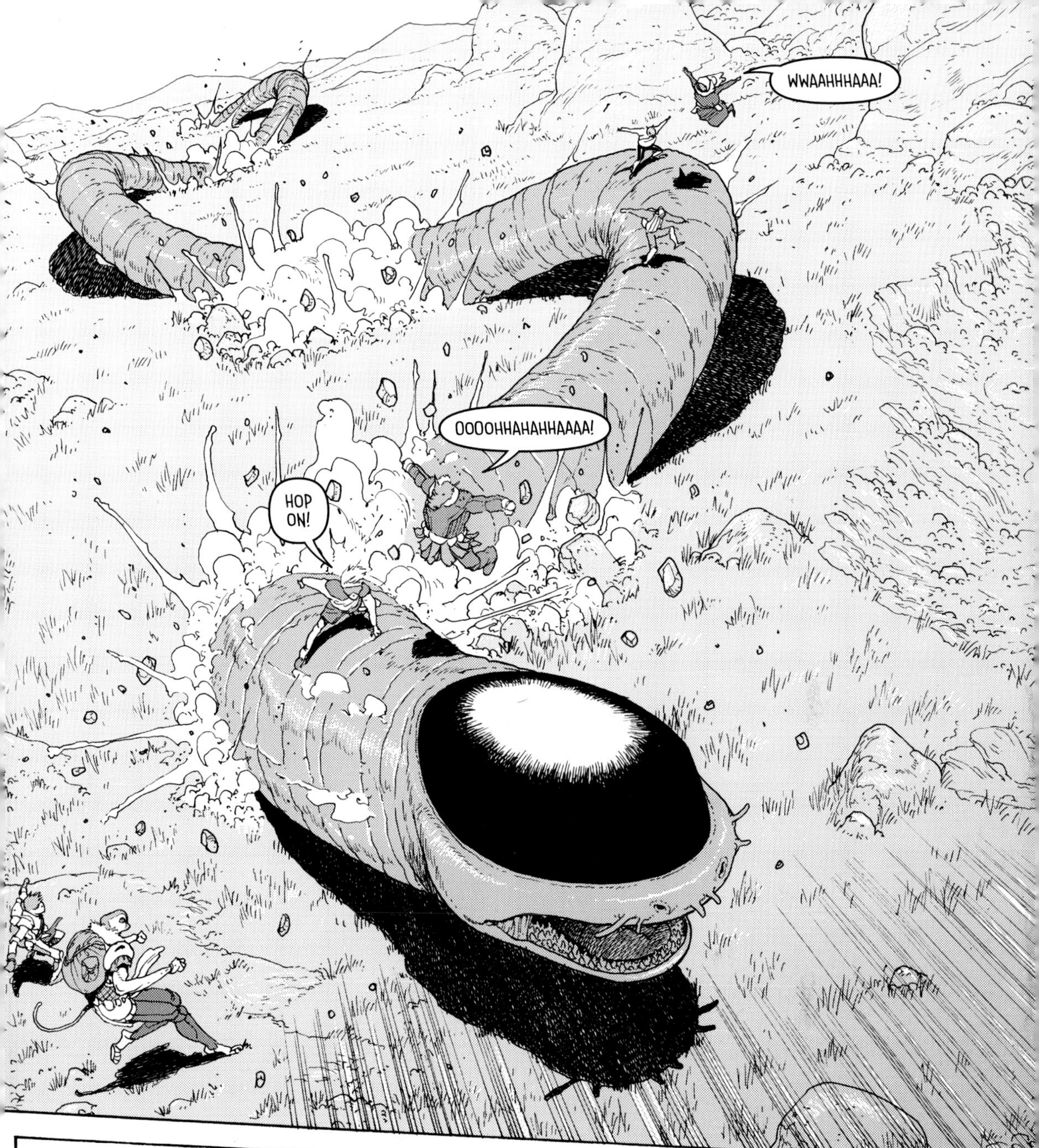
WWAAHHHAAA!
OOOOHHAHAHHAAAA!
HOP ON!
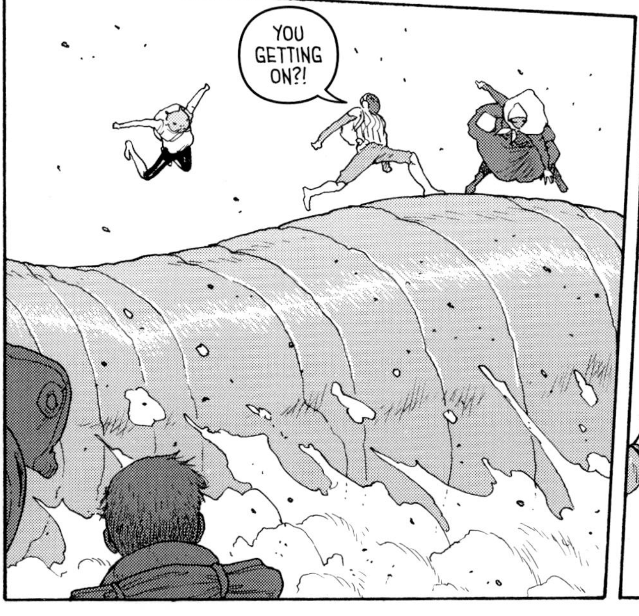
YOU GETTING ON?!
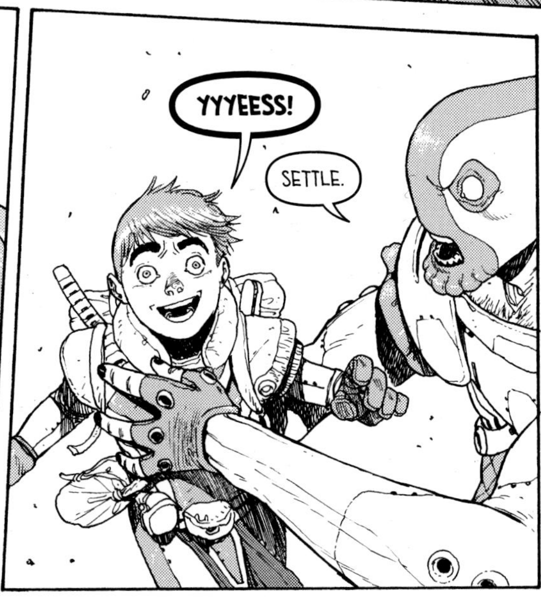
YYYEESS!
SETTLE.

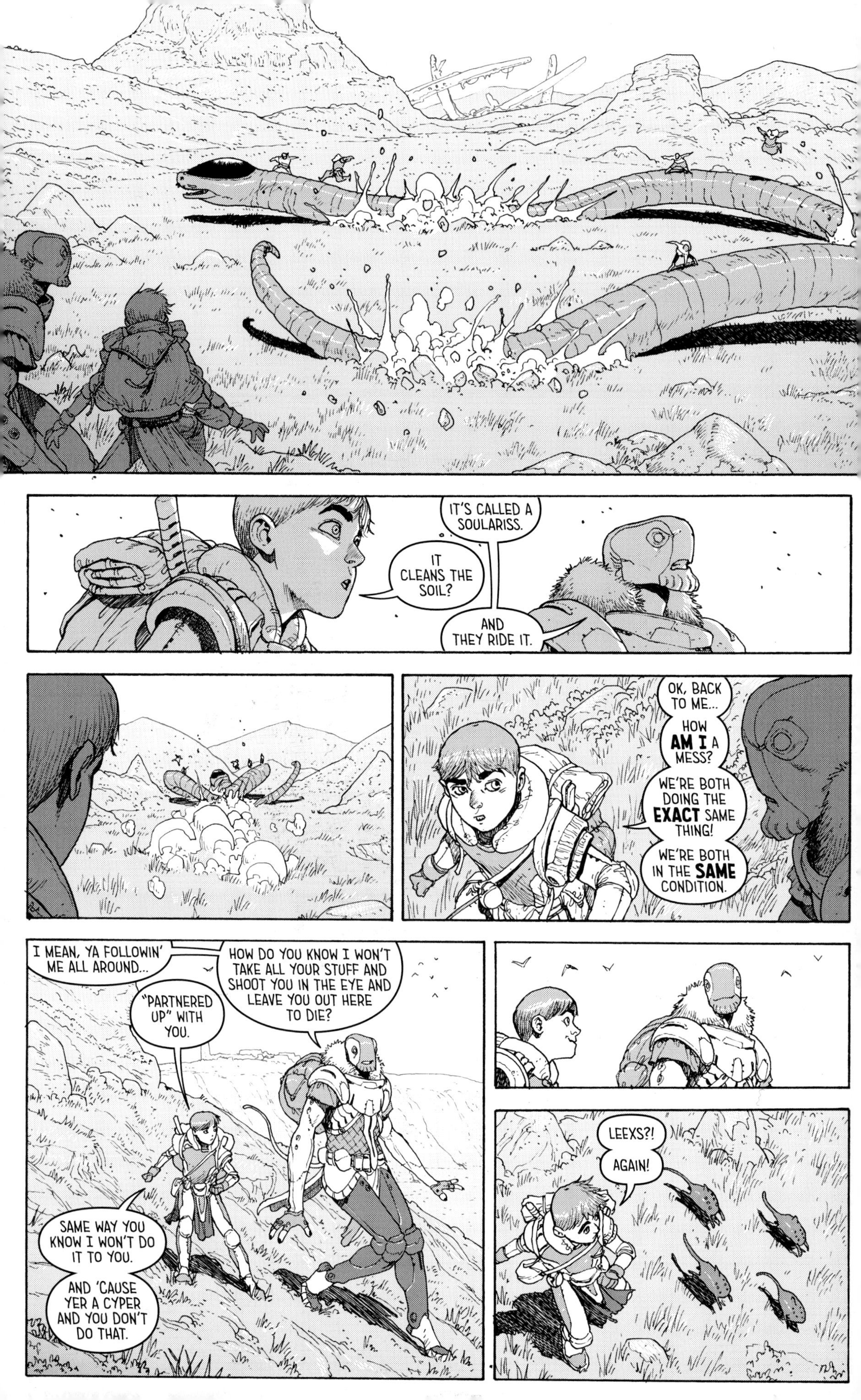
IT'S CALLED A SOULARISS.
IT CLEANS THE SOIL?
AND THEY RIDE IT.
OK, BACK TO ME...
HOW **AM I** A MESS?
WE'RE BOTH DOING THE **EXACT** SAME THING!
WE'RE BOTH IN THE **SAME** CONDITION.
I MEAN, YA FOLLOWIN' ME ALL AROUND...
"PARTNERED UP" WITH YOU.
HOW DO YOU KNOW I WON'T TAKE ALL YOUR STUFF AND SHOOT YOU IN THE EYE AND LEAVE YOU OUT HERE TO DIE?
SAME WAY YOU KNOW I WON'T DO IT TO YOU.
AND 'CAUSE YER A CYPER AND YOU DON'T DO THAT.
LEEXS?!
AGAIN!

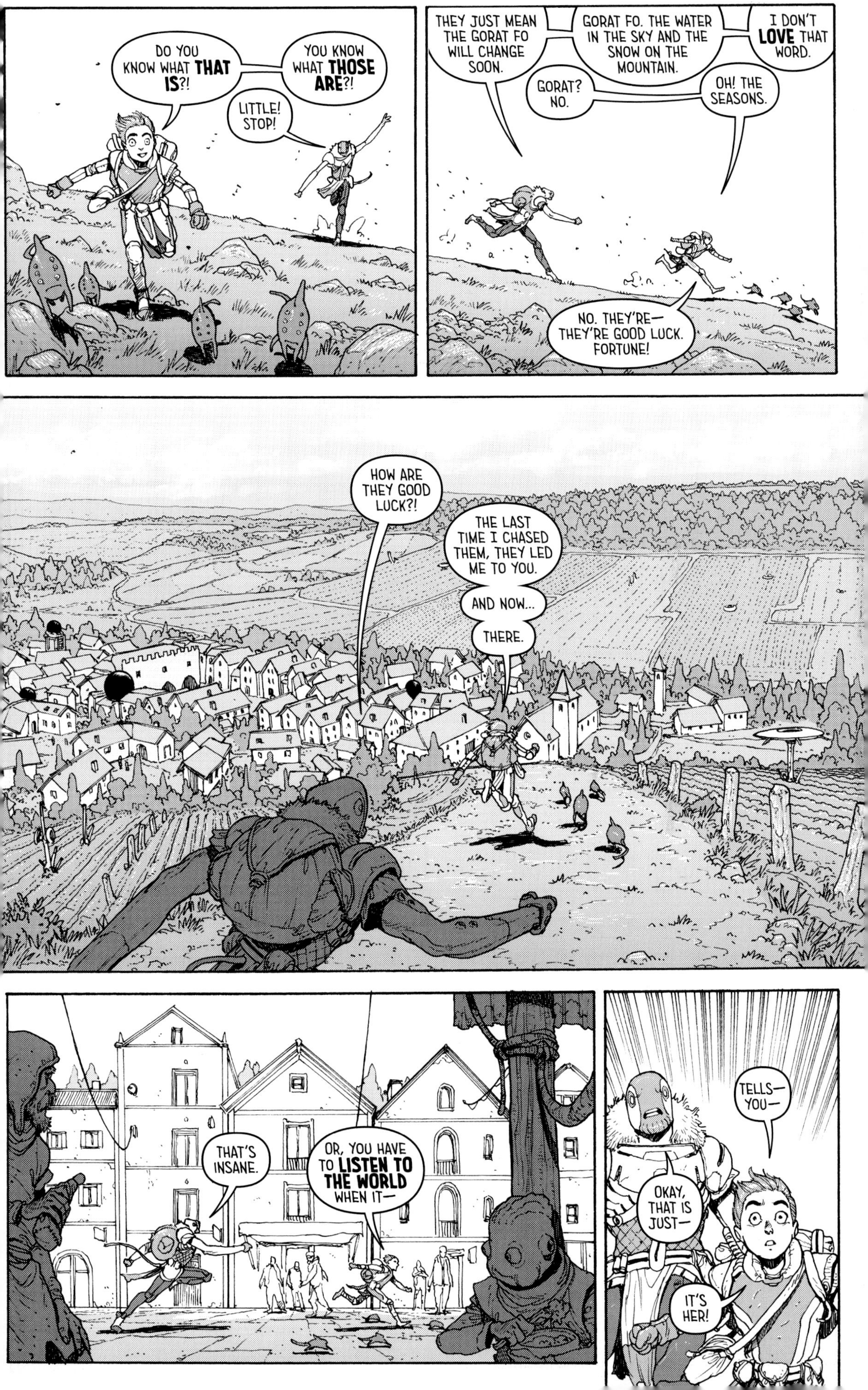

DO YOU KNOW WHAT **THAT IS**?!
YOU KNOW WHAT **THOSE ARE**?!
LITTLE! STOP!
THEY JUST MEAN THE GORAT FO WILL CHANGE SOON.
GORAT FO. THE WATER IN THE SKY AND THE SNOW ON THE MOUNTAIN.
I DON'T **LOVE** THAT WORD.
GORAT? NO.
OH! THE SEASONS.
NO. THEY'RE— THEY'RE GOOD LUCK. FORTUNE!
HOW ARE THEY GOOD LUCK?!
THE LAST TIME I CHASED THEM, THEY LED ME TO YOU.
AND NOW...
THERE.
THAT'S INSANE.
OR, YOU HAVE TO **LISTEN TO THE WORLD** WHEN IT—
TELLS— YOU—
OKAY, THAT IS JUST—
IT'S HER!

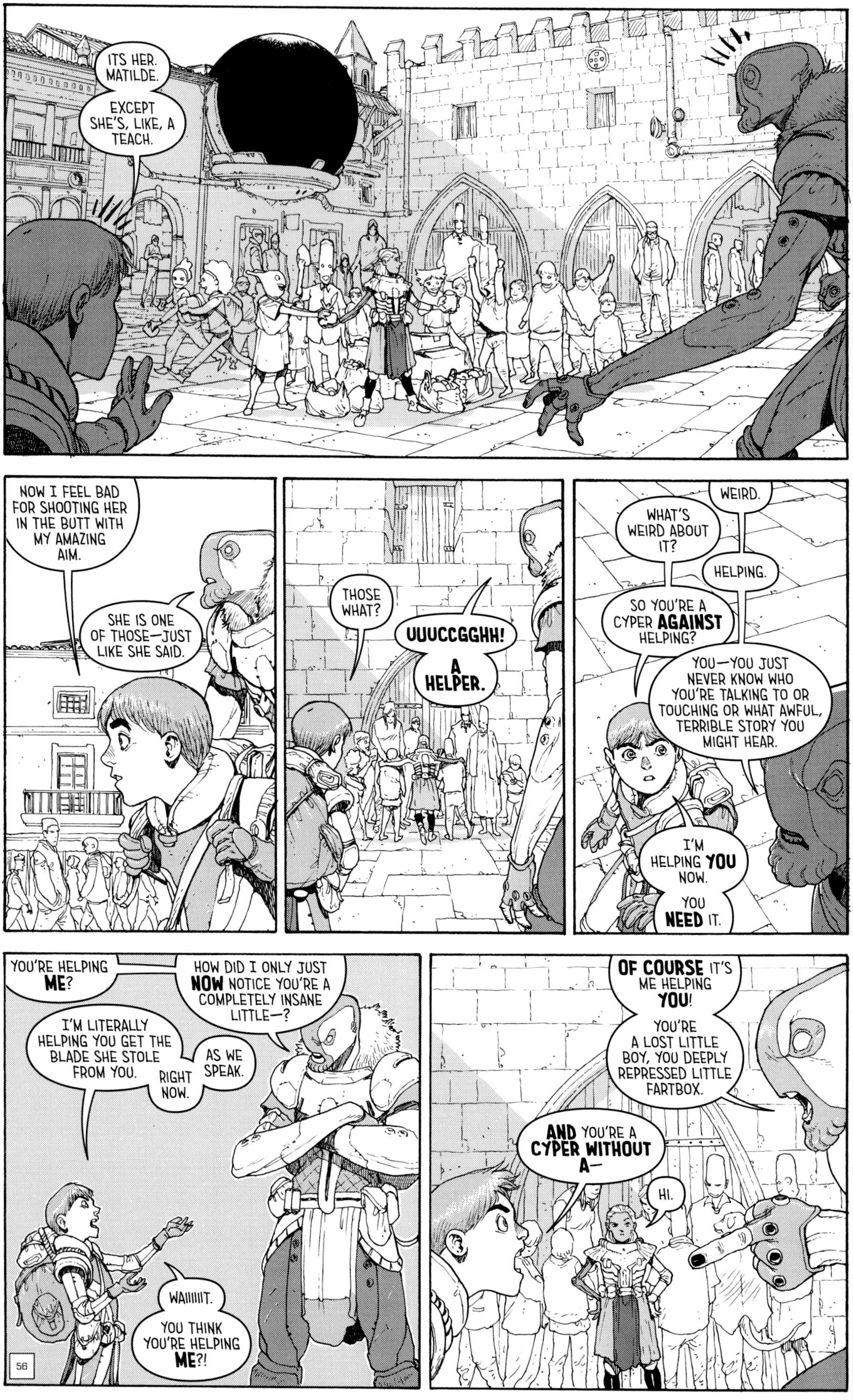
ITS HER. MATILDE.
EXCEPT SHE'S, LIKE, A TEACH.
NOW I FEEL BAD FOR SHOOTING HER IN THE BUTT WITH MY AMAZING AIM.
SHE IS ONE OF THOSE—JUST LIKE SHE SAID.
THOSE WHAT?
UUUCCGGHH!
A HELPER.
WEIRD.
WHAT'S WEIRD ABOUT IT?
HELPING.
SO YOU'RE A CYPER AGAINST HELPING?
YOU—YOU JUST NEVER KNOW WHO YOU'RE TALKING TO OR TOUCHING OR WHAT AWFUL, TERRIBLE STORY YOU MIGHT HEAR.
I'M HELPING YOU NOW.
YOU NEED IT.
YOU'RE HELPING ME?
HOW DID I ONLY JUST NOW NOTICE YOU'RE A COMPLETELY INSANE LITTLE—?
I'M LITERALLY HELPING YOU GET THE BLADE SHE STOLE FROM YOU.
RIGHT NOW.
AS WE SPEAK.
WAIIIIIT.
YOU THINK YOU'RE HELPING ME?!
OF COURSE IT'S ME HELPING YOU!
YOU'RE A LOST LITTLE BOY, YOU DEEPLY REPRESSED LITTLE FARTBOX.
AND YOU'RE A CYPER WITHOUT A—
HI.

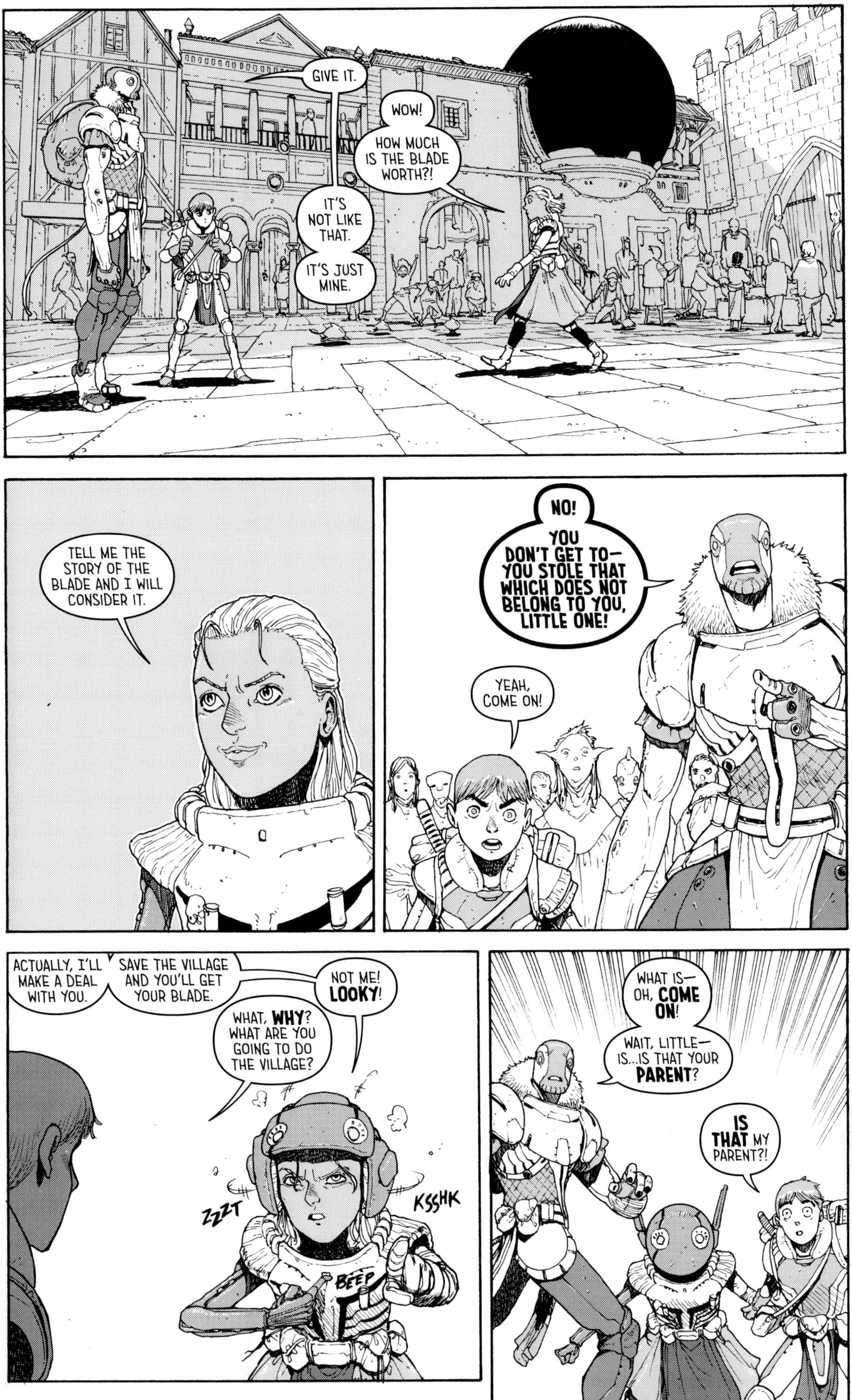
GIVE IT.
WOW!
HOW MUCH IS THE BLADE WORTH?!
IT'S NOT LIKE THAT.
IT'S JUST MINE.
TELL ME THE STORY OF THE BLADE AND I WILL CONSIDER IT.
NO!
YOU DON'T GET TO— YOU STOLE THAT WHICH DOES NOT BELONG TO YOU, LITTLE ONE!
YEAH, COME ON!
ACTUALLY, I'LL MAKE A DEAL WITH YOU.
SAVE THE VILLAGE AND YOU'LL GET YOUR BLADE.
WHAT, **WHY**? WHAT ARE YOU GOING TO DO THE VILLAGE?
NOT ME! **LOOKY**!
ZZZT
KSSHK
BEEP
WHAT IS— OH, **COME ON**!
WAIT, LITTLE— IS...IS THAT YOUR **PARENT**?
IS THAT MY PARENT?!

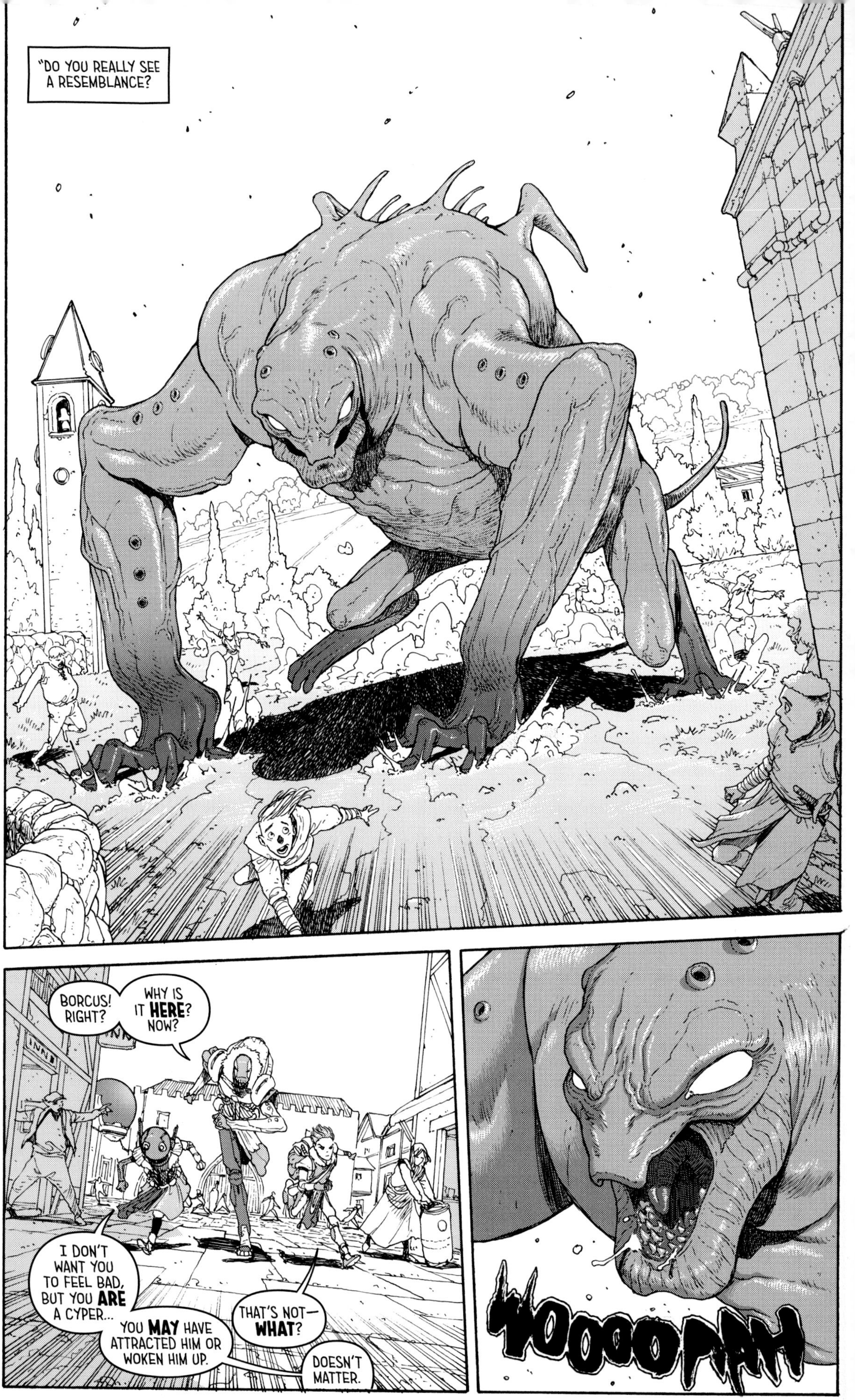
"DO YOU REALLY SEE A RESEMBLANCE?
BORCUS! RIGHT?
WHY IS IT **HERE**? NOW?
INN
I DON'T WANT YOU TO FEEL BAD, BUT YOU **ARE** A CYPER...
YOU **MAY** HAVE ATTRACTED HIM OR WOKEN HIM UP.
THAT'S NOT—
WHAT?
DOESN'T MATTER.
WOOOPAH

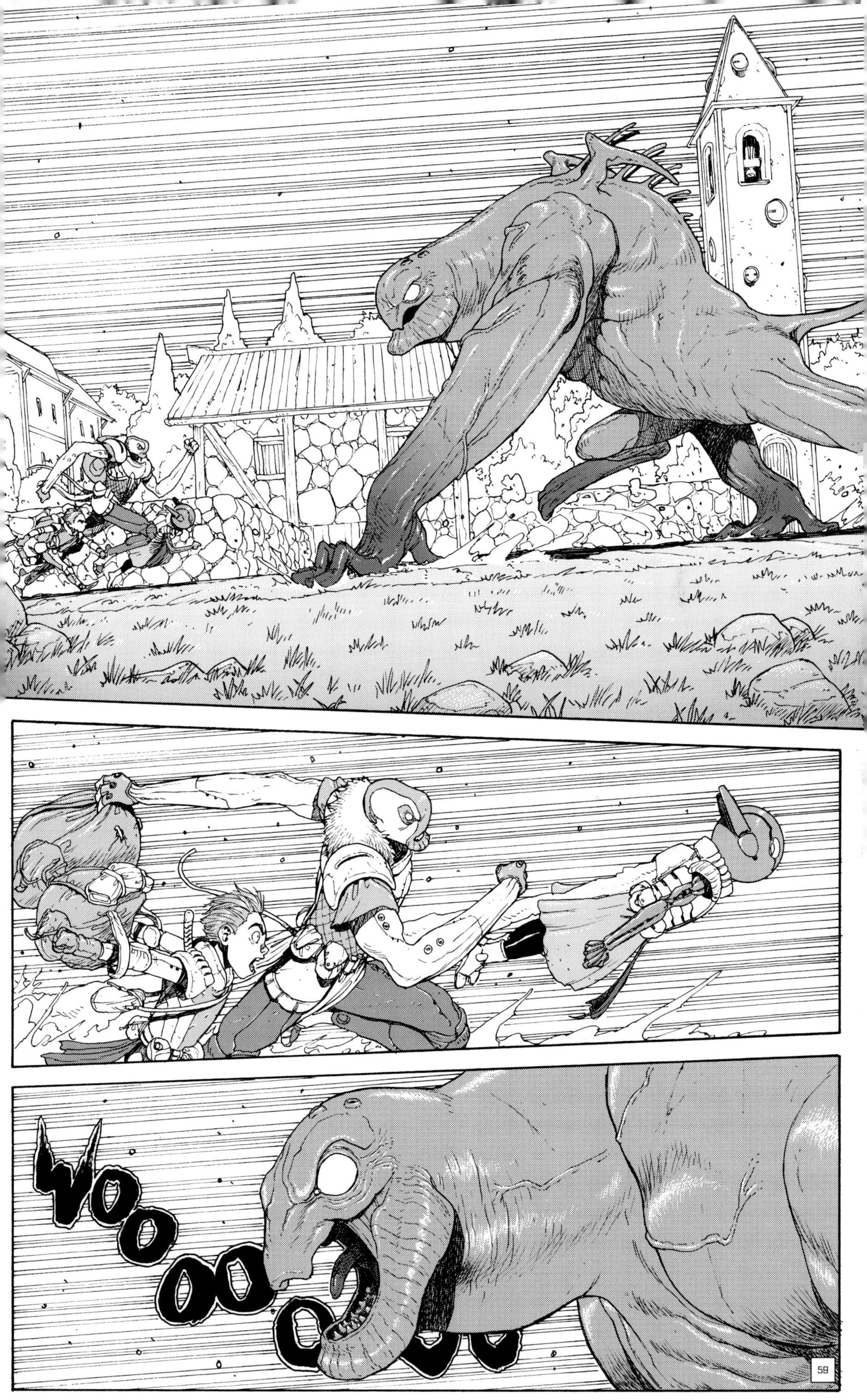
WOOOOOOOO

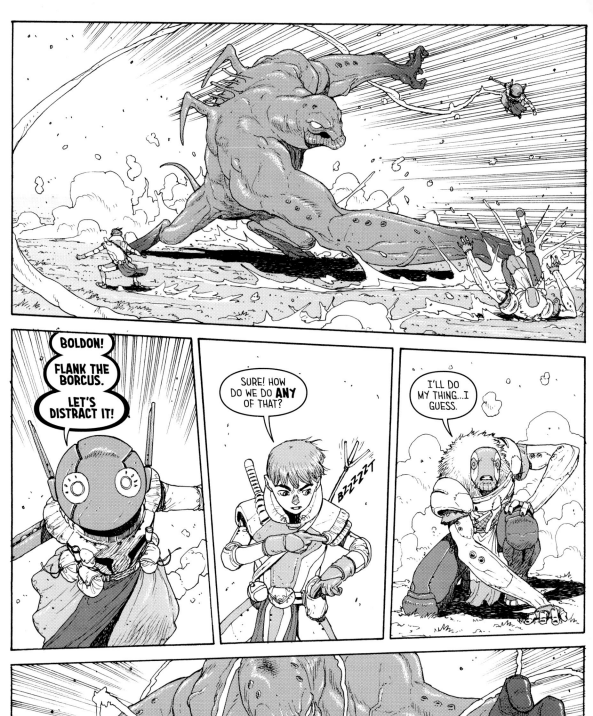

BOLDON!
FLANK THE BORCUS.
LET'S DISTRACT IT!

SURE! HOW DO WE DO **ANY** OF THAT?

BZZZZT

I'LL DO MY THING...I GUESS.

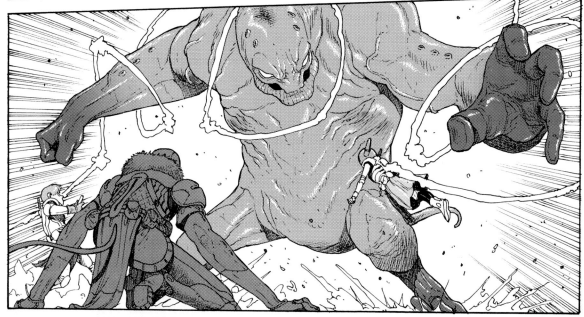

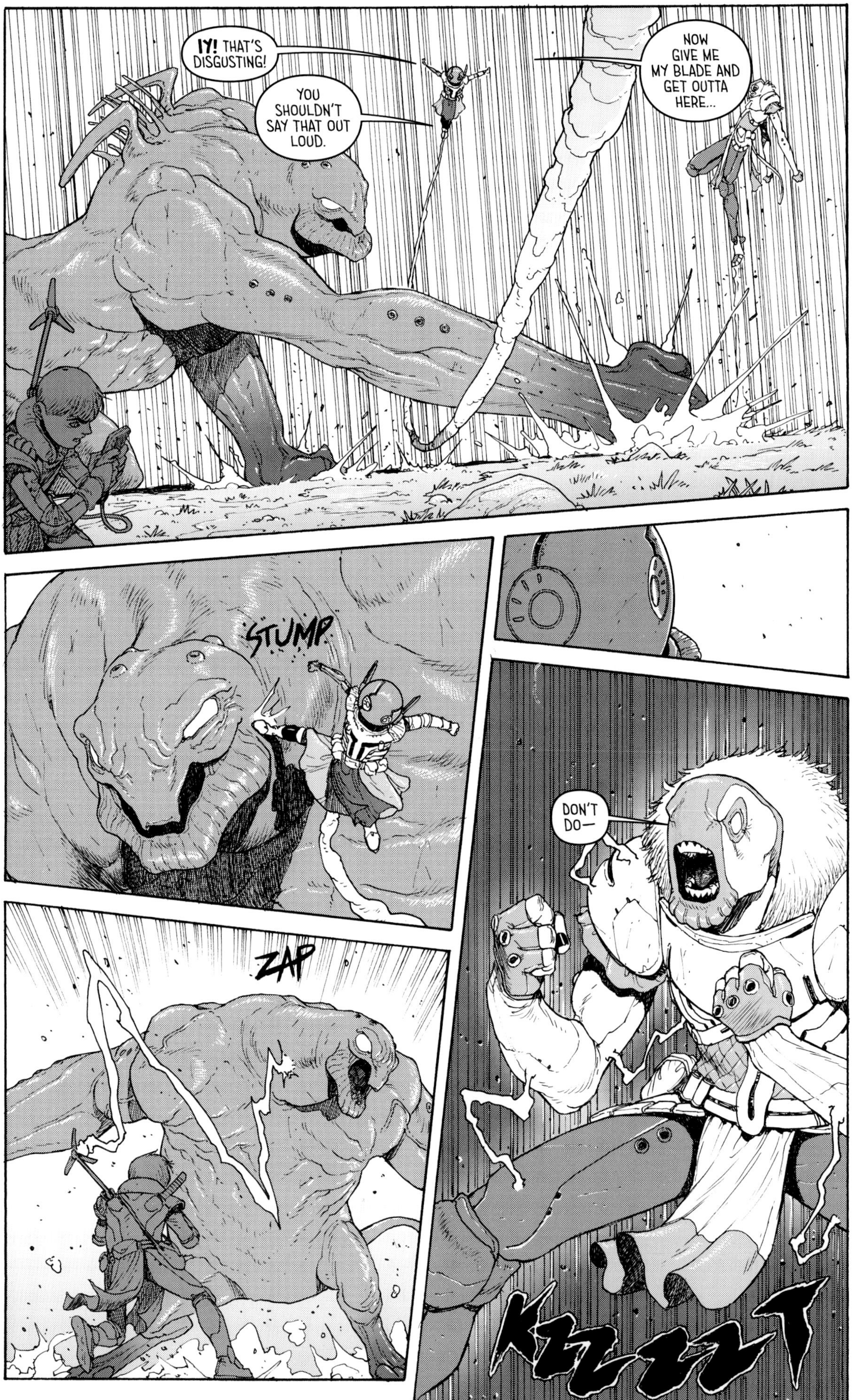
IY! THAT'S DISGUSTING!
YOU SHOULDN'T SAY THAT OUT LOUD.
NOW GIVE ME MY BLADE AND GET OUTTA HERE...
STUMP
DON'T DO—
ZAP
KZZZZT

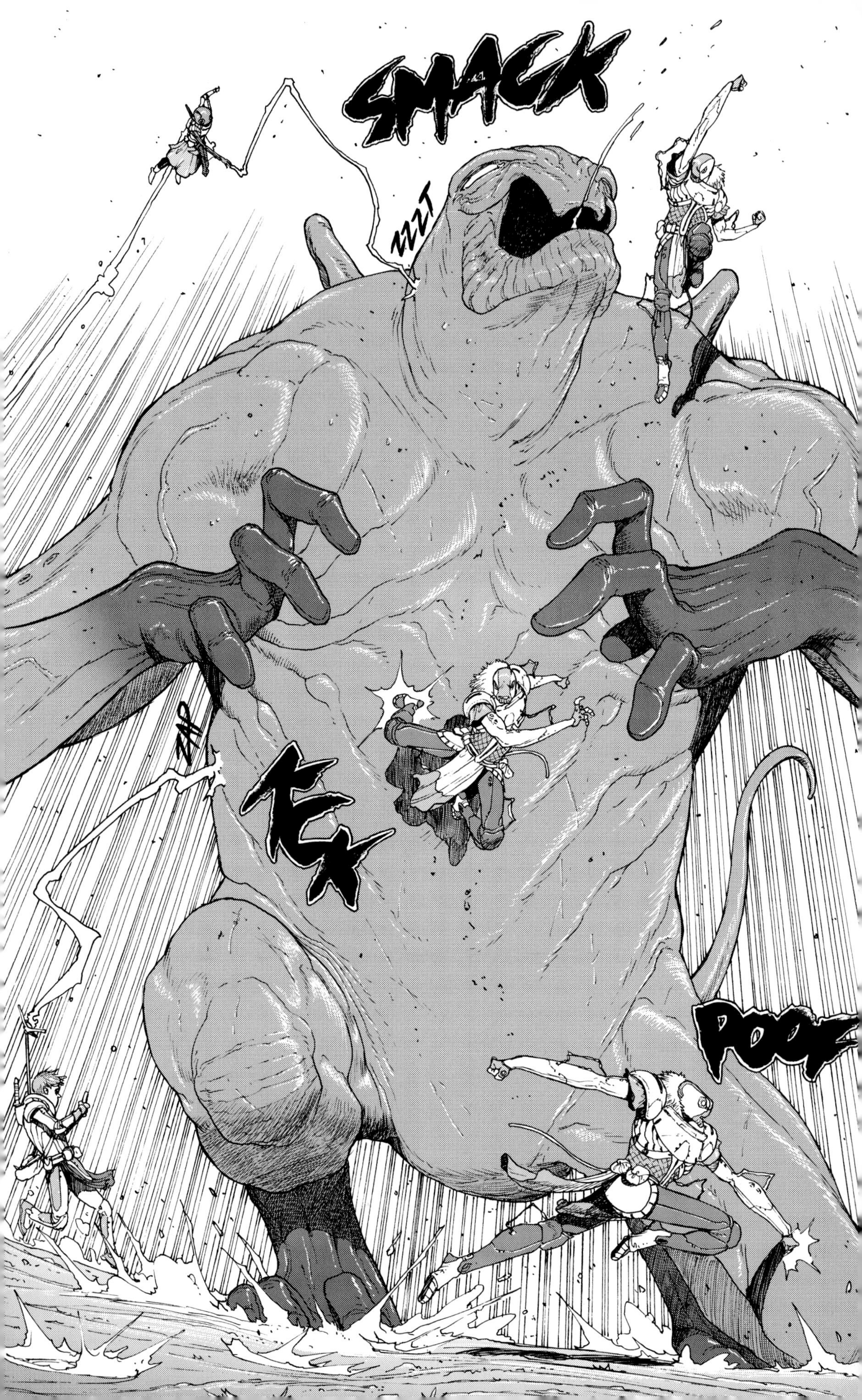
SMACK
ZZZT
ZAP
TCK

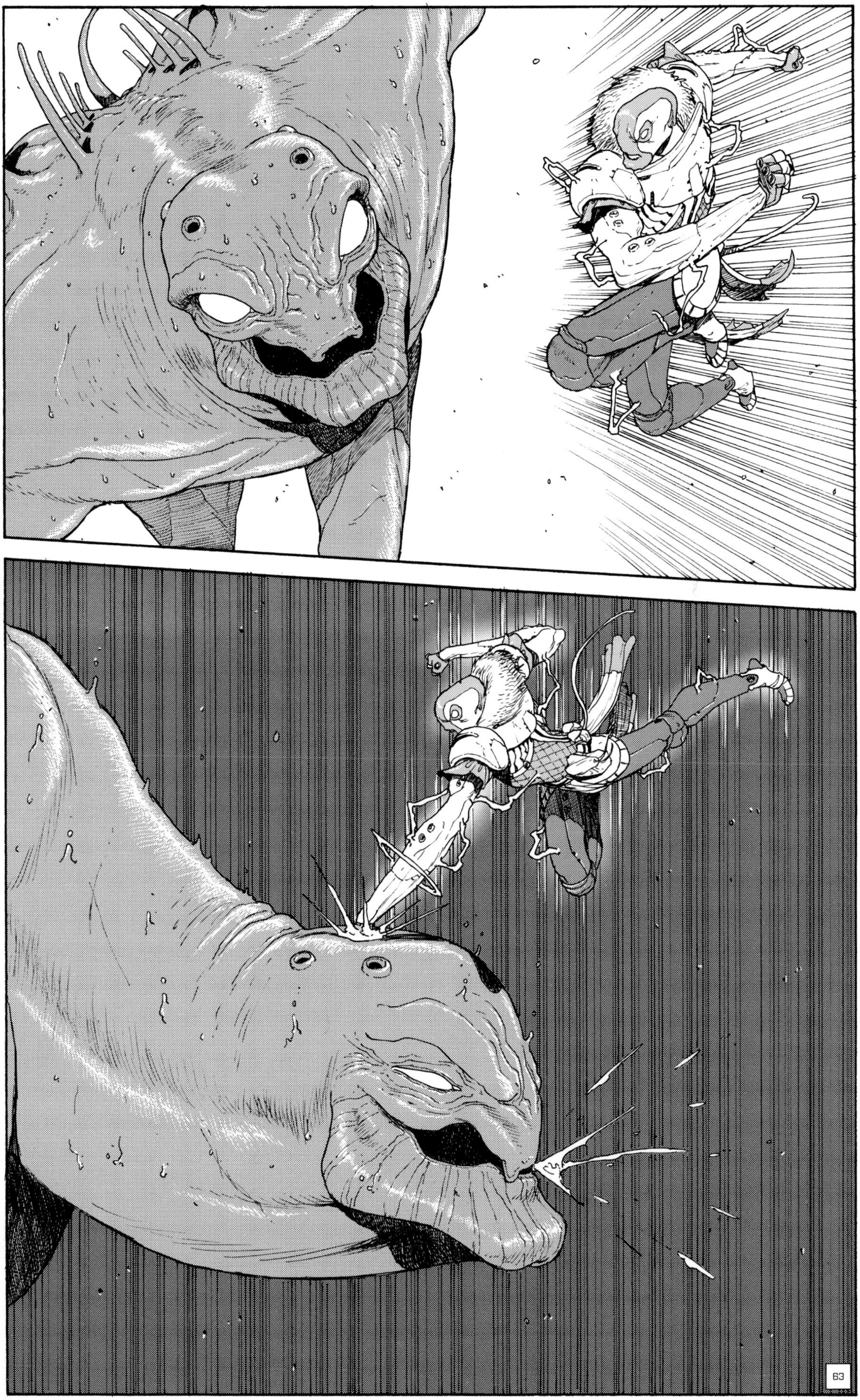

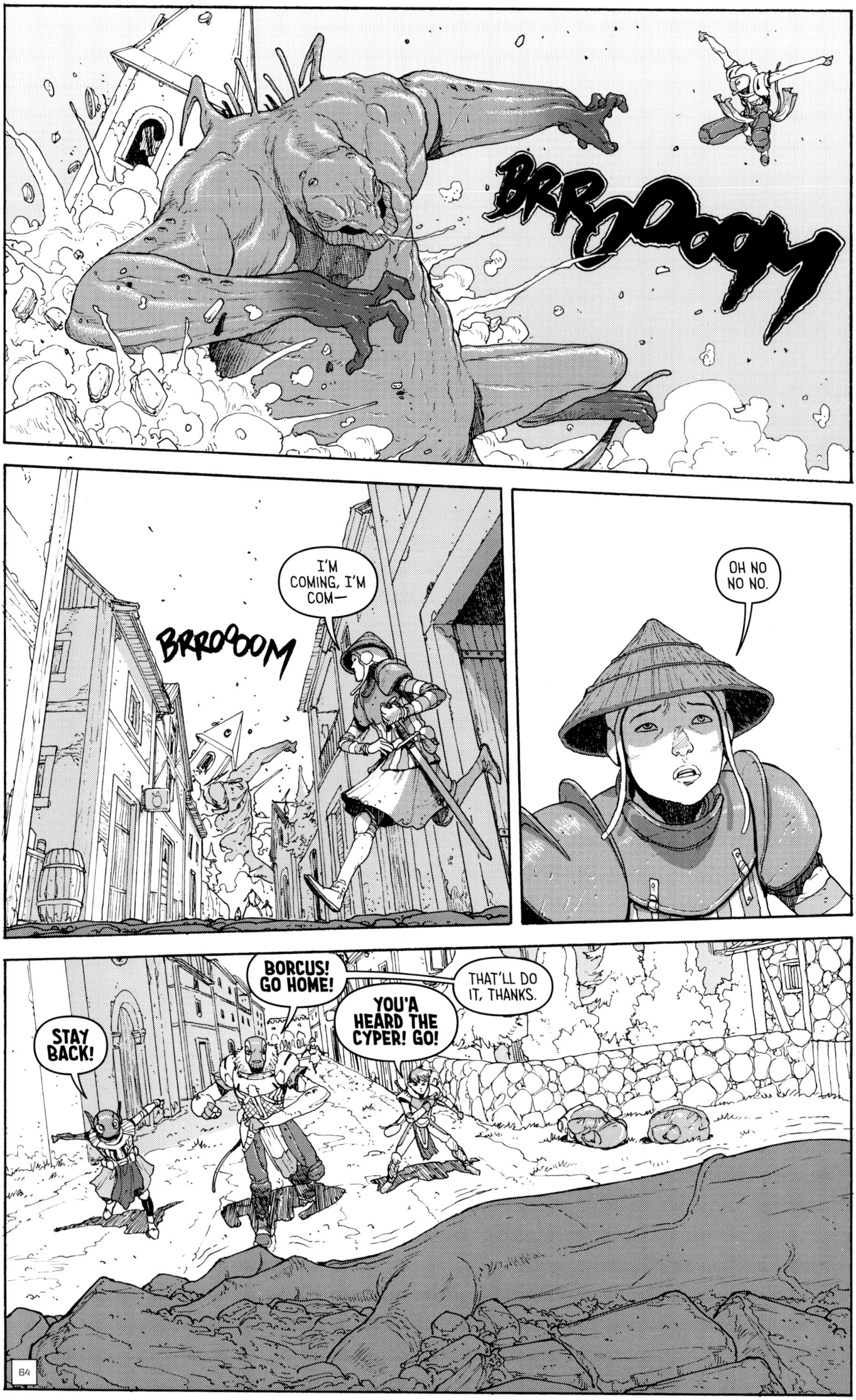
BRRROOOOM
BRROOOOM
I'M COMING, I'M COM—
OH NO NO NO.
STAY BACK!
BORCUS! GO HOME!
THAT'LL DO IT, THANKS.
YOU'A HEARD THE CYPER! GO!

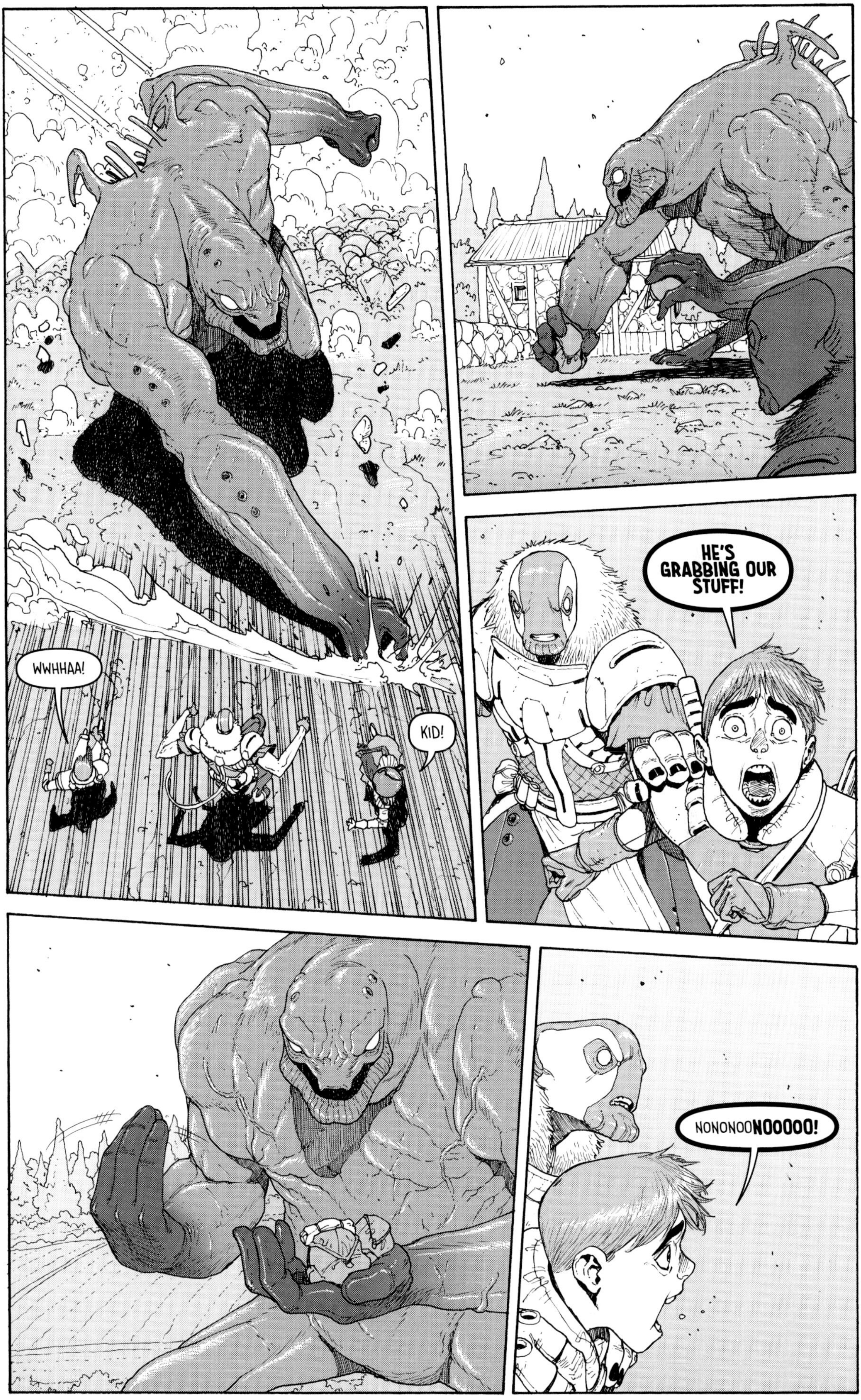
WWHHAA!
KID!
HE'S GRABBING OUR STUFF!
NONONOONOOOOO!

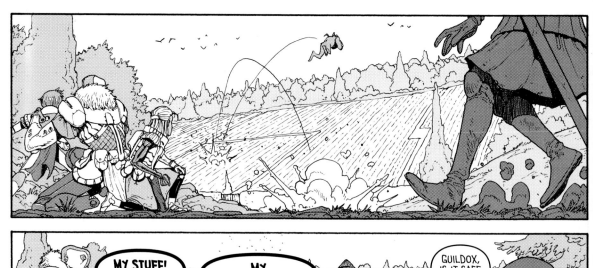

MY STUFF! NNNOOOOOO!

MY STUFFFFFFFFFFFF!

WHAT WAS IN THERE?!

GUILDOX, IS IT SAFE NOW?

THAT CAME OUT OF NOWHERE!

YES, ELDER.

THE BORCUS HAS BEEN CHASED OFF.

I'M GUILDOX, THE VILLAGE PROTECTOR.

I WAS IN THE BATHROOM.

OH! OK.

(NOW I HAVE TO GO.)

I TRAIN EVERY DAY FOR THIS AND I MISSED IT.

MY MUSIC. MY GAMES. MY FOOD.

CLOTHES.

MY CLOTHES!

IN THAT ORDER?

YES!

YOU SAID THOSE LEEXS WERE GOOD LUCK.

OKAY.

SO MAYBE IT WAS JUST THAT ONE TIME.

WANT TO GET OUT OF HERE?

WASN'T MY IDEA TO COME HERE—OH YEAH.

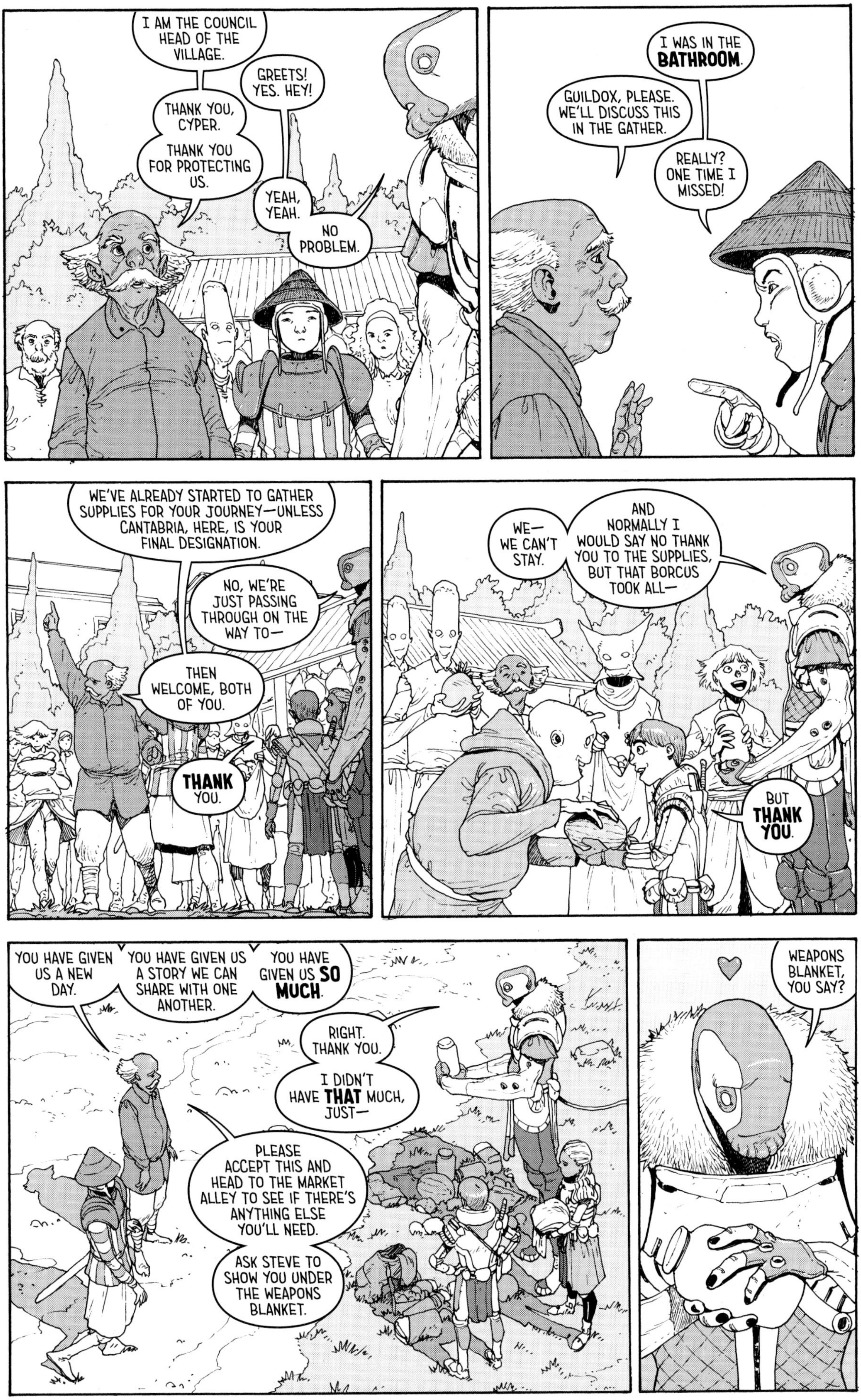
I AM THE COUNCIL HEAD OF THE VILLAGE.
THANK YOU, CYPER.
THANK YOU FOR PROTECTING US.
GREETS! YES. HEY!
YEAH, YEAH.
NO PROBLEM.
I WAS IN THE **BATHROOM**.
GUILDOX, PLEASE. WE'LL DISCUSS THIS IN THE GATHER.
REALLY? ONE TIME I MISSED!
WE'VE ALREADY STARTED TO GATHER SUPPLIES FOR YOUR JOURNEY—UNLESS CANTABRIA, HERE, IS YOUR FINAL DESIGNATION.
NO, WE'RE JUST PASSING THROUGH ON THE WAY TO—
THEN WELCOME, BOTH OF YOU.
THANK YOU.
WE— WE CAN'T STAY.
AND NORMALLY I WOULD SAY NO THANK YOU TO THE SUPPLIES, BUT THAT BORCUS TOOK ALL—
BUT **THANK YOU**.
YOU HAVE GIVEN US A NEW DAY.
YOU HAVE GIVEN US A STORY WE CAN SHARE WITH ONE ANOTHER.
YOU HAVE GIVEN US **SO MUCH**.
RIGHT. THANK YOU.
I DIDN'T HAVE **THAT** MUCH, JUST—
PLEASE ACCEPT THIS AND HEAD TO THE MARKET ALLEY TO SEE IF THERE'S ANYTHING ELSE YOU'LL NEED.
ASK STEVE TO SHOW YOU UNDER THE WEAPONS BLANKET.
WEAPONS BLANKET, YOU SAY?

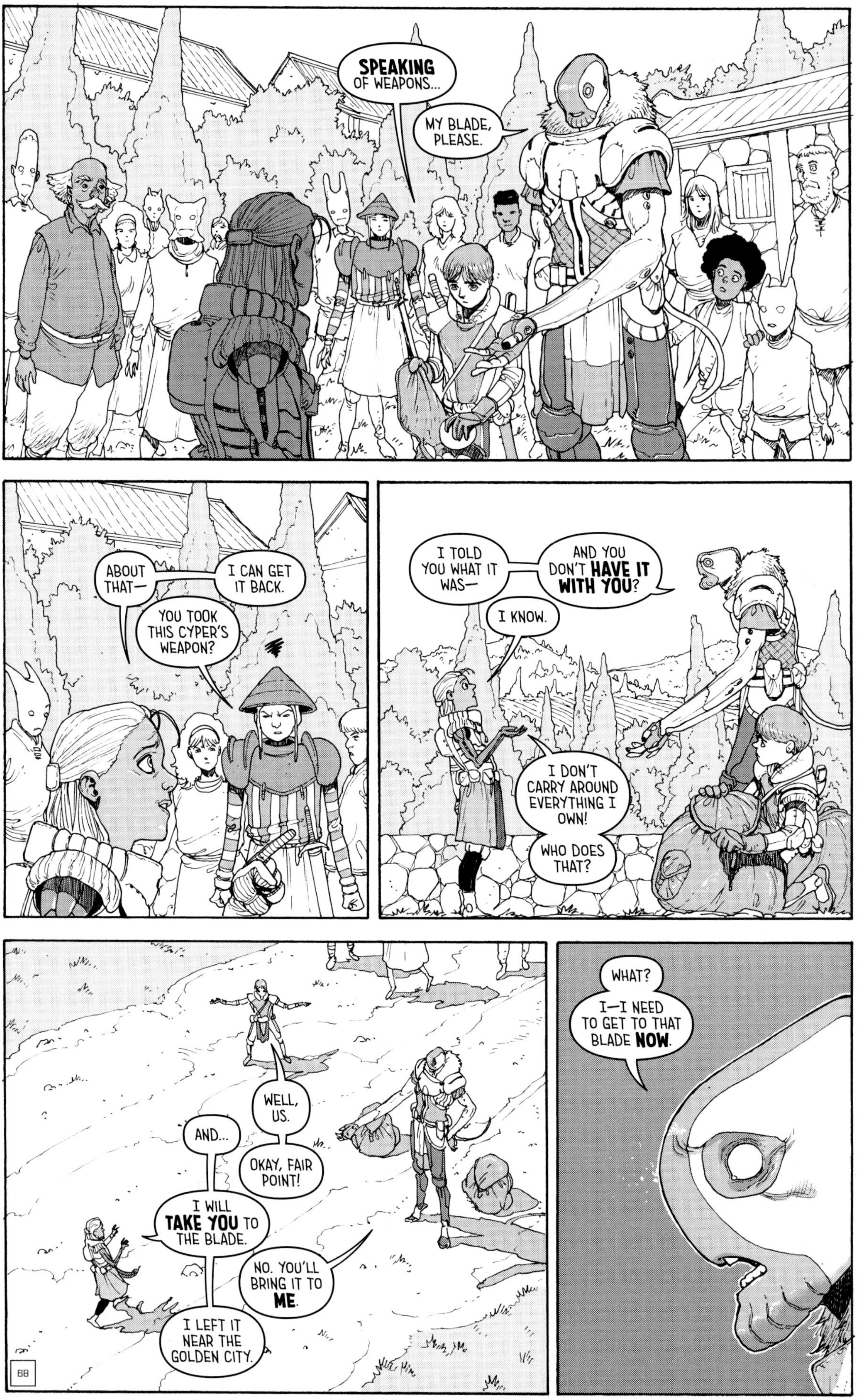
SPEAKING OF WEAPONS...
MY BLADE, PLEASE.
ABOUT THAT—
I CAN GET IT BACK.
YOU TOOK THIS CYPER'S WEAPON?
I TOLD YOU WHAT IT WAS—
AND YOU DON'T HAVE IT WITH YOU?
I KNOW.
I DON'T CARRY AROUND EVERYTHING I OWN!
WHO DOES THAT?
WELL, US.
AND...
OKAY, FAIR POINT!
I WILL TAKE YOU TO THE BLADE.
NO. YOU'LL BRING IT TO ME.
I LEFT IT NEAR THE GOLDEN CITY.
WHAT?
I—I NEED TO GET TO THAT BLADE NOW.

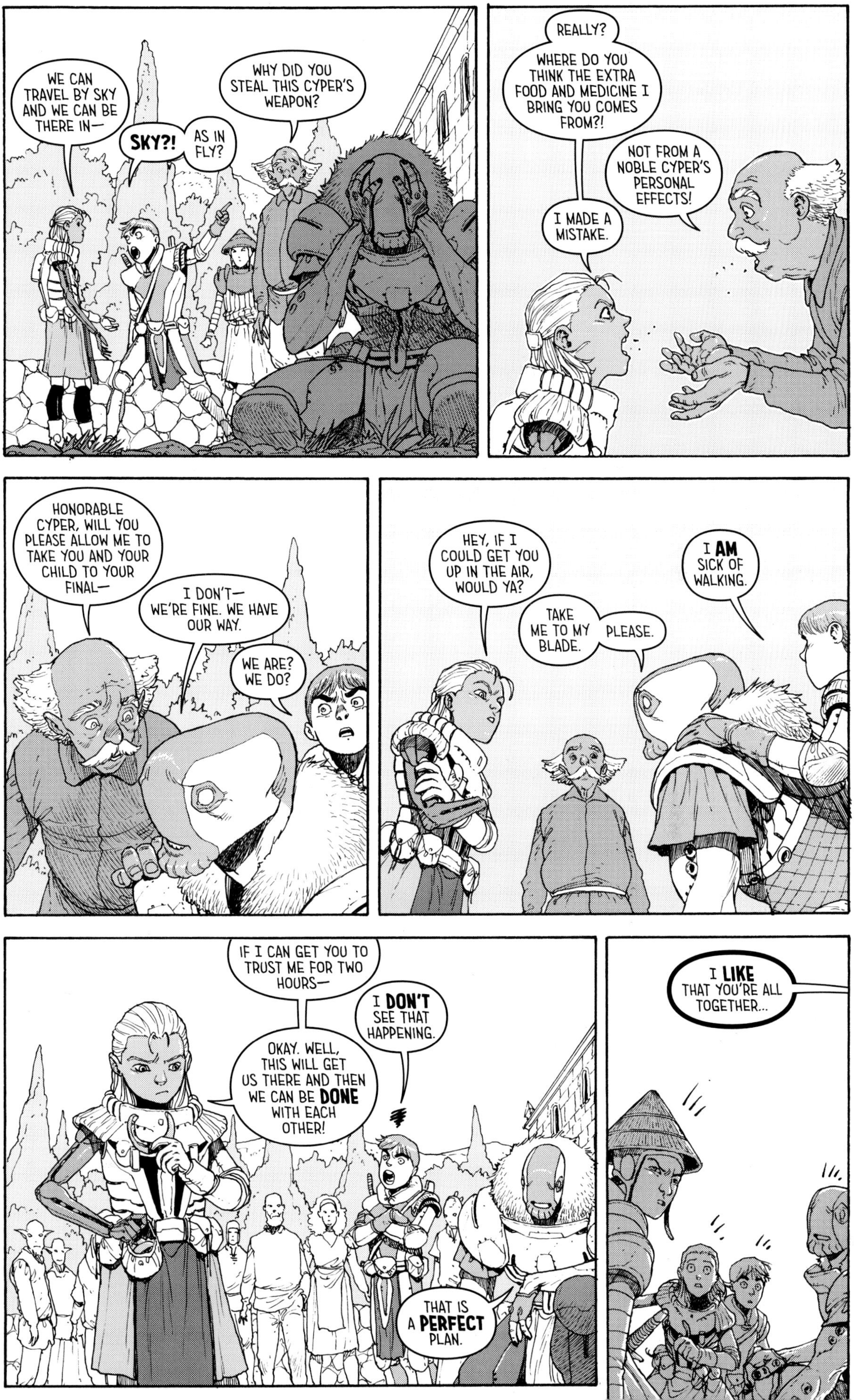
WE CAN TRAVEL BY SKY AND WE CAN BE THERE IN—
SKY?!
AS IN FLY?
WHY DID YOU STEAL THIS CYPER'S WEAPON?
REALLY?
WHERE DO YOU THINK THE EXTRA FOOD AND MEDICINE I BRING YOU COMES FROM?!
NOT FROM A NOBLE CYPER'S PERSONAL EFFECTS!
I MADE A MISTAKE.
HONORABLE CYPER, WILL YOU PLEASE ALLOW ME TO TAKE YOU AND YOUR CHILD TO YOUR FINAL—
I DON'T— WE'RE FINE. WE HAVE OUR WAY.
WE ARE? WE DO?
HEY, IF I COULD GET YOU UP IN THE AIR, WOULD YA?
TAKE ME TO MY BLADE.
PLEASE.
I AM SICK OF WALKING.
IF I CAN GET YOU TO TRUST ME FOR TWO HOURS—
I DON'T SEE THAT HAPPENING.
OKAY. WELL, THIS WILL GET US THERE AND THEN WE CAN BE DONE WITH EACH OTHER!
THAT IS A PERFECT PLAN.
I LIKE THAT YOU'RE ALL TOGETHER...

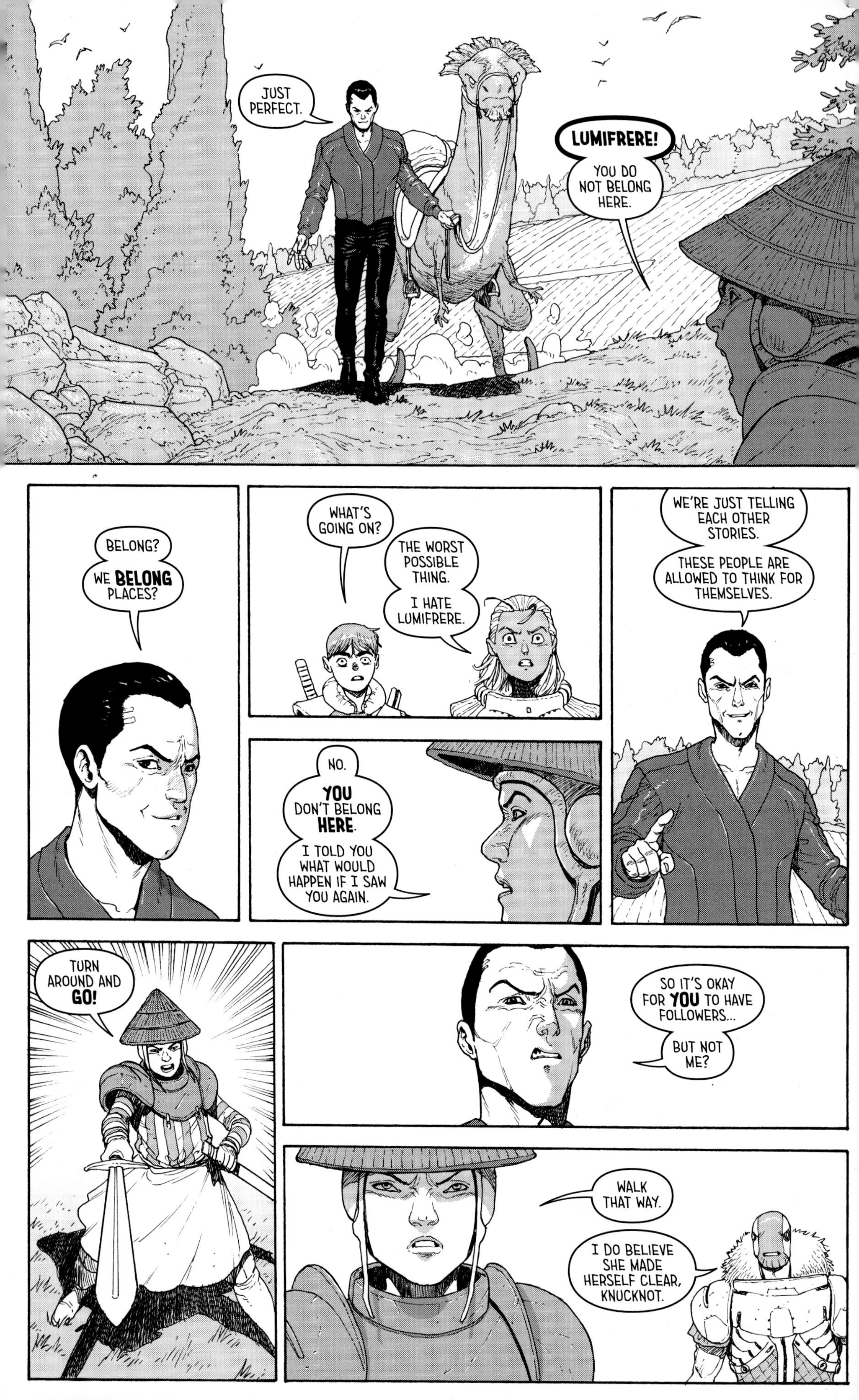
JUST PERFECT.
LUMIFRERE!
YOU DO NOT BELONG HERE.
BELONG?
WE BELONG PLACES?
WHAT'S GOING ON?
THE WORST POSSIBLE THING.
I HATE LUMIFRERE.
NO.
YOU DON'T BELONG HERE.
I TOLD YOU WHAT WOULD HAPPEN IF I SAW YOU AGAIN.
WE'RE JUST TELLING EACH OTHER STORIES.
THESE PEOPLE ARE ALLOWED TO THINK FOR THEMSELVES.
TURN AROUND AND GO!
SO IT'S OKAY FOR YOU TO HAVE FOLLOWERS...
BUT NOT ME?
WALK THAT WAY.
I DO BELIEVE SHE MADE HERSELF CLEAR, KNUCKNOT.

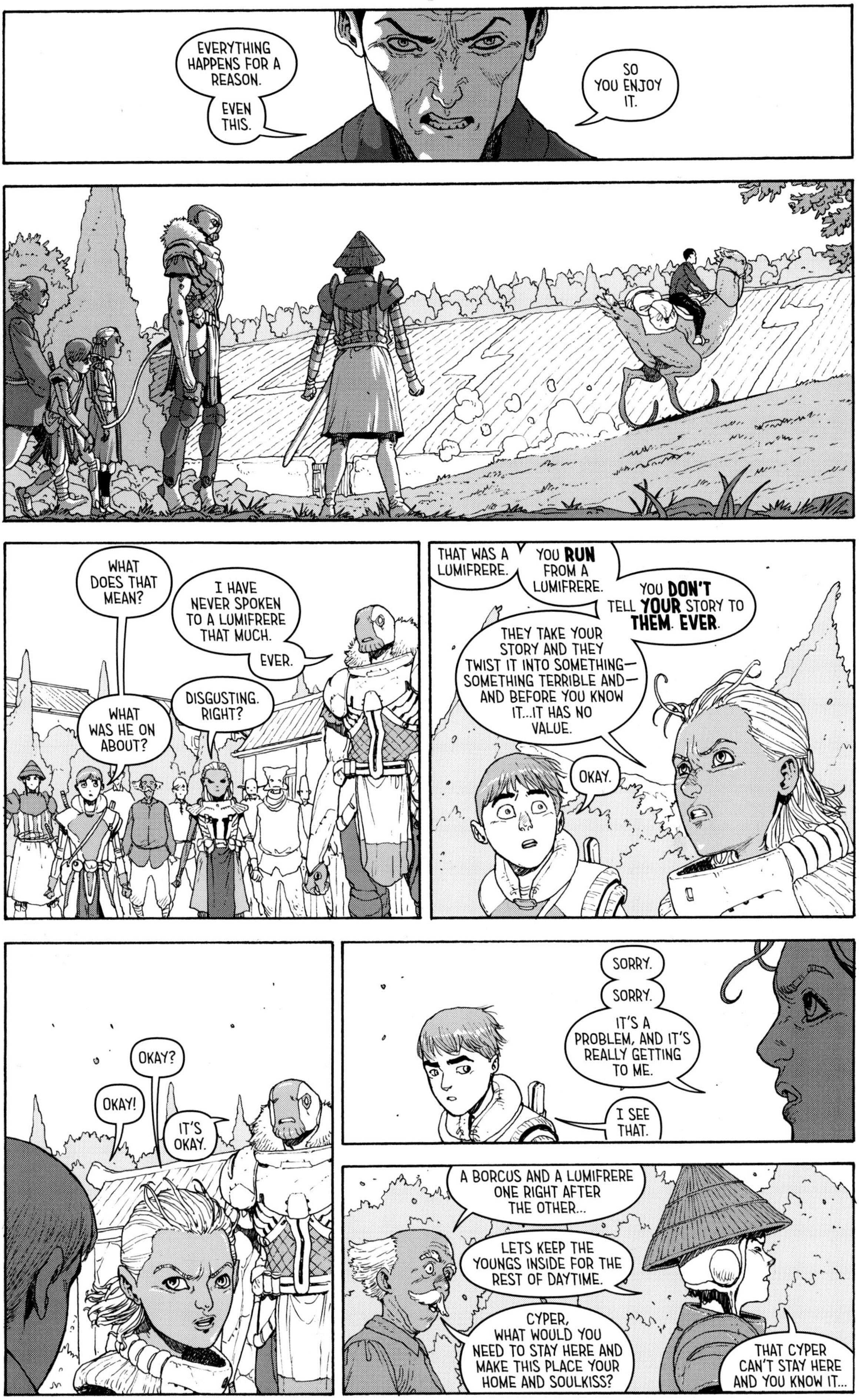
EVERYTHING HAPPENS FOR A REASON.
EVEN THIS.
SO YOU ENJOY IT.
WHAT DOES THAT MEAN?
I HAVE NEVER SPOKEN TO A LUMIFRERE THAT MUCH.
EVER.
WHAT WAS HE ON ABOUT?
DISGUSTING. RIGHT?
THAT WAS A LUMIFRERE.
YOU **RUN** FROM A LUMIFRERE.
YOU **DON'T** TELL **YOUR** STORY TO **THEM**. **EVER**.
THEY TAKE YOUR STORY AND THEY TWIST IT INTO SOMETHING— SOMETHING TERRIBLE AND— AND BEFORE YOU KNOW IT...IT HAS NO VALUE.
OKAY.
OKAY?
OKAY!
IT'S OKAY.
SORRY.
SORRY.
IT'S A PROBLEM, AND IT'S REALLY GETTING TO ME.
I SEE THAT.
A BORCUS AND A LUMIFRERE ONE RIGHT AFTER THE OTHER...
LETS KEEP THE YOUNGS INSIDE FOR THE REST OF DAYTIME.
CYPER, WHAT WOULD YOU NEED TO STAY HERE AND MAKE THIS PLACE YOUR HOME AND SOULKISS?
THAT CYPER CAN'T STAY HERE AND YOU KNOW IT...

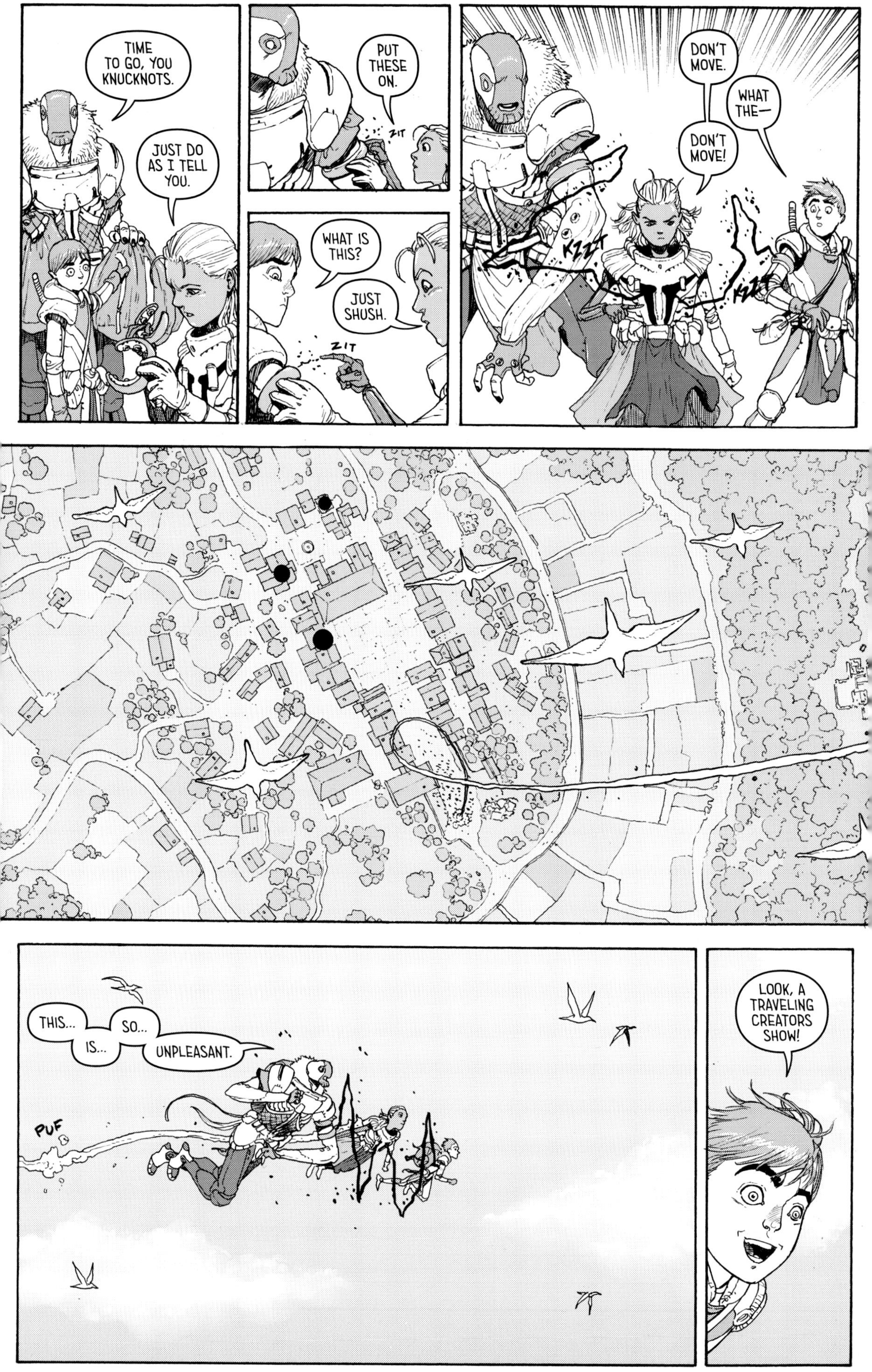
TIME TO GO, YOU KNUCKNOTS.
JUST DO AS I TELL YOU.
PUT THESE ON.
ZIT
WHAT IS THIS?
JUST SHUSH.
ZIT
DON'T MOVE.
DON'T MOVE!
WHAT THE—
KZZT
KZZT
THIS...
IS...
SO...
UNPLEASANT.
PUF
LOOK, A TRAVELING CREATORS SHOW!

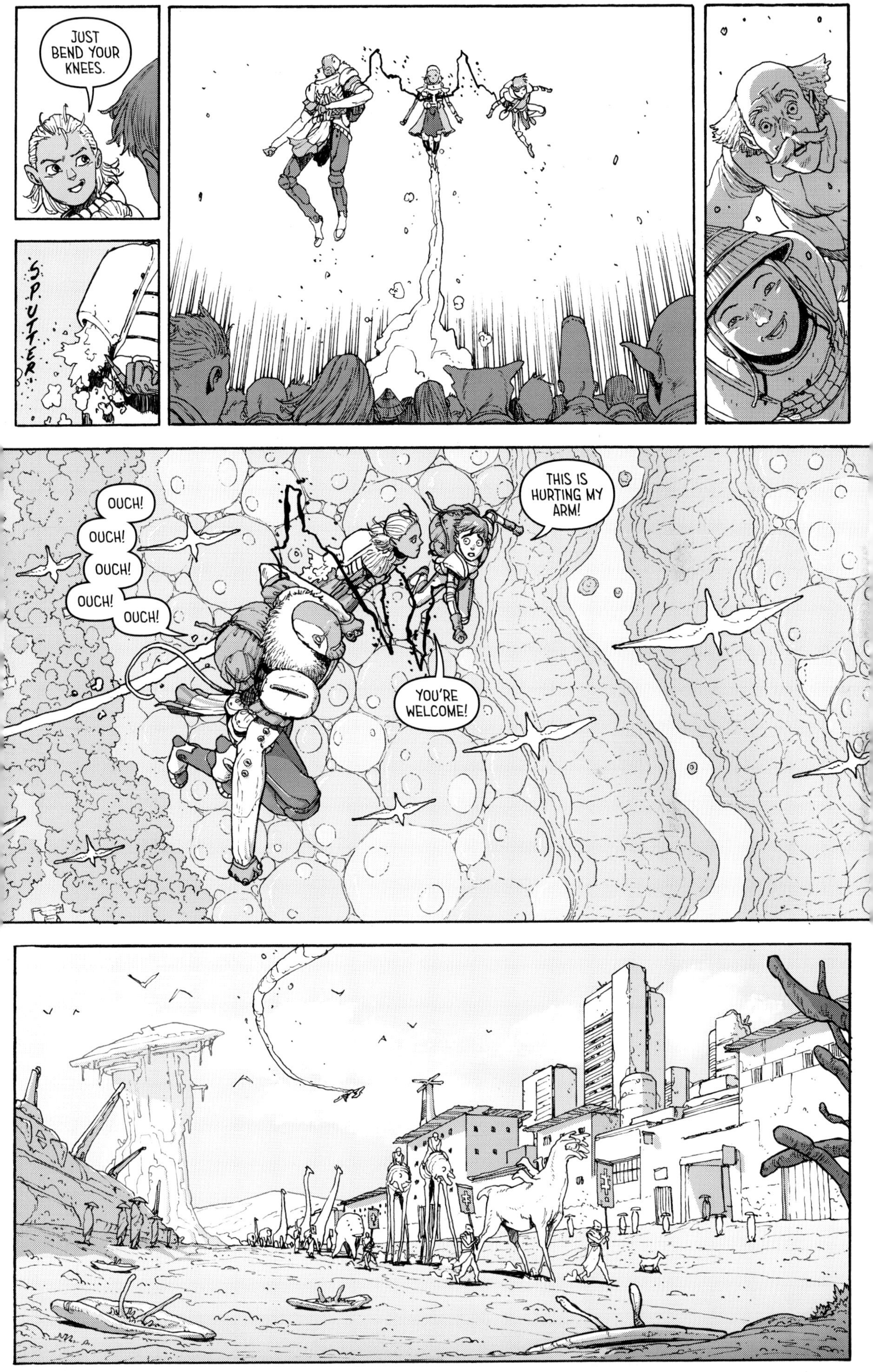
JUST BEND YOUR KNEES.
S.P.U.T.T.E.R
OUCH!
OUCH!
OUCH!
OUCH!
OUCH!
THIS IS HURTING MY ARM!
YOU'RE WELCOME!

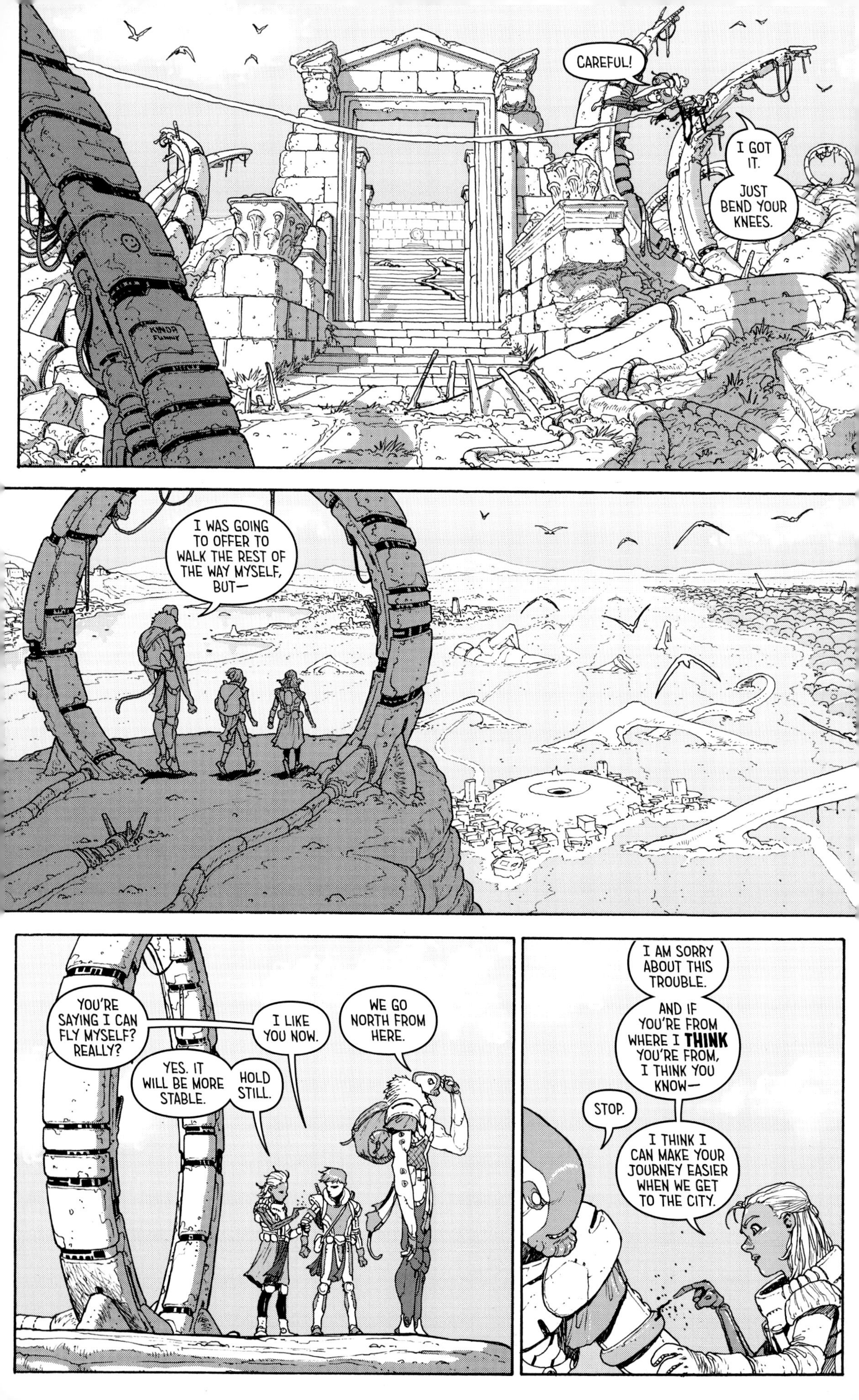

CAREFUL!
I GOT IT.
JUST BEND YOUR KNEES.
I WAS GOING TO OFFER TO WALK THE REST OF THE WAY MYSELF, BUT—
YOU'RE SAYING I CAN FLY MYSELF? REALLY?
YES. IT WILL BE MORE STABLE.
HOLD STILL.
I LIKE YOU NOW.
WE GO NORTH FROM HERE.
I AM SORRY ABOUT THIS TROUBLE.
AND IF YOU'RE FROM WHERE I **THINK** YOU'RE FROM, I THINK YOU KNOW—
STOP.
I THINK I CAN MAKE YOUR JOURNEY EASIER WHEN WE GET TO THE CITY.

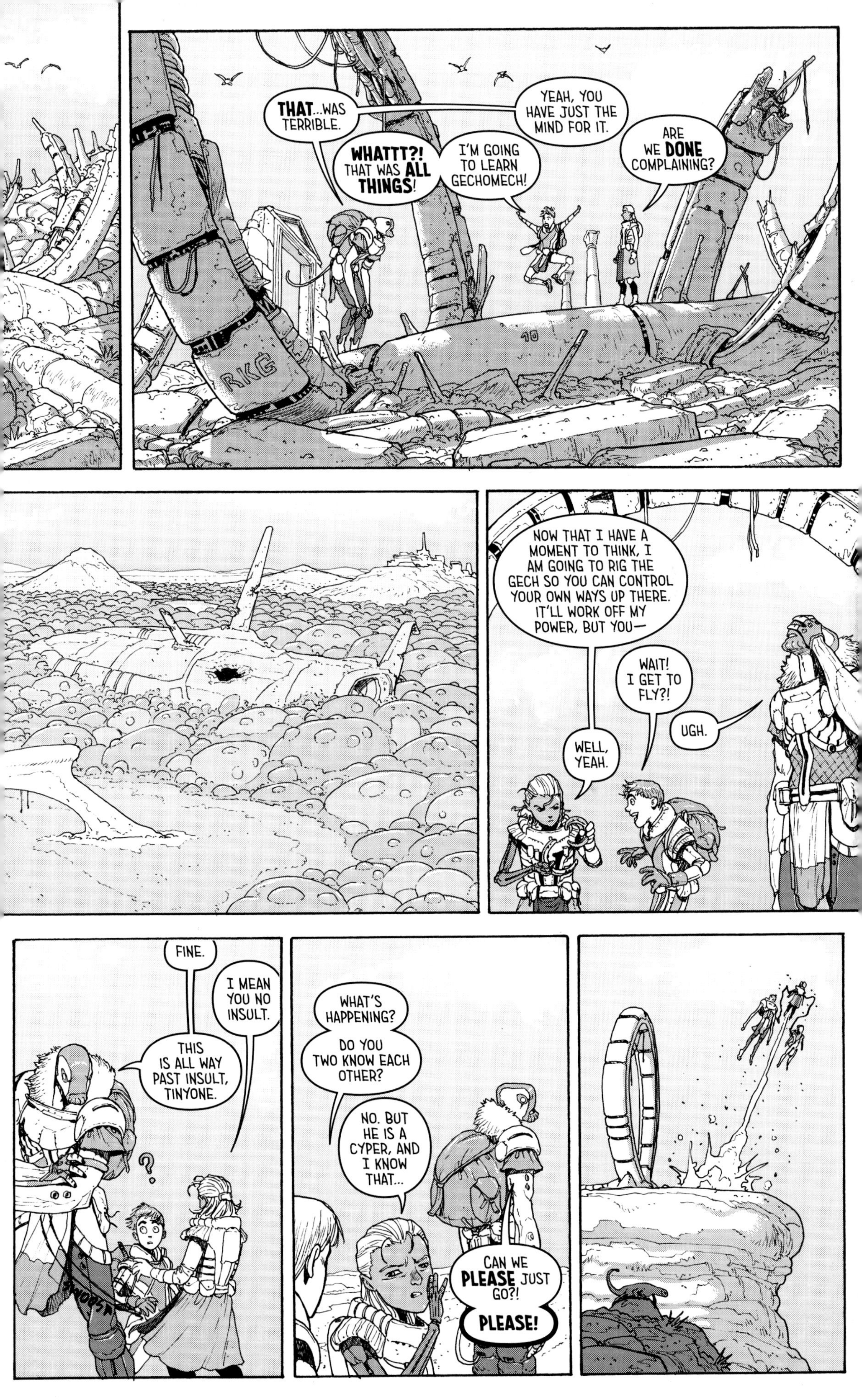
THAT...WAS TERRIBLE.
YEAH, YOU HAVE JUST THE MIND FOR IT.
WHATTT?! THAT WAS ALL THINGS!
I'M GOING TO LEARN GECHOMECH!
ARE WE DONE COMPLAINING?
RKG
NOW THAT I HAVE A MOMENT TO THINK, I AM GOING TO RIG THE GECH SO YOU CAN CONTROL YOUR OWN WAYS UP THERE. IT'LL WORK OFF MY POWER, BUT YOU—
WAIT! I GET TO FLY?!
UGH.
WELL, YEAH.
FINE.
I MEAN YOU NO INSULT.
THIS IS ALL WAY PAST INSULT, TINYONE.
?
WHAT'S HAPPENING?
DO YOU TWO KNOW EACH OTHER?
NO. BUT HE IS A CYPER, AND I KNOW THAT...
CAN WE PLEASE JUST GO?!
PLEASE!

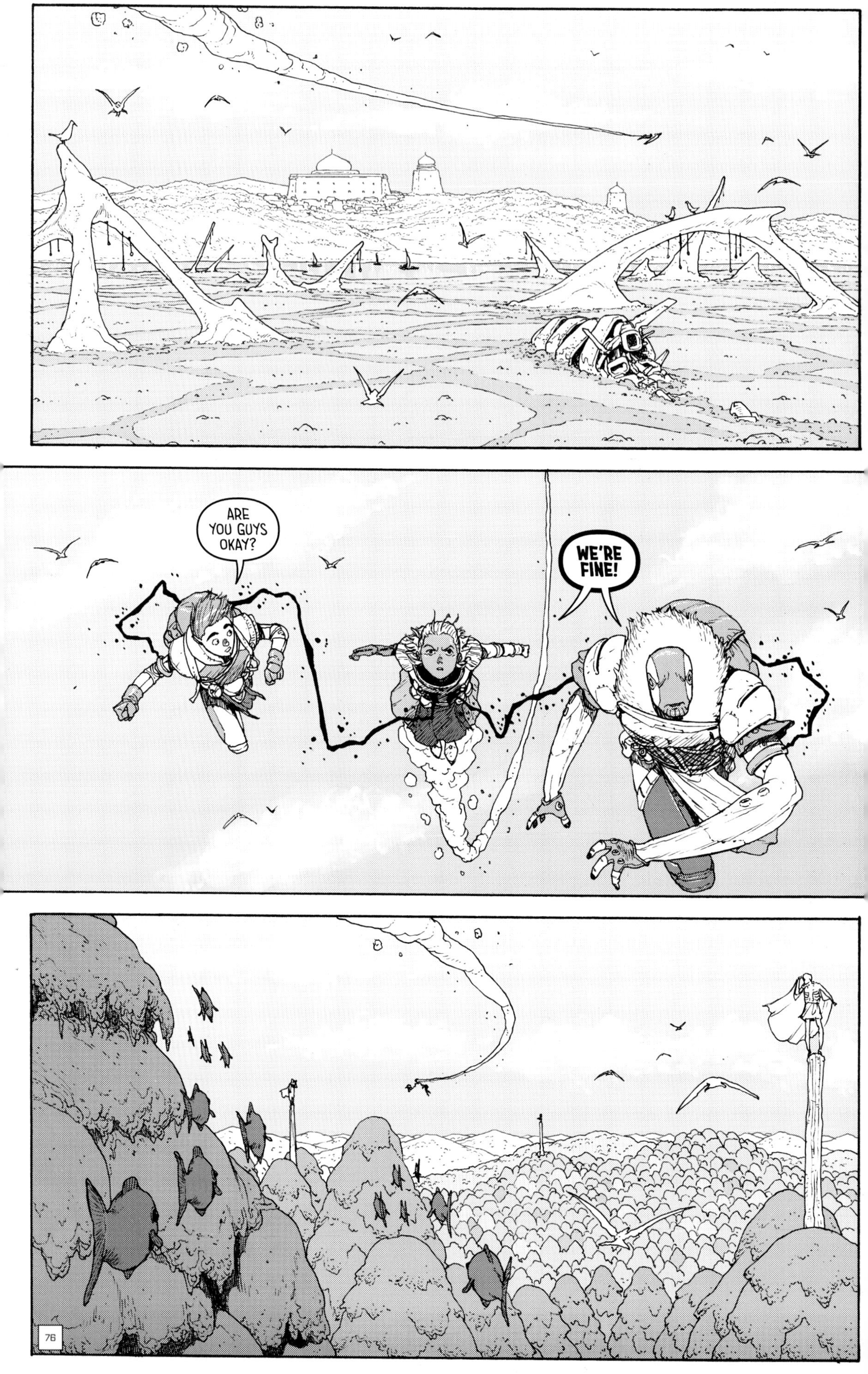
ARE YOU GUYS OKAY?
WE'RE FINE!

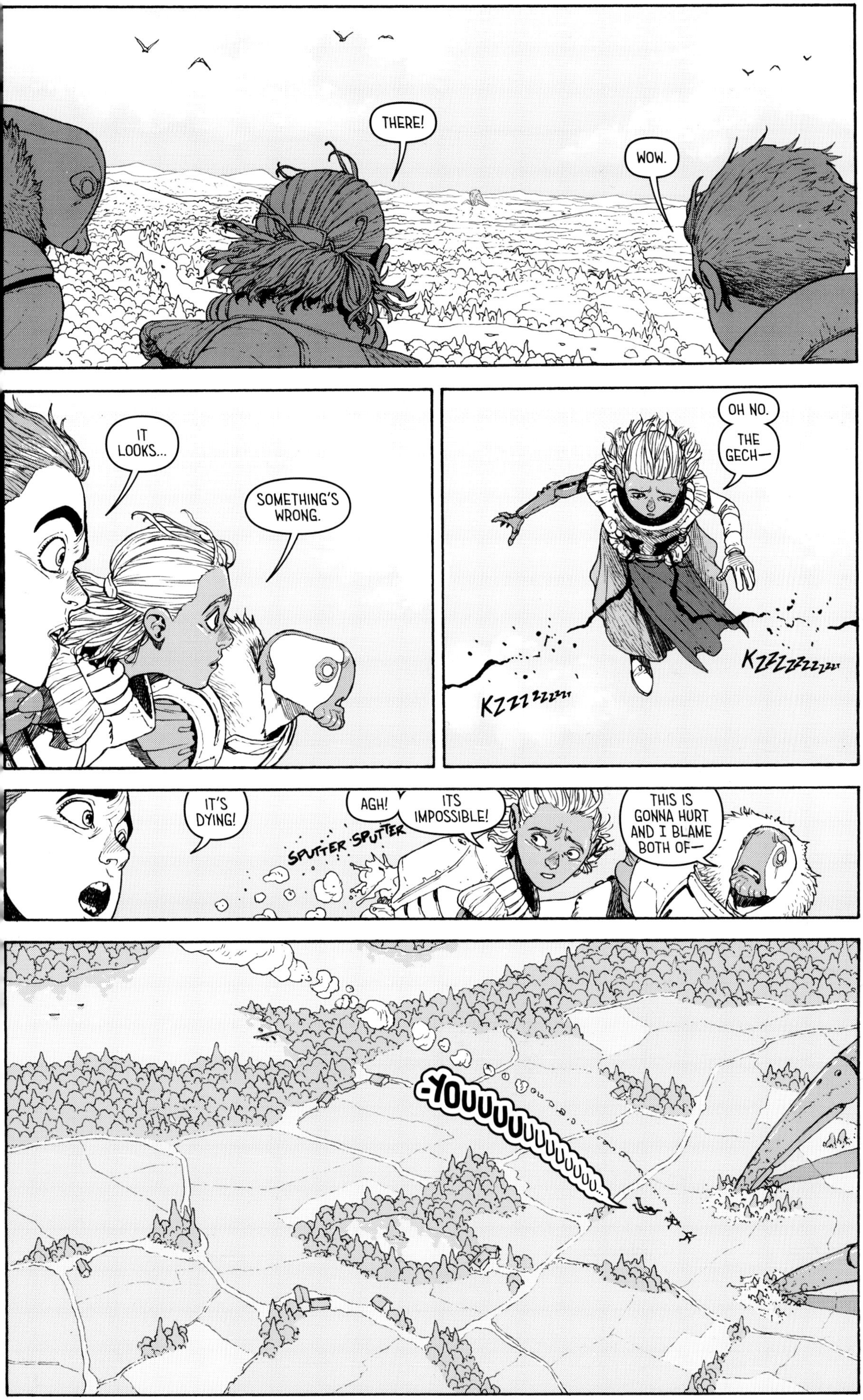
THERE!
WOW.
IT LOOKS...
SOMETHING'S WRONG.
OH NO.
THE GECH—
KZZZzzzzz
KZZZZZZzzzz
IT'S DYING!
AGH!
ITS IMPOSSIBLE!
SPUTTER SPUTTER
THIS IS GONNA HURT AND I BLAME BOTH OF—
-YOUUUUUUUUUUUU...

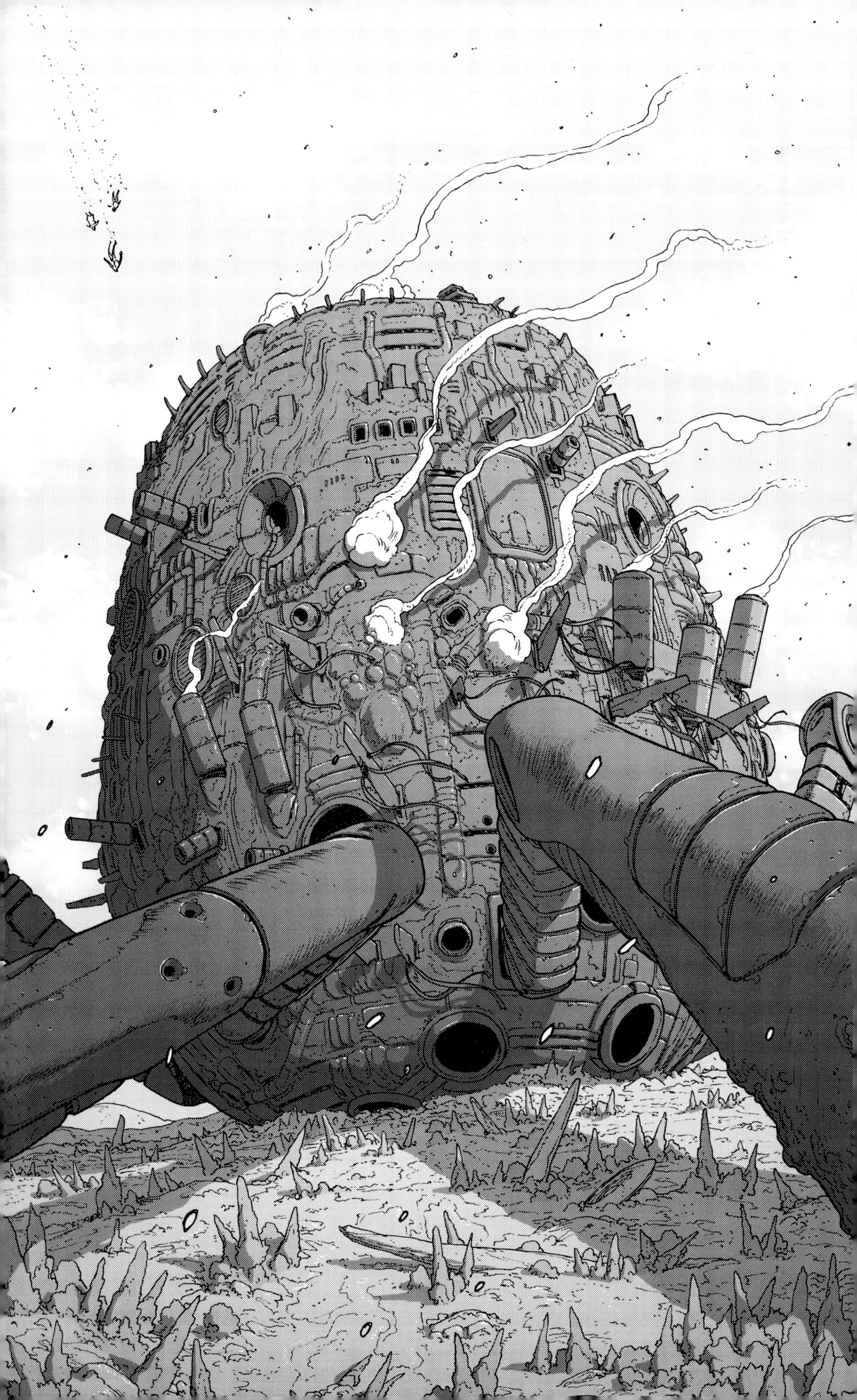

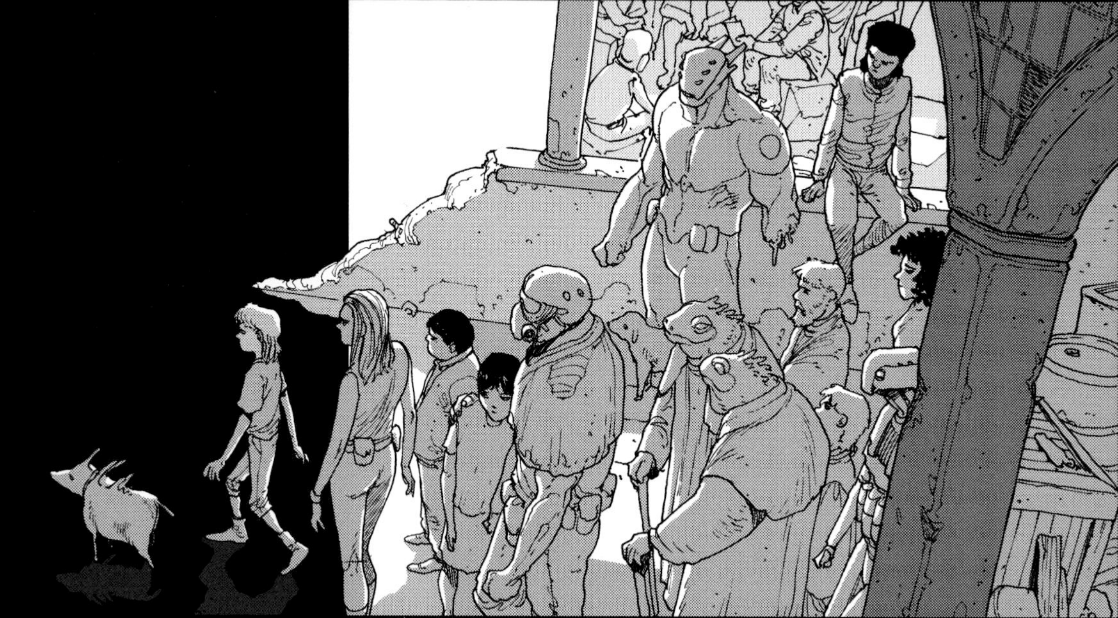

CHAPTER 3

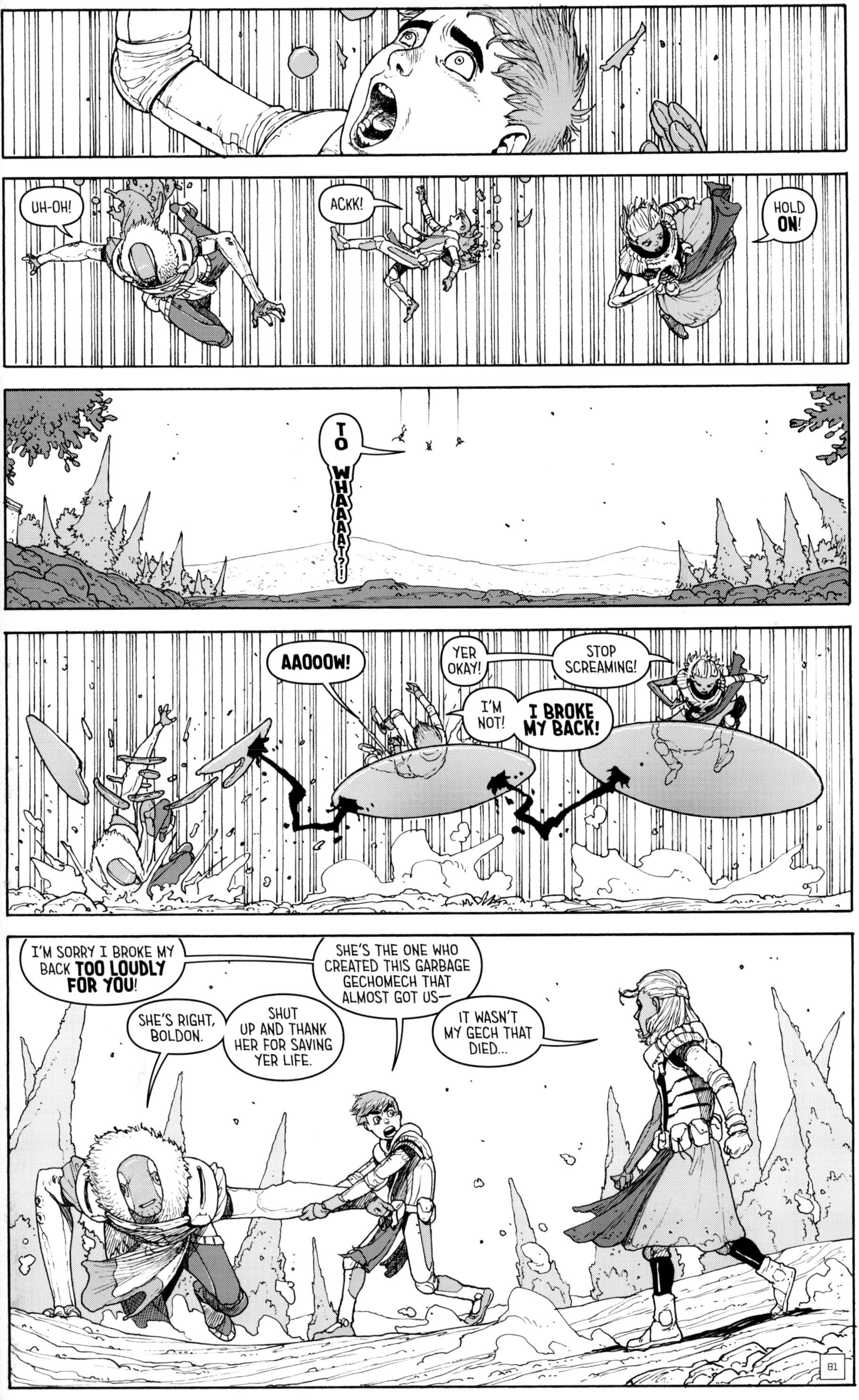

UH-OH!
ACKK!
HOLD ON!
TO WHAAAAT?!
AAOOOW!
YER OKAY!
STOP SCREAMING!
I'M NOT!
I BROKE MY BACK!
I'M SORRY I BROKE MY BACK TOO LOUDLY FOR YOU!
SHE'S THE ONE WHO CREATED THIS GARBAGE GECHOMECH THAT ALMOST GOT US—
SHE'S RIGHT, BOLDON.
SHUT UP AND THANK HER FOR SAVING YER LIFE.
IT WASN'T MY GECH THAT DIED...

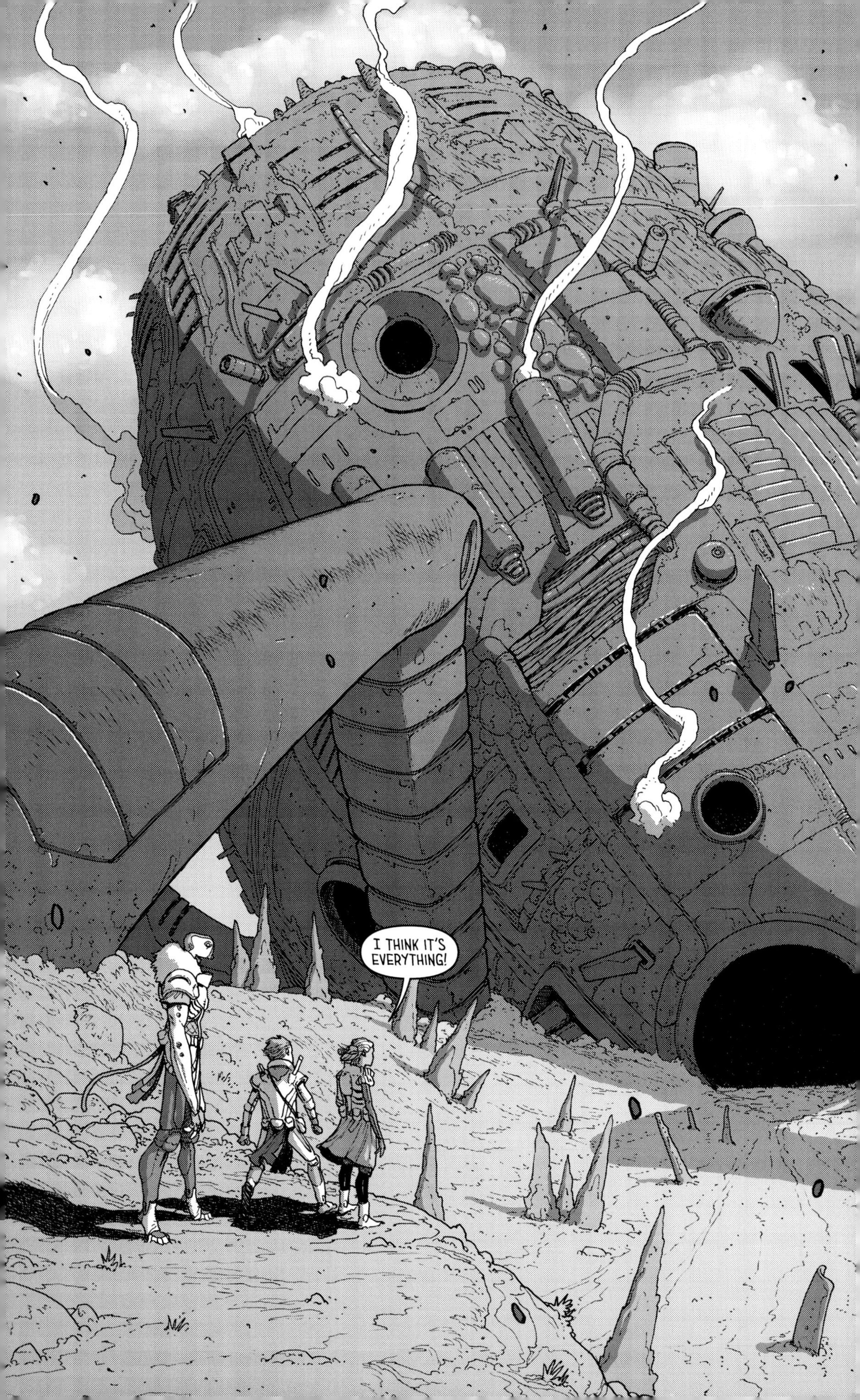
I THINK IT'S EVERYTHING!

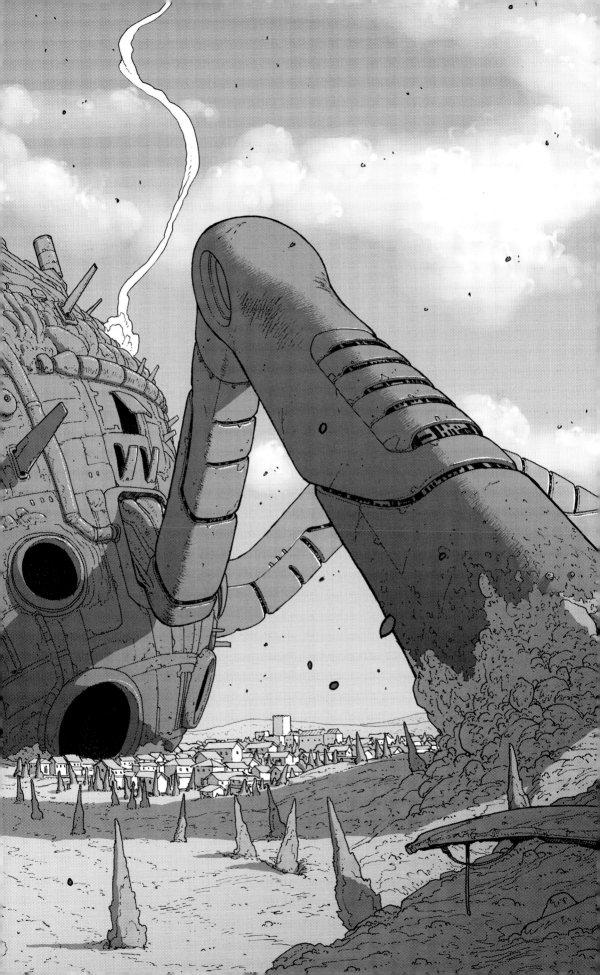

WE **HAVE** TO BE IN THE WRONG PLACE!

WE'RE NOT.

THAT IS THE CITY OF GOLDEN—

STOP TALKIN'.

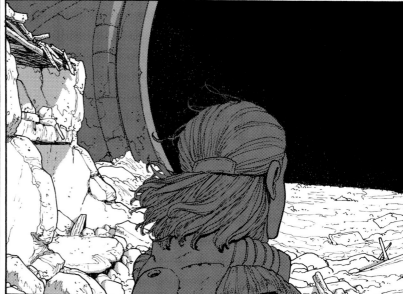

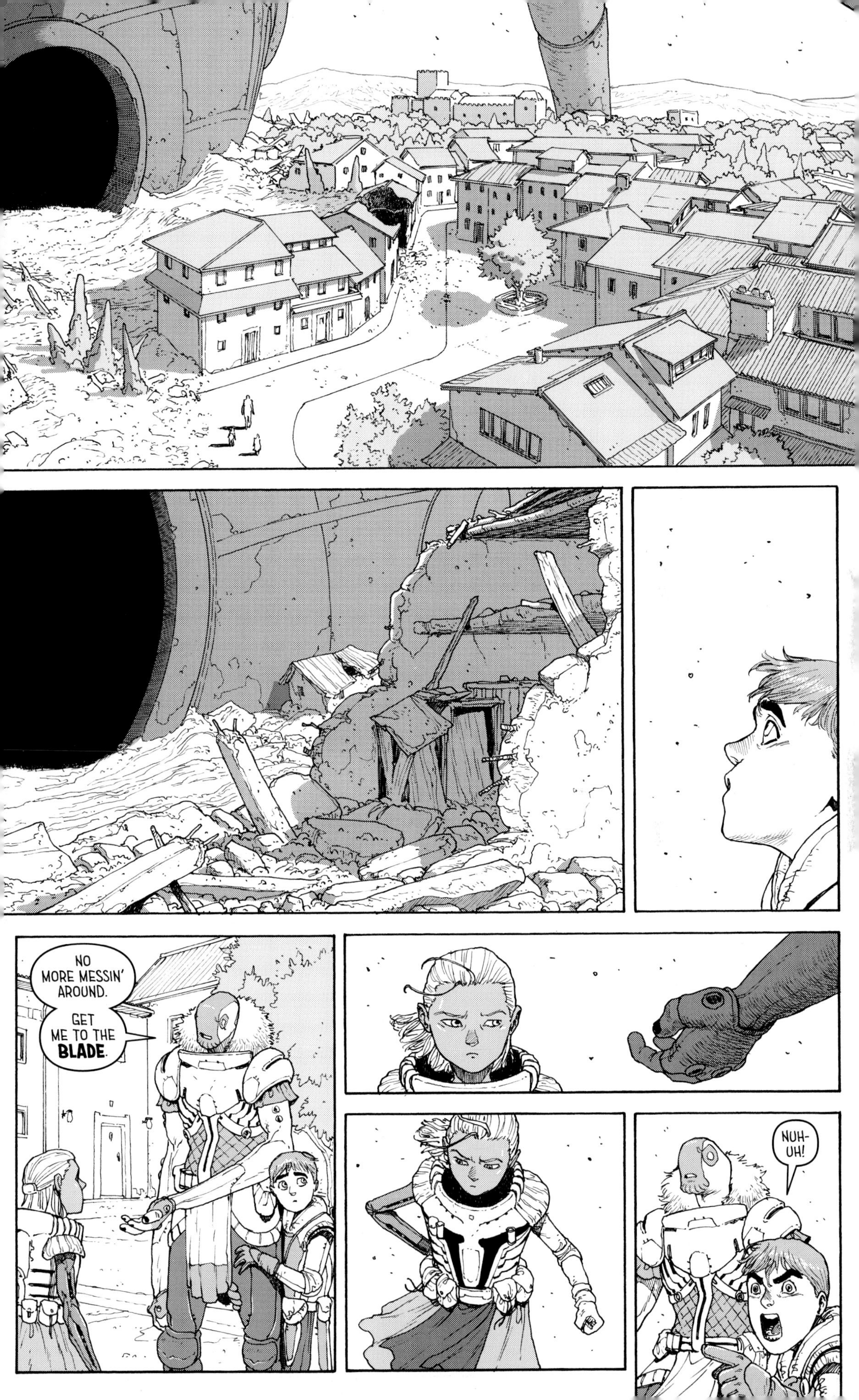
NO MORE MESSIN' AROUND.
GET ME TO THE **BLADE**.
NUH-UH!

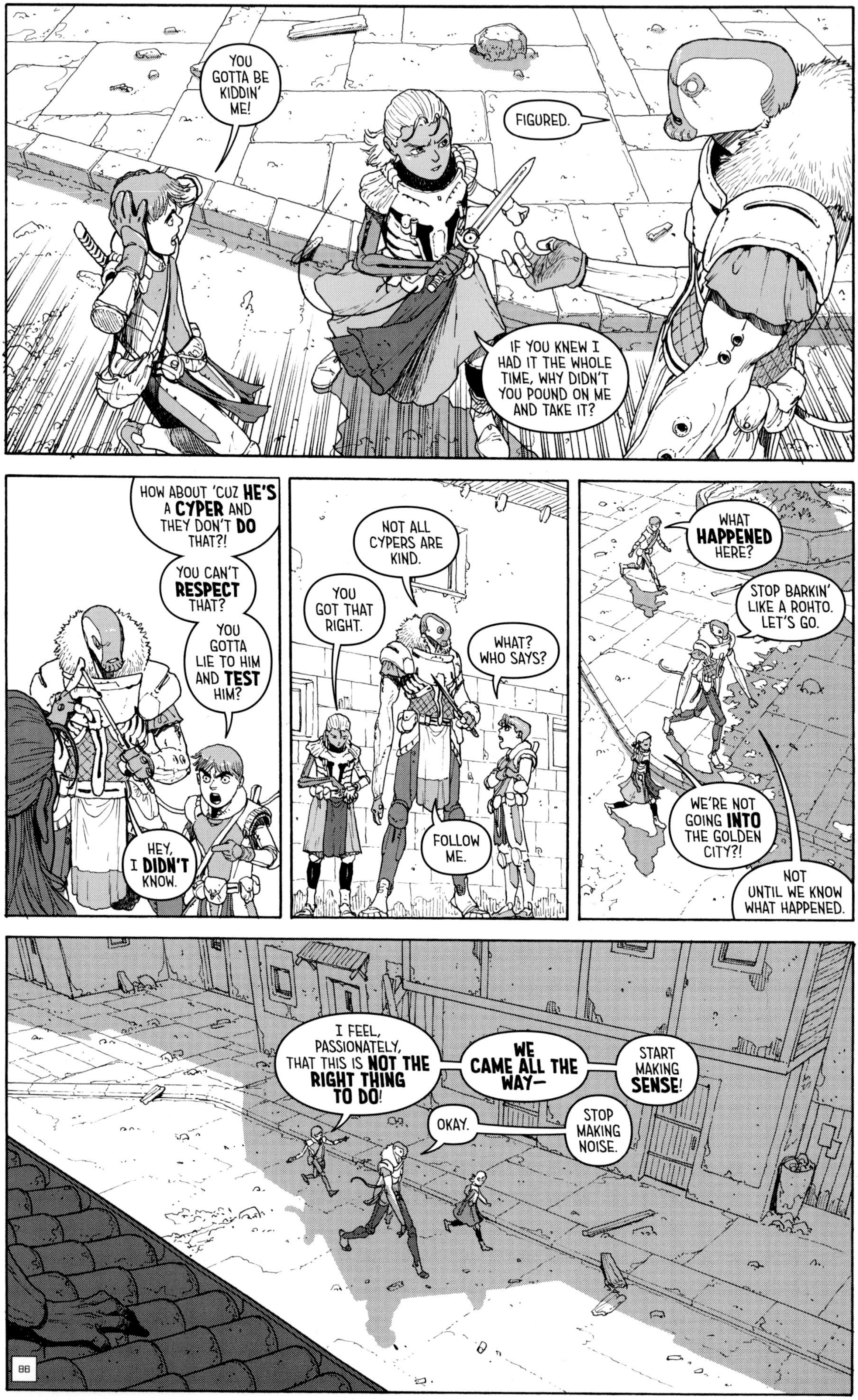

YOU GOTTA BE KIDDIN' ME!
FIGURED.
IF YOU KNEW I HAD IT THE WHOLE TIME, WHY DIDN'T YOU POUND ON ME AND TAKE IT?
HOW ABOUT 'CUZ HE'S A CYPER AND THEY DON'T DO THAT?!
YOU CAN'T RESPECT THAT?
YOU GOTTA LIE TO HIM AND TEST HIM?
HEY, I DIDN'T KNOW.
NOT ALL CYPERS ARE KIND.
YOU GOT THAT RIGHT.
WHAT? WHO SAYS?
FOLLOW ME.
WHAT HAPPENED HERE?
STOP BARKIN' LIKE A ROHTO. LET'S GO.
WE'RE NOT GOING INTO THE GOLDEN CITY?!
NOT UNTIL WE KNOW WHAT HAPPENED.
I FEEL, PASSIONATELY, THAT THIS IS NOT THE RIGHT THING TO DO!
WE CAME ALL THE WAY—
START MAKING SENSE!
OKAY.
STOP MAKING NOISE.

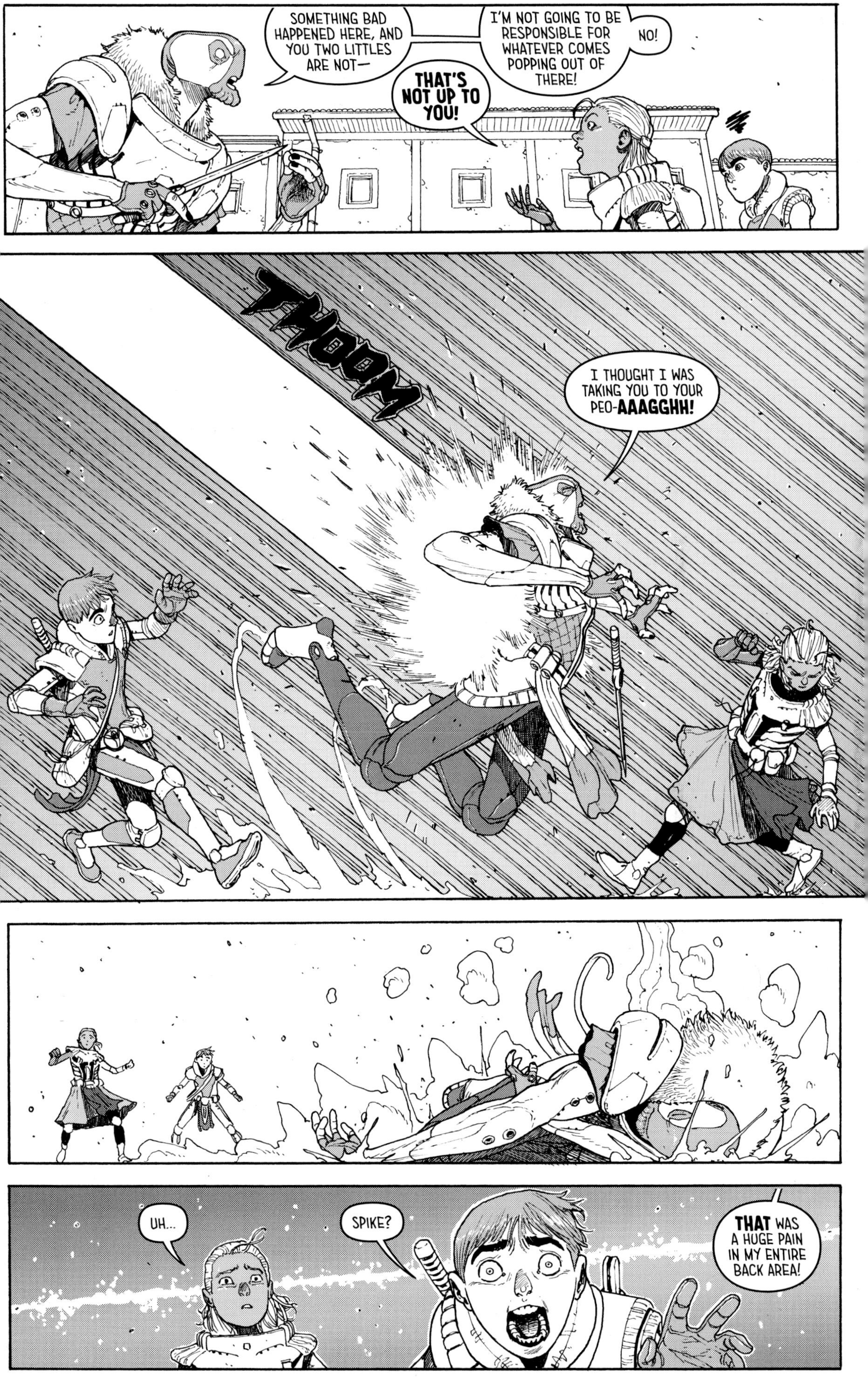
SOMETHING BAD HAPPENED HERE, AND YOU TWO LITTLES ARE NOT—
I'M NOT GOING TO BE RESPONSIBLE FOR WHATEVER COMES POPPING OUT OF THERE!
THAT'S NOT UP TO YOU!
NO!
THOOM
I THOUGHT I WAS TAKING YOU TO YOUR PEO-AAAGGHH!
UH...
SPIKE?
THAT WAS A HUGE PAIN IN MY ENTIRE BACK AREA!

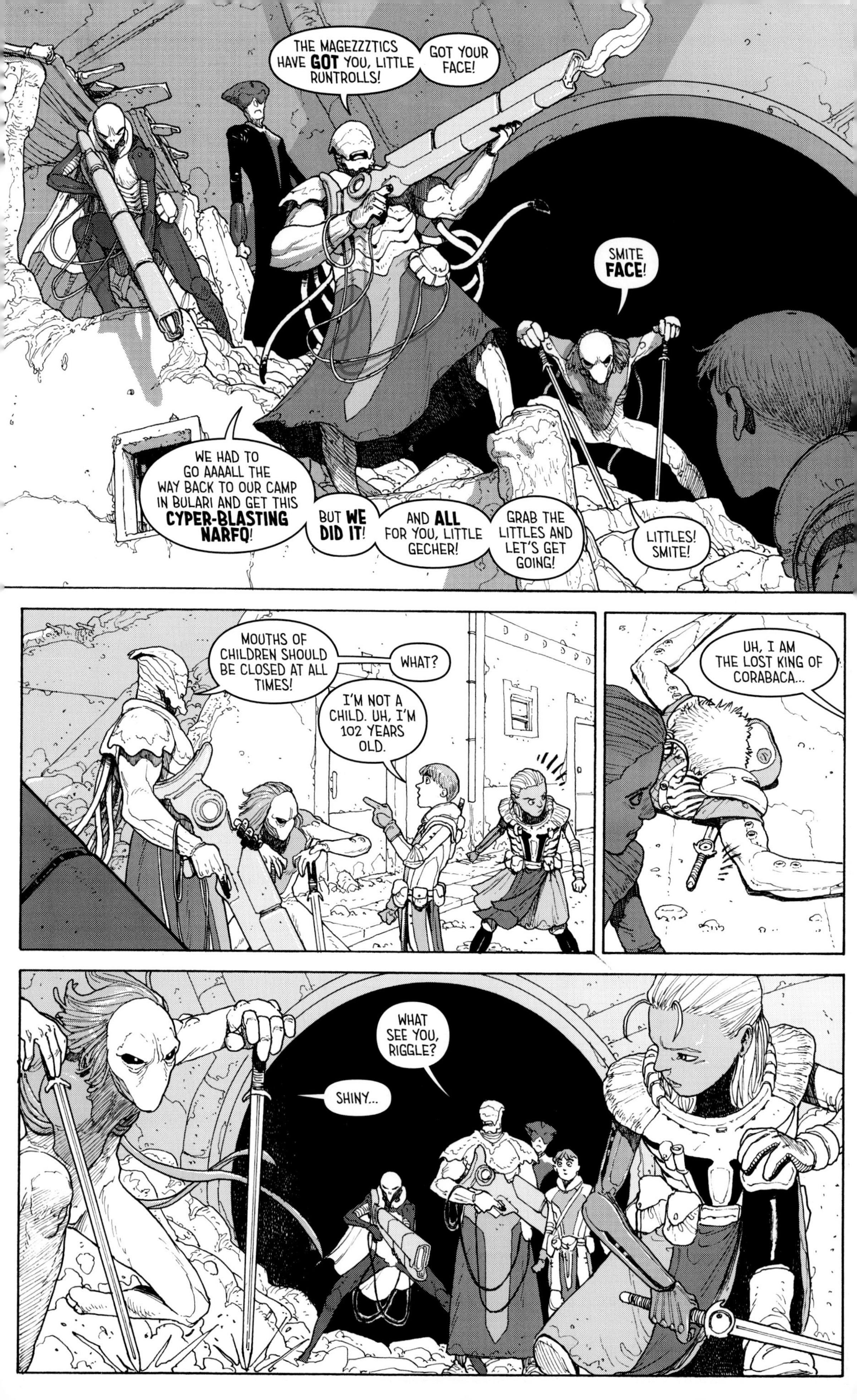
THE MAGEZZZTICS HAVE GOT YOU, LITTLE RUNTROLLS!
GOT YOUR FACE!
SMITE FACE!
WE HAD TO GO AAAALL THE WAY BACK TO OUR CAMP IN BULARI AND GET THIS CYPER-BLASTING NARFQ!
BUT WE DID IT!
AND ALL FOR YOU, LITTLE GECHER!
GRAB THE LITTLES AND LET'S GET GOING!
LITTLES! SMITE!
MOUTHS OF CHILDREN SHOULD BE CLOSED AT ALL TIMES!
WHAT?
I'M NOT A CHILD. UH, I'M 102 YEARS OLD.
UH, I AM THE LOST KING OF CORABACA...
WHAT SEE YOU, RIGGLE?
SHINY...

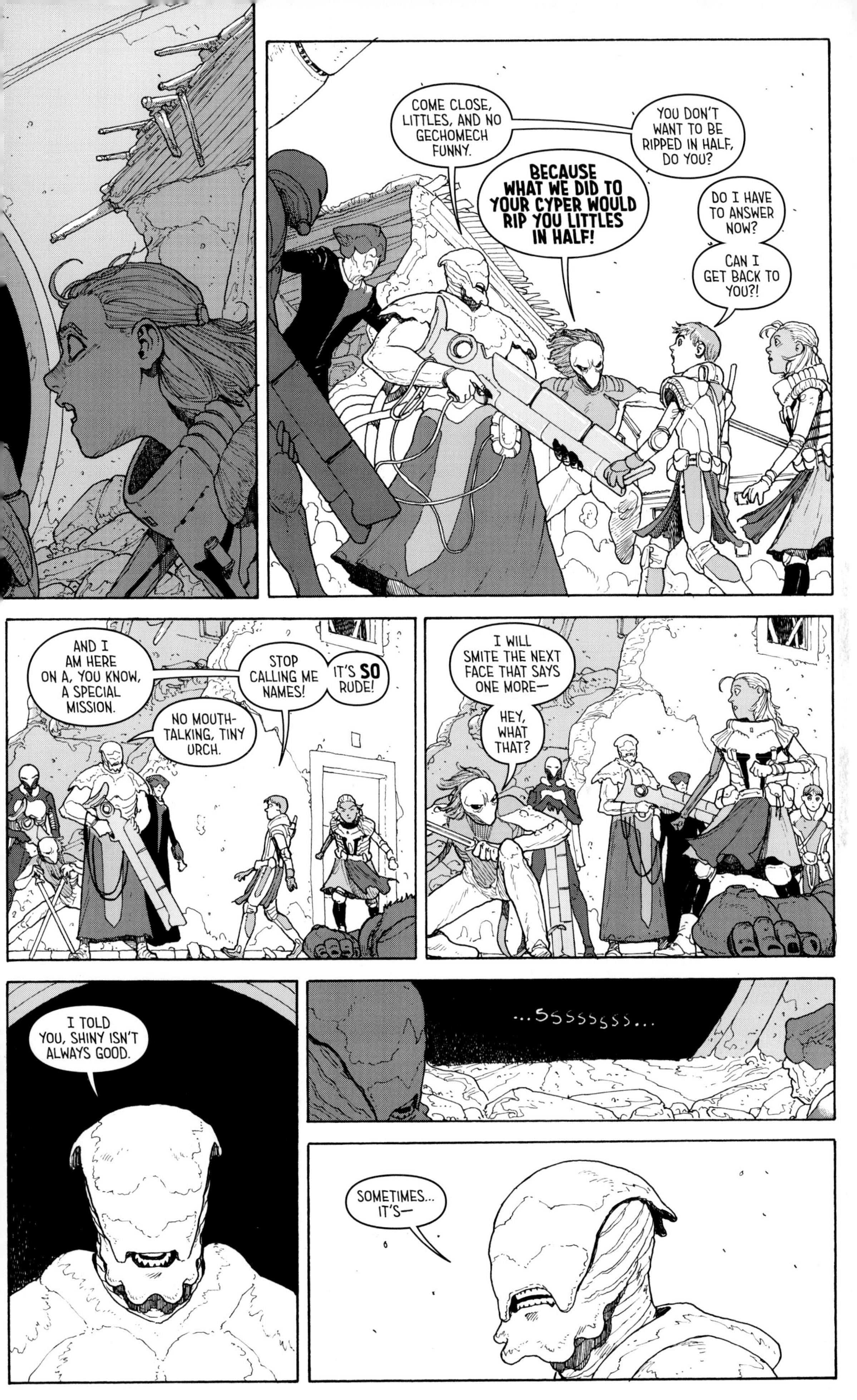
COME CLOSE, LITTLES, AND NO GECHOMECH FUNNY.
YOU DON'T WANT TO BE RIPPED IN HALF, DO YOU?
BECAUSE WHAT WE DID TO YOUR CYPER WOULD RIP YOU LITTLES IN HALF!
DO I HAVE TO ANSWER NOW?
CAN I GET BACK TO YOU?!
AND I AM HERE ON A, YOU KNOW, A SPECIAL MISSION.
STOP CALLING ME NAMES!
IT'S SO RUDE!
NO MOUTH-TALKING, TINY URCH.
I WILL SMITE THE NEXT FACE THAT SAYS ONE MORE—
HEY, WHAT THAT?
I TOLD YOU, SHINY ISN'T ALWAYS GOOD.
...SSSSSSSS...
SOMETIMES... IT'S—

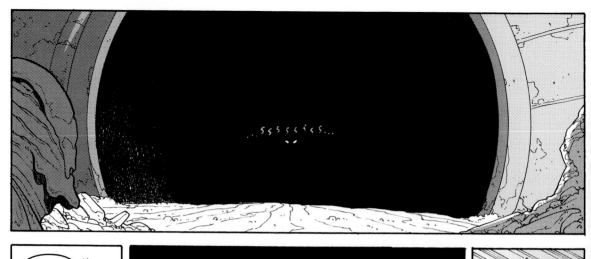

WHAT HAPPENED... HERE?

...ʃʃʃ ʃʃʃ ʃ ʃ ʃs...

MAGEZZZTICS!

WE GO!

WE GO NOW!

SHINY!

MAGEZZZTICS!

WE GO!

SPLAT

SPLAT

WE GO NAAGGHH!

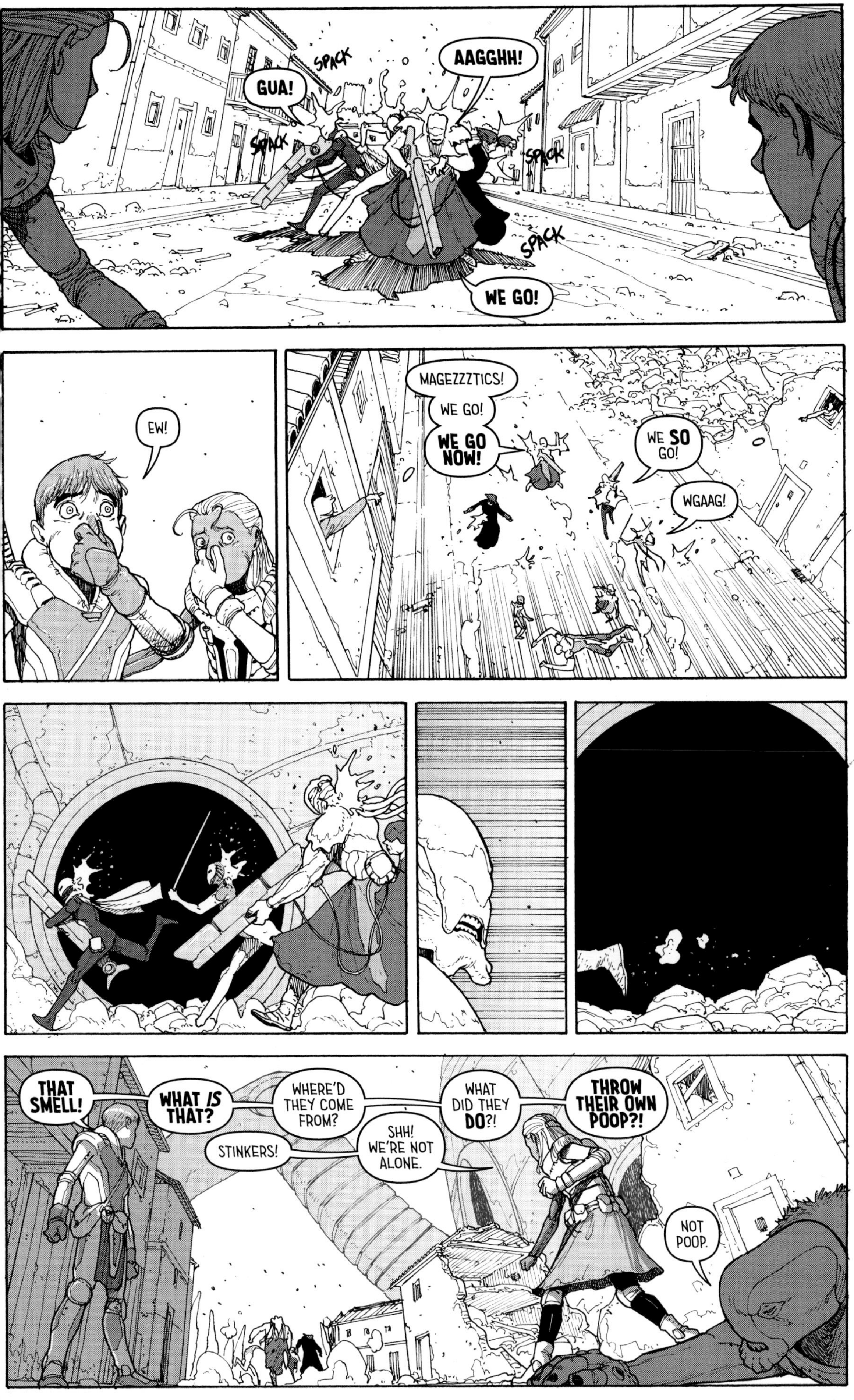
SPACK
GUA!
AAGGHH!
SPACK
SPACK
SPACK
WE GO!
EW!
MAGEZZZTICS!
WE GO!
WE GO NOW!
WE SO GO!
WGAAG!
THAT SMELL!
WHAT IS THAT?
WHERE'D THEY COME FROM?
STINKERS!
SHH! WE'RE NOT ALONE.
WHAT DID THEY DO?!
THROW THEIR OWN POOP?!
NOT POOP.

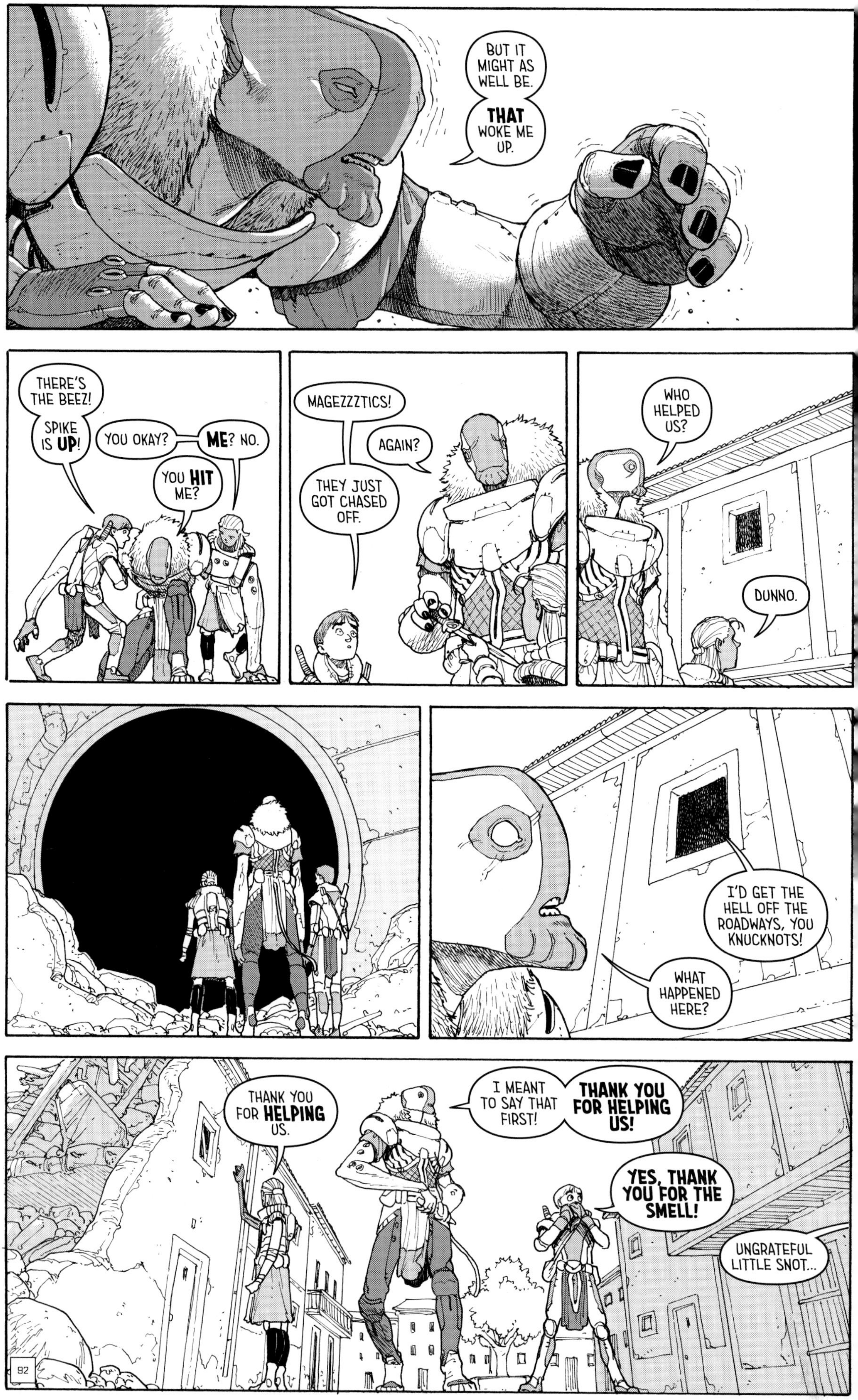

BUT IT MIGHT AS WELL BE.
THAT WOKE ME UP.
THERE'S THE BEEZ!
SPIKE IS UP!
YOU OKAY?
ME? NO.
YOU HIT ME?
MAGEZZZZTICS!
AGAIN?
THEY JUST GOT CHASED OFF.
WHO HELPED US?
DUNNO.
I'D GET THE HELL OFF THE ROADWAYS, YOU KNUCKNOTS!
WHAT HAPPENED HERE?
THANK YOU FOR HELPING US.
I MEANT TO SAY THAT FIRST!
THANK YOU FOR HELPING US!
YES, THANK YOU FOR THE SMELL!
UNGRATEFUL LITTLE SNOT...

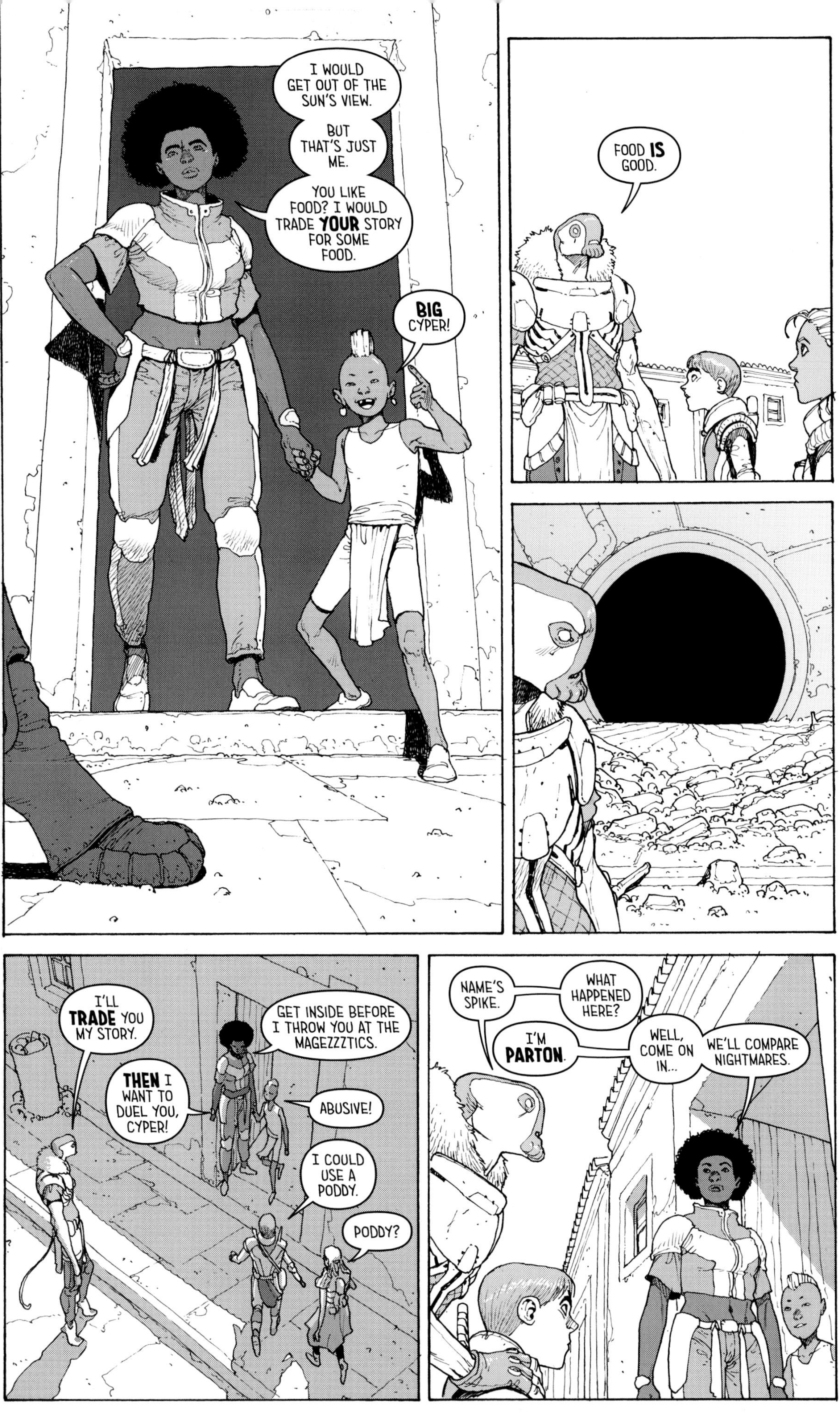
I WOULD GET OUT OF THE SUN'S VIEW.
BUT THAT'S JUST ME.
YOU LIKE FOOD? I WOULD TRADE **YOUR** STORY FOR SOME FOOD.
BIG CYPER!
FOOD **IS** GOOD.
I'LL **TRADE** YOU MY STORY.
THEN I WANT TO DUEL YOU, CYPER!
GET INSIDE BEFORE I THROW YOU AT THE MAGEZZZTICS.
ABUSIVE!
I COULD USE A PODDY.
PODDY?
NAME'S SPIKE.
WHAT HAPPENED HERE?
I'M **PARTON**.
WELL, COME ON IN...
WE'LL COMPARE NIGHTMARES.

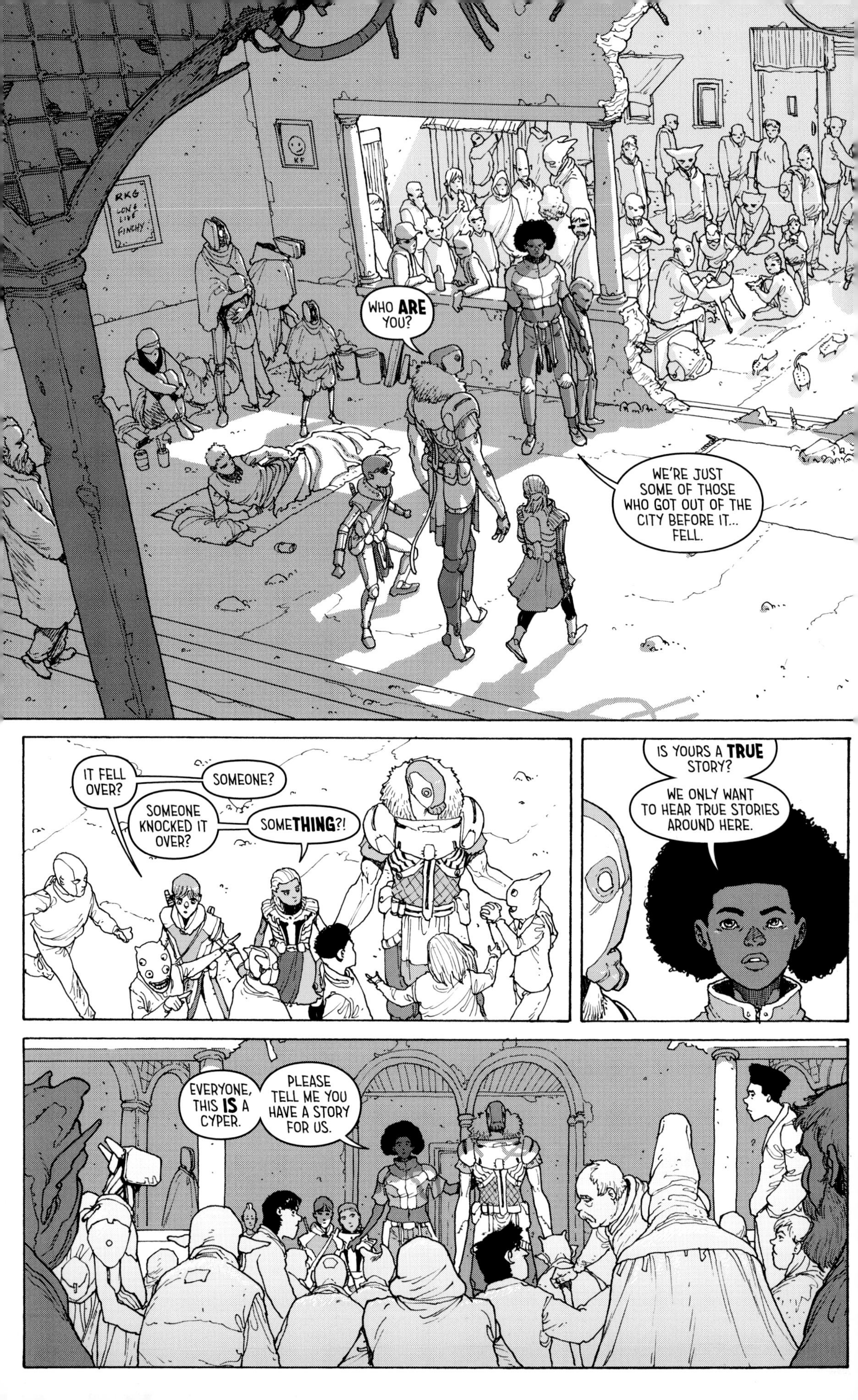

WHO ARE YOU?
WE'RE JUST SOME OF THOSE WHO GOT OUT OF THE CITY BEFORE IT... FELL.
IT FELL OVER?
SOMEONE?
SOMEONE KNOCKED IT OVER?
SOMETHING?!
IS YOURS A TRUE STORY?
WE ONLY WANT TO HEAR TRUE STORIES AROUND HERE.
EVERYONE, THIS IS A CYPER.
PLEASE TELL ME YOU HAVE A STORY FOR US.

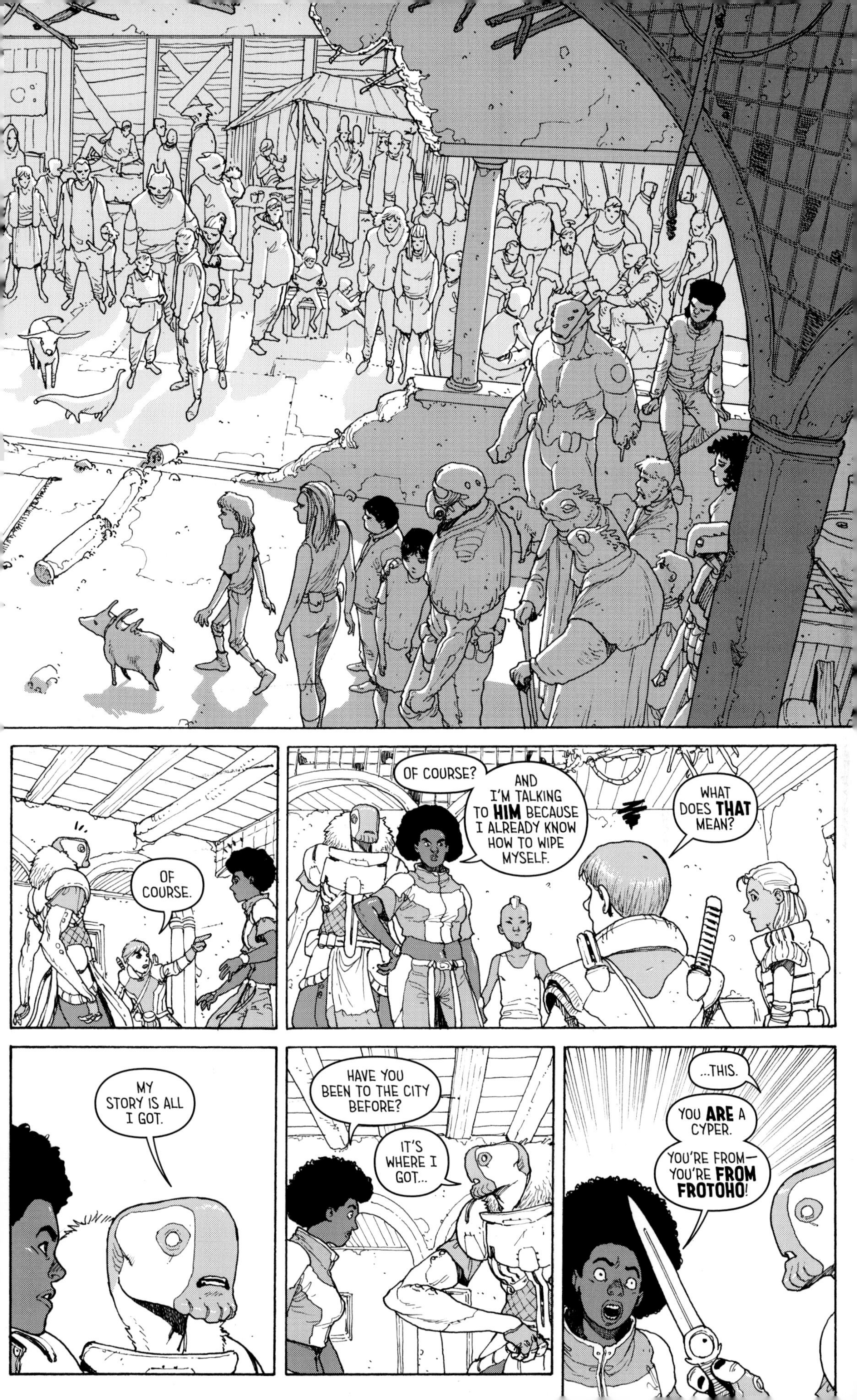
OF COURSE.
OF COURSE?
AND I'M TALKING TO HIM BECAUSE I ALREADY KNOW HOW TO WIPE MYSELF.
WHAT DOES THAT MEAN?
MY STORY IS ALL I GOT.
HAVE YOU BEEN TO THE CITY BEFORE?
IT'S WHERE I GOT...
...THIS.
YOU ARE A CYPER.
YOU'RE FROM— YOU'RE FROM FROTOHO!

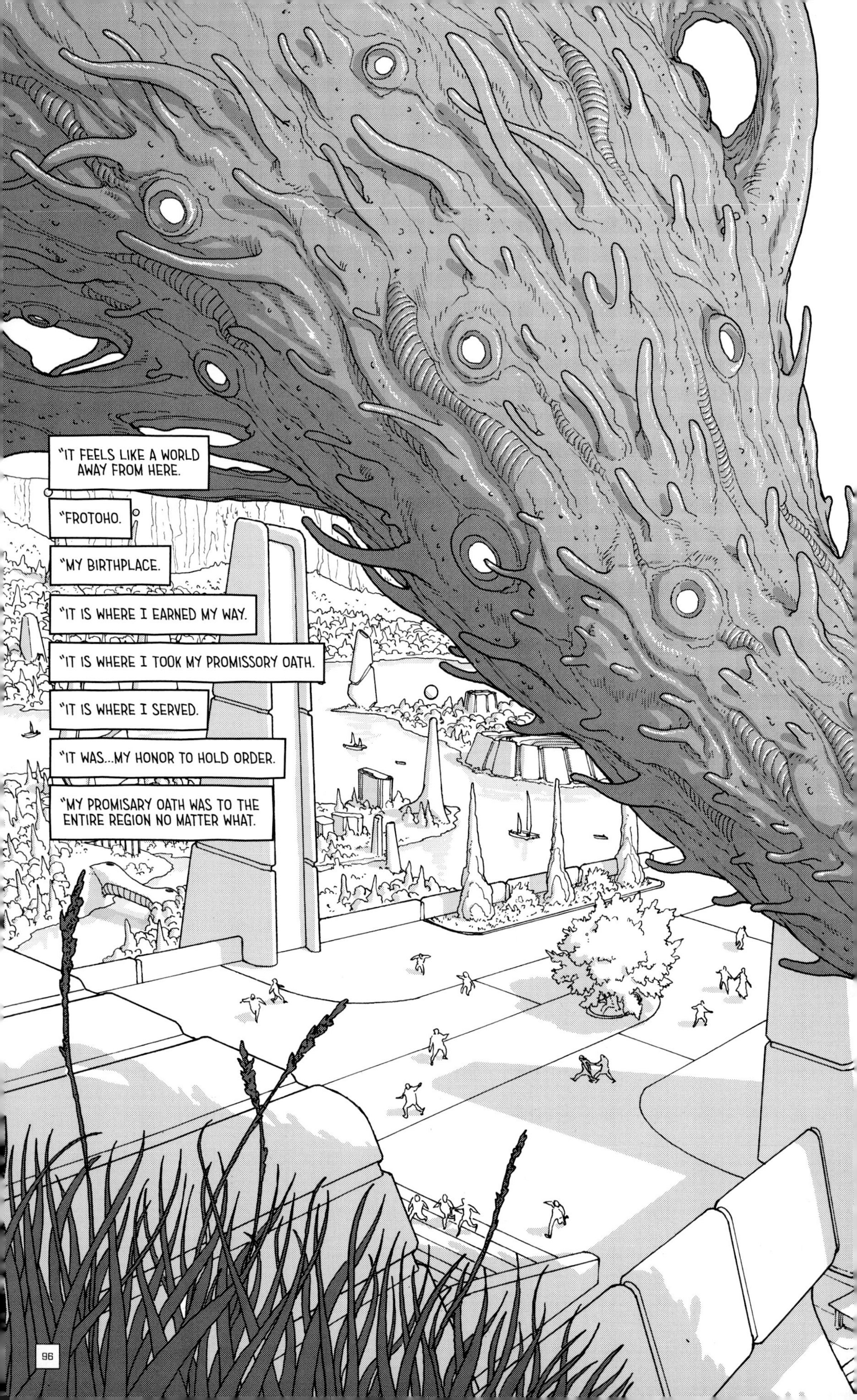
"IT FEELS LIKE A WORLD AWAY FROM HERE.
"FROTOHO.
"MY BIRTHPLACE.
"IT IS WHERE I EARNED MY WAY.
"IT IS WHERE I TOOK MY PROMISSORY OATH.
"IT IS WHERE I SERVED.
"IT WAS...MY HONOR TO HOLD ORDER.
"MY PROMISARY OATH WAS TO THE ENTIRE REGION NO MATTER WHAT.

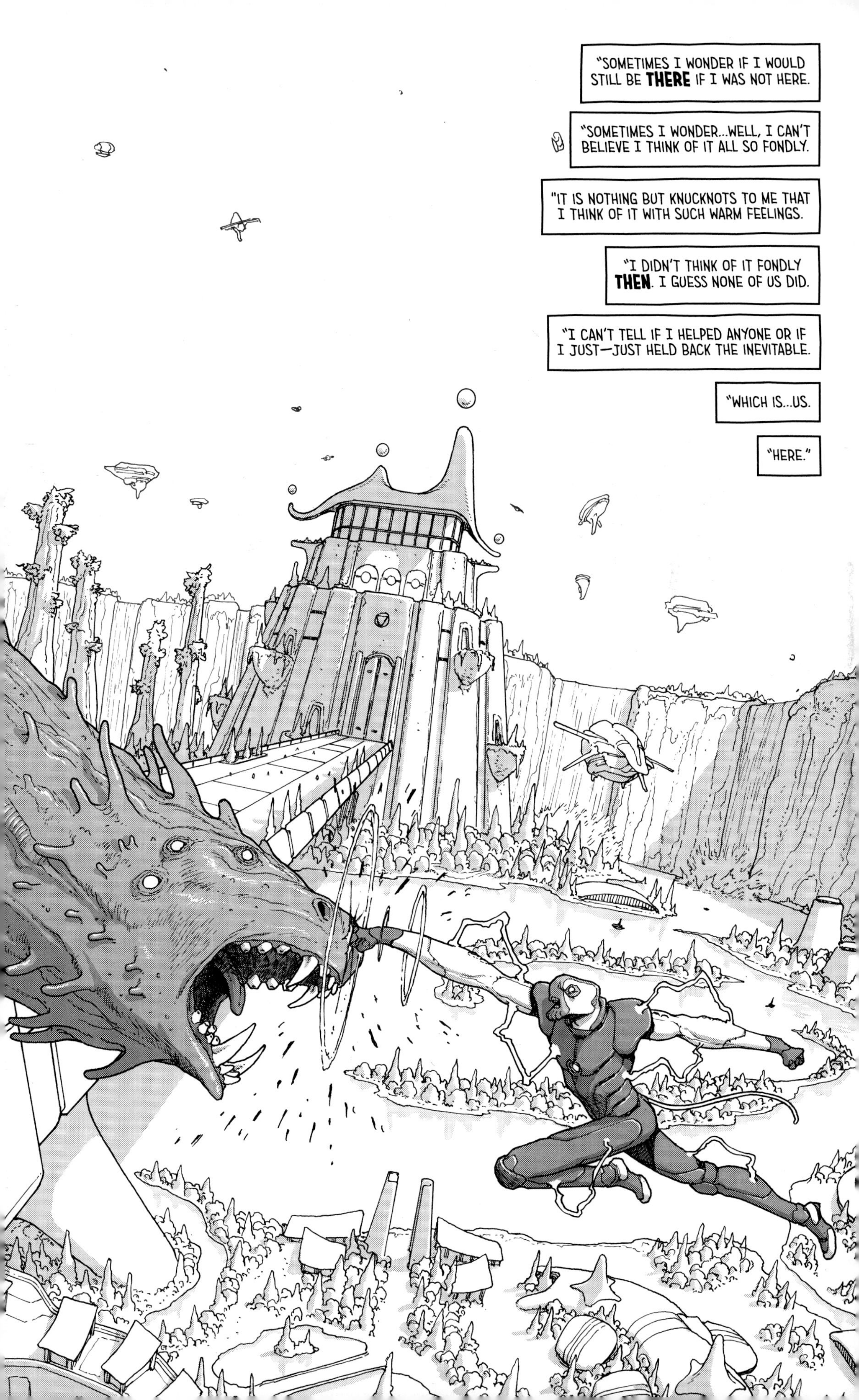
"SOMETIMES I WONDER IF I WOULD STILL BE **THERE** IF I WAS NOT HERE.
"SOMETIMES I WONDER...WELL, I CAN'T BELIEVE I THINK OF IT ALL SO FONDLY.
"IT IS NOTHING BUT KNUCKNOTS TO ME THAT I THINK OF IT WITH SUCH WARM FEELINGS.
"I DIDN'T THINK OF IT FONDLY **THEN**. I GUESS NONE OF US DID.
"I CAN'T TELL IF I HELPED ANYONE OR IF I JUST—JUST HELD BACK THE INEVITABLE.
"WHICH IS...US.
"HERE."

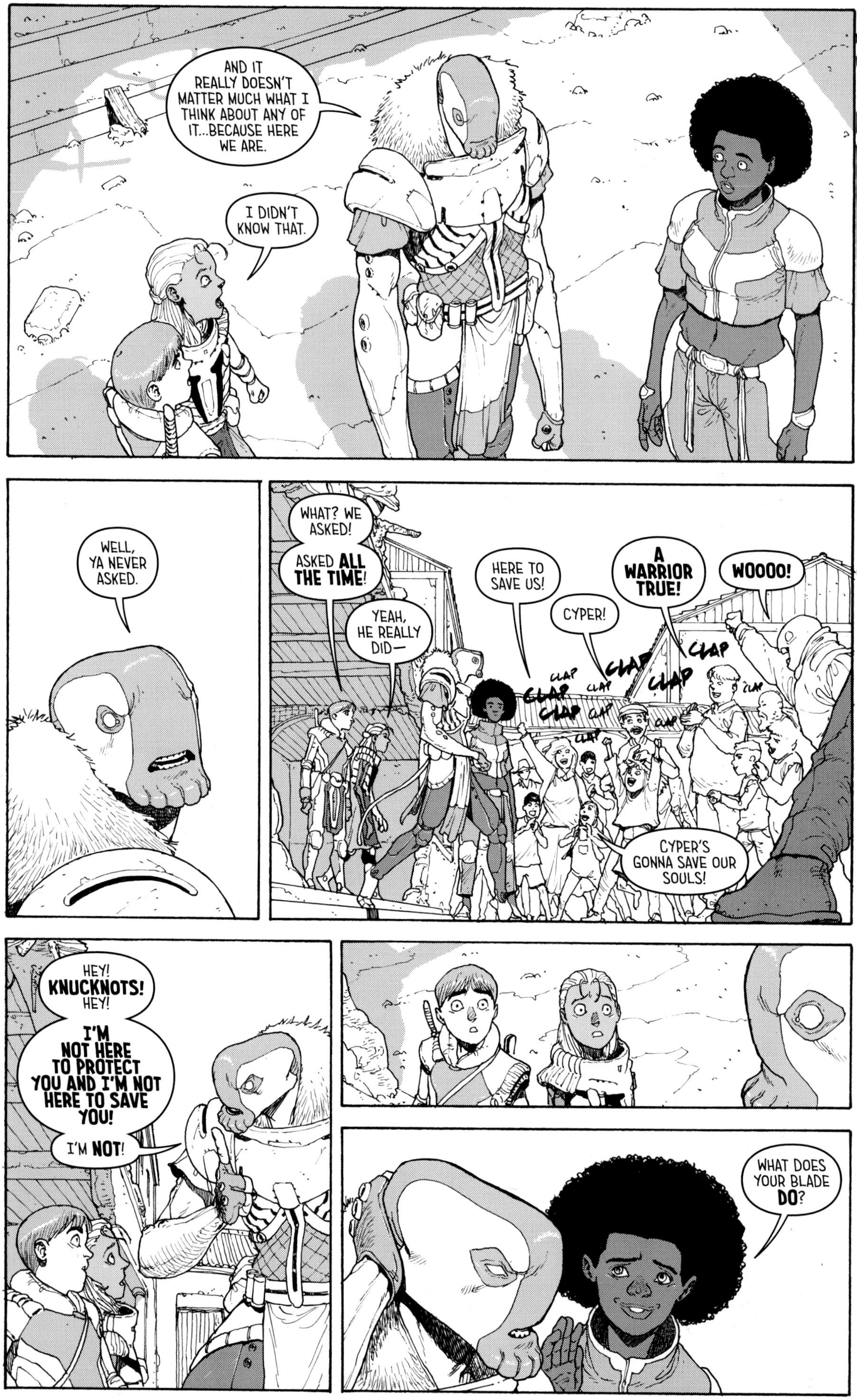
AND IT REALLY DOESN'T MATTER MUCH WHAT I THINK ABOUT ANY OF IT...BECAUSE HERE WE ARE.
I DIDN'T KNOW THAT.
WELL, YA NEVER ASKED.
WHAT? WE ASKED!
ASKED **ALL THE TIME**!
YEAH, HE REALLY DID—
HERE TO SAVE US!
CYPER!
A WARRIOR TRUE!
WOOOO!
CLAP CLAP CLAP CLAP CLAP CLAP CLAP CLAP CLAP CLAP
CYPER'S GONNA SAVE OUR SOULS!
HEY! **KNUCKNOTS!** HEY!
I'M NOT HERE TO PROTECT YOU AND I'M NOT HERE TO SAVE YOU!
I'M **NOT**!
WHAT DOES YOUR BLADE **DO**?

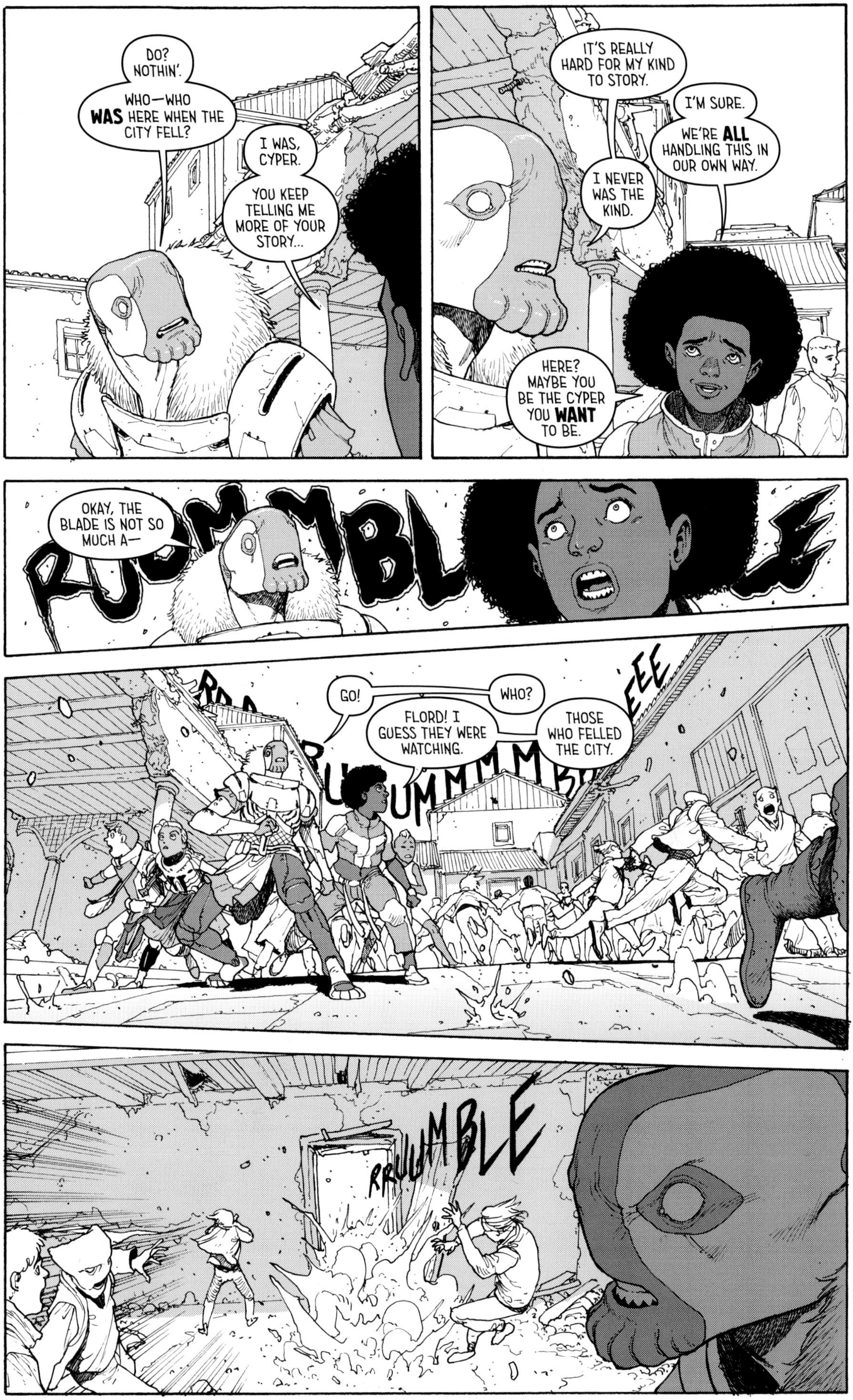
DO? NOTHIN'.
WHO—WHO WAS HERE WHEN THE CITY FELL?
I WAS, CYPER.
YOU KEEP TELLING ME MORE OF YOUR STORY...
IT'S REALLY HARD FOR MY KIND TO STORY.
I NEVER WAS THE KIND.
I'M SURE.
WE'RE ALL HANDLING THIS IN OUR OWN WAY.
HERE? MAYBE YOU BE THE CYPER YOU WANT TO BE.
OKAY, THE BLADE IS NOT SO MUCH A—
RUMMBLE
GO!
WHO?
FLORD! I GUESS THEY WERE WATCHING.
THOSE WHO FELLED THE CITY.
RUMMMMB
EEE
RRUUMBLE

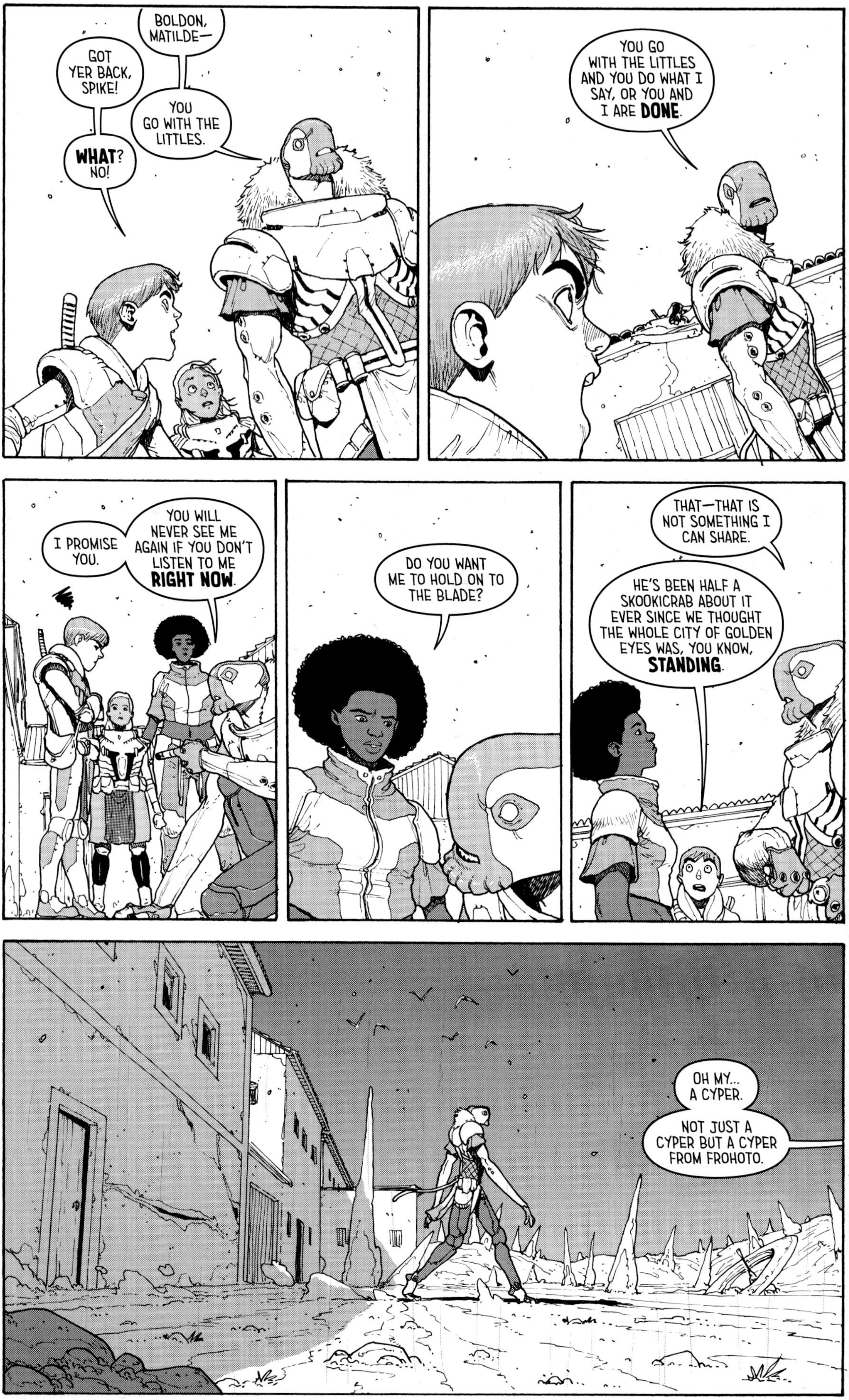
GOT YER BACK, SPIKE!
BOLDON, MATILDE—
YOU GO WITH THE LITTLES.
WHAT? NO!
YOU GO WITH THE LITTLES AND YOU DO WHAT I SAY, OR YOU AND I ARE DONE.
I PROMISE YOU.
YOU WILL NEVER SEE ME AGAIN IF YOU DON'T LISTEN TO ME RIGHT NOW.
DO YOU WANT ME TO HOLD ON TO THE BLADE?
THAT—THAT IS NOT SOMETHING I CAN SHARE.
HE'S BEEN HALF A SKOOKICRAB ABOUT IT EVER SINCE WE THOUGHT THE WHOLE CITY OF GOLDEN EYES WAS, YOU KNOW, STANDING.
OH MY... A CYPER.
NOT JUST A CYPER BUT A CYPER FROM FROHOTO.

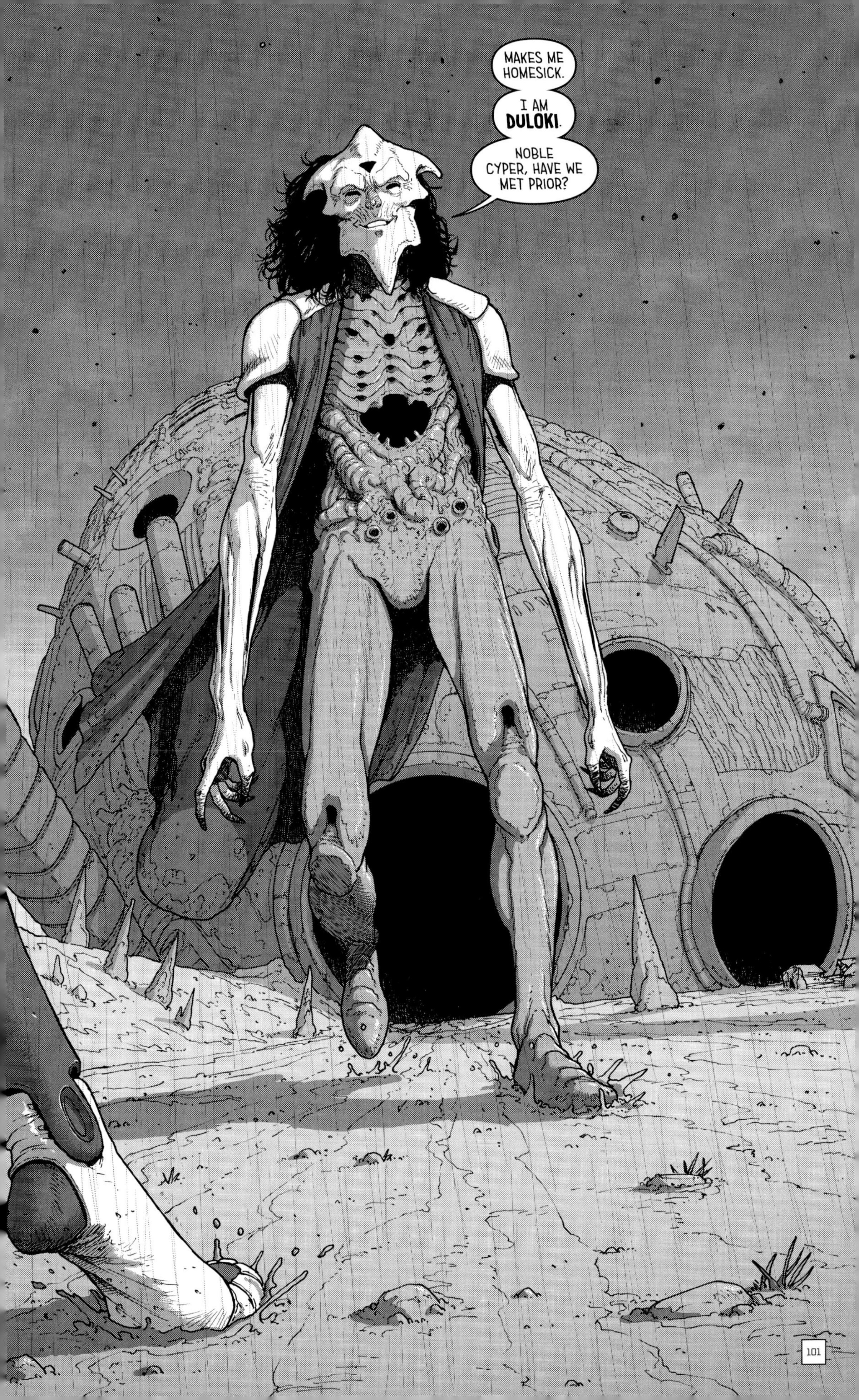
MAKES ME HOMESICK.
I AM DULOKI.
NOBLE CYPER, HAVE WE MET PRIOR?

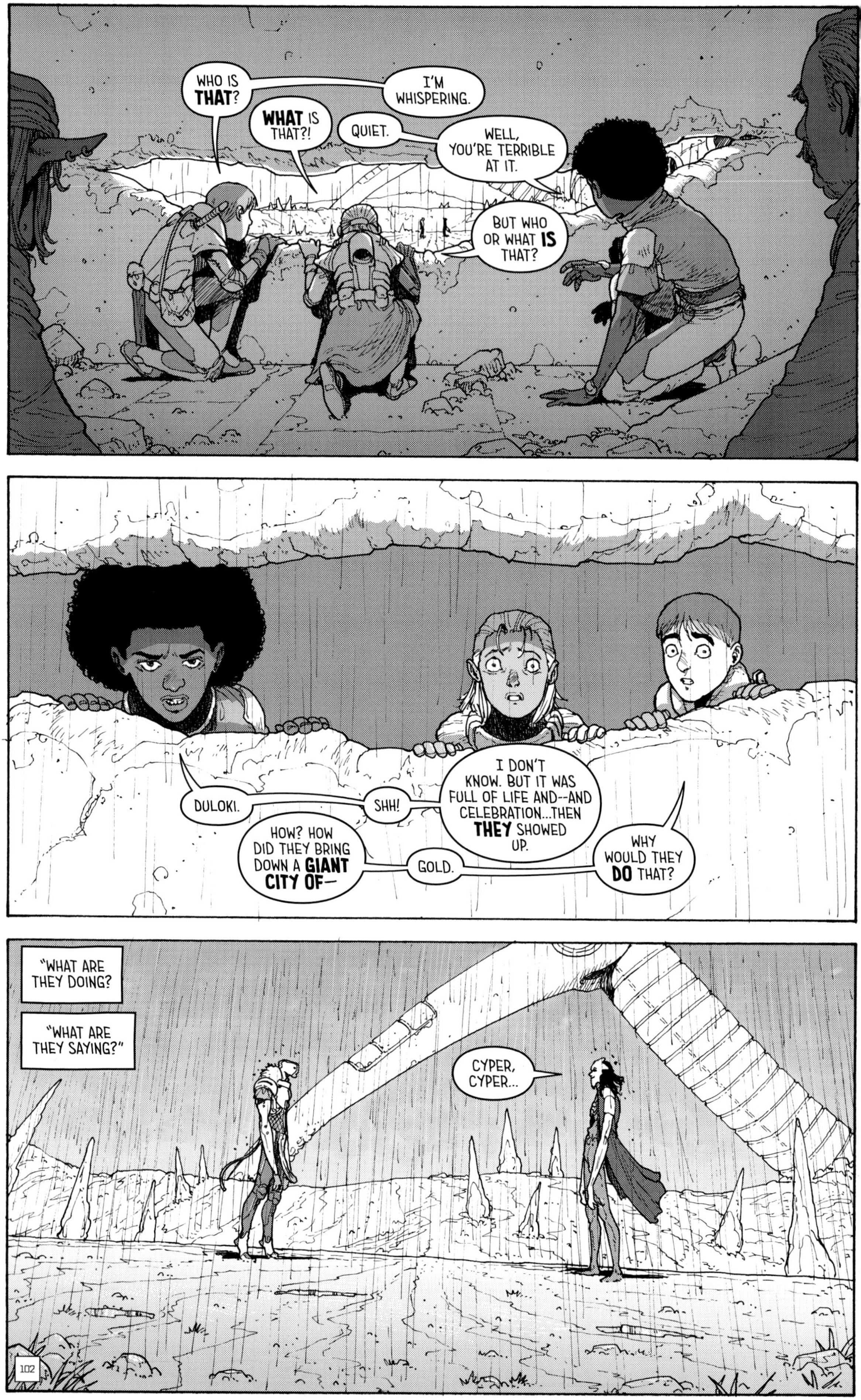

WHO IS **THAT**?
I'M WHISPERING.
WHAT IS THAT?!
QUIET.
WELL, YOU'RE TERRIBLE AT IT.
BUT WHO OR WHAT **IS** THAT?
DULOKI.
SHH!
I DON'T KNOW. BUT IT WAS FULL OF LIFE AND--AND CELEBRATION...THEN **THEY** SHOWED UP.
HOW? HOW DID THEY BRING DOWN A **GIANT CITY OF—**
GOLD.
WHY WOULD THEY **DO** THAT?
"WHAT ARE THEY DOING?
"WHAT ARE THEY SAYING?"
CYPER, CYPER...

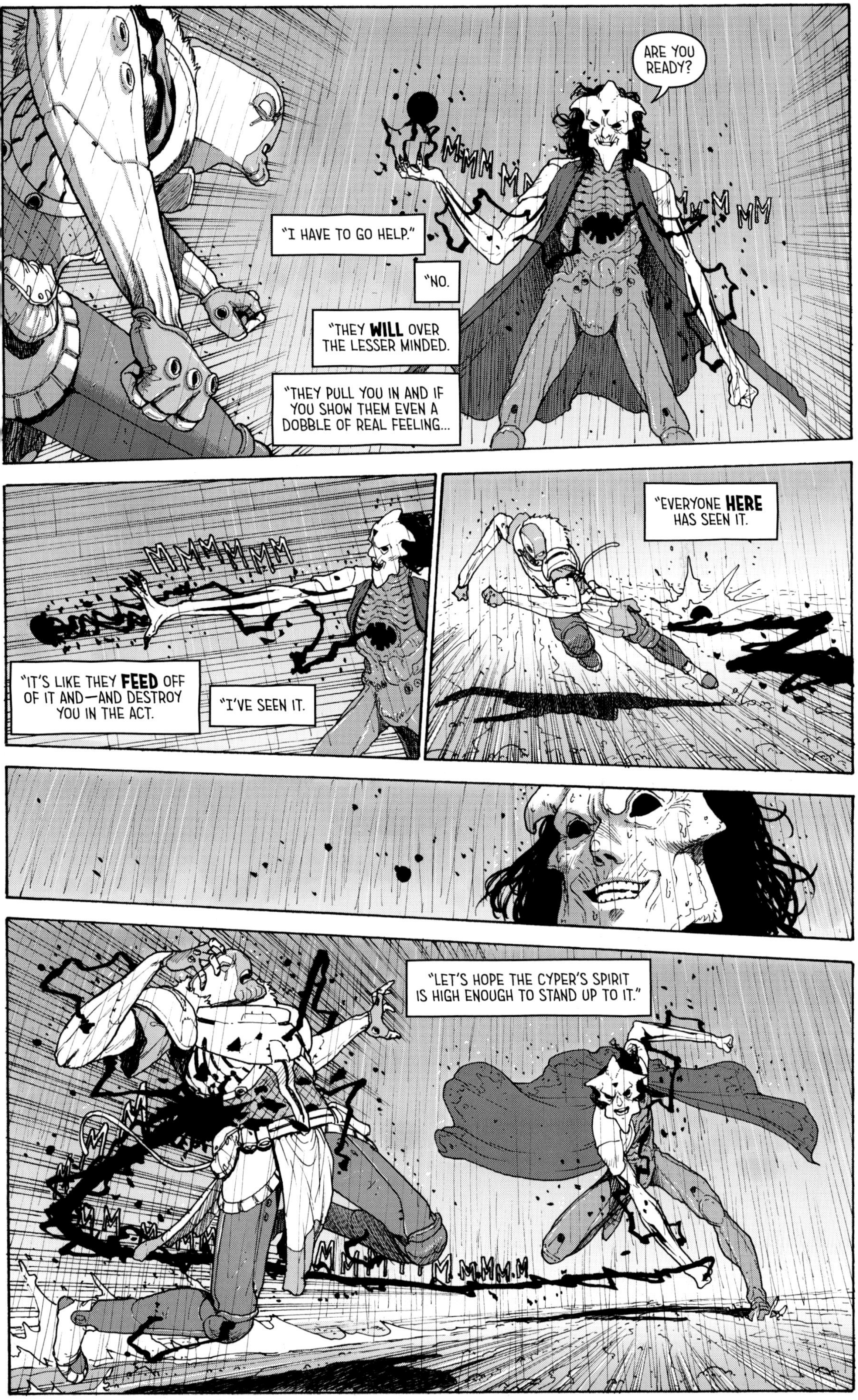
ARE YOU READY?
"I HAVE TO GO HELP."
"NO.
"THEY **WILL** OVER THE LESSER MINDED.
"THEY PULL YOU IN AND IF YOU SHOW THEM EVEN A DOBBLE OF REAL FEELING...
"IT'S LIKE THEY **FEED** OFF OF IT AND—AND DESTROY YOU IN THE ACT.
"I'VE SEEN IT.
"EVERYONE **HERE** HAS SEEN IT.
"LET'S HOPE THE CYPER'S SPIRIT IS HIGH ENOUGH TO STAND UP TO IT."

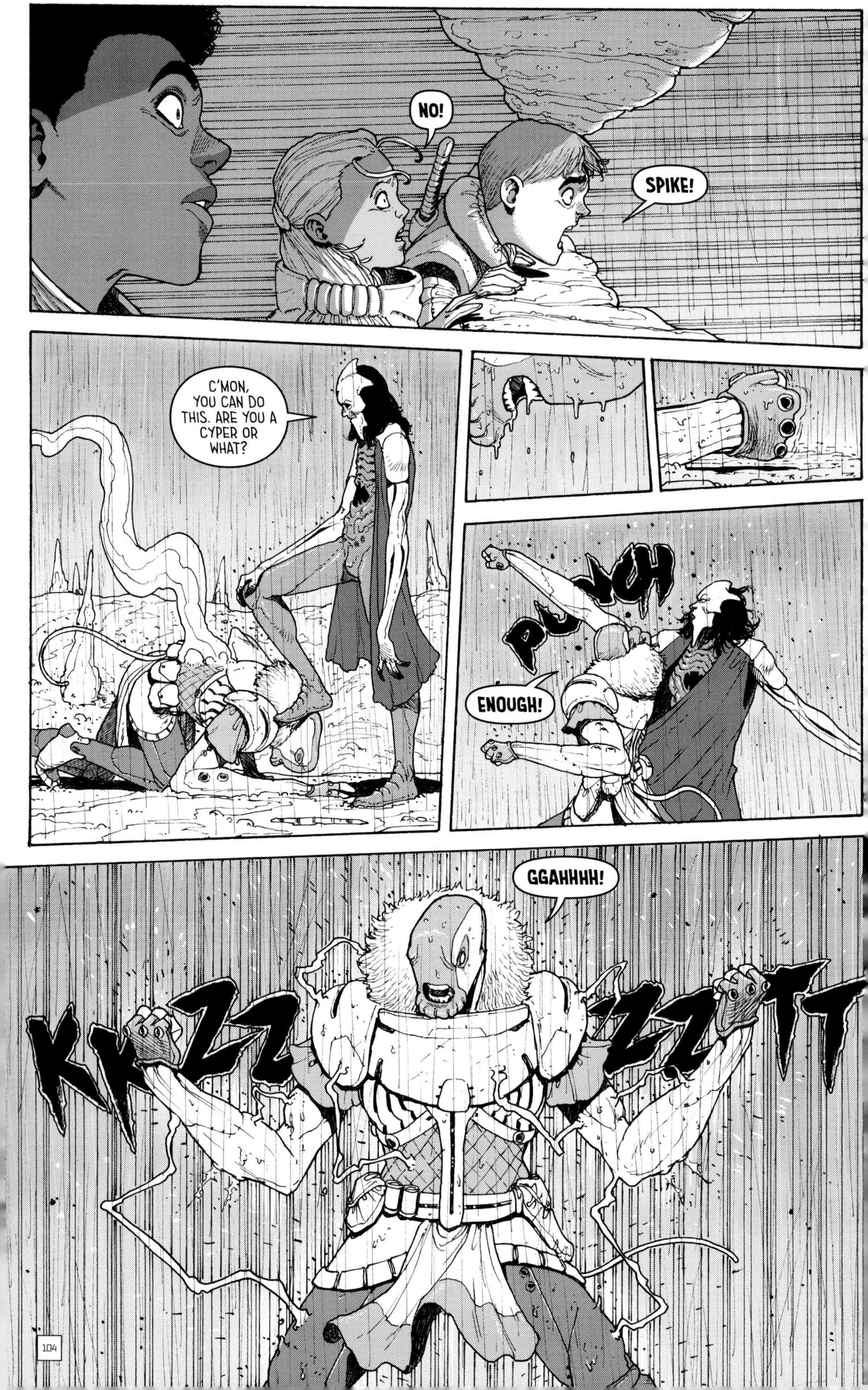
NO!
SPIKE!
C'MON, YOU CAN DO THIS. ARE YOU A CYPER OR WHAT?
PUNCH
ENOUGH!
GGAHHHH!
KKZZZZZTT

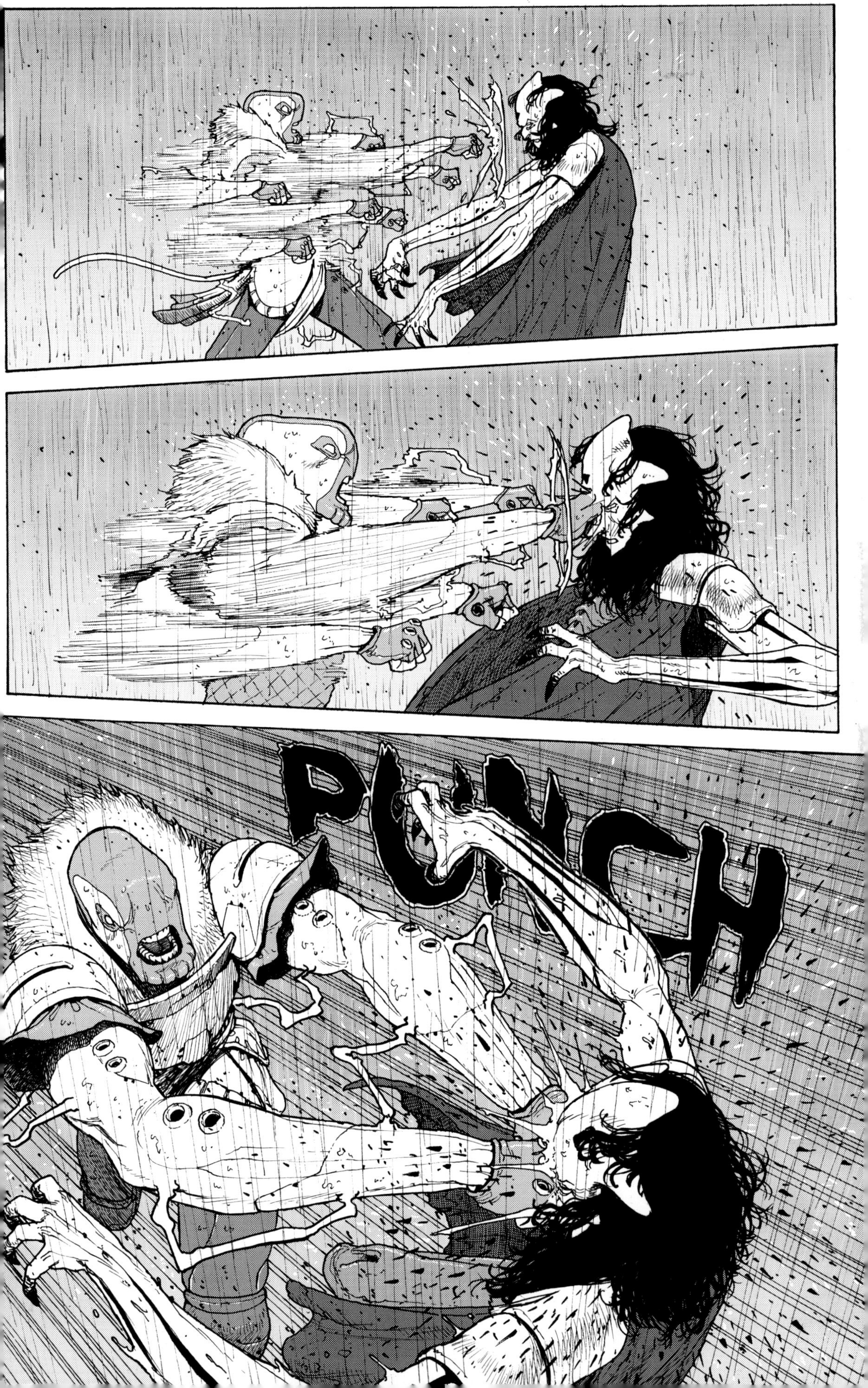
PUNCH

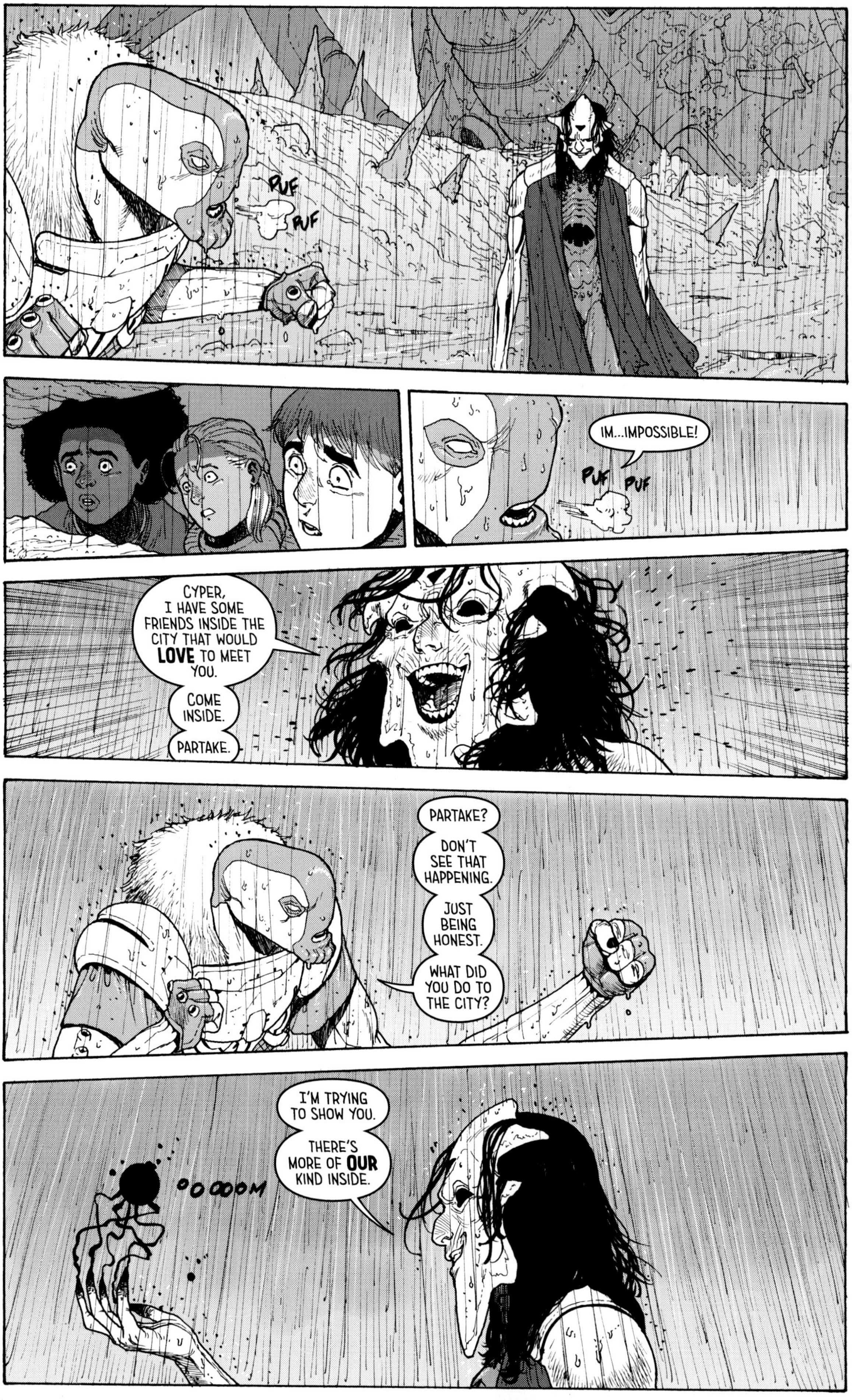
PUF
PUF
IM...IMPOSSIBLE!
PUF
PUF
CYPER, I HAVE SOME FRIENDS INSIDE THE CITY THAT WOULD **LOVE** TO MEET YOU.
COME INSIDE.
PARTAKE.
PARTAKE?
DON'T SEE THAT HAPPENING.
JUST BEING HONEST.
WHAT DID YOU DO TO THE CITY?
I'M TRYING TO SHOW YOU.
THERE'S MORE OF **OUR** KIND INSIDE.
OOOOOM

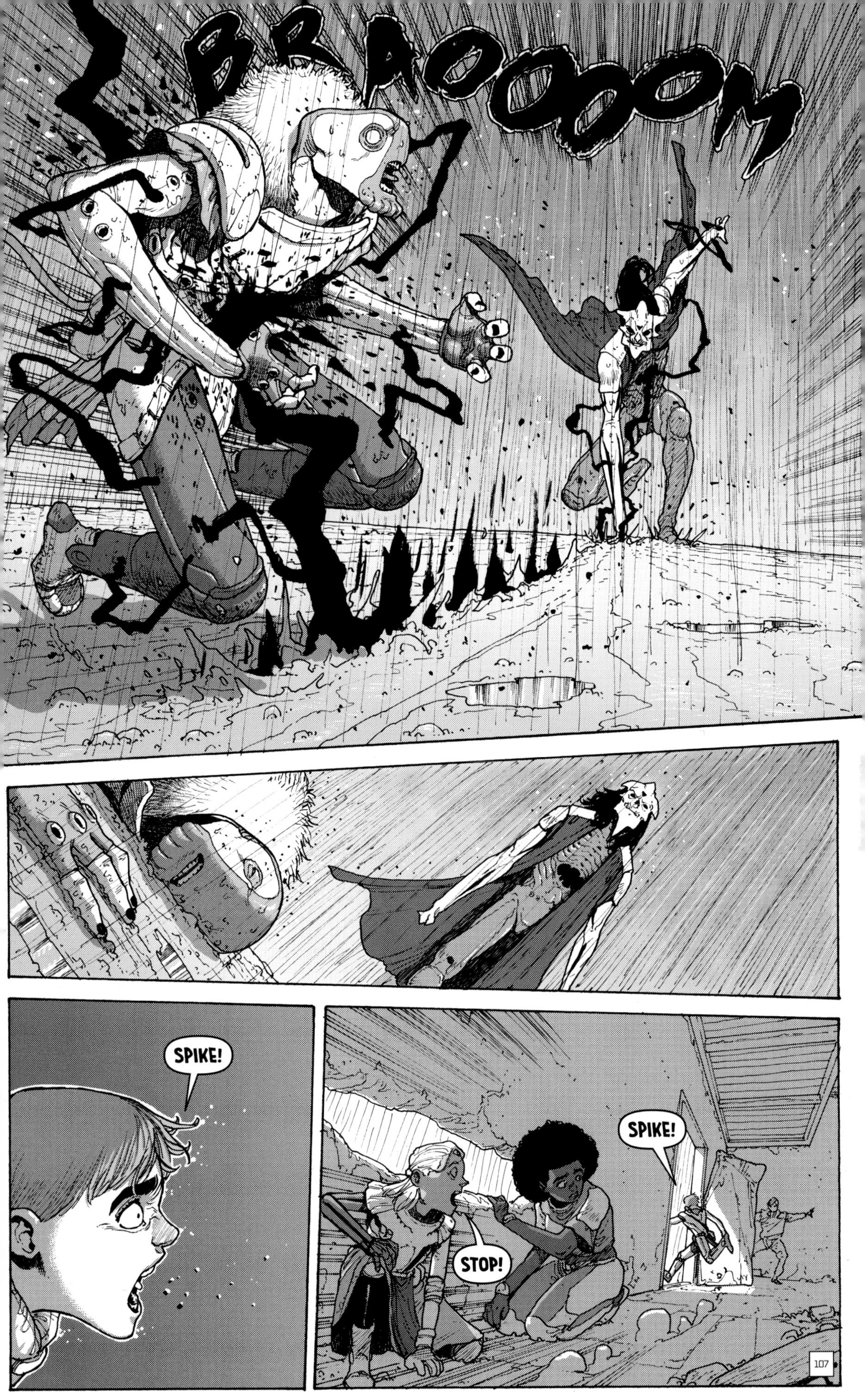
BRAOOOOM
SPIKE!
SPIKE!
STOP!

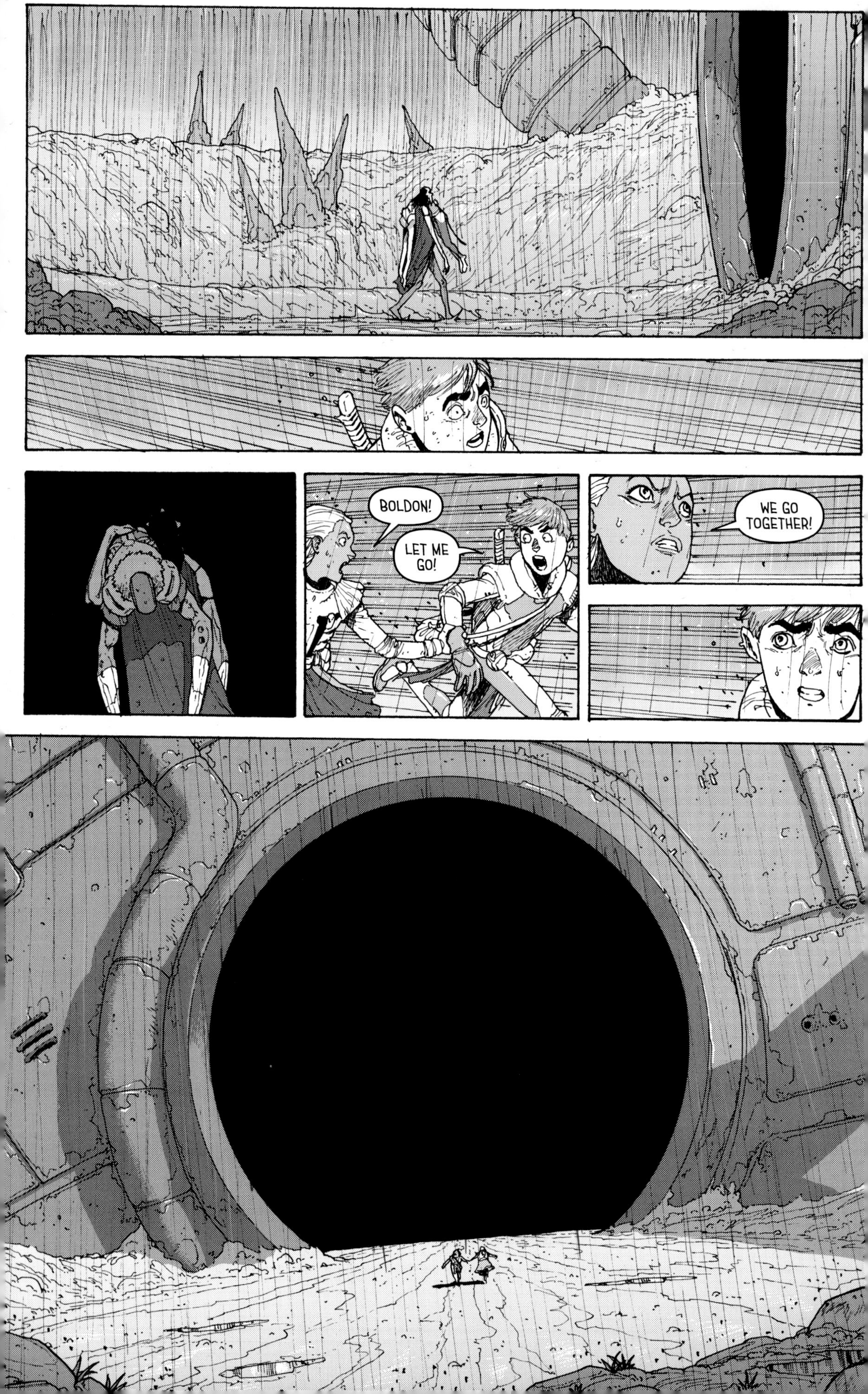
BOLDON!
LET ME GO!
WE GO TOGETHER!

CHAPTER 4

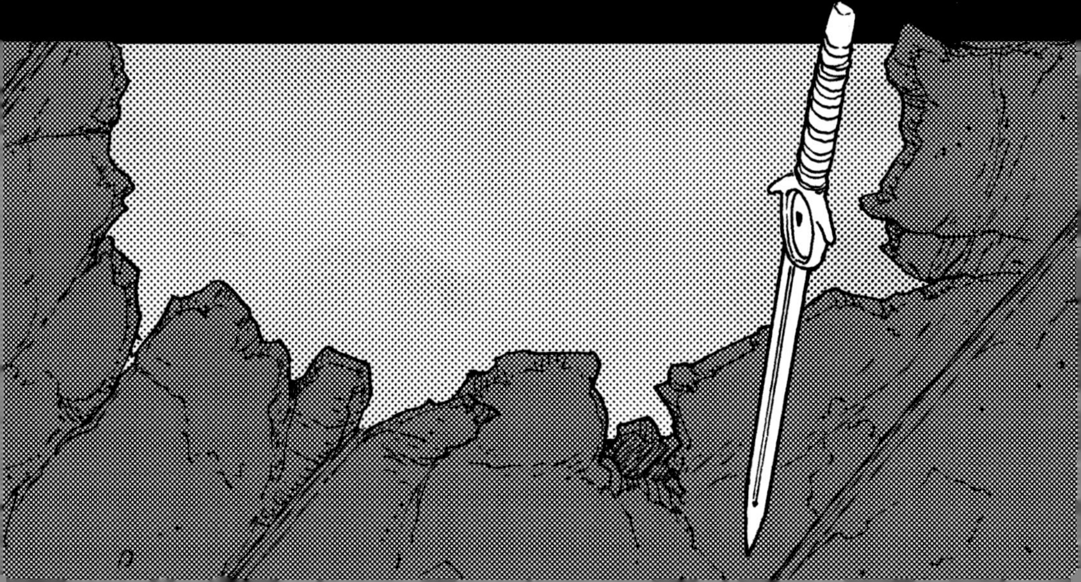

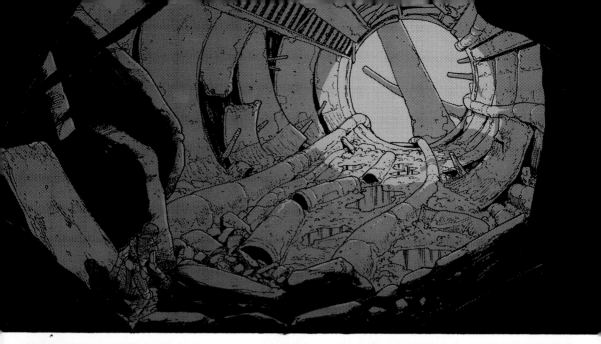

KNUCKNOTS!

AAGGH!

BOLDON! SHH!

WELL THEN STOP *SCARING* ME, MATILDE!

I'M NOT *TRYING* TO SCARE YOU.

AND I'M *NOT* SCARED.

I DIDN'T SAY YOU WERE.

I SAID YOU WERE *LOUD* AND I DON'T THINK *THIS* IS THE PLACE FOR LOUD.

THIS PLACE?

WHAT—WHAT *IS* THIS?

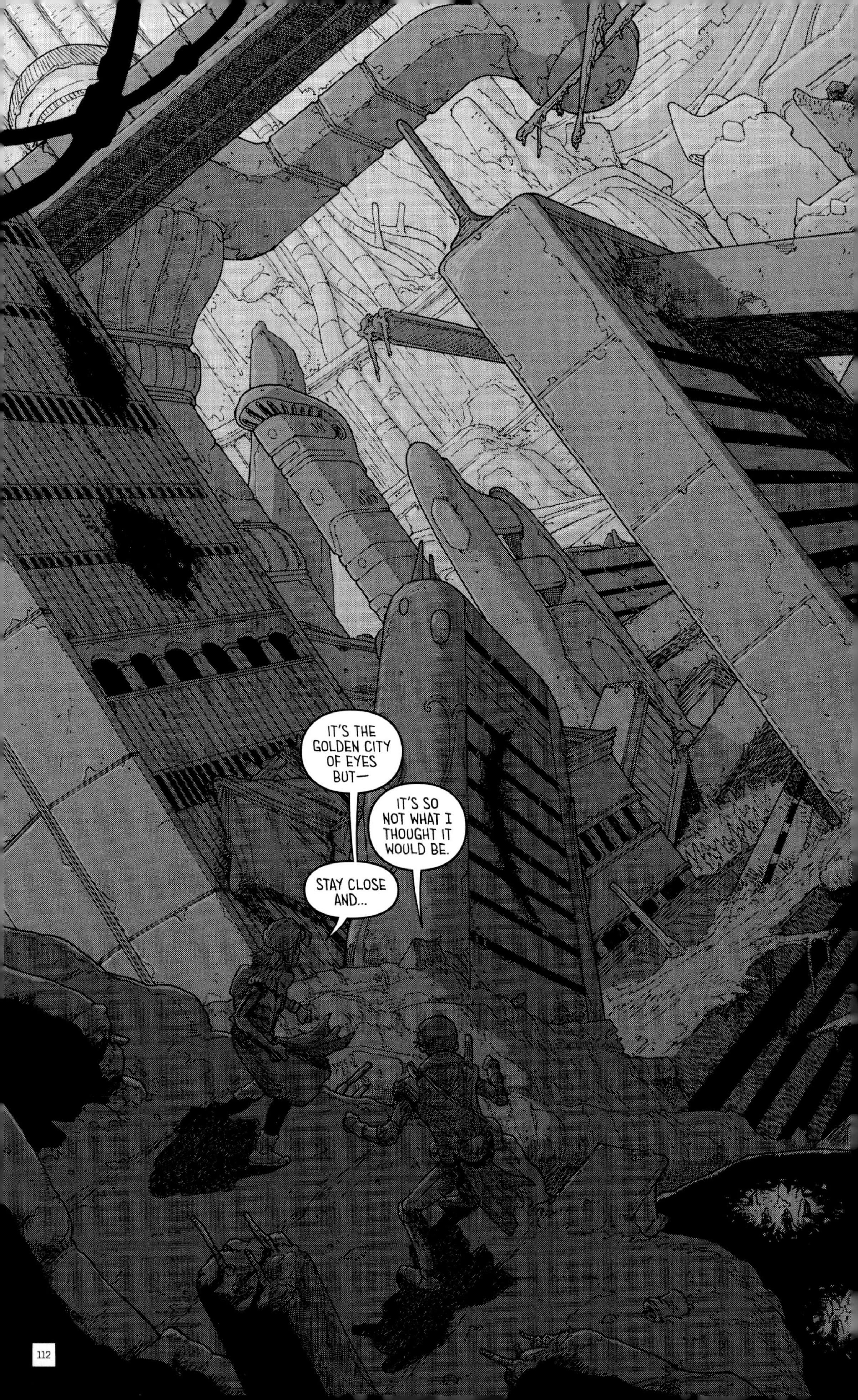
IT'S THE GOLDEN CITY OF EYES BUT—
IT'S SO NOT WHAT I THOUGHT IT WOULD BE.
STAY CLOSE AND...

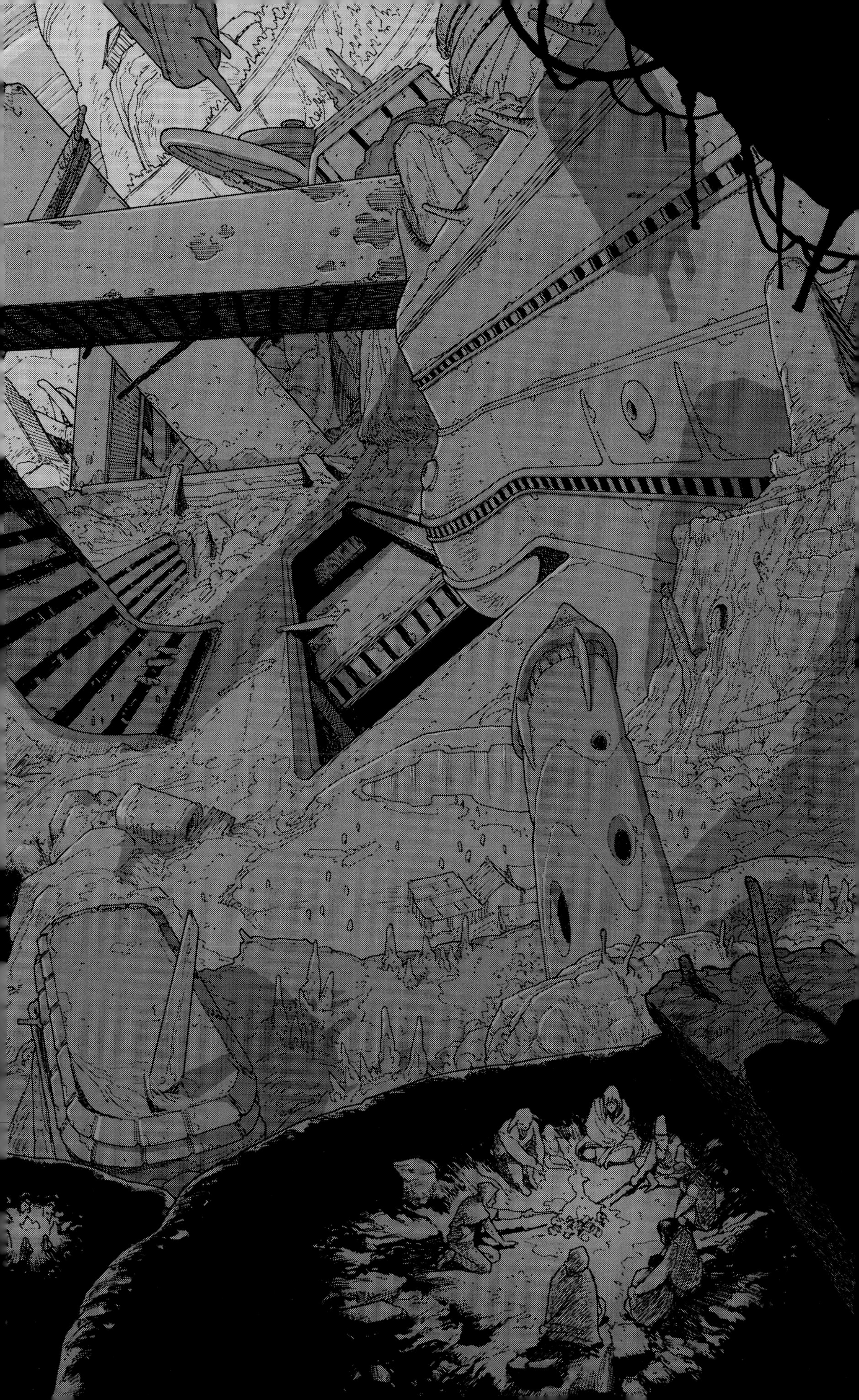

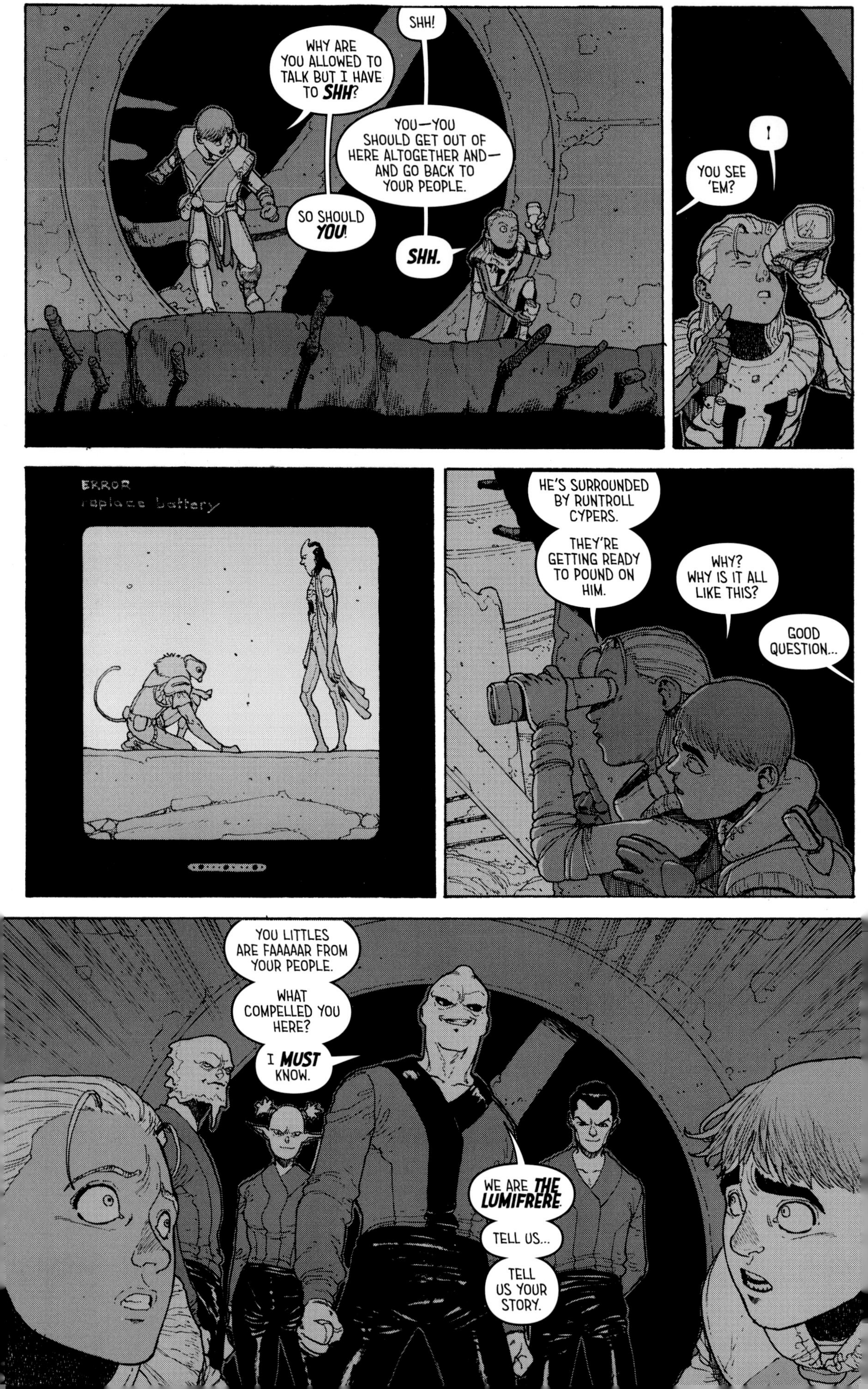
WHY ARE YOU ALLOWED TO TALK BUT I HAVE TO SHH?
SHH!
YOU—YOU SHOULD GET OUT OF HERE ALTOGETHER AND—AND GO BACK TO YOUR PEOPLE.
SO SHOULD YOU!
SHH.
!
YOU SEE 'EM?
ERROR
replace battery
HE'S SURROUNDED BY RUNTROLL CYPERS.
THEY'RE GETTING READY TO POUND ON HIM.
WHY? WHY IS IT ALL LIKE THIS?
GOOD QUESTION...
YOU LITTLES ARE FAAAAAR FROM YOUR PEOPLE.
WHAT COMPELLED YOU HERE?
I MUST KNOW.
WE ARE THE LUMIFRERE.
TELL US...
TELL US YOUR STORY.

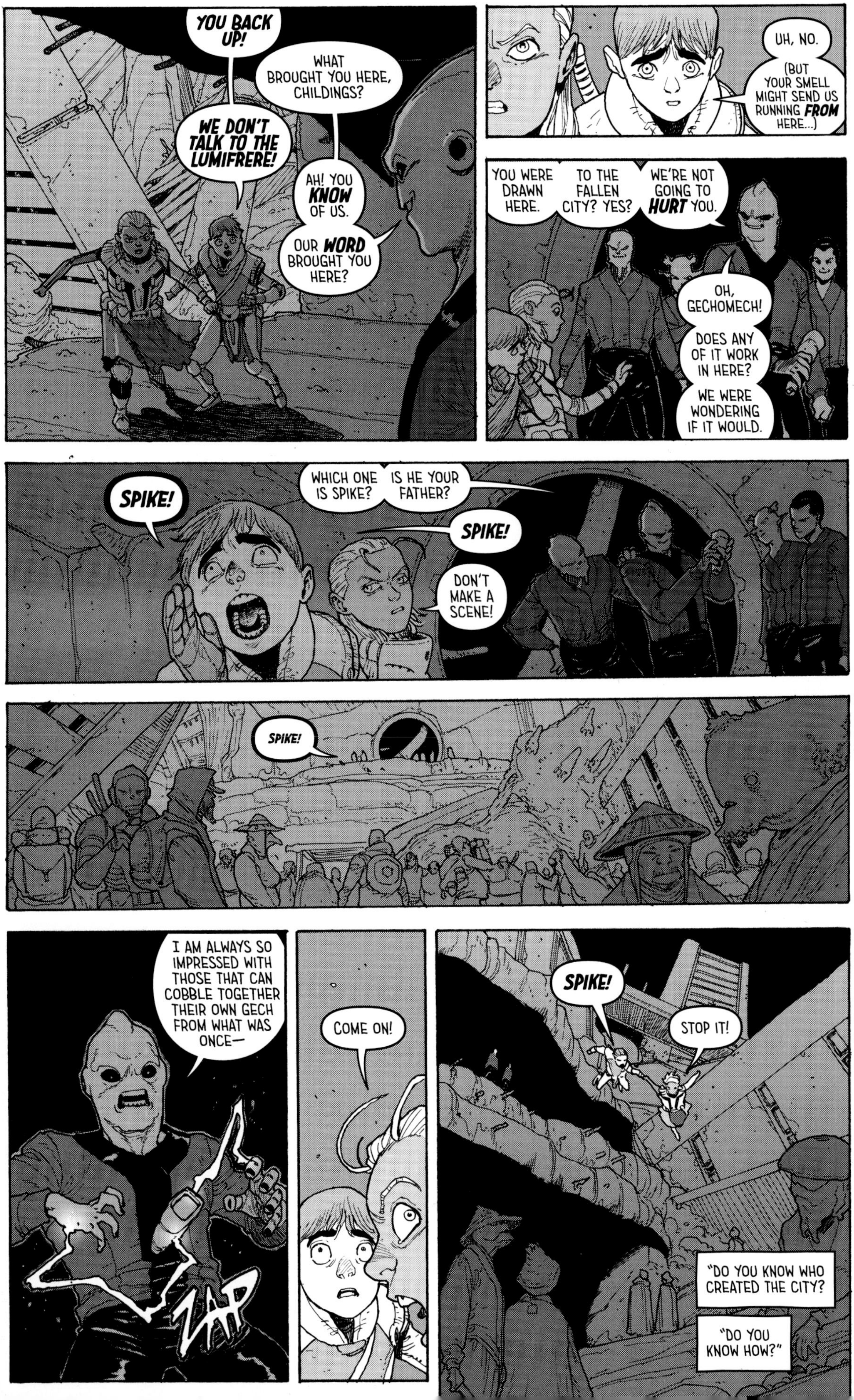

YOU BACK UP!
WE DON'T TALK TO THE LUMIFRERE!
WHAT BROUGHT YOU HERE, CHILDINGS?
AH! YOU KNOW OF US.
OUR WORD BROUGHT YOU HERE?
UH, NO.
(BUT YOUR SMELL MIGHT SEND US RUNNING FROM HERE...)
YOU WERE DRAWN HERE.
TO THE FALLEN CITY? YES?
WE'RE NOT GOING TO HURT YOU.
OH, GECHOMECH!
DOES ANY OF IT WORK IN HERE?
WE WERE WONDERING IF IT WOULD.
SPIKE!
WHICH ONE IS SPIKE?
IS HE YOUR FATHER?
SPIKE!
DON'T MAKE A SCENE!
SPIKE!
I AM ALWAYS SO IMPRESSED WITH THOSE THAT CAN COBBLE TOGETHER THEIR OWN GECH FROM WHAT WAS ONCE—
ZAP
COME ON!
SPIKE!
STOP IT!
"DO YOU KNOW WHO CREATED THE CITY?
"DO YOU KNOW HOW?"

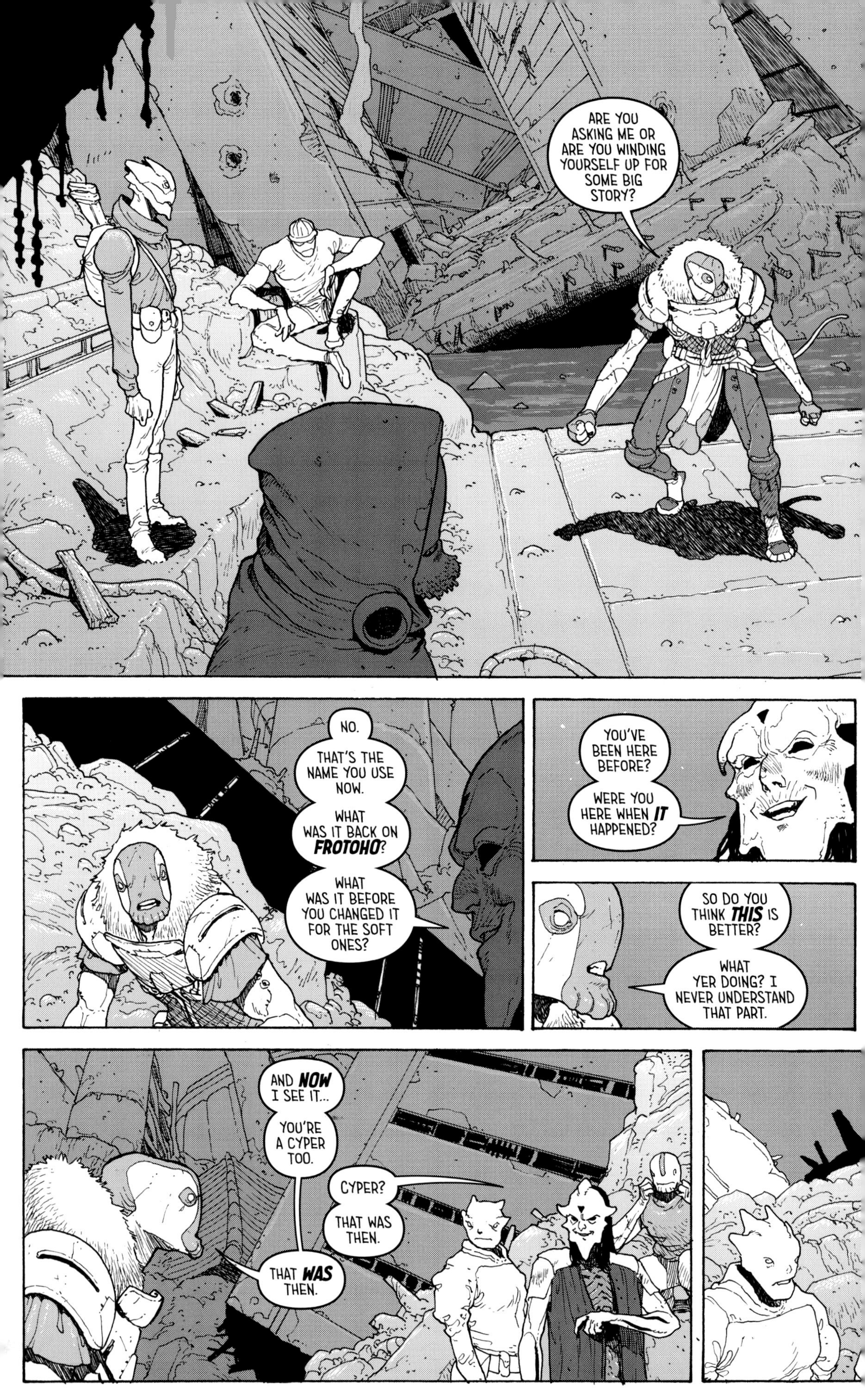
ARE YOU ASKING ME OR ARE YOU WINDING YOURSELF UP FOR SOME BIG STORY?
NO.
THAT'S THE NAME YOU USE NOW.
WHAT WAS IT BACK ON FROTOHO?
WHAT WAS IT BEFORE YOU CHANGED IT FOR THE SOFT ONES?
YOU'VE BEEN HERE BEFORE?
WERE YOU HERE WHEN IT HAPPENED?
SO DO YOU THINK THIS IS BETTER?
WHAT YER DOING? I NEVER UNDERSTAND THAT PART.
AND NOW I SEE IT...
YOU'RE A CYPER TOO.
CYPER?
THAT WAS THEN.
THAT WAS THEN.

NO. I AM ASKING, CYPER TRUE.

I HAVE HEARD SEVEN ENTIRELY DIFFERENT STORIES ABOUT HOW THIS PLACE BECAME *THIS* PLACE.

SEVEN.

ITS FRUSTRATING.

SO THAT'S WHY YOU AND YOUR PALLIES CAME HERE AND TRASHED IT?

WHAT'S YER NAME, CYPER?

I TOLJA: SPIKE.

IS WHAT BETTER, CYPER TRUE?

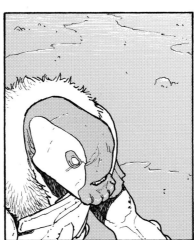

I CAN TELL JUST FROM LOOKIN' AT YA.

YOU *WERE* HERE WHEN EVERYTHING...WENT EVERYWHERE.

YOU HAVE THE REAL STORY. YOU KNOW THE TRUTHS OF THE WORLD.

TOO BAD YOU WEREN'T HERE EARLIER! NONE OF THESE LOCAL KNUCKNOTS WE BOXED AROUND KNEW ANYTHING.

AH! SO, YES, WE'RE CYPER BROTHERS TRUE!

I COULD TELL.

I COULD TELL OUTSIDE.

NOW WE'RE GETTING TO SOME TRUTHS!

HEYO!

THIS ONE CARRIES THE SECRETS OF *US.*

TELL US, SPIKE. TELL US THE TRUE STORY OF THE GOLDEN CITY.

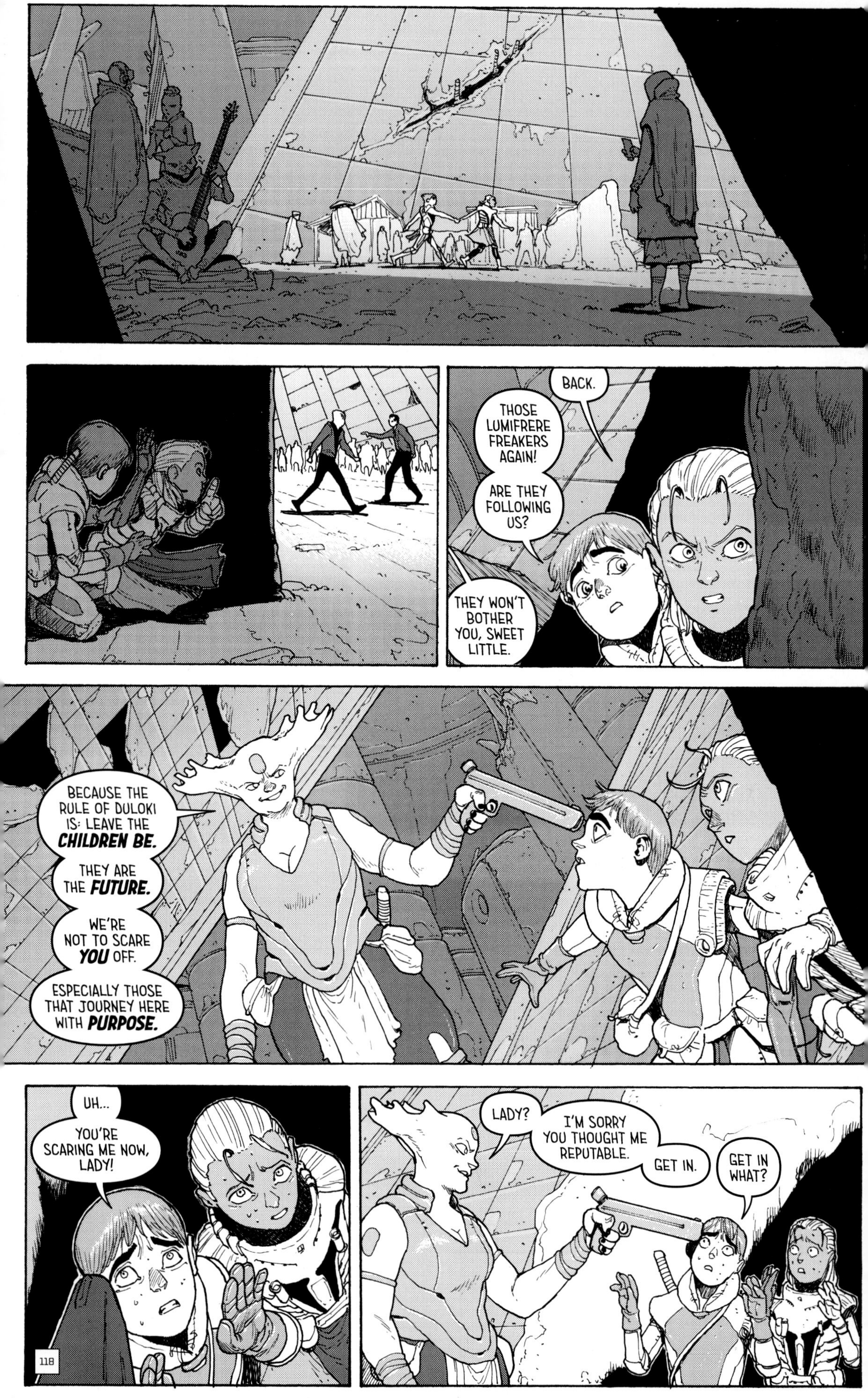

THOSE LUMIFRERE FREAKERS AGAIN!
BACK.
ARE THEY FOLLOWING US?
THEY WON'T BOTHER YOU, SWEET LITTLE.
BECAUSE THE RULE OF DULOKI IS: LEAVE THE **CHILDREN BE.**
THEY ARE THE **FUTURE.**
WE'RE NOT TO SCARE **YOU** OFF.
ESPECIALLY THOSE THAT JOURNEY HERE WITH **PURPOSE.**
UH...
YOU'RE SCARING ME NOW, LADY!
LADY?
I'M SORRY YOU THOUGHT ME REPUTABLE.
GET IN.
GET IN WHAT?

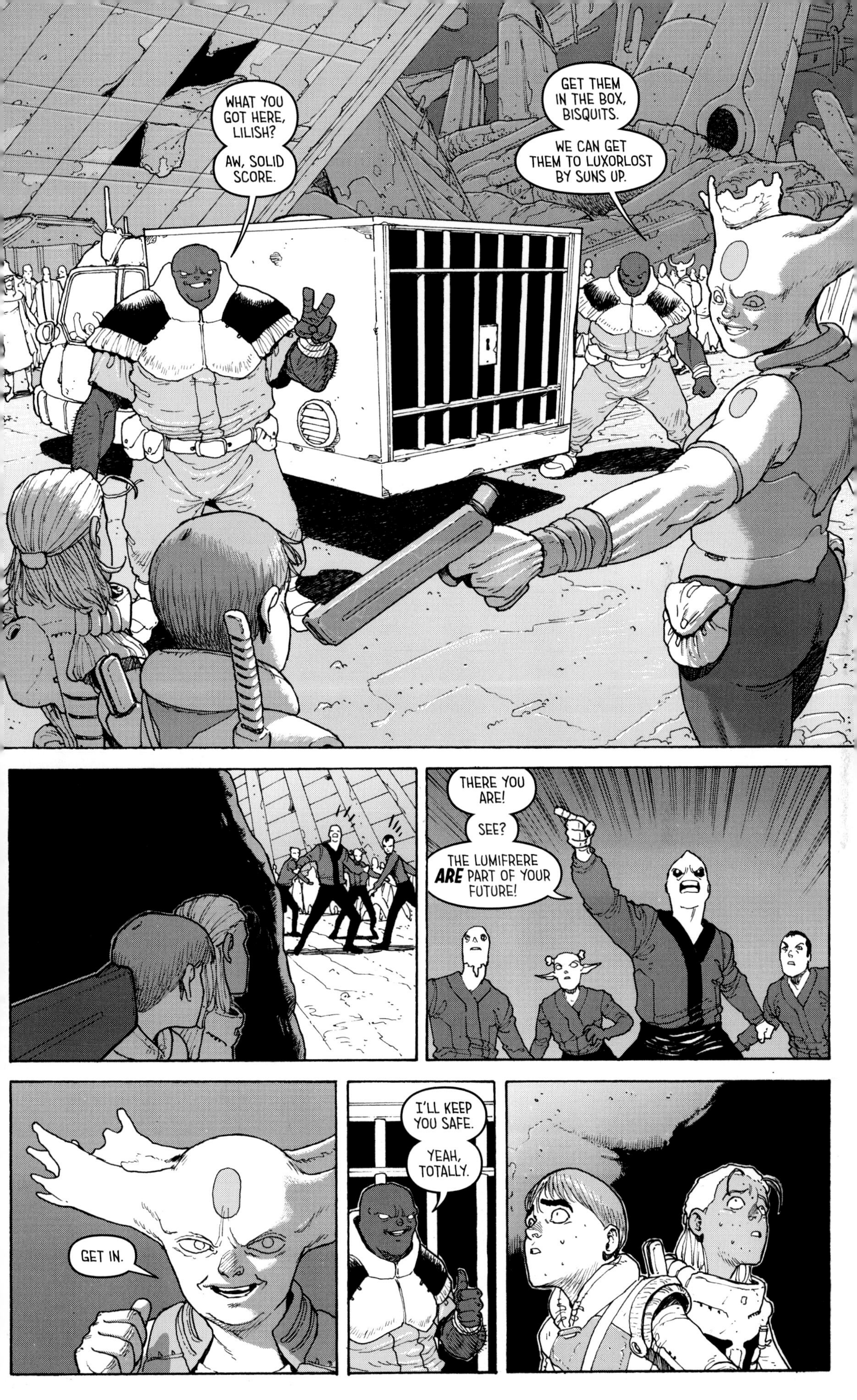
WHAT YOU GOT HERE, LILISH?
AW, SOLID SCORE.
GET THEM IN THE BOX, BISQUITS.
WE CAN GET THEM TO LUXORLOST BY SUNS UP.
THERE YOU ARE!
SEE?
THE LUMIFRERE **ARE** PART OF YOUR FUTURE!
GET IN.
I'LL KEEP YOU SAFE.
YEAH, TOTALLY.

OK, I SEE YOU'RE NOT THE STORYTELLIN' TYPE.

SOME AREN'T.

IT AIN'T THAT...

IT'S JUST IF *THAT* DON'T STOP BREATHIN' ON MY NECK *I'M* GONNA SOCK IT SO HARD IN THE SNOOT IT'LL FORGET HOW TO BARK.

CAN'T BELIEVE IT!

GONG

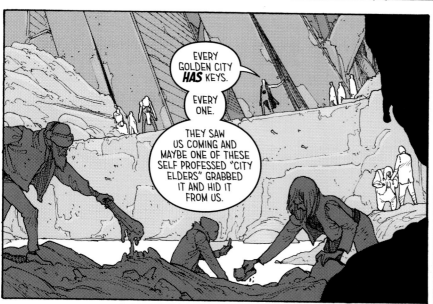

EVERY GOLDEN CITY *HAS* KEYS.

EVERY ONE.

THEY SAW US COMING AND MAYBE ONE OF THESE SELF PROFESSED "CITY ELDERS" GRABBED IT AND HID IT FROM US.

HARD NOT TO TAKE THAT AS A COMPLIMENT.

WE SCARE THEM *THAT* MUCH?

WHY DON'T YOU TELL US WHAT BROUGHT YOU HERE TODAY, CYPER?

HOW HAVE WE NOT CROSSED PATHS BEFORE?

THE WORLD'S A BIG PLACE.

I CAN'T BELIEVE YOU KNOCKED THIS OVER!

US?!

HOW *IS THIS* A GOOD THING FOR ANYONE?

US?

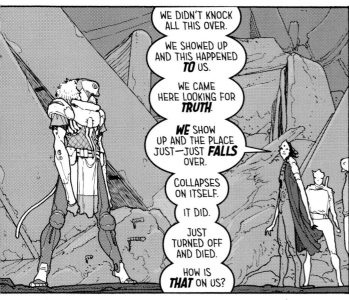

WE DIDN'T KNOCK ALL THIS OVER.

WE SHOWED UP AND THIS HAPPENED *TO* US.

WE CAME HERE LOOKING FOR *TRUTH*.

WE SHOW UP AND THE PLACE JUST—JUST *FALLS* OVER.

COLLAPSES ON ITSELF.

IT DID.

JUST TURNED OFF AND DIED.

HOW IS *THAT* ON US?

THAT'S WHY WE HAVE ALL THESE FLINTY KNUCKNOTTERS CRAWLING AROUND...

SOMEONE HAS *THE KEY TO THE CITY ENGINE*.

WE'LL FIND IT AND THEN WE CAN START *THIS* CITY *RIGHT*.

MAKE IT *OUR* BASE. OUR CENTERPIECE.

MAYBE EVEN FINALLY FIND OUT THE TRUTH THAT BROUGHT US ALL HERE.

THING IS: YOU'RE A CYPER.

YOU *ALL* TOOK AN OATH.

OATH?

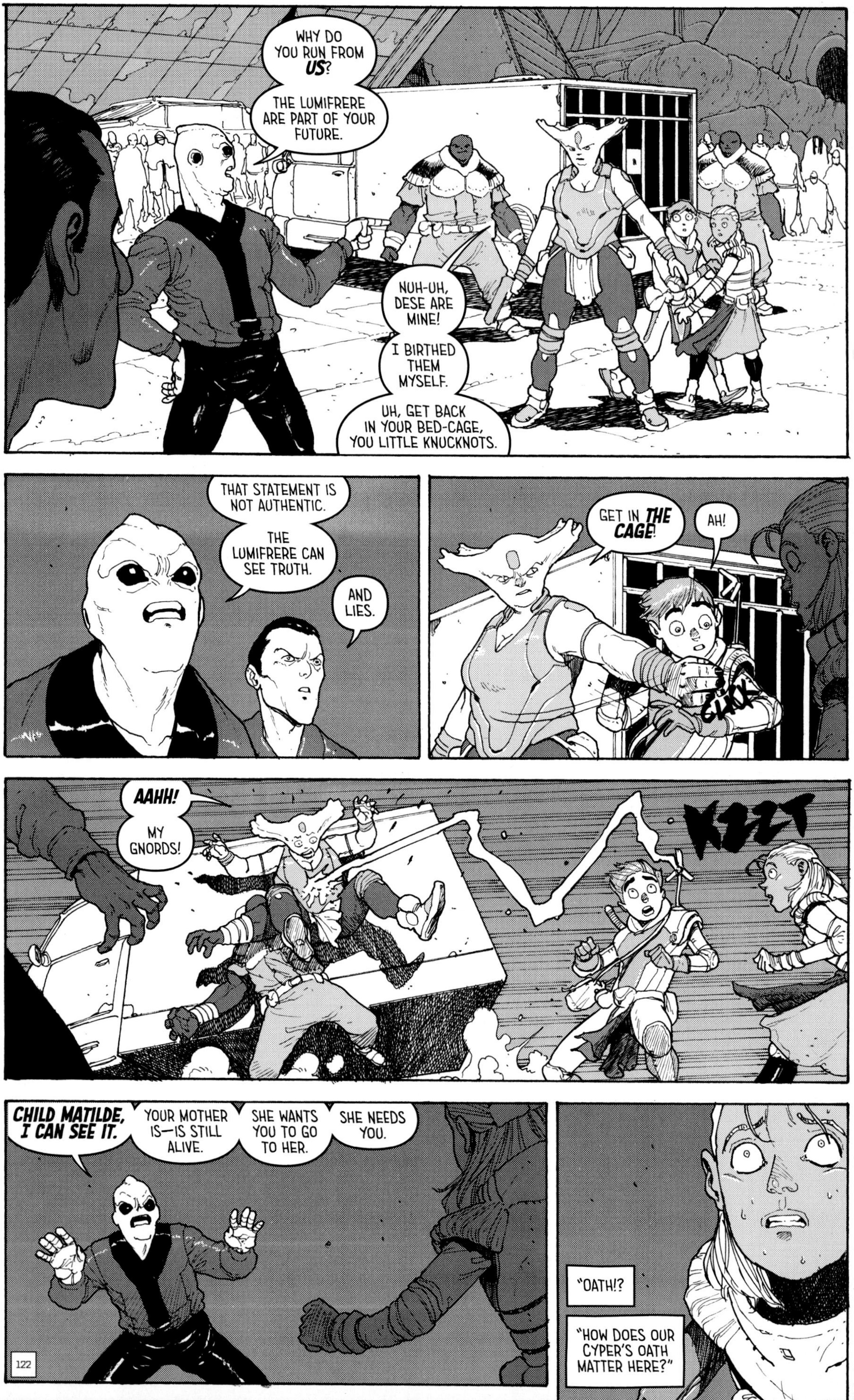
WHY DO YOU RUN FROM US?
THE LUMIFRERE ARE PART OF YOUR FUTURE.
NUH-UH, DESE ARE MINE!
I BIRTHED THEM MYSELF.
UH, GET BACK IN YOUR BED-CAGE, YOU LITTLE KNUCKNOTS.
THAT STATEMENT IS NOT AUTHENTIC.
THE LUMIFRERE CAN SEE TRUTH.
AND LIES.
GET IN THE CAGE!
AH!
AAHH!
MY GNORDS!
KZZT
CHILD MATILDE, I CAN SEE IT.
YOUR MOTHER IS—IS STILL ALIVE.
SHE WANTS YOU TO GO TO HER.
SHE NEEDS YOU.
"OATH!?
"HOW DOES OUR CYPER'S OATH MATTER HERE?"

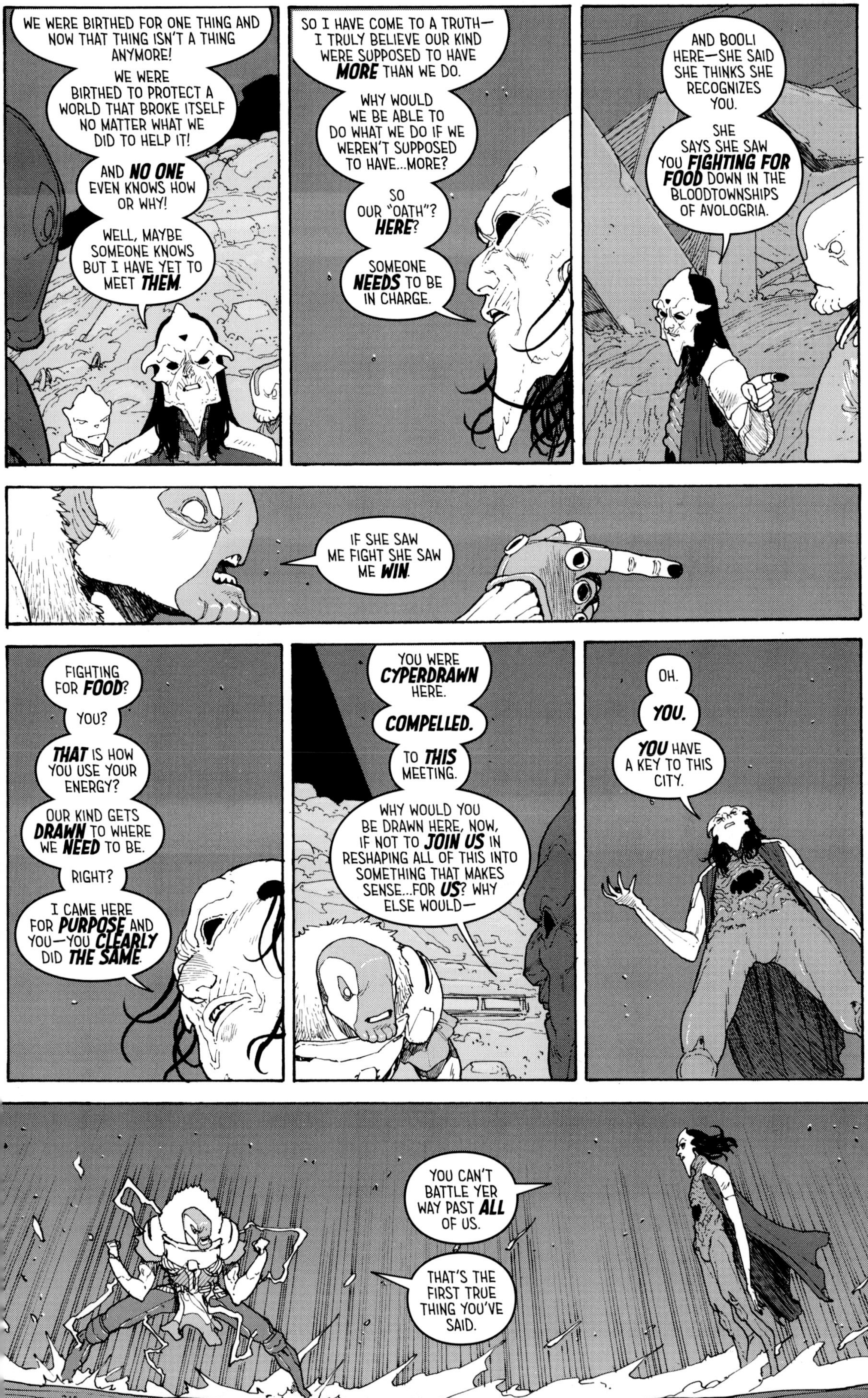

WE WERE BIRTHED FOR ONE THING AND NOW THAT THING ISN'T A THING ANYMORE!
WE WERE BIRTHED TO PROTECT A WORLD THAT BROKE ITSELF NO MATTER WHAT WE DID TO HELP IT!
AND NO ONE EVEN KNOWS HOW OR WHY!
WELL, MAYBE SOMEONE KNOWS BUT I HAVE YET TO MEET THEM.
SO I HAVE COME TO A TRUTH— I TRULY BELIEVE OUR KIND WERE SUPPOSED TO HAVE MORE THAN WE DO.
WHY WOULD WE BE ABLE TO DO WHAT WE DO IF WE WEREN'T SUPPOSED TO HAVE...MORE?
SO OUR "OATH"? HERE?
SOMEONE NEEDS TO BE IN CHARGE.
AND BOOLI HERE—SHE SAID SHE THINKS SHE RECOGNIZES YOU.
SHE SAYS SHE SAW YOU FIGHTING FOR FOOD DOWN IN THE BLOODTOWNSHIPS OF AVOLOGRIA.
IF SHE SAW ME FIGHT SHE SAW ME WIN.
FIGHTING FOR FOOD?
YOU?
THAT IS HOW YOU USE YOUR ENERGY?
OUR KIND GETS DRAWN TO WHERE WE NEED TO BE.
RIGHT?
I CAME HERE FOR PURPOSE AND YOU—YOU CLEARLY DID THE SAME.
YOU WERE CYPERDRAWN HERE.
COMPELLED.
TO THIS MEETING.
WHY WOULD YOU BE DRAWN HERE, NOW, IF NOT TO JOIN US IN RESHAPING ALL OF THIS INTO SOMETHING THAT MAKES SENSE...FOR US? WHY ELSE WOULD—
OH.
YOU.
YOU HAVE A KEY TO THIS CITY.
YOU CAN'T BATTLE YER WAY PAST ALL OF US.
THAT'S THE FIRST TRUE THING YOU'VE SAID.

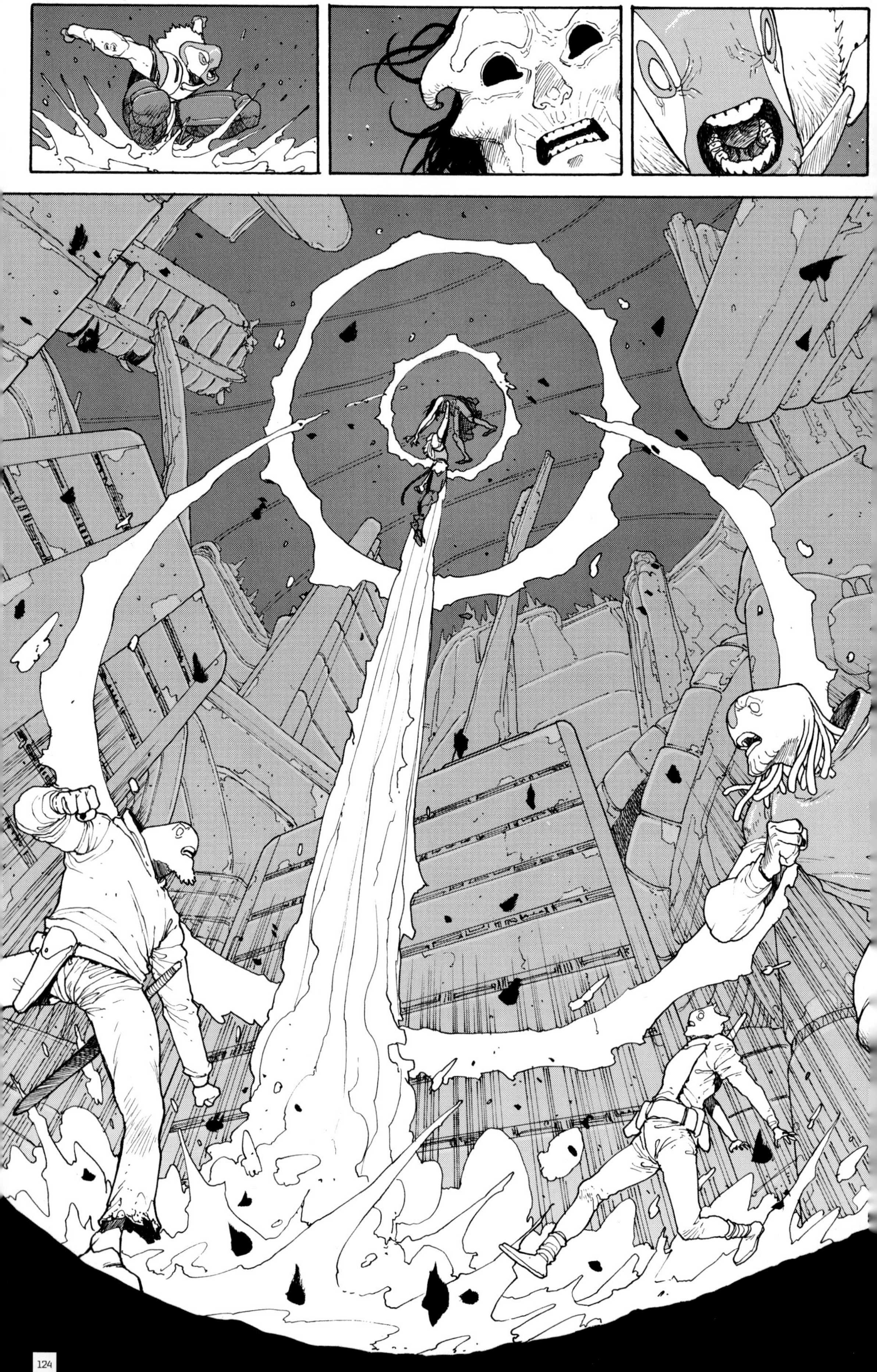

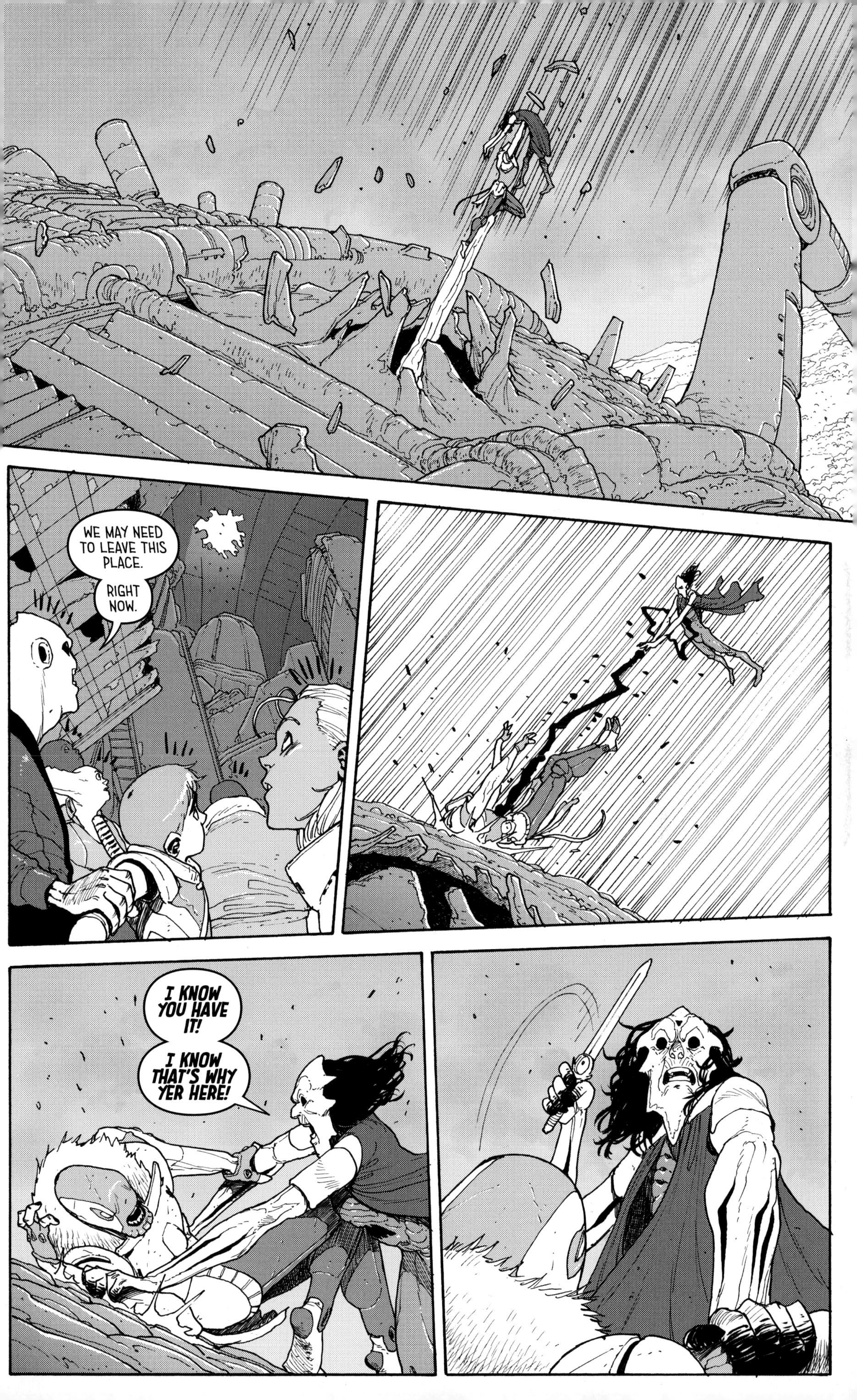
WE MAY NEED TO LEAVE THIS PLACE.
RIGHT NOW.
I KNOW YOU HAVE IT!
I KNOW THAT'S WHY YER HERE!

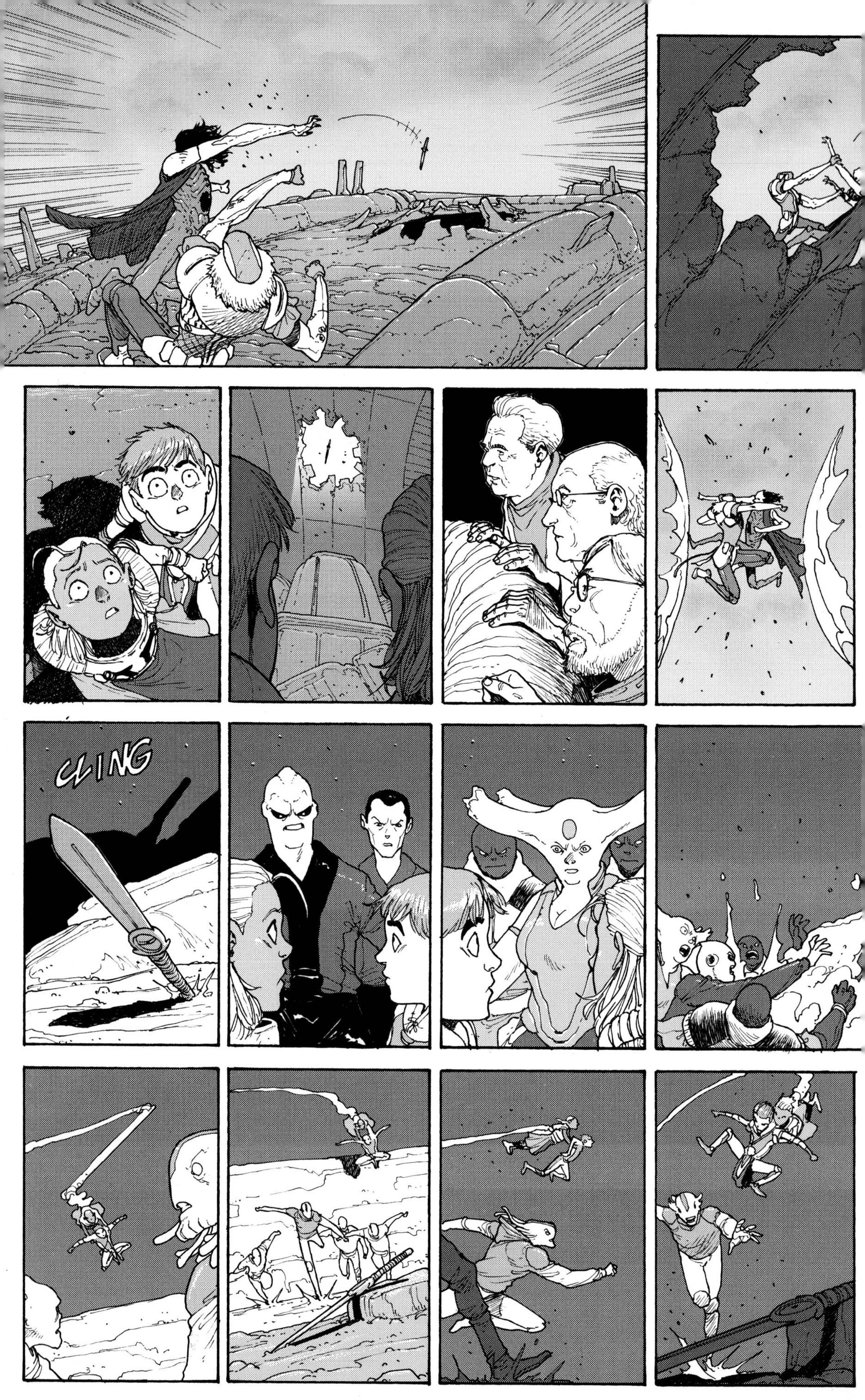
CLING

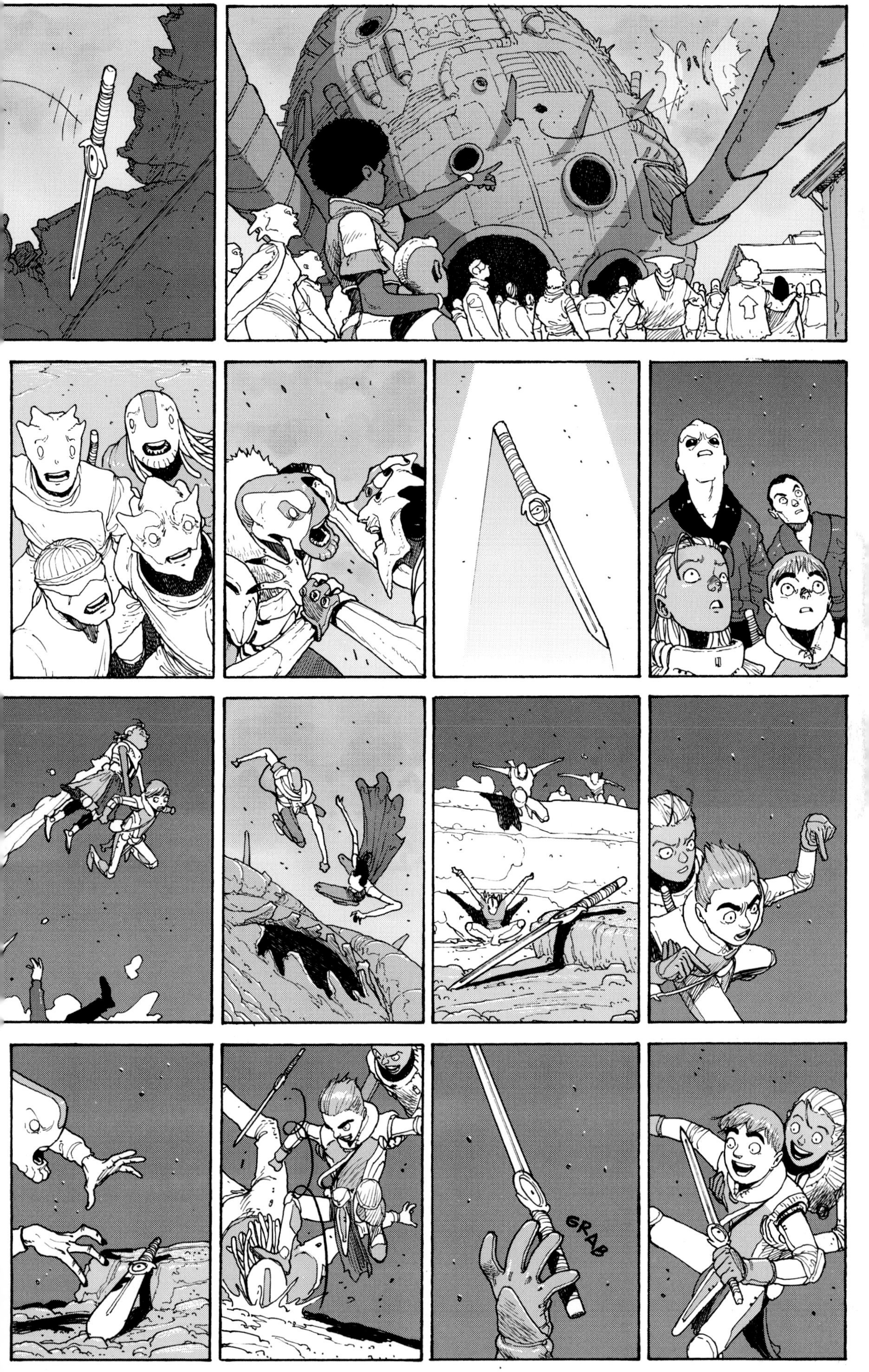
GRAB

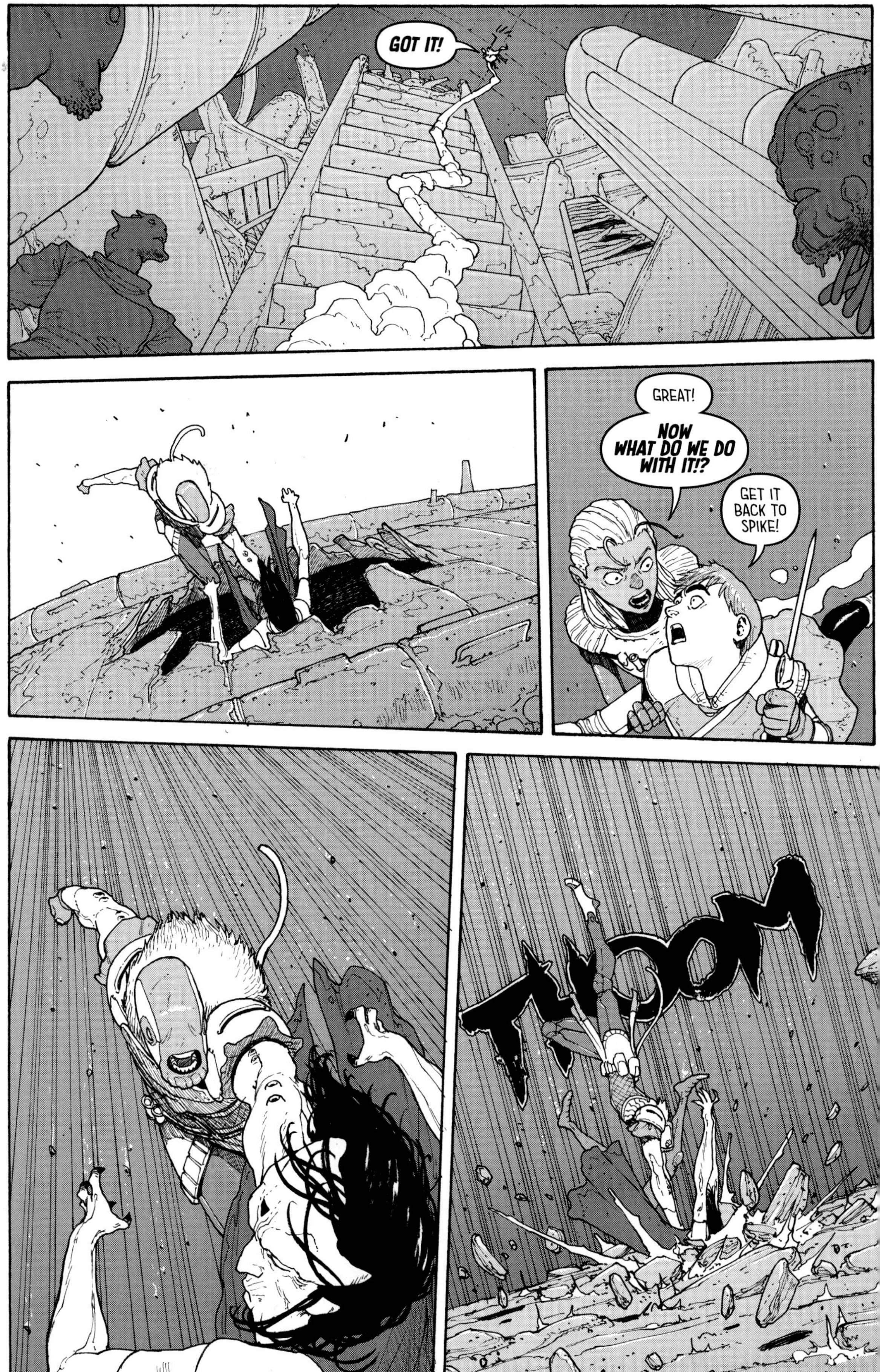
GOT IT!
GREAT!
NOW WHAT DO WE DO WITH IT!?
GET IT BACK TO SPIKE!
THOOM

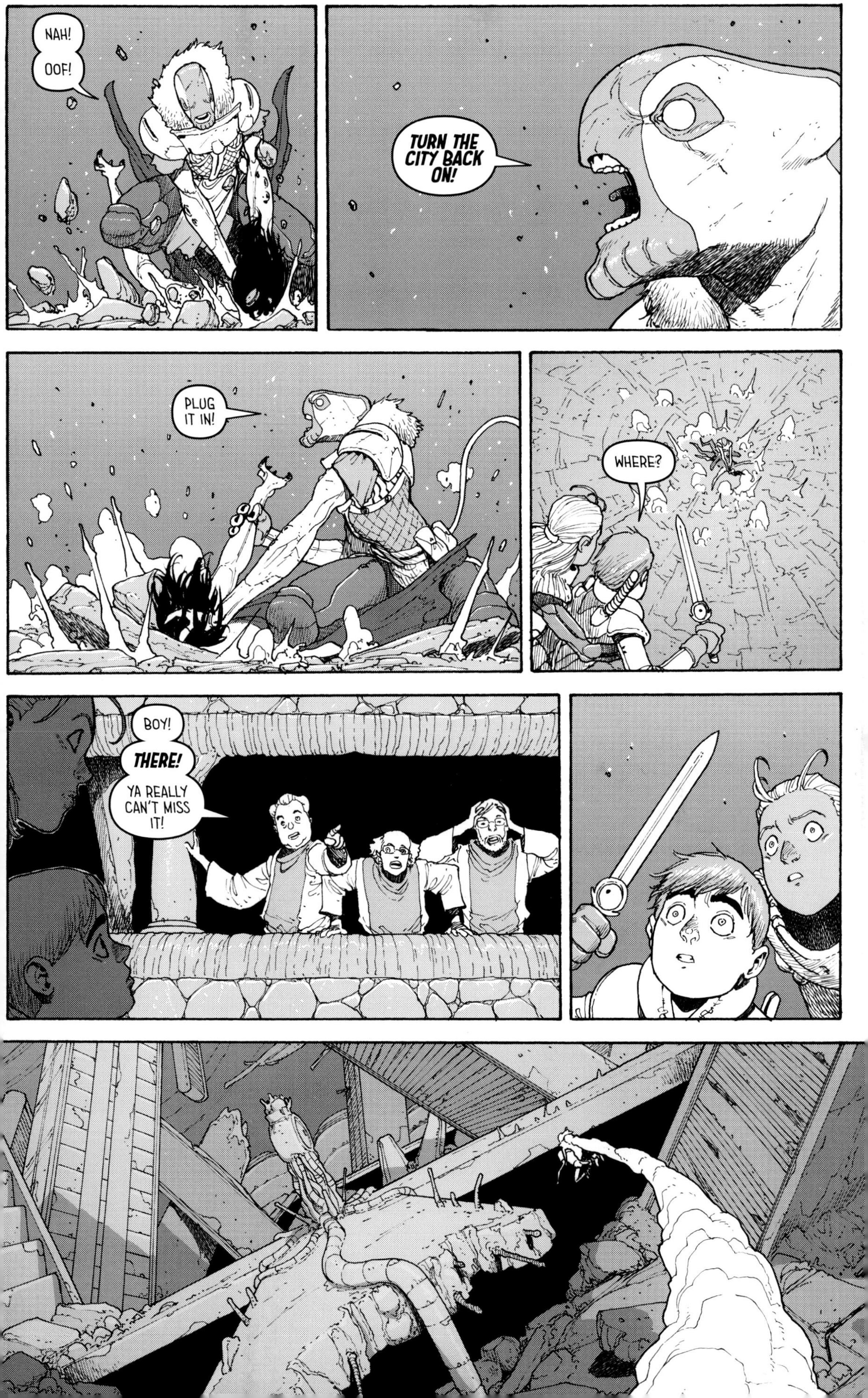
NAH!
OOF!
TURN THE CITY BACK ON!
PLUG IT IN!
WHERE?
BOY!
THERE!
YA REALLY CAN'T MISS IT!

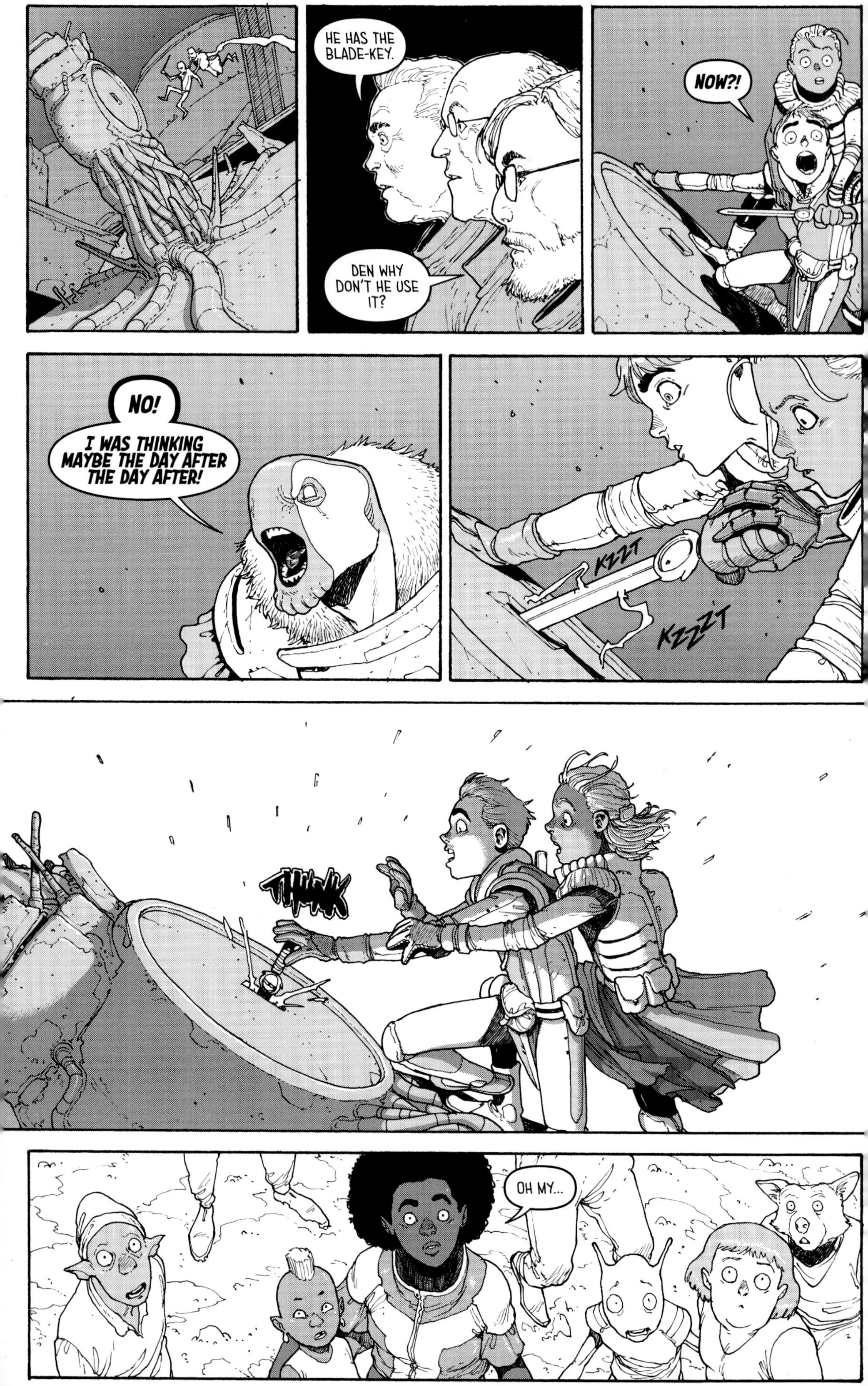
HE HAS THE BLADE-KEY.
DEN WHY DON'T HE USE IT?
NOW?!
NO!
I WAS THINKING MAYBE THE DAY AFTER THE DAY AFTER!
KZZT
KZZZT
THUNK
OH MY...

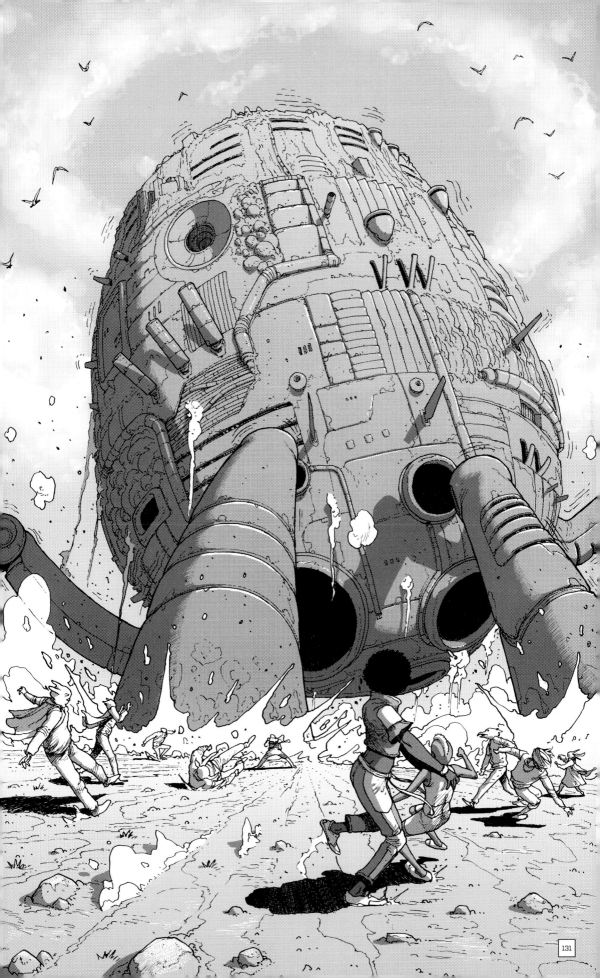

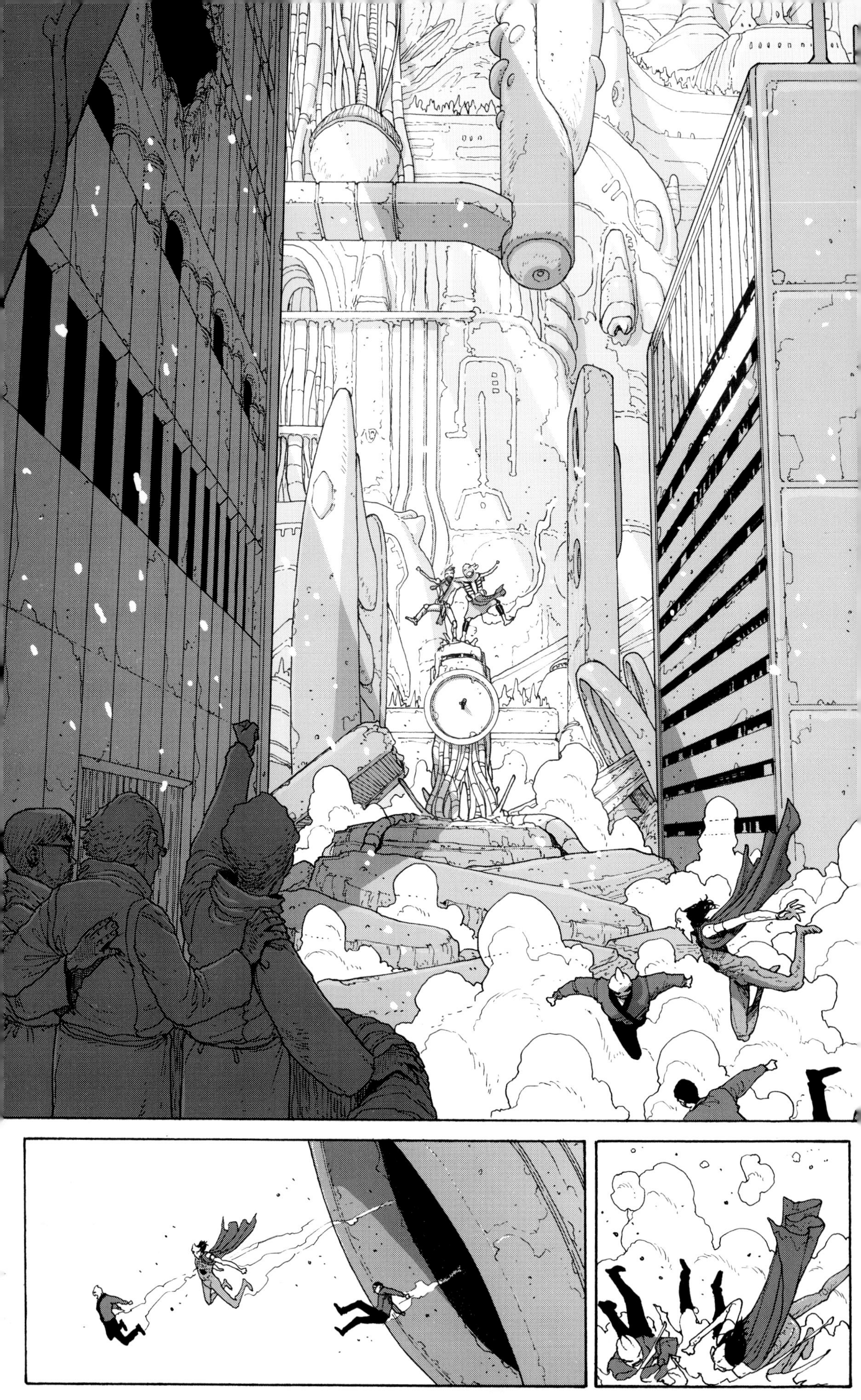

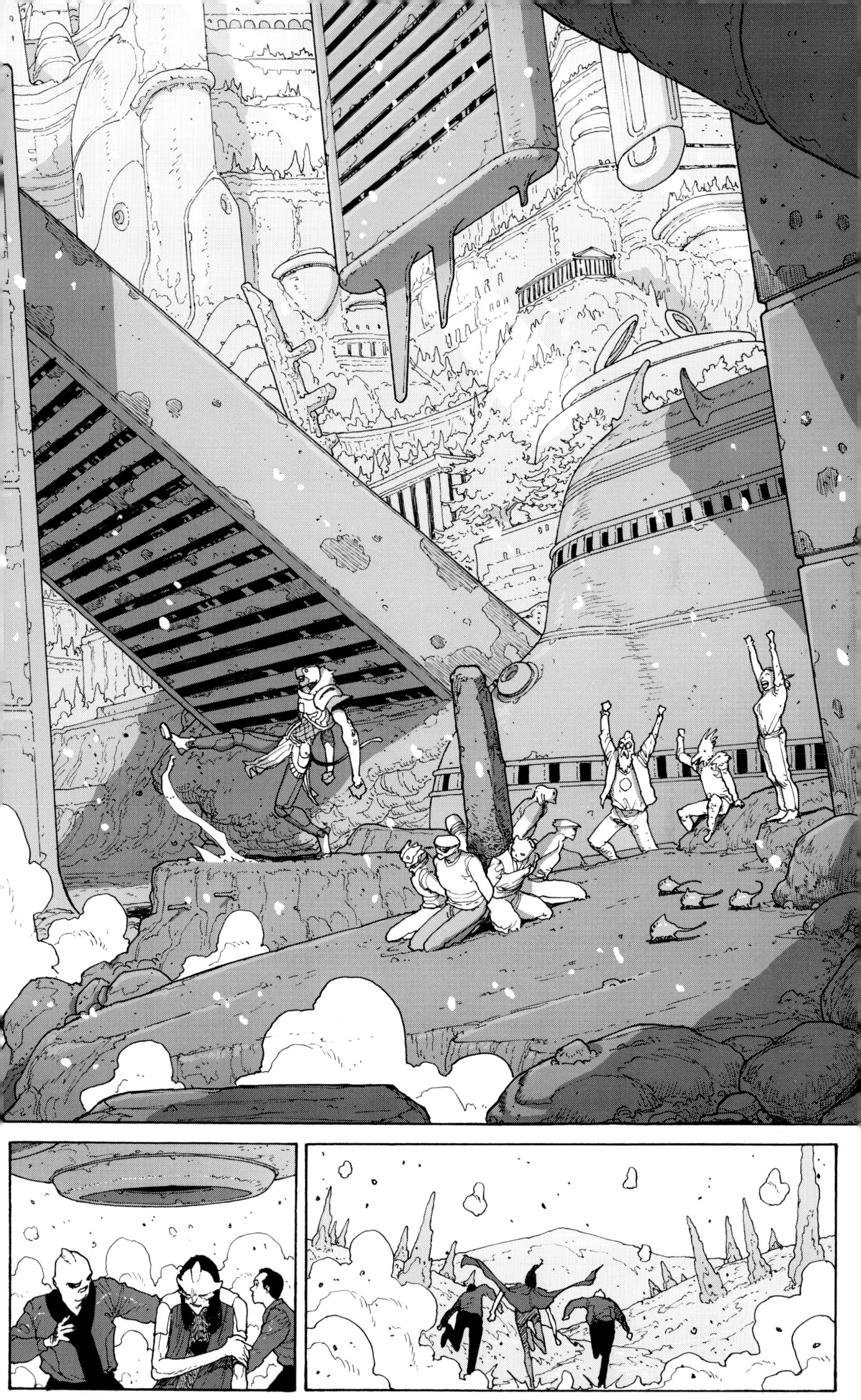

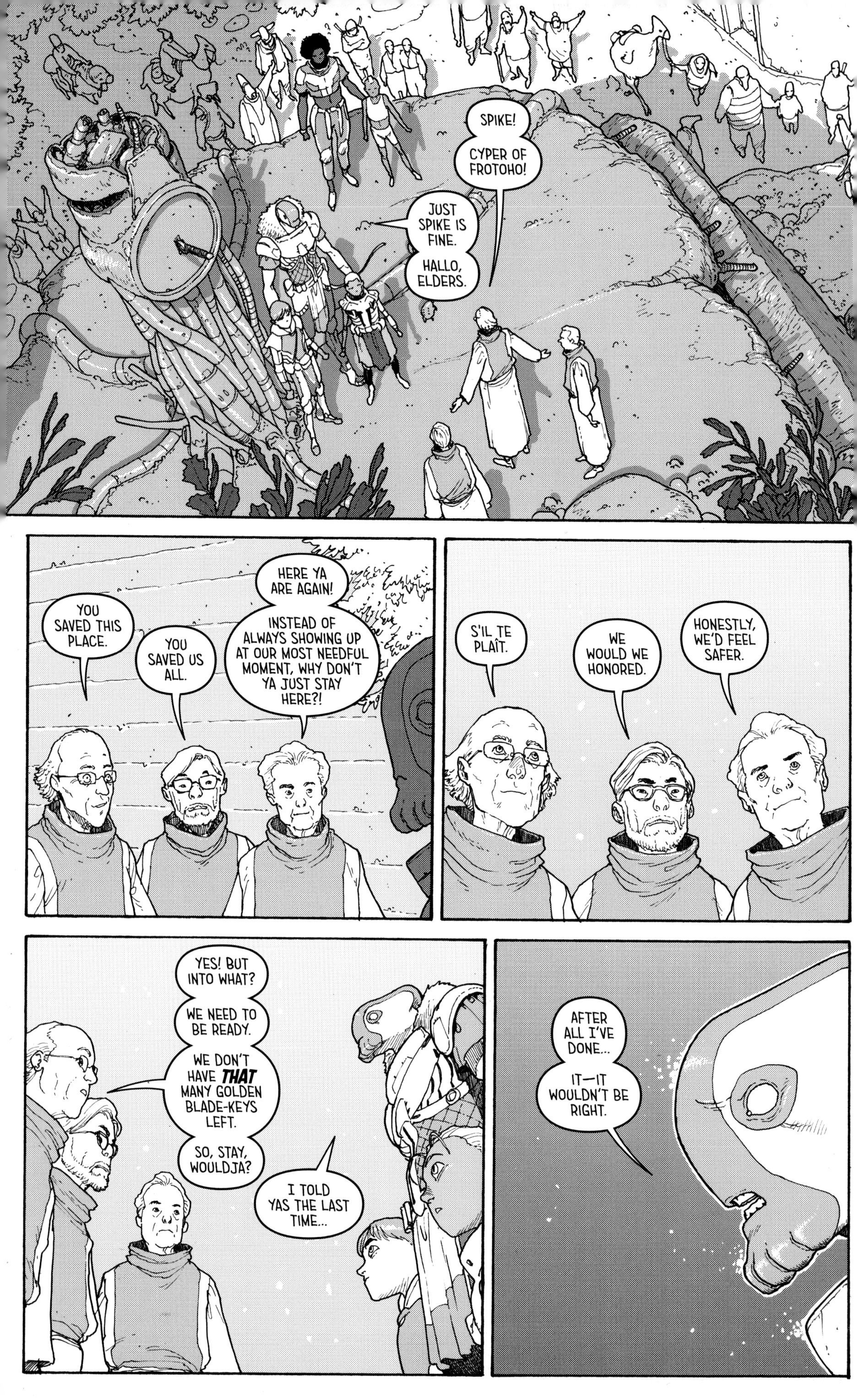
SPIKE!
CYPER OF FROTOHO!
JUST SPIKE IS FINE.
HALLO, ELDERS.
YOU SAVED THIS PLACE.
YOU SAVED US ALL.
HERE YA ARE AGAIN!
INSTEAD OF ALWAYS SHOWING UP AT OUR MOST NEEDFUL MOMENT, WHY DON'T YA JUST STAY HERE?!
S'IL TE PLAÎT.
WE WOULD WE HONORED.
HONESTLY, WE'D FEEL SAFER.
YES! BUT INTO WHAT?
WE NEED TO BE READY.
WE DON'T HAVE ***THAT*** MANY GOLDEN BLADE-KEYS LEFT.
SO, STAY, WOULDJA?
I TOLD YAS THE LAST TIME...
AFTER ALL I'VE DONE...
IT—IT WOULDN'T BE RIGHT.

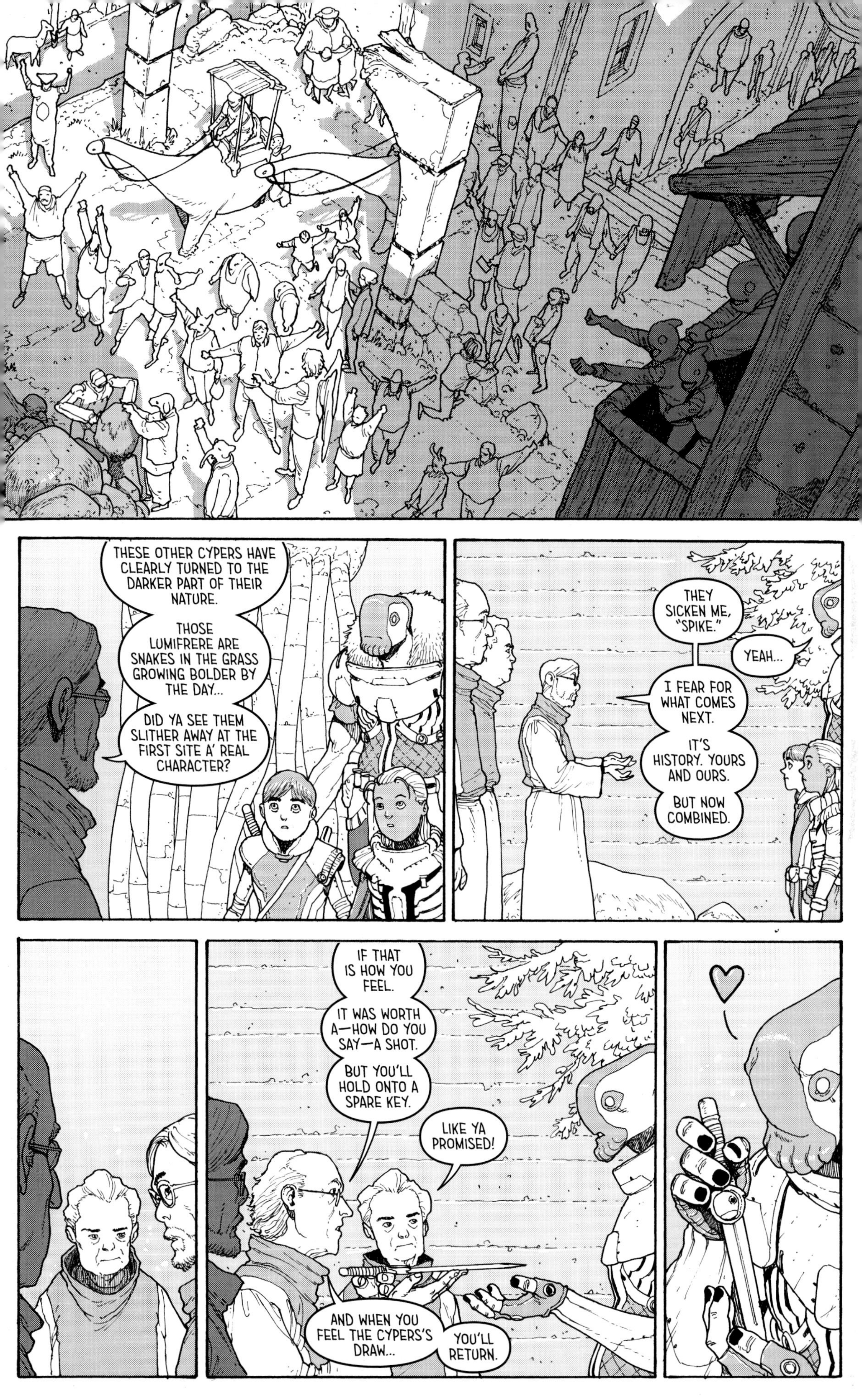

THESE OTHER CYPERS HAVE CLEARLY TURNED TO THE DARKER PART OF THEIR NATURE.
THOSE LUMIFRERE ARE SNAKES IN THE GRASS GROWING BOLDER BY THE DAY...
DID YA SEE THEM SLITHER AWAY AT THE FIRST SITE A' REAL CHARACTER?
THEY SICKEN ME, "SPIKE."
YEAH...
I FEAR FOR WHAT COMES NEXT.
IT'S HISTORY. YOURS AND OURS.
BUT NOW COMBINED.
IF THAT IS HOW YOU FEEL.
IT WAS WORTH A—HOW DO YOU SAY—A SHOT.
BUT YOU'LL HOLD ONTO A SPARE KEY.
LIKE YA PROMISED!
AND WHEN YOU FEEL THE CYPERS'S DRAW...
YOU'LL RETURN.

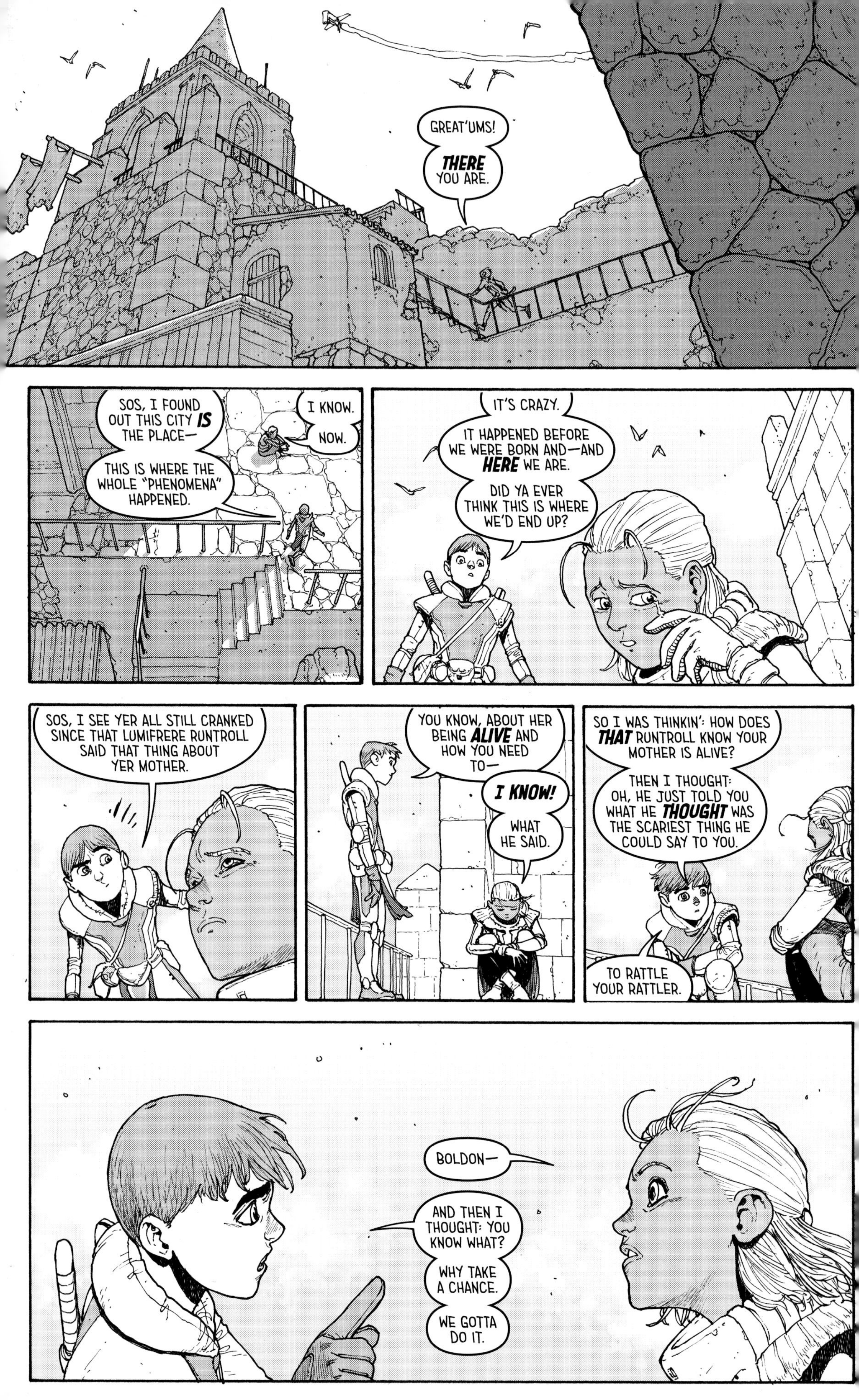
GREAT'UMS!
THERE YOU ARE.
SOS, I FOUND OUT THIS CITY IS THE PLACE—
I KNOW.
THIS IS WHERE THE WHOLE "PHENOMENA" HAPPENED.
NOW.
IT'S CRAZY.
IT HAPPENED BEFORE WE WERE BORN AND—AND HERE WE ARE.
DID YA EVER THINK THIS IS WHERE WE'D END UP?
SOS, I SEE YER ALL STILL CRANKED SINCE THAT LUMIFRERE RUNTROLL SAID THAT THING ABOUT YER MOTHER.
YOU KNOW, ABOUT HER BEING ALIVE AND HOW YOU NEED TO—
I KNOW!
WHAT HE SAID.
SO I WAS THINKIN': HOW DOES THAT RUNTROLL KNOW YOUR MOTHER IS ALIVE?
THEN I THOUGHT: OH, HE JUST TOLD YOU WHAT HE THOUGHT WAS THE SCARIEST THING HE COULD SAY TO YOU.
TO RATTLE YOUR RATTLER.
BOLDON—
AND THEN I THOUGHT: YOU KNOW WHAT?
WHY TAKE A CHANCE.
WE GOTTA DO IT.

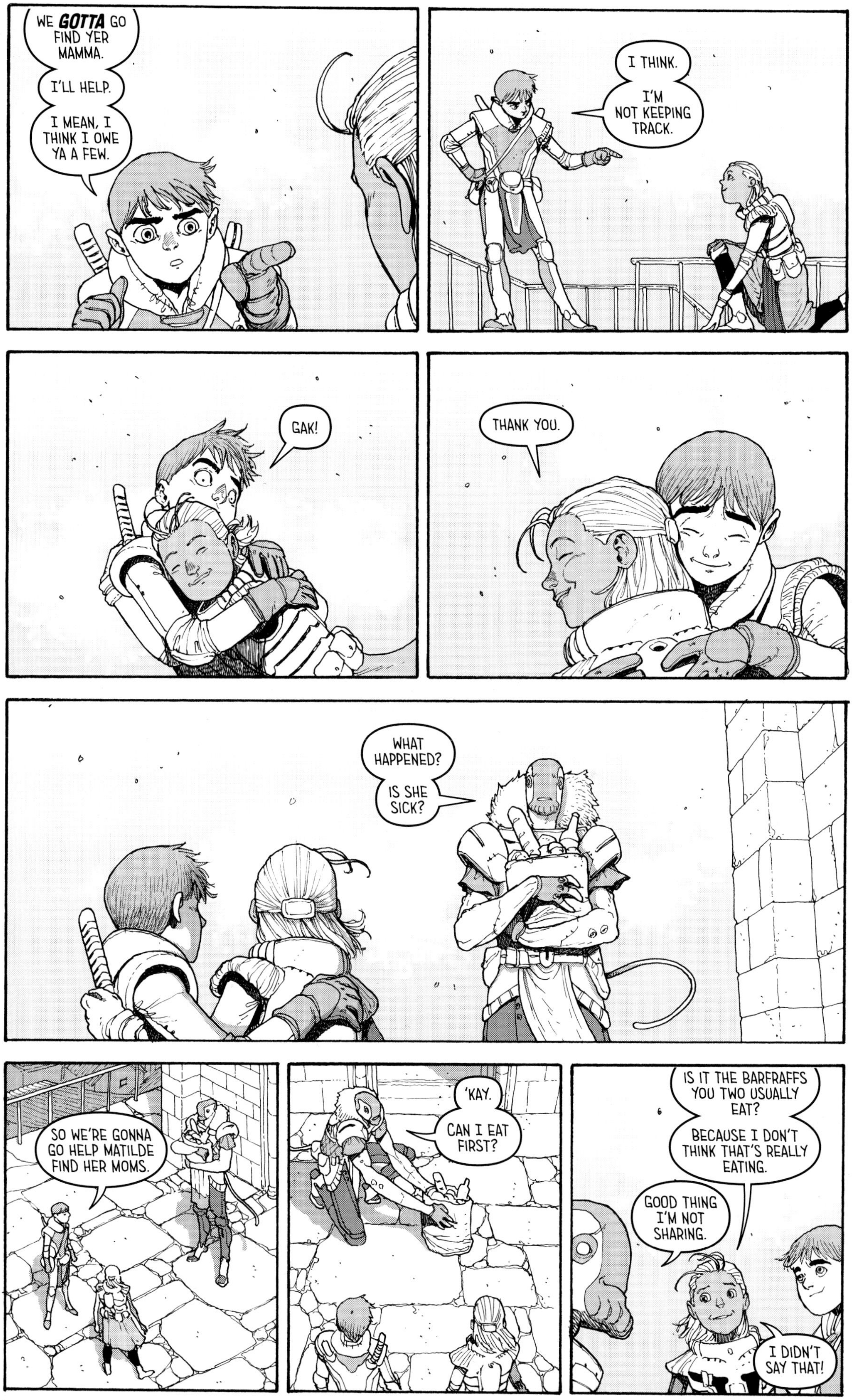
WE GOTTA GO FIND YER MAMMA.
I'LL HELP.
I MEAN, I THINK I OWE YA A FEW.
I THINK.
I'M NOT KEEPING TRACK.
GAK!
THANK YOU.
WHAT HAPPENED?
IS SHE SICK?
SO WE'RE GONNA GO HELP MATILDE FIND HER MOMS.
'KAY.
CAN I EAT FIRST?
IS IT THE BARFRAFFS YOU TWO USUALLY EAT?
BECAUSE I DON'T THINK THAT'S REALLY EATING.
GOOD THING I'M NOT SHARING.
I DIDN'T SAY THAT!

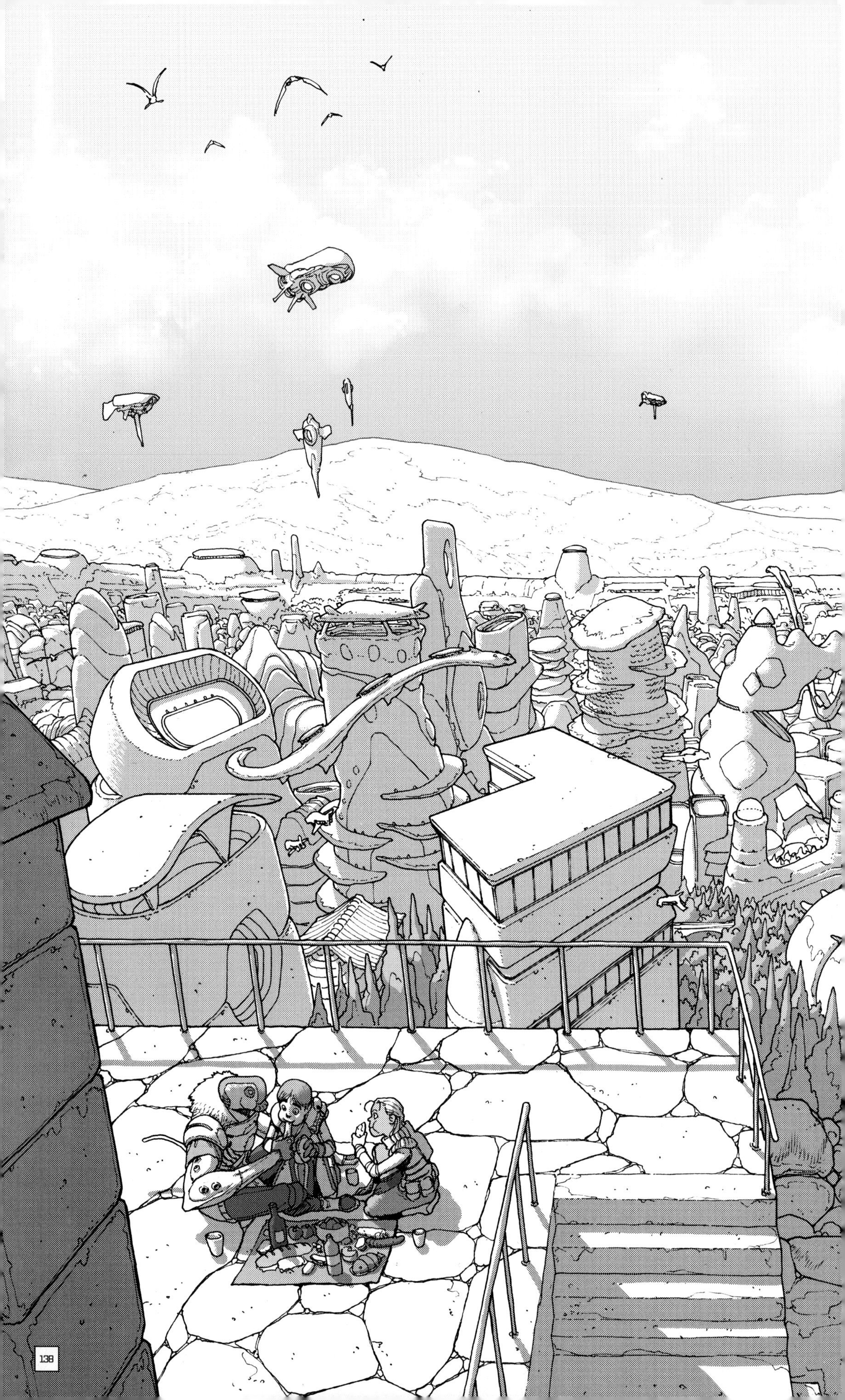

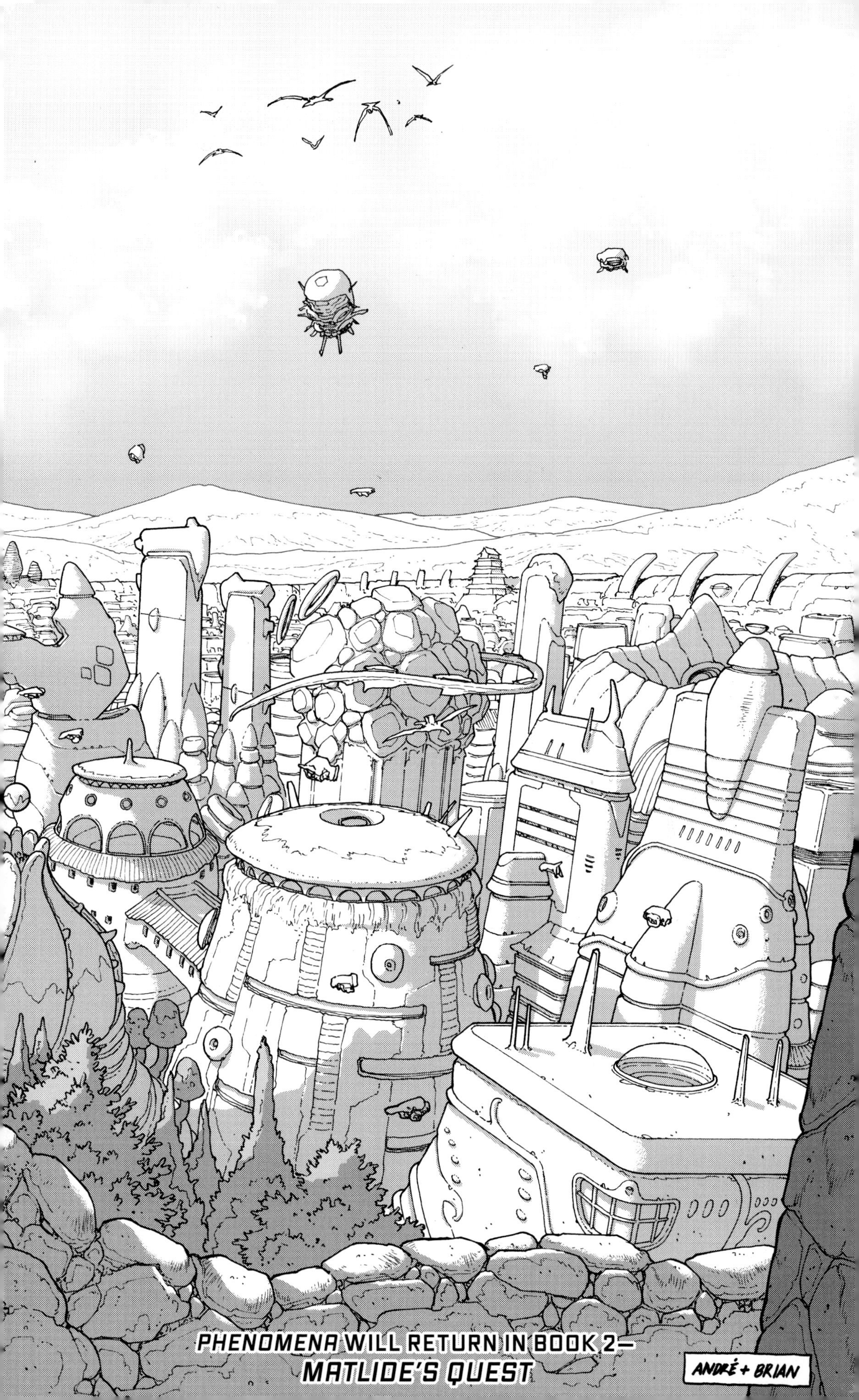
PHENOMENA WILL RETURN IN BOOK 2—
MATLIDE'S QUEST
ANDRÉ + BRIAN

ABOUT THE CREATORS

BRIAN MICHAEL BENDIS is a Peabody Award–winning comics creator, a *New York Times* bestselling author, and one of the most successful writers in comics.

He is the co-creator of Miles Morales, Jessica Jones, Naomi, Iron Heart, and dozens of other characters and stories that populate the Marvel and DC universes, as well as his own original stories.

His Jinxworld line of co-creator-owned comics are published by Dark Horse. Titles include the sci-fi epic *Joy Operations*, the yakuza romance *Pearl*, the spy thriller *Cover*, *Scarlet*, and the alternate history mob story *The United States of Murder Inc.*

At Marvel Comics, Bendis completed historic runs on Spider-Man, Avengers, Iron Man, Guardians of the Galaxy, and a 100-issue run on X-Men, along with the event projects *Avengers Versus X-Men*, *House of M*, *Secret War*, *Secret Invasion*, *Age of Ultron*, *Civil War 2*, and *Siege*. Bendis was also one of the premiere architects of Marvel's Ultimate line of comics and part of the Marvel creative committee that helped set the foundation of the MCU, consulting on all the Marvel movies from the first *Iron Man* in 2008 through *Guardians of the Galaxy Vol. 2* in 2017.

In 2016, Bendis won a Peabody Award for his work as the co-creator of *Jessica Jones* on Netflix from Marvel TV and in 2018 was executive producer and consultant on the Academy Award–winning hit Sony feature *Spider-Man: Into the Spider-Verse* (and its sequel, coming in 2022).

Bendis made his DC debut on the landmark issue *Action Comics* no. 1000 and wrote years-long runs for *Justice League*, *Superman*, *Action Comics*, *Batman: Universe*, and *Legion of Super-Heroes*. He is also the curator of Wonder Comics, an imprint featuring the breakout original *Naomi*.

In 2014, Watson-Guptill published *Words for Pictures: The Art and Business of Writing Comics and Graphic Novels*, based on the class he teaches at Portland State University.

Bendis received an honorary doctorate in the arts from the Cleveland Institute of Art and a certificate of excellence from the Central Intelligence Agency for his work on diversity issues. He has won five Eisner awards, including Best Writer two years in a row, and was honored with an Inkpot Award for achievement in comics.

Brian Michael Bendis lives in Portland, Oregon, with his wife, Alisa; his daughters, Olivia, Tabatha, and Sabrina; his son, London; and his dogs, Splenda and Bowie.

ANDRÉ LIMA ARAÚJO is a Portuguese architect and comics creator, having worked for the major comics publishers in the United States and on an ever-growing body of creator-owned projects. After graduating with a masters from the University of Minho and briefly working as an architect for a year, Araújo began his professional career in comics with Marvel, working on titles such as *Fantastic Four*, *Avengers A.I.*, *Spider-Verse*, *All-New Inhumans*, *Spidey: Freshman Year*, and *Black Panther*, among many others.

He has contributed illustrations to publications such as Duncan Jones's *Madi: Once Upon a Time in the Future* and book covers for Millarworld and Giant Generator. Araújo has also been creating and developing his own comics projects, including *Man Plus* (Titan Comics) and *Generation Gone* (co-created with Ales Kot, Image Comics).

More recently, Araújo worked at DC Comics, where he began his partnership with Brian Michael Bendis on *Legion of Super-Heroes: Millennium* and *Young Justice*. His latest book is the original crime thriller *A Righteous Thirst for Vengeance*, co-created with Rick Remender.

When he isn't working, Araújo likes being with his family, reading history books, driving, and playing video games. He lives in Ponte de Lima, Portugal, with his wife, Luísa, and their three daughters, Matilde, Inês, and Leonor.

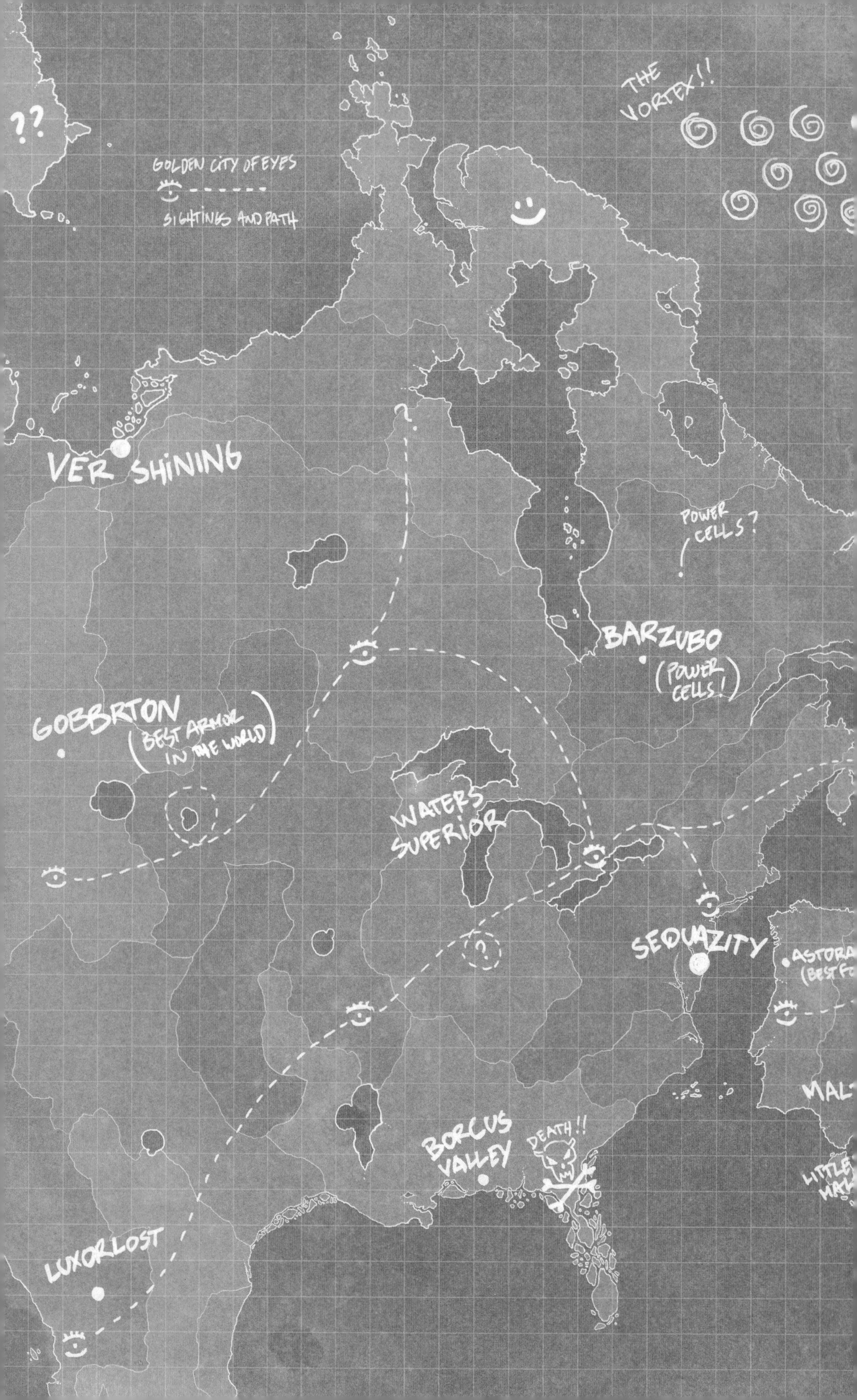
??
GOLDEN CITY OF EYES
SIGHTINGS AND PATH
THE VORTEX!!
VER SHINING
POWER CELLS?
BARZUBO
(POWER CELLS!)
GOBBRTON
(BEST ARMOR IN THE WORLD)
WATERS SUPERIOR
SEQUAZITY
ASTORA
BORCUS VALLEY
DEATH!!
LUXORLOST